"Didn't our night together prove **anything?"**

Obviously Kate wasn't the only one jolting down memory lane. Liam drew her toward him until his body heat—and mere inches—separated them. "I don't know what's happened to you, Just Kate," he whispered. "But I swear I won't hurt you."

She stared into his searing green gaze. "You're not stalking me?"

"No." His quietly sad denial recalled his tenderness and understanding when she'd called an abrupt halt to their lovemaking. Kate pressed her pounding temples. Liam didn't hide his feelings. He laid his cards on the table, as he'd just done.

Battered by conflicted emotions, she glanced at him through her lashes. Self-defense had been her priority for so long, it was her operational default mode. If she let down her guard, admitted he wasn't the man stalking her, it relieved the threat to her safety.

And tripled the threat to her heart.

Dear Reader,

From the moment Liam O'Rourke and Murphy sauntered into *Midnight Hero,* I couldn't wait to tell their story. I was amazed by the change in my easygoing cop! The instant laid-back Liam met Kate, he simmered with intensity. While sensitive to her disability, he encouraged her to spread her wings.

Liam and Murphy also coaxed me from my comfort zone. Like Kate, I was terrified of large dogs. I stuck to my *"no dogs"* mandate through fifteen years of my daughter's begging. But researching K-9s, I was deeply affected by their faithful sacrifices. And my daughter was thrilled when we adopted a puppy.

Cyrus makes me laugh. He's always happy to see me. His intelligence and unconditional love astound me. Like Murphy, he adores takeout. His spirit shines in his lively brown eyes, and his unique personality inspired me…and made Murphy come alive. Peruse pictures on my Web site: www.dianaduncan.com.

Enjoy reading Liam, Murphy and Kate's adventure!

Diana Duncan

DIANA DUNCAN

HEAT OF THE MOMENT

Silhouette®

INTIMATE MOMENTS™

Published by Silhouette Books

America's Publisher of Contemporary Romance

ISBN-13: 978-0-373-27504-5
ISBN-10: 0-373-27504-8

HEAT OF THE MOMENT

This edition published by arrangement with Harlequin Books S.A.

Visit Silhouette Books at www.eHarlequin.com

Printed in U.S.A.

Books by Diana Duncan

Silhouette Intimate Moments

Bulletproof Bride #1284
**Midnight Hero* #1359
**Truth or Consequences* #1373
**Heat of the Moment* #1434

*Forever in a Day

DIANA DUNCAN

Diana Duncan's fascination with books started before she could walk, when her librarian grandmother toted her to work. Diana crafted her first tale at age four, a riveting account of Perky the Kitten, printed in orange crayon. The discovery—at age fourteen—of her mom's Harlequin Romance novels sparked a lifelong affection for plucky heroines and dashing heroes. She loves writing about complex, conflicted men and strong, intelligent women with the courage to dive into the biggest adventure of all—falling in love.

When not writing stories brimming with heart, humor and sizzling passion, Diana spends her time with her husband, two daughters and two cats in their Portland, Oregon, home. Diana loves to hear from her readers. She can be reached via e-mail at writedianaduncan@msn.com or snail mail at P.O. Box 33193, Portland, OR 97292-3193.

Grateful acknowledgment to Officer Matthew Grubb and K-9 Airus. Thanks, guys, for all the help, advice, encouragement and inspiration. Stay safe out there!

*

For Mom...the strongest person I know. You never give in and never give up. No matter how tough things get, you always make me laugh. And you whip up a mean Grasshopper. ;) How can I possibly begin to thank you for all you've done for me? I love you.

For Luis...you adopted our crazy clan without a second thought. Your thoughtful heart and generous spirit have gifted us with so much happiness over the years. I'm proud to call you Dad.

For Boomer, Batesy and Sam, who await us in Heaven. Our loyal and faithful canine companions... your people love and miss you.

Prologue

Las Vegas, Nevada
August 30, High Noon

Kate Chabeau stared down at the sweaty blond man working feverishly between her thighs and waited to die.

Jack Carson raised his head and attempted what she assumed was a reassuring expression. "I know it's tough, but don't squirm."

She clenched her teeth. "Does it usually take this long?"

"Depends on how she's wired."

Slowly, carefully, she eased a strand of long brown hair back from her eyes. "Exactly how good are you?"

"Plenty." Carson's voice grew more strained by the moment. "But this is...beyond me." He eased gingerly from between her legs. "I'm calling in backup."

"They said you had the best hands in Vegas." Perspiration trickled down Kate's spine as he slowly straightened.

"I do." Leaving her sitting immobile in her black Ford Focus convertible, he jogged toward the other members of the bomb disposal squad, convened a safe distance away.

If the best hands in Vegas couldn't disarm the explosive under her seat, then who would save her?

Wait! She bit back the silent scream echoing inside her head. *Come back! Don't leave me to die alone!*

The sun beat down on her exposed head and soaked into her sleeveless black dress, stinging the tender skin beneath. Heat shimmered off the asphalt, a wavery curtain isolating her from the heavily armored police officers surrounding the perimeter. They'd evacuated the parking lot and adjoining buildings, and other than what seemed like hundreds of police vehicles in the distance, hers was the only car in sight. If you didn't include five vans swarming with media personnel.

She scowled. If the vultures got lucky, she might die in time to boost the ratings on the six o'clock news.

How many minutes did she have left? She fought the riptide of fear and glanced at the wilted calla lily on the gray leather upholstery beside her. Its once stark white petals were brown and curling in the heat. Another "gift" from her stalker. The head case had left her lilies and creepy notes, but this was the first bomb.

Her nightmare might finally end here, with her body violently ripped to pieces.

The engine idled a little faster, and her pulse sped into matching BPMs. Could the change in engine tempo trigger the bomb? The young bomb tech had told her she was fortunate her cell call to 9-1-1 hadn't made it explode. She'd been fussing with a melting mocha frappuccino and started the car before she'd spotted the note tucked into the console. The radio station, tuned to "all eighties, all the time," segued into Phil Collin's "In the Air Tonight."

She closed her eyes. How ironic.

Two years ago, the same song had been playing the first time she'd died.

Chapter 1

Two Years Earlier
Riverside, Oregon
March 17, 7:00 p.m.

Breathless and shivering beneath the cold lash of rain, Katherine Chabeau hovered outside the entrance to Delany's Pub.

She'd left her coat behind when she'd fled the hospital, never imagining her car would wheeze to death and leave her stranded. The auto club wouldn't be available for over an hour. And Lord knew, nobody in her family would come to her rescue.

An Irish pub on St. Patrick's Day. What could be warmer? Safer? More abominably cheerful? Kate shuddered. She wasn't a party girl under the best circumstances, and today had taken the prize as the worst day ever. However, she couldn't sit in her dark car in the storm and wait to turn into a human Popsicle.

Over the past year, she'd turned pro at lowering her expectations. She only wanted a steaming cup of cocoa with whipped cream. It was a start.

She attempted to tug open the heavy door before she remembered and switched hands. How long before that became automatic? Heated air, chatter and lively music cannoned into her. The hair on the back of her neck prickled. Suddenly reluctant, she hesitated. Time ground to a halt for a weird, intense moment…as if Fate were holding her breath.

Kate squared her shoulders. *Get a grip.* She was simply walking into a pub. So why did her stomach roll as if she were making a life-or-death decision as she stepped inside?

Jostled by the roiling sea of green-clad revelers, she finally spotted a hallway leading to the restrooms. She pushed inside the door marked Lassies, and then glanced in the mirror. *Blech.* She looked as hideous as she felt.

A random act of violence had stolen her career, incinerated her dreams. Then her fiancé had betrayed her. After the first hit six months ago, she had anticipated tonight's blow. Braced herself to take it on the chin and keep on keeping on. She'd been prepared to kiss her past goodbye.

But not her future.

No matter how badly her throat ached to release the grinding pressure, she would *not* cry. Kate raised her chin. When the tough got sucker punched, they climbed right back into the ring. She grimaced. She looked like she'd gone nine rounds with Rocky. Her specter-pale face was devoid of makeup except for streaky mascara rimming her brown eyes, dark and flat with shock. Her shoulder-length brown hair hung in ropy hanks, and rain splotched her white silk blouse and black wool skirt. Her stockings were soaked, her black Kate Spade pumps—her reward to herself after a grueling stretch of physical therapy—beyond salvation. She shivered, and goose bumps pimpled her damp skin.

After liberal use of paper towels and the hand dryer, she dared another mirror check. Still more Halloween than St. Patrick's Day. And she was shaking, cold to the bone. Kate rubbed her hands over her arms. She might never be warm again.

Inside the pub, she found an empty bar stool in the corner. When she asked for hot chocolate, the bartender offered an Irish chocolate, with a wee dash of whiskey to warm her insides.

Exactly what the doctor ordered. And a heck of a lot better than hemlock. The promise of whipped cream on top sealed the deal. She ordered two. After all, she wouldn't be driving.

She turned her back on the din and huddled over her drinks. The chocolate was excellent, but it didn't alleviate the cold, or fill the emptiness. Why did being in a crowd always make her feel so much lonelier?

"It should be a felony for such a beautiful lady to look so sad." The husky male baritone speaking behind her was richer and more intoxicating than the whiskey-laced chocolate.

Kate glowered into her mug. She wouldn't fall for that load of gilded blarney on her best day, but especially not when she looked like roadkill. She swiveled. "I'll bet you reel them in by the bucketful with—" She strangled on her retort as she got a glimpse of the speaker.

Gorgeous Hunk Alert. Capital *G,* capital *H.*

Charcoal dress slacks and a pearl-gray shirt hugged the guy's big body like they'd been tailor-made to showcase hard, sinewy muscles. Wavy black hair framed his sculpted features. Defined cheekbones complemented a well-shaped masculine nose and strong chin. And, oh, his mouth! Full lips so sexy and kissable, she couldn't help licking her own in response.

He wasn't wearing green. He didn't need to. Eyes as clear and brilliant as emeralds—warm, intelligent eyes fringed by smoky black lashes—sparkled down at her.

She had stared in awe at faces like his gracing marble statues in the vast, echoing galleries of the Louvre.

Over six feet of perfect male magnificence.

Her muse hummed with pleasure, and her fingers clenched with the urge to snatch up a paintbrush. Pain shot up her arm, and loss swamped her. She swallowed a bitter surge of grief. She could never paint again. "G-go away. I'm not after a pickup."

His eyes darkened with concern. "Neither am I. You looked like you could use a friend."

No, he probably thought she looked desperate enough to fall into his brawny arms. "I have enough friends." Mr. Magnificent didn't need to know she'd stopped answering the phone and socializing over the past year. Like she needed more pitying gazes and awkward platitudes. She'd rather drive a clown car for the circus.

He nodded. "Can I call one of them for you?"

Was he for real? "No, thanks."

"Liam O'Rourke." He held out a long-fingered hand. "I'm at loose ends, myself. My partner, Murphy, is in the hospital."

She should've known. Gorgeous. Gallant. Gracious. *Gay.* Her shields lowered. She kept her right hand loosely curled around her mug and nodded hello. Nothing personal. She couldn't shake hands with anyone these days. "I didn't realize you were…sorry I was snippy. I'm having kind of a bad—" *Decade.* "Night."

"No problem. I like a woman with spark." A smile slid across his beautiful mouth, and the room tipped on its axis.

Hello! What was *that?* Even if he wasn't gay, she did *not* need more anguish. "I thought you were feeding me a line."

His smile widened into a playful grin. "Nah. Or I'd have said, 'Help me find my lost kitten. It wandered into the cheap motel across the street.'"

Laughter bubbled out, surprising her. She'd thought her laughter long dead. "I'm Kate."

He cocked his head. "Kate…?"

The impulse to ditch Katherine Chabeau's predicament struck her. She'd borrow a strategy from a favorite book and think about it tomorrow. Grab the chance to be fun and flirty Scarlett instead of dependable-as-dishwater Melanie. "Just Kate."

"Just Kate." He savored her name on his tongue like melted chocolate, and warmth prickled over her skin. "You don't need rescuing, then. Damn, and I wanted my damsel in distress medal."

She'd stopped shaking the moment she'd seen him. Mr. Magnificent was a major distraction. "Sorry, I know the upkeep on white chargers is a killer."

"Worse, the claymore is hell on tailored suits." The couple beside her moved to the dance floor, leaving empty seats. Rather than assuming he was welcome, Liam looked at her, his twinkling gaze silently asking permission.

She inclined her head. "Rack your broadsword and sit down."

"You know your armory, Just Kate." Chuckling, he slid onto the stool, a fluid portrait of strength and agility. *Yowza.*

"I minored in medieval history at Western."

He arched a wicked, glossy brow. "Me too, at U of O."

The bartender greeted Liam warmly and remarked with concern on his and Murphy's brush with the Grim Reaper. Liam exchanged pleasantries with him and ordered an Irish coffee.

Reassured that the bartender obviously knew Liam well, she sipped her chocolate. "A close encounter with the Grim Reaper sounds serious. I hope your partner will be all right."

"The prognosis is good." His Adam's apple jerked, the only indication of the distress beneath his even tone. "He's under sedation. The doc wouldn't let me stay in his room, so my family dragged me here." He pointed out his vivacious, redheaded mother and three tall, dark and buff brothers, who smiled and waved in response. Holy crow. Women probably lined up for blocks to paddle in that gene pool. "They said the diversion would help."

"They're right." She'd spent far too much time in hospitals lately, and had firsthand experience with the strain.

His full lips quirked. "Not until five minutes ago."

He was being polite. Casual conversation with a drowned rat wasn't *that* appealing. "Have you and Murphy been together long?"

"Almost three years." He took a swig of his Irish coffee.

She hesitated, not wanting to offend. "Did the hospital bar you because of his condition, or are they stuck on legalities?" His brows lowered, and she rushed in. "If he's at Mercy, I know a lot of the staff, and I could pull some strings—"

He choked on his coffee. "Hellfire!" Resonant laughter rumbled out. "If my brothers get wind of this, I will *never* live it down."

"I don't understand. I thought your family was supportive."

His exquisite mouth tilted in a grin. "You've obviously never been here before, Just Kate. This is a cop bar. Murphy and I are police officers. All the O'Rourke boys are SWAT cops."

Partners, not *partners.* "*Oh!* Yikes!" She shifted, not nearly as comfortable. At least he was amused. A less secure guy would be furious over her assumption. "What…ah…what happened to him?"

His grin faded. "He took a bullet for me today."

"How awful! That has to be hard to deal with."

He scrubbed his hand over his face. "I'm not sure I can work without him. It's like losing my right arm."

Kate bit the inside of her cheek so hard she tasted blood, but the retort escaped anyway. "I know all about that."

Liam frowned. "You've lost someone close?"

"In a way." Darn it, why was this so awkward? She should be used to it. After today, she'd *have* to get used to it. She shoved down anguish and waved her maimed right arm in feigned nonchalance. Red jagged scars and twisted, useless muscles were partially disguised by bangle bracelets. "Old football injury."

She stared into her mug, braced for camouflaged disgust, mumbled excuses, a speedy escape. *Nice knowing you, gorgeous.*

"Kate." *Hmm. Still here?* She warily glanced up. Compassion glinted in his eyes, but no pity…or distaste. "Forgive me," he murmured. "I didn't realize. I wasn't being flip."

She geared out of defensive mode. "I know, it's okay. I'm used to it." She'd fended off comments from none-of-your-business nosy to breathtakingly cruel. After today, she'd better toughen up, fast. Jaw set, she awaited his questions. Steeled herself to recite the painful account of a vicious dog attack.

Instead, his bone-melting smile flashed. "Dance with me, Just Kate."

"I…don't dance well." Since her injury, she'd become clumsy, as if her disability had thrown her entire body off balance. But she'd never been able to dance. She couldn't loosen up and find the rhythm. And she hated being a public spectacle.

Liam gestured at the gyrating couples on the dance floor. Several had obviously imbibed the green beer a tad too freely. He stood, his long, lithe body relaxed and confident. "That's not stopping anyone else."

It was only a dance. So why did she get the same eerie tingle as when she'd stepped over the threshold and into the pub? As if she were making a life-altering choice.

It wasn't fear. No creepazoid vibes emanated from him, and serial killers didn't travel with cop brothers and mom.

The DJ had been playing Irish bands all night, and the music segued into U2's "With or Without You."

"C'mon." Liam winked at her. "I won't lead you anywhere you don't want to go."

What did she have to lose, except her questionable dignity? "Don't blame me if you end up in the hospital alongside Murphy."

"Gamble is my middle name."

"Your mother must be clairvoyant," she shot over her shoulder as he steered her onto the crowded dance floor.

"More like wishful thinking." Laughing, he faced her. "It's actually Michael. She and Pop gave us all 'saintly' middle names." He sobered. "Is it okay if I hold your hand to lead?"

Nobody had touched her hand in over a year except medical personnel. Nobody had wanted to. "Y-yes."

He offered his palm…and waited.

She stared at his palm, battling panic. He wouldn't ask if he didn't mean it. Wouldn't offer, then yank away in revulsion.

"Trust me," his husky voice admonished. She looked up into his tender gaze, and he gave her a reassuring smile. "I won't hurt you." His somber tone infused the words with deeper meaning, as if he were making a sacred vow.

She'd experienced the worst of betrayals by people who'd professed to love her. She should be beyond trust. Yet, she was willing to trust *him.* Why? Her movements jerky, she laid her hand in his. His warm fingers gently enclosed her scarred, stiff ones. For so long, there had been only numbness. Or terrible pain. But the instant they touched, all the tiny nerve endings in her hand shimmered with pleasure, and her breath caught.

Before she could recover from the jolt, he cradled her hand against his shoulder. His right arm slid around her waist, and his broad palm nestled against the small of her back and tucked her close to his powerful body.

He began to sway, and she tripped and stepped on his foot. He smiled at her. "Follow the tempo inside you, not the music."

Her cheeks flamed, and she ducked her head. "My tempo can't carry a tune in a bushel basket."

"Relax, sweetheart." He drew her close again. "It's a dance, not nuclear disarmament."

She chuckled, and it was suddenly easy to melt into his embrace. She rested her cheek on his chest, where his heart beat strong and steady. He was so warm, yet he smelled as fresh as a winter rainstorm.

Heat radiated from him, enveloped her in a bright glow. Warmed her clear through, to where she was cold and dead inside. Instead of trying to keep time with the song, she followed *his* rhythm. Awareness hummed through her veins, trembled in her belly. The music wove a magical spell, cocooning them alone on the dance floor.

Liam lightly rubbed her back. "You're a natural."

"Only with you," she whispered so low she was sure he wouldn't hear. But his arms tightened around her as if he had.

All too soon, the song ended. Instead of releasing her, Liam kept her for another dance. And another. With every step, every sensual graze of their bodies, heat grew. Their unspoken connection strengthened. The air sizzled between them.

Liam treated her to another Irish chocolate. Sheltered at a cozy table in the corner, she gloried in the keen intelligence and rapier wit beneath his gorgeous exterior.

He treated her as if she were special, not fragile.

She excused herself for a visit to the Lassies' room and bumped into the auto club driver searching for her in the mob near the front. Instead of laboriously writing a check left-handed, she shoved cash at him to tow her car to the garage.

Hours later, Liam pulled back at the end of a dance. She stumbled, and he slid his arm around her. When he touched her, she wasn't clumsy. Wasn't cold. Wasn't alone anymore. And she craved him more than the most scrumptious, expensive chocolate.

He brushed a lock of hair back from her face. "It's getting late. I'll walk you to your car."

Kate crashed back to earth. The ball was over, and she once again turned into a plain old pumpkin. She forced a smile to disguise her disappointment. "I'm traveling by cab."

"In that case, can I offer you a no-strings ride home?"

Maybe there was a sprinkle of magic left. The Kate who had emerged like a wobbly butterfly from her chrysalis over the past few hours looked up into those intriguing Irish eyes and replied, "That would be nice, thanks."

When he discovered she didn't have her coat, he draped his suede jacket over her shoulders. Envious female glares and speculative murmurs about "love 'em and leave 'em Liam" followed them out into the downpour. With his looks and natural charm, he'd have his pick of a different girl every night.

What did it matter? For now, the handsome prince was hers.

He insisted she wait under the covered entryway, and she couldn't resist nuzzling the collar of his coat. The butter-soft charcoal suede smelled of him, like rain-washed piney woods.

Liam pulled up in a white vintage Mustang, and she splashed through the deluge. He was already out with the door open, and she clambered inside.

She brushed raindrops off his sleeve as he slid into the driver's seat. "You should have stayed in here where it's dry."

He grinned and pulled out into the street. "As Gram always said, 'I'm not sugar or salt or anybody's honey. I won't melt.'"

His teasing was a refreshing change. His easygoing charm and sunny grins swept away the damp fog of misery. Smiling, she studied the immaculate ivory leather interior. "Great car."

His grin lit up the night. "A '66 Mustang GT convertible. This pony has the famous 'K-code' four-barrel 289, pumping out a lusty 271 horsepower…" He caught her bemused expression. "TMI?"

"Not too much info at all, but I don't speak hotrod. I fill my car with gas and drive it. You obviously adore yours."

"Pop towed the hunk of junk home on my fourteenth birthday. Over the years, we rebuilt every nut and bolt. Once, when we worked late into the night, he confided a crazy—" He broke off, abashed. "TMI again. Anyway, the pony holds a lot of memories."

His wistful tone clued her in. "Your dad is…gone?"

"He died a year after we finished the car." Pain flickered in his eyes, but his tone was jaunty. "So, Just Kate, where can my white charger sweep you away to?"

Obviously, he preferred to keep things light. One of those party-hearty guys who abhorred commitment. Who despised complicated. Everything about her was complicated these days.

Two streets before the entrance ramp to the freeway, he glanced at her, and his hand covered hers where it rested on the seat. "Have dinner with me Saturday night."

In the intimate confines of the car, his intent gaze—focused on her alone—made her forget the heartache. His warm, gentle touch vanquished the pain. Her bleak nightmare faded in the glow of his easy laughter.

And she didn't want to let him go.

"I…" She hesitated, unsure how to ask for what she wanted. Unsure how far to take it. She'd never been bold. Never been brazen. She'd always squelched her wants and needs. Expecting nothing was so much less painful than battling disappointment. Katherine Chabeau had never gone after what she wanted. Because of that, so much was now lost to her.

Maybe it was high time "Just Kate" started.

Liam stopped for a red light, and taut silence hummed between them. "Would you be more comfortable with lunch?"

"Liam…take me home."

"A coffee?" His fingers gently squeezed hers. "Hell, I'll settle for a hot dog from a downtown pushcart."

The tightness in her chest eased and she laughed. "I meant take me to *your* home." She merely wanted to spend more time with him. Get to know him better. "I'd like to see where you live."

Ten minutes later, Liam ushered her inside a dilapidated two-story Craftsman. Disconcerting electricity arced from his palm to the small of her back, stealing her breath. How could his touch make her reel like she'd been struck by lightning? What was she *doing,* going home with a stranger? Oddly, she felt as if she'd known Liam forever. She'd never experienced a wild, out-of-control attraction to anyone…not even her fiancé.

Maybe that's why he cheated on you.

Liam switched on the lights. "I plan to restore this grand old duchess to her former glory, as time and money allow."

"I used to restore antique paintings for a living. There's nothing more fulfilling…except creating your own masterpiece."

He glanced at her misshapen arm, his emerald gaze tender and wise. Somehow, she sensed he understood her injury meant more than the loss of employment. That it meant the death of her dreams. He pushed aside a toolbox. The hard hat on top bore the Habitat for Humanity logo. "I'll give you the fifty-cent tour."

She indicated the hard hat. "You volunteer for Habitat for Humanity? What, you don't get enough construction at home?"

He winked at her. "Don't ya know, Just Kate," he drawled in a lilting Irish brogue, "that idle hands are the devil's tools?"

She smiled back at him. "Oh, I'm sure your hands are always engaged in one activity or another, Ace."

His grin flashed white and wicked. "Busy hands are happy hands, sweetheart."

His naughty grin made her dizzy inside, like a ride on the scrambler at the state fair. Good grief. Now he didn't even have to touch her to turn her on. She feigned interest in the crown molding. "About that tour…"

His exquisite lips quirked. He knew the effect he had on her. She only hoped he was suffering half as much. He tossed his head, shaking his thick, black mane. "Follow me."

He moved with self-assured loose-limbed grace and power, like a champion thoroughbred racehorse who knows he can defeat every competitor on the field. She obediently followed him into the living room. Heck, she'd follow him into an active volcano. She glanced around. "This would be a perfect home to raise a family. It's got good, solid bones, and lots of space."

"Or a great party house." He flicked a switch. "I wired in surround sound." Phil Collins's evocative voice floated out, and she grinned approval. He nodded. "You like eighties music, too."

"Love it. I consider Phil Collins the modern equivalent of a medieval balladeer. All his songs tell a story."

He gave her a considering look. "You've quite the poetic soul, Just Kate."

She'd thought her soul dead and buried alongside her laughter. Wrong on both counts.

Only half her mind was on the house as he showed off the remodel. He asked her about color and style preferences, and seemed genuinely interested in her opinions. The interior was all lean lines, rich oak built-ins and warm, cozy hues. The house smelled pleasantly of sanded wood and fresh paint.

Most of her attention was riveted on Liam. All rippling muscles, sexy smiles and hot, sensual glances. He smelled erotically of warm, clean man.

He led her to the kitchen. "I just started working in here."

His charisma had started working on *her* the moment she'd seen him. She leaned against the gray granite countertop, and glanced around the gutted room. "When do you expect to finish?"

His intent gaze caught and held hers. "I like to take my time on every project. Lavish thorough, complete attention on each step before moving to the next."

Pleasure tingled over her. In the background, Phil started singing about rain. "A detail man."

"Take these cabinets." He moved until he was mere inches in front of her. His broad hand lovingly caressed a cabinet door above her head. "I sand until the pores grow warm and open to accept the stain. Then I rub in the tint until they glow."

Mesmerized, she watched his hand, imagined his long, clever fingers caressing her. Desire curled low and liquid in her belly. "You…ah…you're dedicated to your work."

"It's not work if you enjoy it." Awareness zinged between them. "Sometimes I forget to eat, forget everything but the gut-deep satisfaction of creating."

She loved that feeling. Missed it with her entire being. She stared into those deep, sparkling green pools and lost herself in his undiluted joy. Lost her grip on reality. "You sound like an artist."

"I am, if you consider art an unflinching expression of true self, no matter the medium." He raised her injured fingers to his lips and placed a soft, gentle kiss on her bent, scarred knuckles. Beauty, kissing the Beast without hesitation. Heat undulated, spread, bathed her in sunlight. He smiled. "Isn't art anything that arouses an emotional response, both in the creator and the observer? Anything that pulls both inside the experience and makes them participants?"

Enveloped in the warm radiance of shared understanding, her withered spirit blossomed. With a turn of the kaleidoscope, the broken pieces inside her coalesced into a rainbow picture. She'd been a good girl all her life. Followed the rules. Tried to do the right thing. What had it gotten her? Hurt. Betrayed.

Crippled, in both body and soul.

For the first time in over a year, she felt neither ugly nor awkward. Her body had been primed for him since the first dance. Now her mind and heart followed, tangoed headlong into reckless abandon.

"There's a room you haven't shown me that I'd like very much to see." She tilted her head and edged closer, until their bodies touched. "Your bedroom."

He inhaled sharply. "Kate." He took a step back. "I'm trying like hell to be a gentleman with you."

She moved close to him again. "Well, stop it."

"This is different from anything…you're different—"

Yes, she was damaged goods. The lovely, warm anticipation inside her shriveled, and she turned away. "I understand."

He gently grasped her chin and urged her to face him. "No, you don't. Hell, *I* don't." Confusion swam in his eyes, and his mouth slanted in a wry grin. "I want you, and after being held against me all night you have to know how much. But I don't want to cross any wires and blow this."

Relief tangled with uncertainty. He *did* want her, but didn't want complicated. They were in agreement. "Not a problem. You want me. I want you." She rested her left hand on his arm, and tension vibrated in his muscles. "Seems very simple."

He uttered a shaky laugh. "Maybe I don't want you to think I'm easy."

"No worries, Ace." She trailed her fingers up his arm and brushed her body against his. "I think you're very, very hard."

He closed his eyes, swore under his breath. "You wreck me, Kate." Then he captured her mouth. His lips so warm, so firm, tasted of sweet chocolate, heady whiskey and hot, aroused man. She nestled into him, waking from a long, cold sleep. His tongue glided inside, and an explosion detonated behind her eyelids.

He knew exactly what she wanted, what she needed, and gave generously. His talented mouth and seeking hands rocketed her to the edge. She kicked off her pumps, he toed out of his shoes and was barefoot in an instant. Her blouse fluttered to the floor, followed by her lacy white bra. One-handed, she fumbled with his shirt. Their mouths fused in the scalding kiss, he reached to help, finally ripped in frustration. Buttons skittered across the linoleum, and his shirt followed her blouse. At the sight of him, the world tilted and left her giddy. He was so beautiful, his wide chest bronzed and rippled with heavy muscle.

His hot, callused palms rushed over her. His big hands tugged down her skirt, then slid her stockings over her calves. She craved his touch like a barren desert craved rain, and rubbed against him as he stripped off his pants and briefs. The crisp hair covering his chest grazed her sensitive nipples, and her knees wobbled. He groaned and lifted her onto the counter.

He stepped between her thighs. Through her lace panties, his thick heat pressed where she ached for him, and her head fell back. His lips nuzzled her throat, roved to her breasts and drank her in. His hands stroked, spiraled her higher with every intimate caress. His tongue swirled over her nipple, sending a lightning flash of heat straight to her belly. Dimly, her mind registered a foil packet crinkling.

Her skin tingled, her blood pounded hot and hard in her ears. Her heartbeat galloped at a frenzied pace. And she wanted more. She arched into his greedy mouth. "Liam, please!"

His fingers hooked the waistband of her panties and rent the soft lace. The granite countertop was cool and smooth beneath her naked bottom. His skin was burning hot against her naked front. His heady male scent flooded her senses, as intoxicating as champagne. She needed him more than her next breath. She pulled him to her. "Now," she gasped.

"Wait!" Panting, he stepped back and rested his forehead against hers. "Not here. Not like this."

"Here is good. This is fine."

"No. I want you in my bed." He scooped her up and she wound her legs around his waist and her arms around his neck. To the erotic beat of drums and the echoing strains of "In the Air Tonight," Liam carried her upstairs. Every step caused her moist, sensitized center to ride the hard ridge of his arousal.

Phil Collins's sensual lyrics mirrored her need; she'd been waiting for this moment all her life. "You can have me wherever you want me." She writhed against him. "Just hurry!"

His breathing rapid, he chuckled unsteadily. "Keep that up, and I'm gonna forget how to walk."

She moaned in pleasure and kissed his neck, devoured his essence. "As long as you don't forget how to do anything else."

He laid her on the bed. Light from the hallway gilded the passion-taut lines of his face as he drank her in. His glowing admiration made her feel more beautiful than a Monet garden, more precious than Michelangelo's *Pieta.*

Seconds later, he followed her down, his solid body heavy and powerful on top of her. The possessive glint in his emerald eyes was all male. "I'll remember everything about you. Always, my sweet Kate." In one smooth motion, he sank deep inside her.

She was prepared for the quick stab of discomfort. But not the shock of searing intimacy. Not the heart connection.

Not the ultimate bond of soul-to-soul.

In a horrifying instant, her fatal mistake hit home. She'd struggled back from the shattering brink of loss and betrayal, convinced she had nothing more to lose.

But she'd been dead wrong.

Her beautiful kaleidoscope picture shattered. If she let Liam O'Rourke as deeply into her heart as she had her body, he would have more power to ruin her than the two traumas combined. Love 'em and leave 'em Liam could destroy her. When things inevitably got complicated, his rejection would hurtle her over the edge into the depths of hell. And she would never resurface.

Liam froze above her. "Dammit, Kate, *why?*"

Dying inside, she choked out, "I'm…sorry." She stiffened, braced for his wrath. She *deserved* it. "I can't…do this."

He cupped her face in his hands. "Okay. It's okay. I didn't realize— *Hell,* Kate, why didn't you *tell* me you were a virgin?"

"I'm sorry," she whispered on a sob. "I never intended…" *To expose my heart. To make myself fatally vulnerable to you.* "I didn't know it would be so…" *Soul-shatteringly intimate.*

"Don't cry, sweetheart." Horror darkened his eyes. "*I'm* sorry. I didn't mean to hurt you."

"You didn't." Mortification sickened her. She was as clumsy in bed as everywhere else. "Could you please…get off me?"

"Sure." Slowly, gently, he withdrew and rolled to the side.

Humiliated, and feeling more alone than ever, she covered her face. "I don't expect your forgiveness, Liam. But I *am* truly sorry."

"Stop apologizing." He drew her into his embrace. She hid her face in his shoulder, but he grasped her chin and made her look at him. "What just happened here?"

"I made a mistake. I thought it would be…different." She'd thought he could make her forget. Instead, he'd made her remember who and what she was. Or rather, *wasn't.*

Made her see the potential for her own devastation.

She couldn't trust *anyone.* Not even herself.

His expression tender, his tone patient, Liam kissed the tip of her nose. "Talk to me, Kate. What's going on?"

Nearly blind with panic, she blurted out the only thing she could think of to stall him. "I'd like to…shower first."

"Sure, sweetheart. Use the first floor bath, the rooms up here aren't finished. I'll order Chinese food. Then we can eat and talk." As she gingerly eased off the bed, he sat up and swung his long legs over the mattress. "Let me help you downstairs."

That's all she needed to complete her descent into hell. "I'm fine, thanks anyway." She turned and fled.

In the kitchen, she gathered her scattered clothes. Clutching them, she locked the bathroom door and turned on the shower.

Upstairs, horror assaulted Liam, and he lowered his head into his hands. He'd just abruptly ended Kate's virginity. She'd been more than ready, but if he'd known, he'd have taken far more time with her. Been much more gentle, stayed in control.

He scrubbed his palms over his face. Who was he blowing a smoke screen for? If he'd known, he'd never have taken her to bed. Even that small expectation of commitment would have sent him hurtling into a tactical retreat. Confusion slammed into fear. Except he hadn't been able to resist Kate. The instant he'd spotted her in the bar, he'd been drawn to her side. Every defense he'd deployed had been useless against basic physics.

An irresistible force pulling in an immovable object.

He clenched his jaw. He loved women, loved everything about

them, but he never dated the same girl twice. After his fiancée had cold-bloodedly warbled "buh-bye" to their three-year relationship without so much as blinking, he'd made a decision to avoid entanglements. *He* did the leaving, before anyone could abandon him.

A gust of wind rattled the house, and he jerked upright. How long had he been absorbed in self-recriminations while the shower ran on and on? He shoved his legs into his slacks and zipped them while he sprinted downstairs. "Kate?" He knocked on the bathroom door. "Are you all right?"

No response.

"Kate!" He curled his fist and pounded. "Answer me!"

Dead silence.

Gut-wrenching panic ripped through him as he shook the locked doorknob. Had she passed out? He kicked in the door. Icy wind blasted through the open window, blowing the curtains aside. There was no trace of Kate...except for her torn panties in the trash can. She had vanished into the storm.

Chapter 2

Las Vegas, Nevada
Present Day, August 30, 12:15 p.m.

Shaking from the memory, Kate jolted back to the present. How ironic. She'd finally rebuilt her life…and was about to die.

She peered through the undulating heat curtain. TV cameras recorded every nuance as Carson, the young bomb tech, stood in the distance engaged in fierce conversation with a taller guy who had his back to her. Snug, faded denims showcased the new man's athletic build, and like Carson, he wore combat boots. Longish, wavy black hair brushed the collar of his navy T-shirt. Bold white lettering on the shirt's broad back proclaimed: *I am a bomb tech. If you see me running, try to keep up.*

They *weren't* going to send in the comedian? Both men turned and walked toward her car. Maybe the Joker was her only hope. Hardly reassuring. Tall, dark and so-not-funny took the lead, and the cameras followed his progress. There was something wrenchingly familiar about his loose-limbed saunter. Something heart tugging about the confident tilt of his head. Kate's breathing sped up. He broke through the shimmering curtain, and his face swam into view. Kate gasped. Reeled.

Oh, God! The last man she ever expected to see. The last man she *wanted* to see. Especially during her last moments!

Liam O'Rourke!

His hair was longer, his hard-muscled body leaner, his sculpted features more rugged. Two years had matured his good looks from just unbelievable into devastatingly handsome. She knew the instant he recognized her. He faltered, stumbled, and his beautiful face turned to stone. Then he recovered, schooled his features and strode full speed ahead.

He reached the car, and his sexy mouth twisted sardonically. "I'll be damned. A blast from the past."

Carson hurriedly caught up with him. "Meet Officer Liam O'Rourke. He has the best hands in the Western Hemisphere."

She stared up into Liam's thick-lashed emerald eyes that still glowed with the secrets of the universe. "Yes, I know."

"Just Kate." The smoky intimacy in Liam's deep voice told her he remembered that the last time they were together they'd both been naked. "Long time no see."

In spite of the relentless heat, a shiver trembled over her. "I didn't know you were a bomb tech."

He turned to Carson. "I'll take it from here. Bug out of the hot zone." Carson jogged away, and Liam swiveled back to her. "No. You didn't stick around long enough to find out."

Her gaze skittered from the censure on his gorgeous face to the dying calla lily. Over two years later, he was still angry. Could he be the man who was stalking her? Had he pretended to be surprised to see her? Nobody would know more about planting a bomb than a bomb tech. But why come to her aid? Confusion and fear spun in a sickening whirl. Maybe to make her trust him?

"I need to get between your legs." His demand cut into her turbulent thoughts.

She blinked. "I beg your pardon?"

"Hello." He gestured with a pair of wire cutters. "Improvised incendiary device under the seat."

Gad, she was in sorry shape if the mere sight of him had made her forget she was sitting on a bomb. "Oh, right."

He flashed her a wicked grin as he slipped between her bare legs. "Déjà vu, Just Kate?"

She was so not going *there.* "You're a long way from Oregon."

"Riverside SWAT is engaged in tactical cross-training for Homeland Security with Vegas SWAT and the FBI." His bristled cheek grazed her calf in a sensual caress, and her toes curled.

Fate had again thrown her into his path during a crisis. "Once more, we're both in the right place at the wrong time."

"Guess this is your lucky day."

"Yes, I'm so fortunate that some nut job wants to blow me to kingdom come."

His warm breath feathered over her instep, making her stomach jitterbug. "If I weren't in Vegas, he'd have succeeded."

"I sincerely hope that arrogance isn't misplaced."

"Relax." He chuckled. "You're in the best hands in the Western Hemisphere."

Been there, done that, had abandoned the torn panties. She didn't doubt his prowess…in bed. Whether she trusted him with her life was another question. Her temples throbbed. She despised giving up control, hated not having a choice.

Six hours after she'd run out on him, she'd boarded a one-way flight to Europe. As the 747 had lifted into the sky, she'd prayed for forgiveness. And hoped that somehow she would find the strength to resurrect her spirit from the grave of despair.

Over the past two-plus years, she had reinvented herself. She'd rebuilt her shattered psyche an excruciating step at a time. She was a woman reborn. *Nobody's* pawn. *She* was in charge of her fate.

Until the stalker had upped the ante.

Liam's strong fingers gripped her ankle. "I need more room. Prop your right leg over my shoulder."

Flushing, she did as he directed. No need to stress over the bomb. She'd expire from embarrassment. If she lived, tonight's entry dictated to her electronic journal would be a lulu! *Dear Diary, an old lover I never wanted to see again saved me from getting blown to smithereens by a crazed stalker.*

He whistled. "Nice piece of work! Never run into one built quite like this."

"That's what Carson said." He'd also informed her that, because of the close quarters, the bomb tech couldn't wear protective gear. Liam was as vulnerable as she was. She bit her lip. "Can you deactivate it?"

"No worries." His voice was muffled as his big, warm hand eased her thighs farther apart. "I don't seem to have a problem not causing an explosion where you're concerned."

Her flush burned hotter. As if she needed a reminder of her ultimate humiliation. Even more humiliating, her body still craved his…like a dangerous narcotic. She'd locked away her longing over the years of agonizing withdrawal. But her subconscious insisted on tormenting her with dreams of being in Liam's bed. Dreams that left her trembling with need and aching with desire that no amount of cold showers could quench.

Why did her mind continue to inspire passion that her body was incapable of consummating?

"I'm gonna shift you into a better position."

"Is that a good idea?"

"All my ideas are good." Several seconds passed. "Except one," he muttered. "Once upon a time." His wide palm covered her thigh, and she jumped. "Easy. Hold real still." He pressed the lever, and her seat hummed slowly backward.

He returned his focus to beneath her. Long, tense heartbeats of thick silence ticked past. Perspiration beaded on her upper lip, and she fought not to fidget.

"Hmm." Liam's dubious exclamation made her go rigid. That didn't sound promising. "What's your favorite color?"

"Why?"

"Trying to determine which wire to cut."

Belatedly, she remembered the man had claimed his middle name was Gamble. "You're gambling with our *lives?*"

"More like an educated guess." He laughed. "Live life on your own terms, Just Kate."

"I d-don't…" Her voice shook, and she cleared her throat. "I don't have a favorite color." Not anymore. She only saw the world through her camera lens…in shadowed shades of gray.

"Black it is." His unruffled reply was as jaunty as ever. Metal bit into metal, unnaturally loud in the heavy silence.

"Son of a bitch!" Liam gritted, and she flinched. He segued into fast motion. "I suggest you offer up any last prayers. Fast." Rapid-fire snaps echoed from under her seat.

Hot, suffocating air jammed in her lungs. She cringed, braced for the fireball that would end their existence.

Nothing happened.

Liam's broad back rose and fell. He emerged from beneath her and knelt between her thighs. His dark hair was tousled, and his eyes sparkled as if he'd stepped off a thrill ride instead of cheating death by seconds. "That was interesting."

The horizon spun in crazy loop-de-loops. "It's over?"

"Yeah." He shot her a wry smile. "After the big buildup, the finish is often anticlimactic."

"Stop it," Kate whispered. Her shoulders sagged and she wove from side to side.

"Whoa! Head down." Liam pushed Kate's head between her knees. Her soft cheek brushed his, and her sun-warmed hair trailed over his skin like silken licks of flame. His belly clenched. When he'd recognized her, the world had screeched to a halt. His brain had blanked out. He'd forgotten how to walk.

He'd had to force aside stunned shock and snap his focus back to save her life. Now that the danger had passed, Kate consumed all his attention.

Her shiny chestnut hair was longer, down to her midback. She'd gained much-needed weight, and the ragged, angry red scars mottling her right arm had faded to pink. The biggest difference was in her face. The raw pain that had been torturing her when they'd met had ebbed to haunted shadows in her big brown eyes.

He buried his face in her hair and breathed in her essence. She smelled the same, like the elegant, expensive flower gardens gracing estates where he used to mow lawns for spending money.

His heart stumbled, mimicking his body's reaction when he'd recognized her. Two-plus years of soul-searching. Twenty-nine months of questions. One hundred and sixteen weeks of living hell receded into the past as he held Kate in his arms.

Liam had never confided in anyone about Kate. Why talk, when only action achieved results? Hell, he didn't understand why he was so confused and hurt—so obsessed over tracking down a woman he'd known mere hours. So he'd suffered in silence and camouflaged his pain behind a good-time-guy smoke screen.

But *everything* had changed for him that night. His life, his beliefs, his heart had been flipped upside down and yanked inside out. He'd spent four months searching for her and the following two months serial dating—trying to forget her. He'd eventually stopped dating, but he'd never forgotten Kate. Even as recently as an hour ago, he'd studied women's faces as he passed them on the street, hoping, *needing* to find her.

No other woman tripped his pulse. No other woman weakened his knees. No other woman hurtled adrenaline through his system with the same thrilling rush he got when he disarmed a bomb.

No other woman terrified him.

Just Kate.

"I still remember the way you taste," he whispered into her silky hair.

She flinched away like he'd burned her and jerked upright. "Are you stalking me?"

Yanked out of the past, he blinked. *"What?"*

"Notes, flowers…and now a bomb. Is this your way of exacting revenge because I ran out on you—"

"Hold the phone, babe. How could I send notes and flowers when I didn't even know who the hell you were?"

"You're a cop, you could have easily found out."

"I searched for you for months. But I had no last name, address, make or model of vehicle. Nobody at the bar remembered seeing you before. I didn't know where you worked. Mercy Hospital wouldn't release patient information. I had *squat.*"

Her eyes widened in bewilderment, her long lashes dark against her pale face. "Only my first name," she whispered.

"Just Kate." He scrubbed a hand over his face in frustration. "Do you know how many variations of *Kates* live in the vicinity of Riverside, Oregon? One thousand, four hundred and eighty-two." He clenched his jaw. "None of them were you."

"You called over a thousand women?"

"I could hardly trot around with a pair of torn panties and see who they fit."

Her lips went white. "*Why* did you try so hard to find me?"

He'd convinced himself it was because he wanted to ensure she was okay. He wasn't a player. He'd never taken a woman to bed without a clear understanding of terms.

Just Kate.

When he messed up, it was his duty to fix it. "Out of all the men in the bar that night, why did you go home with *me?* Why did you give away your virginity to *me*?"

Trembling, she stared down at the tips of her French manicured toenails. "I didn't intend to sleep with you."

"You could have changed your mind at any time. Refused me at any time." He nearly choked as he spilled out the terrible fear that had tortured him for two years. "I never would have forced you. You had a choice, even at the last second. One simple *'no'* would have stopped me cold. You *do* know that?"

She raised her head and met his gaze, her fawn's eyes steady. "Yes, of course. I simply got…carried away."

"'Oops, I lost my virginity to a stranger by *accident*?'" He drilled her with a hard stare. "No way. You had an agenda."

"You're still mad, after all this time." Alarmed confusion chased across her face, but she didn't deny she'd only used him. "That *could* give you incentive to stalk me."

"Not in this lifetime." In spite of his ire, she aroused every protective instinct he possessed. "But I will find out who is stalking you. And neutralize him."

Her wary expression said she didn't believe him. Frustration burned. He'd been callously used before. Brutally dumped. But only Kate had the power to hurt him with a look.

He'd never left a woman unsatisfied. He'd sure as hell never made one cry in his bed. Or scared one enough to run away. Yet Kate had slept with him once and thought he was some kind of freaking *psycho?* He would damn well prove her wrong.

That wasn't his ego talking. Her opinion of him mattered more than he cared to admit.

He hollered, "Murphy!" The big German shepherd bounded over, and Liam motioned. "Murphy, search!"

"Murphy is a *dog?*" Kate went rigid as Murphy circled the car. "You said Murphy was your *partner.* A cop, just like you."

"K-9 Murphy *is* a cop. He graduated from a training academy, just like me. It's a felony to assault him, just like me. He apprehends bad guys and faces bombs, just like me."

Murphy reached the open door and stuck his nose inside, sniffing loudly. He should have sat in passive alert when he scented the accelerant, but he continued to sniff. Liam frowned.

Kate gasped. "What's he doing?"

"I want him to locate the bomb. It reinforces his training. There are nine basic scents of explosive components. Some dogs can do twelve. Murphy knows eighteen." Why didn't he recognize the device inside Kate's car? Though he'd know it from now on. Liam's frown deepened. First the weird schematics, and now this.

Kate scrambled up onto the seat. "Get him away from me!"

What was up with her overreaction? "He won't touch you. He's trained not to touch *anything* during a search, so he won't detonate an explosion. He needs to learn the scent."

Kate huddled on the seat. "I don't care! Make him leave."

Bewildered, Murphy fixated on Kate. The big dog tensed, waiting for a cue from him. *Okay partner, what now? You're not treating this scared female like a bad guy.*

"Down, Murphy. She's a friend." Murphy sat. Liam turned to Kate, his heart sinking. "Why are you terrified of dogs?"

She squared her shoulders. "I am not terrified. I'm just not comfortable around them."

Yeah. And the A-Bomb was simply a few cranky atoms. Liam shook his head. How was this possible? He and the woman he couldn't forget weren't sexually compatible. She not only despised him, she also despised his partner and best friend. He'd rather she take a razor blade to his jugular.

Liam offered her his hand. She ignored it and clambered out on her own. He clenched his jaw. She mistrusted him as much as the dog. More than her appearance had changed. She'd erected a shield around her heart as tough and impenetrable as Kevlar. Doubt assailed him. Had their disastrous encounter caused that? He'd never run up against a problem that couldn't be solved with a few strategically placed explosives.

Just Kate.

The answer was as obvious as the difference between a hearing aid and a hand grenade. Maybe Kate *wasn't* who he'd thought she was. Maybe he'd imagined the connection between them. Maybe all this time, he'd been chasing a dream.

Then why was the idea of walking away from her like a roadway spike strip through his chest?

Liam signaled the waiting teams all clear. The incident commander jogged over, followed by the bomb disposal squad and SWAT. The FBI agent heading up security training beat them all. Special Agent Chuck Hanson's merciless squint would do Dirty Harry proud, and his skin had been baked by the desert sun to the same color and texture of his rattlesnake skin boots.

Liam normally worked well with the Feds. One of his best friends from high school was a Feeb. Which was why the Riverside SWAT team had received an invite to the regional training. However, getting along with Hanson took effort. The man had a hard-on for his job that made him a real pain to work with. The teams had deflected his attitude and verbal jabs all week.

The Vegas and Riverside SWAT teams—including Liam's brothers Aidan, Con and Grady—secured the area while the bomb disposal unit secured the car. Hanson thrust his face into Kate's, and she shifted uneasily. "Special Agent Chuck Hanson, FBI." He flashed his badge. "I need to see some ID. Now."

Liam moved to Kate's side. "She's the victim, Hanson, remember?"

"Special Agent Hanson, O'Rourke. You're no longer needed on site. Dismissed." So much aggression thrummed in his graveled voice and taut stance that Murphy rumbled out a low growl.

Hanson gripped the butt of his holstered pistol. "If you can't control that animal, I will."

Liam had a reputation as the easygoing brother. A joke was often the most effective weapon. However, he couldn't find anything remotely funny about the current scenario. He signaled Murphy to heel, which put Liam between his dog and Hanson's gun. "I don't know what's lodged up your arse, and don't give a flying Finnegan. But don't take it out on Kate. And if you draw down on my dog, there won't be any question about what's lodged where."

"Are you threatening me, pretty boy?"

Liam rested his palm on the Glock in his thigh holster. Growing up in the middle of four brothers had taught him a thing or two about testosterone. As a K-9 officer, he'd been trained to project as the alpha male in the pack. If good old boy wanted a pissing contest, he'd oblige. "Just the facts, *Chuck.*"

"Liam," His oldest brother Aidan called from behind him. "What do you want the bomb squad to do with the device before we tow the car? Leave it or detach it?"

The question broke the simmering tension, no doubt as Aidan intended. Hanson eased his hand off his weapon. Liam turned and caught dual, *"What the hell?"* stares from both Aidan and next-to-oldest brother Con.

Ignoring his puzzled brothers, he reached into the car for Kate's purse, which he passed to her over his shoulder. "Leave it. I want to study that double antitamper switch." He swiveled back to see Kate awkwardly fishing out her wallet. Not for the first time, he wondered what kind of accident had caused her injury. He hadn't asked when they'd first met because, A: it was none of his business, and B: he'd sensed her extreme sensitivity to the topic. If she wanted him to know, she'd tell him.

She held out her driver's license with a shaking hand. "Someone's been stalking me for over a year. He's left notes and calla lilies, but this is the first time he's tried to hurt me."

Hanson took the license. He reached inside his brown suit jacket—which he insisted on wearing in spite of the withering heat wave deep-frying Las Vegas—and extracted a cell phone. He stabbed out a number. "Run wants and warrants on Katherine Marie Chabeau." He spelled her name, rapped out her birth date, model of car and license plate number.

Liam concentrated on tamping down his fury and studied Kate's graceful profile. *Katherine Marie Chabeau.* He now knew her full name and birthday. She was a Gemini. So was his baby brother, and she shared a few of Grady's personality traits. Dual-natured, elusive and complex fit her to a *T.*

And in spite of everything Liam still *didn't* know, he would fight legions of both heaven and hell to protect her.

"No warrants, no priors, ten-four." Hanson tucked away the phone. "You received a message from this 'stalker'? Show me."

Kate bit her lip. "I know this sounds crazy, but they sort of…crumble into ashes after I open and read them."

Hanson looked at Liam, skepticism burning in his gaze. "You're the bomb tech. Explain that."

Hmm. "Hell, you can make a bomb out of toilet bowl cleaner and tinfoil." Liam shrugged. "Have you seen the disposable thermal heating pads that activate when you open the package? If the right combination of chemicals were applied to paper and sealed airtight, it's theoretically possible to create a note that would 'destruct' after a few moments exposure to oxygen."

"Theoretically?"

"I've never lab tested the idea. Obviously, Kate's stalker has mastered advanced chemistry." To a scary degree.

Hanson snorted at Kate. "I think you've been watching too many movies, little lady. What the hell is really going on?"

"I'm telling the truth! The lily is still in my car."

"Anybody can buy flowers. What did the note say?"

"The same thing they all say. 'I burn with passion for you, Katherine.'" She shuddered. "Except this one had an addition—'I'm through with you.' I thought maybe he was finally going to leave me alone."

Liam tensed. Just the opposite.

Hanson rubbed his chin. "You *just happen*ed to see the bomb in time?"

"When I started the engine, the lid popped off my mocha frappuchino. I leaned down to pick it up." She gulped. "That's when I saw the contraption under my seat."

Bile rose in Liam's throat. She'd come so close to dying. Mere chance, and a hankering for chocolate had saved her.

Hanson stared at Kate's license for several long, taut moments, then stared at her. "Are you the Katherine Chabeau who is the spokeswoman for Renée Allete, the French photographer?"

She nodded, and Liam did a double take. Another freaky coincidence. A collector's book of photographs sat on his coffee table, open to one of Renée Allete's black and whites. He'd been thumbing through the pages in a gallery, and the picture had hit him like a battering ram. He'd been compelled to buy the book.

"Renée Allete is conducting an auction at the Venetian the day after tomorrow." Hanson looked pleased with himself. "A bomb scare would generate a buttload of free publicity."

Kate's jaw dropped. Before she recovered enough to reply, Liam jumped in. "Watch the mud slinging, Hanson. I neutralized that incendiary device. It came damn close to killing us both."

"Or that's what Ms. Chabeau wanted you to think."

"That bomb was no publicity prank. It was built by someone who knew what they were doing, and it was intended to kill. My dog didn't recognize the accelerant."

Hanson frowned suspiciously as he returned Kate's license. "A professional job."

Kate fumbled with her wallet. "I've made police reports about every note, in every city. Madrid, Rome, London..."

"You've recently been in those specific cities?" Hanson's eyes narrowed. "Turn around and put your hands on the car." He reached inside his jacket for his cuffs. "I'm taking you in."

Kate gasped. *"What? Why?"*

"Suspicion of terrorist activities." He spun Kate and pushed her against the car. "I said turn around." He yanked her left arm behind her and slapped on the cuffs, then the right. He gave no consideration to her disability, and she uttered a soft cry of distress. He shoved her legs apart and frisked her.

Rage flashed through Liam's veins, as fast and hot as a match igniting gunpowder. His years of training, his cop's discipline exploded in a red haze.

He lunged for Hanson's throat.

Chapter 3

1:00 p.m.

Liam crashed into a wall of male bodies in battle gear. As the bloodred haze faded, he recognized his brothers. It took all three of them to muscle him to the other side of the car.

Murphy growled and snapped. If it had been anyone else manhandling him, the dog would have torn them apart. Liam struggled to break free. "Get off me!"

Aidan immobilized him in a loose chokehold. "What the *hell* got your shorts in a wad?"

Liam was forced to watch while Hanson marched Kate to his black SUV. "He hurt my woman! He has his hands all over her!"

Aidan, Con and Grady exchanged silent communication. They clearly thought he'd lost his ever-loving mind.

Maybe he had.

Grady, the SWAT team's paramedic, fisted his fingers in Liam's hair. "Look at me." He tipped Liam's head back. "Did you inhale exhaust fumes when you disarmed the bomb?"

Liam's snarled retort made his brothers' eyebrows shoot into their hairlines.

Grady shrugged at Aidan. "He's not foaming at the mouth, but maybe his rabies shots aren't current."

Con's grip on his arms relaxed slightly. "Chill out, bro. What's going on?"

Murphy finally reached his limit and leaped, fangs bared. Liam mustered enough self-restraint to call him off. "Murphy! Down!" Growling and trembling with agitation, Murphy reluctantly backed off and put his belly to the ground.

Liam set his teeth as Hanson revved up the SUV and peeled out of the parking lot, taking Kate away. "Turn. Me. Loose."

With Hanson gone, his brothers released him, but surrounded him in a deceptively casual circle. Liam sucked in a frustrated breath. He wasn't going anywhere until they let him.

Murphy moved to his left side and pressed against his thigh, offering silent backup. *I'm here. Say the word, and we'll take these cocky pups down.*

He ruffled the dog's thick fur. "Kate is the woman from Delany's Pub, two years ago on St. Patrick's Day."

That long ago night in Delany's Pub, the instant he'd seen her, Liam had felt as stunned and disoriented as if a flash bang had exploded in his face. He feared Pop had been right.

Pop had made a fantastical claim one evening when they were working on the Mustang. He'd said every O'Rourke male inherited the ability to know his soul mate the instant he saw her.

The O'Rourke men fell in love with one glance.

Out of four sons, Pop had told only him. Liam hadn't quite believed the wild story, but had never forgotten it. As a bomb tech, he knew appearances were deceptive.

What you *couldn't* see was what got you killed.

But over the past two years, Liam had watched Aidan and Con happily marry women they'd loved at first sight. Aidan and Zoe had just returned from their honeymoon in Jamaica.

Liam rested his hand on Murphy's head, taking comfort in his partner's loyal support, his solid, unshakable presence. How had it all gone so wrong for him? Maybe Pop had foreseen disaster. Maybe he'd known Liam would need the knowledge to sustain him until he could find *her* again.

Kate. The woman he'd loved and lost the same night.

The night a family trait had turned into a terrible curse.

Liam stroked Murphy's soft coat. "She's…" *I think she might be* The One. *I have to know. Even though the idea makes me want to gear up in a blast suit. Even though I've only been with her once. Even though she hates my guts, hates my dog and believes I'm stalking her.* Yeah. *That sounds nice and sane.*

He struggled for an explanation that wouldn't have Grady reaching for the white jacket that tied in the back. "Hanson will steamroll Kate. I have to protect her." Would she thank him? Or run away again? He had to help her, regardless.

Three sets of serious stares regarded him for several seconds. Then Grady grinned. "Yee-haw! Love 'em and leave 'em Liam finally met a woman he couldn't turn his back on."

Would she take the opportunity to stomp all over him? Then walk out, leaving a bloody hole in his heart…just like Michelle?

Aidan nodded at Liam, his brown eyes dark with empathy. "A man's gotta do what he's gotta do."

Con cocked his head. "But play your hand smart, not hard, little brother."

If they hadn't intervened, he'd be cooling his heels in jail. Useless to Kate. He glanced at the thronged reporters in the distance. Oh yeah, the media would have salivated over footage of him assaulting a federal officer. "I hear ya."

Aidan's wife Zoe was somewhere in that media mob. She'd convinced Riverside station KKEY to let her accompany the SWAT team to Vegas and cover nonclassified sectors of regional Homeland Security training. Zoe was smart, sympathetic and chock-full of integrity, but even she wouldn't have been able to put a positive spin on Liam throttling a Fed. The last time he'd fully unleashed his temper was his freshman year in college. That had been over a girl who'd ended up dumping him, too.

He'd *never* lost it on the job. For Kate's sake, he'd better get it together. Fast. Tactical strategies, not tantrums. "Stand down, guys. I'm over my case of the stupids."

His brothers opened the circle around him. With Murphy trotting at his heels, Liam sprinted toward his Mustang, parked at the outer perimeter. "Hate to leave when the party's just getting started, but I have a damsel in distress to rescue."

Grady's groan carried on the baking air. "He's a goner."

Police officers crowded the room where Kate perched stiffly on a metal chair. They'd removed the cuffs to fingerprint her, but her arms were again bound behind her. The stocky incident commander sat across the table, still in full body armor. A balding man Hanson had addressed as Jerry guarded the door with his hand on his pistol as if she might make a break for it. She rolled her eyes. Like she was crazy enough to try.

A redheaded detective and a gray-haired captain from the Vegas police stood beside Hanson as the FBI agent fired out questions. The local cops had angrily argued about jurisdiction after Hanson had brought her in, over an hour ago.

They'd Mirandized her, but she hadn't been charged. Hanson badgered her with questions, but wasn't accepting her answers.

None of them were listening to her.

Kate glanced at her pale reflection in the wall mirror. Who was on the other side looking in? Her arms ached, and the tension winching her temples had intensified into a screaming headache. Great time for one of her migraines. She needed a clear head to get out of this. She shifted in the unforgiving chair. If only she could rub away the pain.

Stay calm. Once she made everyone see it was all a huge misunderstanding, she'd be free to go. "Could you please remove these handcuffs? They're hurting me."

"Sure." Graveled voice falsely cheerful, Hanson gestured at a table that held a sweating water pitcher and clean glasses. Everyone but her had something to drink. "Tell us who you work with, and we'll uncuff you, get you water, aspirin, whatever."

Her headache must be obvious, big surprise. Jerry could probably hear her pulse clanging against her skull across the room. "I've explained, it's just me and my admin assistant."

"Her name?"

His name was Etienne Duplais. And she wasn't about to sacrifice him to Hanson. Confronted by police, Etienne would completely lose his English. If he found out she'd been arrested, he'd pitch the mother of all hissy fits. Who knew what he'd say? Her young protégé was impassioned and impetuous, but his artistic elan was infallible. "Not important. I work alone."

"So you're admitting you planted the bomb yourself?"

"*No!* The person who has been stalking me planted the bomb!"

"With mysterious notes that self-destruct?" He snorted. "You don't expect us to swallow that?"

"It's the truth!" Liam had explained how. Two years ago, all her instincts had told her she could trust the handsome SWAT cop. After being held in his arms again today, the feeling was even stronger. She glanced at the mirror once more, almost imagining she felt his presence. But Liam had gone into a huddle with his brothers when she'd been arrested. Though her innocence *must* be obvious, they apparently hadn't wanted to argue with the FBI. Liam hadn't shown up at the police station, either.

Why would he? They'd had a one-night stand, a long time ago. She'd used him and then fled. But she'd never forgotten him. Never gotten over him. He'd changed her life.

Heck, he'd *saved* her life.

He claimed he'd tried to find her for months. What kind of obsession inspired that much persistence? She shook her head. How could she believe her instincts to trust him, when intellect demanded she at least consider that Liam might be the stalker?

Maybe he wasn't absent because he didn't care, but because he cared far too much. In all the wrong ways.

She met the FBI agent's icy gray gaze, and took a slow breath. A handsome prince would not be charging to her rescue. She had to rescue herself…like always. "I want to call my attorney. I'll make bail before you finish the paperwork."

Hanson bared his teeth. "Not so fast, Ms. Chabeau. We can hold someone we suspect of planning an attack on the U.S.—someone we declare an 'enemy combatant'—in military custody, without charges. Without legal representation. Indefinitely."

She gasped. "You're lying! That's unconstitutional!"

"Homeland Security laws now give us the power to protect our citizens from terrorists."

"If that's the truth, it's horrifying. Who's going to protect citizens from zealots like *you?*"

His smile widened into arrogance. "Spoken like a true anarchist. Your file mentions that you're from France."

Shortly after she'd been brought in, he'd received a stack of computer files, no doubt detailing her life down to her bra size. The government's new powers were frightening. She'd only begun to learn the extent. "I've been living in Paris, but retained my U.S. citizenship. I'm no terrorist. I'm an artist!" She half rose from the chair.

"Most fanatics think they are." He pushed her down. "You've overplayed your hand, this time. The bomb in your car was constructed from a new explosive we have yet to identify. Bomb dogs don't recognize it, X-rays can't detect it. It's as unique and incriminating as a fingerprint. Pointing at you."

The pain in her temples throbbed viciously. "Someone tried to kill me with this new explosive, and you're blaming *me?*"

"I'll spell it out. We've only found this chemical residue after bombings in Europe—linked to an elite terrorist organization." He waved her passport, which had been in her purse. "An organization active in the same cities at the same times you were there. Now we find it in your car. We believe this group's attacks were rehearsals for something much bigger. A major strike. You're our first lead. Our only connection."

Bewildered, she floundered through waves of fear. "I don't know anything about bombs. Someone has been stalking me for a year." It was difficult to speak with her mouth bone dry. She watched Hanson deliberately sip water. "The guy has the money to follow me from Europe, he could have purchased this new stuff."

Hanson plunked the glass down in front of her. "If an unknown individual *is* targeting you, what's the motive?"

"What motivates any maniac?" She refused to point a finger at Liam. Power-hungry Hanson would attack him. Accusations of treason could sink Liam's career. Ruin his *life*. She had nothing more than suspicions. And her uneasiness *could* be guilt over the way she'd treated him. Even on the remote chance Liam was stalking her, she couldn't believe he was connected with terrorists. Let Hanson come up with his own darned answers.

"Maybe someone developed a fixation at an auction. Or when Renée's photographs were featured on that home decorating show and she became American consumers' newest fad." She strove to banish shrillness from her voice. "I'm not important enough to interest terrorists. Even if I had somehow attracted their attention, what would be their reason for trying to kill me?"

"Internal power struggle. The damn nut jobs off each other all the time. Maybe you know more than they want you to. More than you think you do. Cooperate, and we can protect you."

"I am *not* involved in a conspiracy to commit terrorism!"

"We're obtaining warrants to search your residences and Renée Allete's studio in Paris as we speak."

Perspiration trickled down her hairline, and she rubbed her face on her shoulder. Why couldn't she wake up from this hideous nightmare? Or maybe she *had* been killed by the car bomb and landed in hell. It was hot enough. "You won't find anything."

"Time will tell." He shrugged. "Enjoy federal prison."

Nausea welled in her throat. "You can't keep me in custody! It's not only my life at stake here!"

"Are you making threats?"

"No!" She forced herself to enunciate slowly. "My two-year-old niece, Aubrey, was born with a genetic kidney disorder. She needs a transplant, a procedure my brother-in-law's insurance won't cover. The transplant *must* be done while Aubrey's still strong enough to survive…and the hospital won't perform the procedure without being paid first."

Hanson smirked. "How original. You climbed into bed with terrorists to get money for your *niece's operation.*"

"I haven't done anything wrong." Kate stared into his eyes, as flat and cold as the silver mirror. "The auction at the Venetian is to raise the necessary funds. If that auction doesn't take place as scheduled, we won't have the money. Every single thing must happen as planned, on time. This is Aubrey's last chance. Her *only* chance. If you detain me, she could die!"

He shrugged again. "Your camera-shy boss will have to jet over from Paris and conduct the auction personally."

She sighed and gave up. "*I* am Renée Allete. I use a pseudonym and pretend to be the company's spokeswoman because I prefer anonymity." She begged with her gaze, her voice. "You *have* to let me go. A little girl's life depends on it!"

"Thousands of lives depend on identifying the source of this dangerous new explosive." Hanson planted his hands on the table in front of her. "Who else are you pretending to be, Ms. Chabeau? Until we know for certain, you're not going anywhere."

Watching and listening from outside the interrogation room, Liam pursed his lips. *Kate* was Renée Allete. Now he knew why the haunting photo had evoked the same emotions in him as she had. He'd studied the photo nearly every night, and hadn't been able to shake the eerie feeling.

As Hanson denied her plea for her niece's life, her body trembled and her brown fawn's eyes filled with tears. Liam slammed his fists against the glass. He'd been locked out for over an hour while Hanson hammered Kate. This was not his police station…hell, not even his precinct, and he had no authority. Not that he had any over the Feds, anyway. Helplessness was damn near killing him. Especially when Kate's welfare was at stake.

Murphy, tuned into Liam's emotions as always, whined and nudged his hip with his nose. *Keep your survival instincts sharp, partner. It's a dog-eat-dog world.*

Liam looked down at the anxious canine. "It's okay, pal. I'm not gonna smash a desk through the window and feed it to the bastard, piece by large, splintered piece. *Yet.*"

Another five minutes of this torture, and he might break.

"I would hope not." The deep male voice spiced with a melodic Spanish accent spoke from behind him. "'Desking' a federal officer will look lousy on your annual evaluation."

Grinning, Liam pivoted. "It's about damn time!" He did a double take. "Whoa! Aren't you pretty? What's with the hair?"

Alex Cortez lifted one shoulder, displacing his long black curls. He returned Liam's grin. "I have been undercover with a motorcycle gang."

Murphy looked up at Alex expectantly. *Long time, no see!*

Alex scratched Murphy's ears. "What's the emergency, *mi amigo?*"

Liam jerked his thumb toward the interrogation room. "The guy who thinks he's Tommy Lee Jones on crack."

Alex didn't bother looking in the window. "Ah, Special Agent Chuck Hanson."

"Met him before, have you?"

"I've had the pleasure."

Liam grimaced. "There are so many egos and badges duking it out in there, they won't be able to decide what kind of doughnuts to order, let alone figure out the truth."

Alex stared into the window. "What has Hanson done now?"

Liam filled him in, and they devised a ballsy tactical plan. When they concluded their discussion, anger darkened Alex's coffee-brown eyes to nearly black. "My father emigrated from Cuba so his sons could live in a country where such atrocities do not occur. The man makes a mockery of justice." He whipped out his phone. "You have Hanson's number?"

"I've had his number since the second we met."

Alex chuckled. "I'd wager my Harley on it." He spoke into the phone. "Agent Hanson, this is Supervisory Special Agent Alex Cortez. Please step outside, and bring your documentation."

Frowning, Hanson strode stiffly into the hallway. Alex took his time reading the entire file, and then nodded at him. "You will release Ms. Chabeau to me. Immediately."

"And let you nab the credit for an international—"

"Agent Hanson." Alex's low voice sounded lethal. "If you don't like my decision, you may take it up with my partner, Special Agent Pete Lassiter.

Hanson scowled and slammed back into the room.

Liam grinned. Now things were getting interesting.

Hanson jerked Kate into the hallway, her expression scared, her wrists still cuffed. Liam's grin disappeared as his strained patience crumbled. "Murphy, guard."

Murphy surged to his feet, and his warning growl backed Hanson against the window.

Kate squeaked and scuttled away from the dog, and Liam belatedly remembered her fear. He blocked her view of Murphy with his body. "It's okay, he's just gonna keep Hanson in line."

"You'll regret this, O'Rourke." Hanson's attempt at intimidation was neutralized by the fact that, with Murphy snarling inches from his crotch, he didn't dare move anything more than his lips.

"Probably." It took stubborn Irish will to wink at Kate, when what Liam really wanted to do was sweep her into his arms and hold her. Kiss away her fears. Soothe her pain. "But it'll be worth it."

"I'll have your badge for this!" Hanson snapped.

Liam dug out his universal handcuff key. "For transferring custody of a prisoner?" He swiveled to Kate. "Turn around." She complied and he carefully unlocked the cuffs.

Her arms dropped uselessly to her sides, and she turned back to face him. "My arms are numb."

"The circulation will resume in a minute." *And hurt like a bitch.* Liam gently rubbed her wrists. She grimaced, and he fought the urge to smash Hanson's leathery face. "I'm sorry, I know it smarts. Are you all right?" His fingertips brushed the scars on her right wrist. "Do you need to see a doctor?"

Her mouth trembled when he touched her scars. "I'm fine." She nervously eyed Murphy, who kept Hanson flattened against the wall with nothing but his steely brown gaze and a toothy snarl. "As long as the dog stays over there."

"Babe, you're afraid of the wrong dog. Murphy's less dangerous than the jerk he's holding back."

Alex stepped forward. "Supervisory Special Agent Alejandro Cortez, at your service, Ms. Chabeau." He lifted Kate's hand and swept a courtly bow. "I apologize for Agent Hanson, and assure you I'll take disciplinary action."

As Kate's eyes widened, an unaccustomed spear of jealously goaded Liam. He was no slouch with women, but they literally flung themselves at Alex. He elbowed his friend. "Show-off. Everyone calls him Alex, Kate."

Kate's voice was faint, her face white, but she held her spine regally straight. "Thank you, Agent Cortez."

"You're most welcome." Alex inclined his head at Hanson. "Agent Hanson, you're dismissed."

Liam waited several taut beats.

Finally, Hanson gritted, “I can’t twitch until he calls off this friggin’ dog.”

“Murphy, release.”

Aw…all right. Murphy sat back on his haunches, but his vigilant gaze never left Hanson’s face. *But I don’t trust him.*

Smart dog. Before Hanson could move, Liam leaned in and said very quietly, “If you ever put your hands on Kate again, I will let Murphy have your cojones for chew toys.”

Murphy smirked, and Alex doubled over in a coughing fit.

Red mottled Hanson’s neck and streaked across his face. “You can’t threaten me, pissant. I’m your superior.”

“That’s open for debate, Chuck.”

Hanson thrust out his chin. “Blatant insubordination.”

Alex executed his blasé shrug. “Please return Ms. Chabeau’s personal effects, except her passport, which I will retain.”

Muttering, Hanson stormed back into the interrogation room.

Liam sent Alex silent gratitude. “I owe you one.” Behind that angelic face lurked a scarily sharp intellect and bone-deep dedication to justice. “I’d appreciate a copy of the lab analysis on the bomb when it comes in, and intel from overseas.”

“Done.” Alex smiled. He knew he could also call in a favor any time. “I’ll need your Homeland Security pass. As of now, you have only one assignment.”

Liam handed it over without protest. He had his priorities straight.

Hanson marched out and thrust Kate’s purse at her, slapped her passport into Alex’s extended palm and then stalked away.

Kate sidled down the hallway. “I’ll be leaving, now. Thank you for getting me out of there.” Her gaze flicked to Liam, and fear-edged regret glinted in the soft brown depths. “Both of you.”

Alex held up a hand. “One moment, Ms. Chabeau.”

Kate stopped, wariness etching her expression. “Yes?”

“I’m afraid you’re not free to go.”

“But I thought—” Kate blanched. “Why not?”

“Because of the possible threat to national security, we cannot release you until you’re cleared of suspicion. It’s also for your own safety. If you were not targeted by these terrorists before, you may come to their attention now."

"But I have to leave!" She was so distraught, she didn't notice she'd walked closer to Murphy. "My niece's life depends on those photographs being sold at the auction!"

"I realize that, and can accommodate you."

Kate's shoulders sagged in relief. "Thank goodness."

Liam tensed. He was about to be entrusted with the most high-stakes incendiary device he'd ever handled. Pop had either been one hundred percent right, or dead wrong. The way Liam figured the odds, there was a fifty-fifty chance Kate was his love-at-first-sight soul mate. But this time, he couldn't walk away. He had to do his duty. Even if it blew up in his face.

Alex gave Kate his fallen angel's smile. "You are hereby remanded into the custody of Officer O'Rourke."

"What?" Kate rounded on Liam, her face etched with horror.

Alex calmly finished sealing their doom. "Until further notice, you must stay within Liam's sight 24/7."

Chapter 4

3:00 p.m.

Kate rubbed her aching temples as Agent Cortez urged Liam into a private confab. This could not be happening! She'd never done anything more daring than hold her camera out over the railing of the Eiffel Tower to snap a photo. Yet she was suspected of conspiracy to commit international terrorism?

Her headache ramped up, and she riffled through her purse for her migraine medication. She tugged out the bottle and groaned. *Empty.* The refill *had* been in her purse, but a vicious attack two weeks ago had kept her housebound for days. Blind with pain, she'd stored the meds in her bathroom cabinet for easy access.

Barring medication, she needed food...and a chocolate hit. She'd been in the hospital visiting Aubrey at breakfast time, and hadn't had a chance to drink the mocha frappuccino that had saved her life. The FBI interrogation had preempted lunch.

To distract herself from the pain, Kate studied Liam, engaged in vehement conversation with Agent Cortez. The harsh overhead light washed out everyone else, but showcased the SWAT cop's compelling features—wavy blue-black hair, defined cheekbones and strong, square jaw. She'd never met a more striking man. Her artist's eye saw a magnetic, devastating, dripping-with-testosterone alpha male. She automatically reached for her camera, and her stomach dropped. Her beloved Leica had been left in the car, which was in police impoundment.

Cortez finished his speech—a warning, judging by his quiet ferocity—and Liam's complexion drained of color.

Commanding Murphy to stay, Liam pivoted and strode toward her as the FBI agent sauntered away. Liam's eyes glittered with a storm of emotions. Rage, determination and something that looked suspiciously like suppressed fear whirled through the emerald pools as fast and lethal as a tropical typhoon.

This was not the lighthearted Irish charmer who'd enchanted her two years ago. This man was serious business. All cop. Dangerous. Lethal.

What had Cortez told him? Kate took an involuntary step back. Damn fate's sick, twisted meddling. She'd vowed never again to be anyone's pawn. Yet, she'd been gift bagged by the FBI and delivered into Liam's clutches. The man who had witnessed her ultimate mortification. The man for whom she still had far too many turbulent feelings.

The man who *might* be stalking her.

Liam stopped and studied her face. "Are you *afraid* of me?"

In *so* many ways. "No," she lied. "I need to see about my camera before we leave."

To her relief, he accepted the change of subject. "It was in your car?"

She nodded. "I never go anywhere without it. If it sits in the evidence room too long, who knows what will happen to it, or my film. I have some irreplaceable candids of Aubrey." Her spirits sank. "They won't release it, will they?"

"Don't be so negative, Just Kate." He called Murphy to him.

As the enormous canine advanced, she instinctively retreated before she caught herself and stopped. "Does he have to come?"

"I know you don't like him, but he stays with me."

Wonderful. Liam and Murphy, both threats, in different aspects. Nightmares dogging her every step. At least he made the German shepherd stay back.

They trooped down one floor of metal stairs to the basement. Liam had Murphy sit beside the doorway, and Kate followed Liam to the desk blockading the fenced-off property room.

She couldn't help but admire the view. *Admire?* She could barely staunch the drool. Liam's navy cotton T-shirt strained across impossibly broad shoulders and outlined ripped muscles. Her gaze drifted lower, and she swallowed hard. Drat. Those snug jeans cupping such a nicely shaped behind should be declared a controlled substance.

The SWAT cop's stroll was a rhythmic, confident prowl. Not quite a swagger, but almost. A man who knew exactly where he was going and what he wanted.

A man who wouldn't take no for an answer.

The gray-haired cop behind the desk shot down their request faster than a fleeing suspect. Once Liam chatted him up and then offered his Glock for some "seasoned advice," the officer agreed to page his supervisor.

Where Liam was concerned, luck was a lady. And Lady Luck was with Kate for once in this day of disaster. The supervisor was a woman. Never mind that the bottle blonde was practically old enough to be Liam's mother. He flashed his shield and his smile—tough call to say which was shinier. After five minutes of O'Rourke charm bombs lobbed her way, the supervisor surrendered Kate's camera. Kate took satisfaction in the fact that the woman wasn't too bedazzled to forget to make him sign a receipt. Until she saw that blondie had jotted her phone number on Liam's copy.

She clamped down on fury as she marched toward the stairs. Every emotion-based decision she'd ever made had caused a catastrophe…including sleeping with Liam. She couldn't afford to lose it. She had to remain in control. Unfortunately, she'd been legally chained to the one man who could make her come undone.

Adding to her humiliation, it wasn't because he had any special feelings for her. He had the same effect on *all* women.

He paused at the base of the stairwell. "Why are you pissed off? We got your camera back."

She shook her head. "I'm fine."

"And I'm Lucky the leprechaun." He blocked her way. "What's wrong?"

She sighed. "Okay, you've officially been appointed my keeper. I'll do whatever is necessary to save Aubrey."

"Ah." He pursed his lips. "It's all right to be angry. If my life had been flipped sideways, I'd be torqued, too."

"Don't worry about my emotional state. I certainly don't." At least she hadn't until a smooth-talking, sexy-walking Irishman had disintegrated her composure. "This arrangement will be on *my* terms. Simple and uncomplicated."

"You mean boring."

"Maybe so. But we'll do it *my* way."

"An old, but popular song in Sin City." His seductive mouth quirked. His sexy, knowing smile could cause a revolt in a convent. He sobered. "But when it comes to your safety, I'm not taking any risks. When I say *'jump,'* you ask, *'how high?'*"

"Give the man an inch, and he thinks he's a ruler." She planted her hand on her hip. "Try jumping off the stratosphere."

His lips twitched. "For someone who isn't mad, you're doing a better impression than the guy playing Elvis at the Mirage."

She hung onto her cool by a fragile hair. "We're stuck with each other. Let's leave feelings out of it. Not get personal."

"Good tactical plan." His wry expression matched his tone. "But way too late, babe. The igniter cord was lit on that fuse a long time ago. The blowout can only be contained for so long."

Her cell phone rang, sparing her an undignified retort about what he could blow out where. By the mischievous twinkle in his eyes, he'd read her mind. How did Liam O'Rourke eclipse her common sense? Make her lose focus of her goals? Erase her hard-won progress and hurtle her a hundred giant steps backward into the past? She snatched the phone from her purse.

"Kate?" Edging out a burst of static, her brother-in-law Daniel's anxious voice thrummed over the line. "We need you."

Her heart skipped a beat. When she'd left earlier, Aubrey had been okay. "Daniel? Has something happened to Aubrey?"

"She's…upset…" More static broke up the message. Maybe being in the stairwell was scrambling the signal. "Come to…hospital."

"Can you hear me?" Kate shouted. "I'll be there as soon as I can." The crackling increased, and she lost the signal.

She squelched gnawing anxiety. Someone in the family needed to stay calm, and she'd been elected, by default. "We need to go to the hospital."

Liam's handsome face sharpened with concern. "Is Aubrey okay?"

"Daniel said she was upset about something. The reception was terrible. She was fine this morning."

"Is your whole family living in Vegas, now?"

"Yes, except me. Dad moved the company headquarters here two years ago. Taxes are cheaper, and the climate goes easy on his arthritis." For Kate, the climate was easier the farther away she was from her sister's histrionics, her mother's criticism and her father's indifference.

They jogged up to the main floor, and Liam commanded the dog to heel, which put Murphy behind him, on his left.

Kate scurried to his other side. In another lifetime, she'd accompanied Pookie Bear, her sister's toy poodle, to obedience school. Sis had typically flaked out after two lessons, and Mom had made Kate take him. "Don't dogs heel on the right?"

"K-9s are trained to go left, to keep clear of the officer's gun hand."

She glanced warily at the lethal black pistol holstered on his thigh. The weapon was a grim reminder that she was in police custody. Liam wouldn't hesitate to use the gun to protect her. She bit her lip. What if he *was* the stalker? Or what if he suspected her of terrorism? Would he turn the weapon against her? He might love 'em and leave 'em when it came to women, but Officer O'Rourke was devoted to duty. That devotion could be a very good thing. Or turn out to be a very *bad* thing.

It could swing either way.

The problem was, she didn't know which way.

Destiny was in the driver's seat. The trip was as unpredictable and scary as hurtling around the Arc de Triomphe in a Parisian taxicab. But no matter how terrifying the ride, she *refused* to be a helpless passenger.

They strode outside, and blinding sunlight and suffocating heat slammed her to a standstill. How did people live in a place with the approximate temperature of a pottery kiln? She longed for the serenity of pearly gray skies, misty rain and lush foliage. One reason she'd chosen Paris was the effervescent city's similar climate to the Pacific Northwest.

She reeled, and Liam slid his arm around her waist. "Whoa!" He glanced down at her. "Are you all right?"

She'd die under torture before confessing that she appreciated his support. Or admit she craved contact with him. He smelled scrumptious, as fresh and clean as the rain-washed forests she longed for. She'd never forgotten the toe-curling intensity of his delicious chocolate and whiskey kisses.

Kate ground her teeth, ramping her headache to agony. *Why* was she so conflicted about him? One minute, she wondered if he was dangerous, and the next, fantasized about kissing him.

"I'm fine. Let's go." She shook her head and shot a glance over her shoulder. Since the stalker had insinuated his creepy-crawly self into her life, she'd grown extra vigilant. "It must be a hundred and ten degrees." She fanned her face, which merely wafted scorching air.

A quirk of his glossy eyebrow stole her breath faster than the overheated atmosphere. How did he *do* that? He smiled and strode forward. "But it's a dry heat."

She grimaced at the acrid scent of baking asphalt as they hurried around the side of the building to the parking lot. "So is a crematorium."

He tugged out a remote key chain. His white Mustang beeped twice as the security system disengaged.

"Vintage cars don't usually have alarms."

"I installed one. Pays to be careful."

"You don't strike me as the cautious type, Mr. 'my middle name is Gamble,' Disarms-bombs-for-a-living."

His gaze stroked her face. "Did you know that some cultures believe if you save a person's life, they belong to you forever?" His gaze sharpened. "I take care of what's mine."

She gulped. His deep declaration made her pulse stumble. There were scarier things than being stalked. She yanked open the door and started to slide inside.

"Oh no, you don't." He tugged her toward him so quickly that she lost her balance. Lightning-fast, his arms wrapped around her, and she ended up plastered to his hard-muscled body.

He was big and solid and steady in an uncertain world. For an insane moment, she longed to forget the danger. To rest her cheek against the navy cotton covering his wide chest and let him hold her. Sheltered in his arms, she felt safe, cherished. Dazed, she looked up at him. His searing green eyes held hers captive. Hotter and more intense than the Vegas atmosphere, his laser gaze burned away her doubts. Her fears suddenly seemed groundless and silly.

Night after lonely night, she'd dreamed about Liam's lean, hard body covering hers. About his green eyes staring into hers with smoldering desire. About his full lips and teasing, talented tongue. And then she'd awakened, alone and hurting.

She'd had a brief, wondrous taste of him. Just enough to leave her craving more, as badly as a junkie jonesing for a fix.

His arms tightened, drawing her into an achingly intimate embrace. He lowered his head until nothing more than warm breaths separated them. His full lips parted.

She couldn't move, couldn't blink. Couldn't breathe.

The world slowed…teetered on the trembling edge of flight.

The thick, dark fringe of his lashes swept downward, and her stomach clenched. Anticipation skimmed up her spine.

Murphy made a noise somewhere between a snort and a cough, and Liam tensed, swore, stepped back. "Too hot."

Her reply was a cracked whisper. "Tell me something I don't know."

He flashed an unsteady grin, and gestured at the car, then at her just-above-the-knee black linen sheath and matching sandals. "Sun-broiled leather seats on bare thighs."

She cringed. "Oh. Youch."

"Exactly." He released her, leaving her feeling more alone than ever, and rummaged in the trunk. He quickly returned with several ragged towels. "Murphy doesn't appreciate sitting on hot seats, either. Besides, he drools." He flipped a towel over the front seat.

She hesitated. *Dog drool?*

Liam smirked. "I *do* wash them."

"Of course you do. Sorry." She hopped into the ovenlike car.

Murphy stubbornly sat there, and Liam sighed. "Get in."

Murphy didn't budge. Clearly upset, he barked at Liam, and Kate flinched away. Would he attack?

Liam rolled his eyes. "He hates sitting in the back."

Her brows drew together. "You have *got* to be kidding. We don't have time for this."

Liam shrugged. "Does it look like he's kidding?" He made a hand motion at the scowling dog. "We're in a rush. It's the back or walk, pal."

Grumbling, Murphy climbed into the car and perched on the towel Liam had spread behind the driver's seat.

Liam strode around to the driver's side. He started the engine and flipped the AC to arctic. Before long, they were cool and speeding through afternoon traffic toward the hospital.

Liam glanced at her. "You thought I was going to kiss you back there." He smiled. "I almost did."

What had changed his mind?

His smile widened into a naughty grin. "You wanted me to."

She battled unease. Those vigilant gambler's eyes didn't miss a trick. "Your imagination is only exceeded by your ego."

"Why do you do that?"

"Do what?"

"Deny your feelings?" He gave her a considering look. "'I'm not scared, I'm not mad, I don't desire you.'"

"I wasn't, I wasn't and I don't."

"You're lying."

The sharp-eyed cop was far too discerning. She looked over her shoulder again, out the back window. She never lost the jittery feeling of being watched all the time. "The heat is making you hallucinate."

A frown eclipsed his sunny smile. "Where's the warm, vibrant woman I met on St. Patrick's Day, Just Kate? The emotional, colorful, passionate woman I made love to?"

"She died," she said flatly.

Sorrow laced his low voice. "What happened to you during the past few years, sweetheart?"

"I grew up. Faced reality. Packed away childish dreams."

He shook his head. "Dreams are what keep your soul alive. What keep you going when tragedy and heartbreak bring the world crashing down around you."

The words spilled out before she could stop them. "What would you know about heartbreak? About tragedy? You smile, quirk a beautiful brow, toss off a clever quip, and the world bows at your feet." Though she tried, she couldn't keep bitterness from her voice. "You've probably been handed everything you wanted since the moment you blinked open those bewitching green eyes."

He blasted through a yellow light, and went silent.

Murphy whined and nuzzled Liam's neck, and he reached back to scratch the dog's ears. Liam's expression was carefully neutral, but his rigid posture said she'd hurt him. Badly. How did Murphy know Liam was upset?

"You honestly think I'm that shallow?"

Kate drew a trembling breath. She was less sensitive than the dog. *Ridiculous.* Animals didn't understand human emotions. Murphy just wanted to get in the front. She cradled her aching head in her palms. "I apologize. That wasn't fair. Because I've had a rotten day doesn't give me the right to lash out at you."

"I'm not just spouting platitudes. I've slamdanced with adversity." Liam swerved around a slow moving Cadillac. "I told you that Pop died a year after we finished rebuilding the car. What I didn't tell you was that he was murdered. In our house, during a home invasion robbery."

Shock and horror jerked her upright. "I'm so sorry."

His agonized glance touched her briefly. "I was in my second year at U of O, and my youngest brother Grady was a high school senior. The family was hyped over Grady's soccer game…state championships. Pop had the flu, and had to stay home. He was really torqued about missing the game."

She touched his forearm, warm steel beneath her palm. "You don't owe me an explanation. Don't do this to yourself."

"It's okay. Maybe…I need to say it as much as you need to hear it. It's not something I talk about." Grief sharpened his profile. "Mom and Pop went to our games and school events when they could, and Pop was a Boy Scout leader."

Honored that he trusted her with something so painfully personal, she smiled gently. "*You* were a Boy Scout? Go figure."

"All of us were." He offered her a ghost of his ebullient grin. "Anyway, Grady's team won, and he got Most Valuable Player. Aidan, Con and I shoulder carried him into the house. Mom followed with his trophy. We were singing a goofy, semirisqué cheer at the top of our lungs." He hung a sharp left. "It didn't register that the house had been tossed. Stuff was gone."

"I'm not very close to my family," she whispered. "But I can't imagine anything more horrible."

"There's nothing worse than the fear that someone you love has been hurt. Mom rushed upstairs to the bedroom. Grady and Con ran to the kitchen. I was yelling for Pop, and then I…I stopped calling. My gut felt *wrong*."

She nodded. "I know that feeling." She'd experienced the awful sensation once before, and been proven horribly right.

"Aidan and I barreled into the family room." He shuddered. "And I…I couldn't move, couldn't speak. Couldn't breathe. Blood was spattered everywhere. My heart just…exploded." His voice went hoarse. "The murder had happened in there. Even sick and weak, Pop had fought to the bitter end."

He blew through another intersection. "We searched the debris, but couldn't find him." He blinked, as if seeing the atrocity again. "Only his blood."

"Oh, Liam." She rubbed his arm, offering what little comfort she could.

"Aidan and I didn't want Mom to see the carnage. We blocked the door, but she fought. Both of us could barely keep her out. I think she thought Pop was inside, and was trying to get to him. None of us were too coherent."

"Nobody would be."

"We took her to our neighbor Letty's house. Grady came unglued…it messed him up bad. Aidan made him stay with Mom. Aidan held Con and me together while the CSI team collected evidence. After, Grady came back over. Man, he was blank…a zombie. The four of us went into the family room and started scrubbing away the gore."

Her sister would have dissolved into hysteria, and her mom would have devoted herself to Janine's needs—leaving "more capable" Kate to fend for herself. "I can't believe how strong you all were…even so young."

"No way were we gonna make Mom deal with that." He grimaced. "Seemed like I was on my knees mopping up blood forever. We worked like robots. Did what had to be done. We ripped out the carpet and drove it and Pop's ruined chair to the dump. We climbed into the back of Con's truck and heaved Pop's recliner over the side. The four of us looked at our father's chair sitting in the garbage, blood spattered and broken." He shifted, roared around a truck. "Then we lost it. Put our arms around each other and cried."

Though she hadn't cried in two years, tears burned her eyelids. He'd opened his life, his heart. Revealed his deepest hurt. *Why?* Maybe to show her that she wasn't alone in experiencing bloody loss and betrayal?

Yet Liam seemed happy, while she'd withdrawn into a lonely, brittle protective shell. She forced down the lump in her throat. "I'm glad you and your brothers had each other." Maybe that was the difference. Not trying to handle the pain all by yourself. But she was a pro at flying solo.

"I *felt* alone. We all did. After the memorial service, the house was empty. Cold. I'd never see my father again. Never smell his spicy aftershave in the bathroom in the mornings. Never hear him belting out naughty limericks." His voice caught. "Never get another big, warm bear hug."

Murphy whimpered from behind Liam. The dog planted his wide paws on the seat back and rested his muzzle on Liam's right shoulder…almost as if *he* were offering Liam a hug.

Kate snatched her hand away. Odd how Murphy seemed cognizant of Liam's moods. A freaky coincidence. Animals didn't possess rational motivations. Maybe he needed to go outside.

Liam gripped the wheel until his knuckles whitened as he swiftly negotiated traffic. "I wandered out to the garage. I climbed inside the Mustang and sat, clinging to the steering wheel. Then I revved her up and drove out of the city. I put the top down and let her rip. The solid gearshift in my hand, the roar of the engine and the wind in my face washed away the pain and anger."

He hesitated, then forged ahead. "I swear, I could feel Pop sitting beside me, telling me everything would be okay."

"Maybe he was."

"I've never told *anyone* about that. It sounds certifiable."

"No, I understand completely."

"I thought you might." He gave her a crooked smile.

"Did they ever find out what happened to your dad?"

"Only recently. We just got his remains back." Liam went silent for a moment, then sighed and gave Kate a crooked smile. "It's a long story, for another time."

Their unspoken bond, shared feelings and, most of all, his unflinching honesty gave her the courage to offer a confession. "In my most…desolate moments during those early days in Paris, I treasured the one painting I have by my grandmother. She was also an artist. I never met her, but somehow, through the painting…her essence encouraged me."

"You *do* get it." He shot her a look of wonder. "Whenever I miss Pop, I take this pony out and open her up…and he's there."

"Which explains why you drove to Vegas instead of flying."

He stroked the dog's muzzle, snuggled into his shoulder. "I didn't want to subject Murphy to the cargo hold of a plane."

Murphy flopped down with a gusty sigh. Kate fidgeted with her camera to hide her roiling emotions. Liam's brush with tragedy had caused him to form strong attachments. He possessed love and loyalty for his family, his dog and even his car.

Love and loyalty she'd yearned for her entire life.

His feelings ran deep and touched the loneliness inside her. Aching to respond, she fought the crazy urge to fling herself into his arms. To comfort and be comforted. To soak in his warm strength and understanding. To lose her flaws in the consuming passion her body and soul remembered.

Doubts assailed her. Though her heart was breaking for him, how did he feel about her? Had the trauma of his father's murder unsettled him enough to make him cling too tightly…causing him to stalk her after their night together?

She studied his noble profile, his face heavy with sorrow. If she bought into that theory, then she'd have to take the next logical step and surmise he'd also tried to kill her. Did she actually believe that? Could she go that far?

Could *he?*

Liam glanced at her. "I'll need names, occupations and birth dates of every guy you've dated or had personal contact with the past couple years."

She bit her lip. "I'm not really comfortable giving you that kind of personal information."

"Even if one of them could be stalking you?" He abruptly jerked the car over to the curb. "What is your major malfunction, Kate?"

She blinked. "I beg your pardon?"

"No more bluffing." Fury flared his eyes. "Let's both lay our cards on the table. Go all in. Right here. Right now."

Chapter 5

4:00 p.m.

Kate stared at the livid cop, her thoughts spinning faster than the slot machines at Caesar's. Confrontation was so not her forte. She went out of her way to avoid it. Growing up, her sister had kept everyone in constant upheaval. Everything was done Janine's way…or take the highway. Kate *never* wanted to behave like that. She craved peace, needed the security of stability. "I don't know what you're talking about."

He snorted. "I won a buttload of college debate trophies. Don't try to out-BS a champion BSer."

Taut urgency thrummed inside her. "We don't have time. I need to get to the hospital."

"I'll get you to the hospital, ASAP. First, we settle this. If you don't trust me, I can't help you. Can't protect you. Not trusting me could cost you your life." He frowned. "Two years ago, you went home with me. You trusted me to be your lover." He unsnapped his seat belt and turned toward her. "Trusted me to be your *first* lover. What the hell is it now that puts fear in your eyes?"

She *had* trusted him. When she'd thought she'd never trust anyone again. Except the way Liam made her *feel* wasn't comfortable. She gnawed her lip. The way he forced her to confront her emotions was *awful.* Her parents had continually let her down. Her fiancé had slept with another woman. Her sister was always selfish. Often frantic. Kate had chosen the polar opposite of Janine's rants. In order to survive, she needed a clean, angst-free canvas inside. She strove to maintain constancy, to achieve quiet blankness.

Loss of control equaled disaster.

Liam had hurtled her so far out of her comfort zone that she was in another galaxy. Could that cause her to rationalize uneasiness as suspicion?

She looked at his amazing face, and felt the familiar clutch of desire. It could. Unlike wildfire attraction, suspicion was manageable. Suspicion helped her maintain a safe distance.

Suspicion couldn't stab her through the heart.

Kate marshaled her fortitude. "It's not you who's different. It's me. Perhaps…I…I've learned to expect betrayal."

"I've never betrayed you." Liam's big hands grasped her shoulders. "I just spilled my guts to you. Four hours ago, I saved your life. I sprung your cute little behind out of federal custody—at no small hazard to my career. And I got your camera back, which also put my butt on the line. I love my job. Too much to torch it with a self-indulgent stalker fantasy."

He was right. He'd been honest from the moment they'd met. Today, he'd jeopardized everything he valued, and asked nothing in return. He could have kissed her in the parking lot, and easily squelched every objection. Dissolved her inhibitions. She would have surrendered without a shot being fired.

Her attention locked on his sensual lips, and he arched an ironic brow. Worse, he *knew* it. Instead, he'd exhibited steel-clad self-discipline and stepped back.

Although so many things about Liam confused her, she understood him well enough to realize how tough it had been for him to pull back. He didn't retreat from challenges. Heck, she'd witnessed the adrenaline glitter in his eyes when he'd disarmed the bomb. He *reveled* in them.

"Didn't our night together prove *anything?*"

The past flew up to mock her. Liam's concern for her well-being in the bar that long-ago night. His matter-of-fact acceptance of her disability. Him teasing her into a dance, and holding, kissing her maimed hand without pause.

His awed expression as he'd made love to her, as if she were precious and valuable.

Shared memories flickered in his gaze. She wasn't the only one jolting down memory lane. He drew her toward him. His body heat, his pine-forest scent beckoned her closer, until inches separated them. "I don't know what's happened to you, Just Kate," he whispered. His fury yielded to pained confusion. "But I didn't hurt you then, and I swear I won't hurt you now."

Kate took pride in seeing life as it was, not as she wished it. She stared into his searing green gaze, struggling to discern reality from imagination. "You're not stalking me?"

She expected him to get angry again, spout indignant protests.

"No." His quietly sad denial recalled his tenderness and understanding when she'd called an abrupt halt to their lovemaking. She'd seen him mad before—moments ago, in fact—but his ire flashed as quick and hot as a summer storm. And passed as rapidly. He wasn't sneaky or devious. Not the kind to hold a grudge.

His grip gentled. "The only thing you gain by holding on too tight is an armored truckload of pain."

Kate pressed her pounding temples. How idiotic could she be? A love 'em and leave 'em guy wouldn't stalk a woman. Leaving was what they did best. Liam didn't hide his feelings. If he got angry, he said so. Laid his cards on the table, as he'd just done. He'd fight fast and furious and then it would blow over.

Making up could be incredibly interesting.

Battered by conflicted emotions, she glanced at him through the buffer of her lashes. "I'm trying to figure out the truth."

He frowned. "You *know* the truth."

The scary thing was, she did. Liam hadn't become angry or obsessive that night...only worried about her. Kate expelled a frustrated breath. She'd almost made another emotionally laden decision and messed up *again.* Self-defense had been her number one priority for so long, it was her operational default mode. If she let down her guard, admitted he wasn't the man stalking her, it relieved the threat to her physical safety.

And tripled the threat to her heart.

He smoothed a stray strand of hair behind her ear. "Here's the truth. I'm responsible for protecting you. I'll lay down my life to do so. Believe it."

Her nerves thrummed. She'd rather believe he was stalking her. It was less frightening than their crackling chemistry. If he were "the enemy," it was easier to keep a detached, remote perspective. Fiery attraction would only burn them both.

Yet, even as his gaze held her captive, she *did* believe him. He would willingly die to protect her. Apprehension slithered up her spine. She was in far more danger than before. She'd rather go quick and clean in an explosion than wallow in the torn, blood-soaked remnants of shattered dreams.

Been there, done that. Lost everything.

Cold terror clawed at her defensive shield. Liam might be able to save her life…but he couldn't save her from desire.

Liam warily monitored Kate's silent battle. She'd erected a frozen fortress that no Vegas heat wave could melt, but her vulnerable fawn's gaze revealed far more than she knew.

The idea that she thought he was a superficial, selfish party dude rankled. Worse, it *hurt.* Hellfire, talk about revelations. The appalling impulse to confide in her about Pop had ambushed him—as treacherous as a hidden minefield. Once he'd stepped in it, he was committed to moving forward.

He grimaced. All these years, he'd managed to hide his pain from those who knew him best. After Pop's murder, Liam's self-appointed duty was to cheer up his loved ones. Revive their shattered spirits. Keep hope alive. The last thing they needed was for him to dump his personal angst. His intrepid sense of humor had been his saving grace…and theirs.

If Kate wanted to believe he was stalking her, there wasn't a damned thing he could do to change her mind. Perhaps the spontaneous unload would encourage her to trust him. She *had* to trust him. Had to obey him without question. Or they could both die. Alex's sources had indicated that Interpol suspected *Les Hommes de la Mort* of the bombings. Phillipe Marché, an infamous bomber who had terrorized Europe in the late seventies and early eighties had founded the ruthless international terrorist organization—The Men of Death. If they *were* involved, Kate was in mortal danger.

The woman he'd met two years ago had been intuitive, intelligent and fair-minded. Willing to take a chance on him. At least he'd thought so. He studied her face, so still and pale her delicate features might have been chiseled from ice, and a chill crawled down his backbone.

Had he gambled his life—and Kate's—on a fantasy?

Her summer meadow scent, so at odds with her cool facade, filled his head, buzzed his senses. He chafed at the delay. As a SWAT bomb tech, he'd been trained to make fast decisions. To ad-lib, and get it right. Or people died. For a man used to taking immediate action, who didn't let *anyone* make judgment calls for him, waiting was pure torture.

Resignation shadowed her gaze, followed quickly by fear. Not fear of him. Fear of the truth. "I didn't mean to seem ungrateful for all you've done. But I needed to sort through the facts. I *have* to protect myself. In every way." Her lips trembled. "I believe you. Thank you, Liam, for risking everything for me."

He released a silent sigh. Believing had her on the ropes. "I'd do it again in a hot second."

"I don't understand why," she whispered.

"Because, like it or not, you need me, Just Kate." His fingers tightened on the smooth skin of her bare shoulders with the desire to yank her to him. To wrap his arms around her and kiss her until he drove the sorrow from her wide brown eyes. Until the worry lines around her mouth softened and her lips surrendered to his. Until her body went limp with sated pleasure beneath him. "It's a risk I'm willing to take."

Kate moistened her lower lip with the tip of her tongue, and the unconsciously sensual gesture constricted his abdominal muscles. He'd never forgotten her hot, sweet taste. The way she'd trembled with passion in his arms. How her soft curves melded into his hard angles, as if she'd been made only for him. Damn, the heavy beat of blood through his veins was scalding.

"We're through." She pulled back. "I need to get to the hospital. *Now.*"

"Right." Slammed headfirst into reality, he commanded himself to release her. He'd damned well better put passion on a short leash. He'd been assigned to protect her, but he wasn't about to hand any woman his heart. Especially Kate. He couldn't trust her not to detonate the charges and blast it to pieces.

Kate already walked out on him once. Just like Michelle before her. Michelle had taken his heart *and* his engagement ring. Tossed three years into the crapper without a backward glance. Burn me once, shame on you. Burn me twice, and I'm a gullible idiot with kibble for brains.

He fastened his seat belt, and merged into traffic. For two years, he'd corralled his feelings for Kate by pouring time and energy into renovating his house. He'd hammered, sanded and painted to keep from going crazy with questions he couldn't answer.

Now she'd been tossed back into his life…and the scenario was as dicey as juggling live ammo.

Their past might be history, but it was far from over.

He checked the rearview mirror and swore. "We've picked up a tail."

Kate swiveled. "I've been watching. I always watch. I didn't see anyone."

"Gray SUV three cars back." He'd bet it was Chuck's flunkies. The Fed was a Gila monster. Once he clamped his jaws down, he didn't let go until you chopped off his head. However, Liam wasn't taking chances with Kate.

"Hold on." He depressed the clutch and shifted. "Murphy, floor!" Murphy jumped to the floor behind the driver's seat.

Liam swerved into the right lane, looked in the mirror and swore again as a black Triumph motorcycle broke from the pack. The leather-clad, dark-helmeted biker zoomed past two cars on the shoulder, engaged in active pursuit. A sawed-off shotgun rode at his side. Liam's senses screamed to red alert. *That* wasn't the FBI. "Make that two. An SUV and a bike."

Kate unbuckled her seat belt, clambered up and knelt on the seat facing backwards.

"What the *hell* are you doing? Get strapped in!"

"Photographic evidence." She pointed her camera at the back windshield and the shutter whirred with rapid-fire shots.

"Sit, dammit!" Liam yanked the wheel into an abrupt right turn. Downshifting, he sped across both lanes, ignored blaring horns behind him and swung a left.

"It's my life, my career in jeopardy. If I prove I'm being stalked, the FBI will leave me alone and go after *him.*" Kate clung to the seat and clicked away.

He shifted into fourth and hit the gas. After a fast right, then a left, he did another mirror check and smirked. The Mustang had left the bulky SUV in a distant cloud of dust.

The Triumph was a different game. Playing for keeps…winner take all. Liam had the edge in power, but the biker proved he had him beat to hell in maneuverability by careening down the sidewalk. As pedestrians fled, Liam calculated the seconds until a gap would appear in the flood of approaching cars. "Plant your butt in the seat and snap your freaking seat belt! *Now!*"

His take-no-prisoners order had her scrambling to obey, and he grinned. "Now we're cooking. Hang onto your boxers."

With Kate safely strapped in, Liam was in his element. He double stomped the brake and clutch, shifted and wrenched the wheel. Tires shrieking, the car skidded and whirled three hundred and sixty degrees in the middle of the street. Kate yelped as Liam shifted again, swerved to avoid the onslaught of oncoming vehicles and slammed down the gas pedal.

The Triumph bumped off the sidewalk and spun to follow. The bike wobbled, the rider corrected. For a split second, he almost made it. Then the motorcycle toppled. Spokes spinning, sparks flying, the Triumph dragged its passenger along the asphalt.

Liam burst into laughter as they roared in the opposite direction. "Pony one, bad biker dude zero."

Murphy hopped onto the seat, thrust his nose in the air and chimed in with a hearty, "Roo, roo!" *We kicked tail, partner!*

"Holy crow!" Kate flung shiny strands of chestnut hair out of her eyes. "You're both *deranged.*"

"Yep." Liam chuckled. "We do demented for a living."

She jerked down her crumpled hem, which had climbed her long, shapely thighs. Outgunning the AC, a flash of heat blasted him. *Damn.* She frowned. "You certainly are good at it."

He flashed her a grin. "Thank you."

Her lips twitched. "That wasn't an endorsement."

"We left the bogie sprawled in the street."

She turned, gazed out the back windshield. "Oh, look. There's my stomach."

"Admit it, Just Kate. That was the wildest ride you've had in…" He shot her a teasing glance. "Two and a half years."

A reluctant smile curved her sexy mouth. "Yeah, you're a thrill a minute, Ace."

Liam called 9-1-1 to assist the downed cyclist and requested that the local cops hold him for questioning.

He hung up, and Kate looked away from him, out the window. "The answer to your question is zilch."

"Come again?"

"Zero. No dates since you and I…"

"All right." He wanted to know more, but knew he had to stay focused. "Tell me everything about this stalker. Exactly when did it start? What do the notes say?" He spent the rest of the drive interrogating Kate. He mentally filed away every detail. His priority was to protect her, which would hamper his investigation. But one way or another, he would find the whack job and put him away, and clear her reputation.

As they strode through the double glass doors of the hospital, Kate pointed at Murphy. "Animals are prohibited."

"K-9 Murphy is allowed to go anywhere I am."

Rejecting Liam's repeated reassurances about her safety, Kate refused to ride in an enclosed elevator with Murphy.

The dog rolled his eyes and heaved a long-suffering sigh. *Your female isn't the brightest squeaky toy in the box.*

Liam hiked five flights of stairs without objection. Kate would get used to Murphy. After spending time with the dog, women doted on him like a favorite child. The mutt's loyal, loveable, goofball personality couldn't fail to grow on her.

Outside room 514, a tall blonde wearing an elegant beige suit sobbed in the arms of an older woman. "I can't stand it!"

Kate sprinted down the corridor. "Has something happened?"

The gray-haired woman, whom he surmised was Kate's mother, patted the hysterical blonde. Her hazel eyes shot Kate a reprimand that could freeze gasoline. "You took *your* time."

Kate sighed with patient resignation. "Unavoidable delay."

"It's bad enough that your father can never get away from the office." The older woman bestowed another accusatory stare. "Your sister needs the entire family's support. She's upset."

"So I gathered. Does she have cause to be?"

"You know Janine has always been fragile." Mrs. Chabeau's expression and tone were both starchy. "Don't snipe at her because you're stronger and more capable."

Kate's voice was carefully modulated. "I wasn't—"

The blonde wailed louder. "She never understands what I'm going through! I can't take this stress anymore!"

Kate briefly closed her eyes, visibly reined in her temper. "What's going on? Where is Daniel?"

Mrs. Chabeau stroked Janine's hair. "He went to the cafeteria about an hour ago. He desperately needed coffee."

Kate's chest rose and fell in a trembling breath. "It can't be that serious, or he wouldn't have left Aubrey."

Mrs. Chabeau frowned. "If you'd been here, you could have gone for him, and he wouldn't have had to leave her."

Liam's best intentions to remain uninvolved disintegrated under the assault on Kate. He strode forward in her defense. "Kate's had a stressful day herself."

Her mother turned her frosty stare on him. "Our family business is none of your affair, young man."

Kate waved him back. "I'm fine."

"The doctors threw us out of Aubrey's room, to run *more* tests!" Janine shrieked. "They said my baby is going to die!"

"Shh!" Kate grabbed the half-open door and swung it shut. "Mother, tell me *exactly* what the specialist said."

Kate's mother glanced down the hallway. "Here comes Daniel now."

Clearly frustrated, Kate whirled and assumed a neutral expression as a blond man sauntered toward them. Liam caught the distinct vibe that she wasn't wild about her brother-in-law.

The guy was around Liam's height, fit and gym honed. His short hair was gelled to tousled perfection. His shoulders were squared, his pale blue gaze direct, his walk a self-assured strut. The ultimate all-American boy. Even as Liam mentally rolled his eyes, his instincts prickled. Cocky, fair-haired frat boys were never as innocent as they appeared.

Kate waited for Daniel. "Has something happened?"

Daniel's cool gaze measured Liam, didn't miss a detail. No challenge glinted in his eyes, merely interest. "Who's this?"

"Daniel Tyler, Officer Liam O'Rourke." Kate made an impatient gesture. "Um…he…" She trailed off uncertainly. "He's…"

Liam extended his hand. "Security detail for the auction."

Daniel's glance flicked to Murphy. "You rented an off-duty cop and his watchdog?" His hand briefly clasped Liam's. "I could have arranged for professional security through the company's resources. We can't afford to cut corners."

Liam counted to ten. In Gaelic. Murphy picked up on his edginess and curled his lips back. Liam felt like showing some fang himself. *Rent-a-cop, my arse. I'm gonna check him out so thoroughly, I'll know his cholesterol count.*

Kate gave Daniel a tight smile. "Officer O'Rourke and his…partner are fully qualified. Now, *what* is going on?"

Janine sniveled into her mother's shoulder. "I can't bear to hear it again. I need to go home, take a pill and lie down."

"Of course you do, sweetie." Mrs. Chabeau's gaze pinned Daniel. "We'll be in the car. Don't keep us waiting."

Daniel nodded. "No, ma'am. I'll be right there."

Without a word, she led Janine down the hallway.

"Daniel, what's up?" The pressure was starting to tell on Kate. She looked like she wanted to scream, and Liam didn't blame her. More than ever, he appreciated his family's close-knit ties and unfailing support. She exhibited the patience of a saint. This crew leached *all* the "fun" out of dysfunctional.

"Aubrey's remaining kidney function is in decline. They had to do another dialysis this afternoon. She has less time than we thought." Daniel's face furrowed, and his fingertips brushed Kate's good arm. The casual gesture rose Liam's hackles. The guy needed support, but Liam didn't like him touching her.

Tension pulsed between Kate and her brother-in-law. She gulped, struggling to sustain her calm demeanor. "We'll have the money in forty-eight hours and the transplant can proceed."

Daniel frowned. "Everything has to go off without a hitch. The doctor said Aubrey won't last another week."

She blanched impossibly paler. "Don't worry, she's going to be fine. I *refuse* to accept any alternatives."

"We know we can count on you." He sighed. "I'd better get your sister home before she has a nuclear meltdown. After the doctors are done, call me with any news."

Kate nodded. "Of course."

Daniel patted her shoulder, and she stiffened. "Thank heaven *someone* in the family is dependable." He inclined his head at Liam in dismissal and strode away.

Don't put the guy's lights out. People reacted to stress differently. Obnoxiousness wasn't out of line for a parent trapped in an intensely emotional situation without spousal support. Especially for a CEO, used to being in charge. Besides, Ma would kick his butt if he punched a grieving father.

Kate reached for the doorknob to Aubrey's room. "I'll see if they're almost finished." Liam followed, with Murphy tagging behind. She whirled, color surging into her cheeks. "You stay here! I am *not* letting a vicious dog anywhere near that baby!"

Liam frowned. She wasn't crazy about his partner, but Murphy had done nothing to warrant mistrust. He spread his hands. "Down, girl! Watch the slander. Murphy is *not* vicious. A K-9 is trained to bite for three reasons." He ticked them off on his fingers. "At the handler's command. To protect his handler. To protect himself. Murphy would *never* hurt a child."

Trembling, she crossed her arms over her chest. "You have no control over his actions. You couldn't stop him."

Why the unreasonable fear? "Wrong. He's better trained than any soldier. He will not attack without provocation."

She stared at him, her eyes as flat and cold as ice chips. "I refuse to jeopardize Aubrey's welfare."

He gestured at the dog, who cocked his head and held up a paw. *I think we got off on the wrong paw. Shake?*

"Look. He wants to be your friend."

She'd gone pale again. "With friends like that, who needs enemies? He stays out!"

Puzzled, Liam ordered the dog across the hall. People were intimidated by large dogs, especially K-9s. They were *meant* to intimidate. But Kate's extreme phobia didn't make sense. Unless…

He studied her frozen defensive stance. Body turned slightly sideways, Kate appeared perilously close to tears. Her left arm was cradled protectively over her crippled hand. She hugged her purse and camera to her and rocked on her heels as if she expected imminent assault.

Damn! As he stared at her scars crisscrossed beneath the stacked bangle bracelets, horrifying realization settled in a sick, suffocating weight on his chest. He clung to the shattered hope that he was wrong…all the while knowing he wasn't. "What type of dog attacked you, sweetheart?" he asked gently.

Shock jolted her features before she lowered her chin. "I only remember a huge black blur and snarling fangs." Her voice went deathly quiet. "Torn flesh. Blood and pain."

Heart aching, he tugged her to him, and she didn't resist. He enfolded her in his arms. "I wish you'd told me before."

"Why? Would you have sent Murphy away?"

He could never do that. Murphy was his partner. A faithful friend who offered unconditional love and the quality he valued most… steadfast loyalty. Murphy had put his life on the line for him more than once. Had unhesitatingly stepped between him and a bullet. "Unless Murphy and I live together, I can't be a K-9 officer. And as a bomb tech, I'd have to trust my life to someone else's dog, or a robot." He'd rather direct traffic.

He hoped like hell he wouldn't eventually be forced to choose between Murphy and Kate. As they worked together, she would learn to trust Murphy. He had to believe that. "I can't compromise your safety. We're a team. Better, stronger together. But I would have understood. Kept more distance between you and him." She was still shaking, and he rubbed her back. "Can you tell me what happened?"

"It was about a year before you and I met. Janine wanted to take her toy poodle to the park. She's never had good judgment, and since I'm five years older, Mom always expected me to keep an eye on her. Janine let PB off the leash because he was getting in her way while she flirted with some guy."

"PB?"

"Pookie Bear, or Pookums, as Janine called him." They grimaced in unison, and Kate offered a crooked smile. "Gag me. I couldn't shout that around the neighborhood, so I shortened it."

He snorted. "Don't blame you one iota, honey."

"PB wandered away. We heard horrible growling and ran to find him. He'd wriggled under the fence beside the walkway and had been attacked by an enormous black monster." She bent her head, the shiny waterfall of hair hiding her face. "Janine started screaming her head off. I didn't stop to think. I vaulted the fence and jumped into the fray."

He massaged the back of her neck, and some of her stiffness yielded to his touch. "Very brave."

"Most people think it was very stupid."

"Too many people don't understand the devotion between dogs and their humans. Did you save him?"

"Yes. And Janine gave him away while I was in the hospital, because he was 'too much trouble.'"

He swallowed bitterness. As a cop, he'd seen the slimy underbelly of humanity. Man's disregard for man wasn't news. Sibling rivalry stretched back to Cain and Abel. So why was he so revolted by her sister's heartless indifference? Because if the drama queen had exerted minimal effort and kept the damned dog, Kate *might* have bonded with him and avoided her phobia. He stroked her hair. "It's too little, too late…but I'm sorry."

"It was my own fault. After four surgeries and a year of physical therapy, my PT told me I'd never regain my fine motor skills." She inhaled a shuddery breath. "Another impulsive, bad decision that cost me everything."

Kate was wounded—both body and soul. An artist who could no

longer paint because of a dog attack. Did he honestly believe she could overcome the tragedy and trust Murphy? He'd had his heart broken before. Trust was a fragile web. Once ripped to shreds, it didn't mend easily. And the patched strands were never as strong.

His spirits nosedived. She'd said *another* impulsive decision that had cost her everything. Did she consider sleeping with him one of those bad decisions? Was that why she'd run away? He closed his eyes and rested his cheek against her silky hair, but found no comfort. "Even though you paid a terrible price, you saved a life. That counts for something."

"Yes. I don't regret rescuing PB. I never have." She pulled back, putting space between them.

Their connection shriveled, froze over. Her fears blocked his way…a barricade he couldn't scale. A locked door he couldn't batter down. Sweet Kate. Haunted by her past and terrified of the future.

She was whiter than the vertical blinds lining the windows. "I should check on Aubrey."

Ten-four. Snap out of it, O'Rourke. Duty calls. "You've been under considerable strain. When did you eat last?"

She dismissed his concern with a shrug. "I don't have time. After I see Aubrey, I need to finalize auction details."

Sorrow clashed with anger. For a guy who dodged life's curve-balls, his emotions were taking too many hits. "That's your thing, isn't it? Rescuing everyone. Taking care of everyone. No matter what it costs you." He cupped her face, stroked her cheek with his thumb. Her fair skin was smooth and cool beneath his palm. Too cool. "Who worries about you? Who takes care of you?"

She raised her chin. "*I* take care of me."

"From what I can see, not very damn well."

She jerked away, her defensive stance unable to conceal her vulnerability. "I'm a big girl. I don't need mommying."

Good thing, because her mother seemed decidedly unconcerned about her welfare. "Do I look like a mommy to you?"

Her smile wobbled at the corners. "Big brother, then."

"I don't want to be your brother." What *did* he want to be? He gave her a long, appraising look. "Don't you get lonely?"

"No."

"Renée Allete's photographs say differently."

She gasped, turned aside. "Renée's photos are compositions arranged to artfully contrast light and dark. No more."

"What about 'Man in the Shadows?'" The photo that had first grabbed his attention. A silhouette of a man with his back to the camera, leaning in one of a row of darkened brick archways and staring out at the fog-shrouded Seine. Captured from a distance in the middle of the night, the poignant black and white evoked a visceral image of stark loneliness.

She wrestled with composure before turning back. "I appreciate that you feel responsible for me. But you're only accountable for my physical safety." Sadness swam in her big brown eyes, and her voice was gentle. "I don't want my emotional well-being to become another of your duties. It's best for everyone if we keep it just business between us."

He donned a mental blast suit against the sting. Strapped a layer of Kevlar around his rioting feelings. She was determined to keep her distance, and he'd damn well better heed the warning siren. Stick to his decision to stay uninvolved. Liam scrubbed a hand over his face. Or it could swing around and bite him. Big-time. Whenever he'd tried to cling to anyone, they'd slipped through his fingers. Nobody had to light a case of dynamite under him. He'd stay with what worked—easygoing and casual.

He would use humor to buffer the fierce attraction, subdue the intense emotions threatening to implode between them. Hell, that was his freaking forte. Laugh and the world laughed with you. Cry, and you had salty Guinness.

He'd vowed to treat her just like any other job. And that's exactly what he'd do. When it was over, he'd walk away. If he played it smart, he'd escape with all his vital organs intact.

The door swung open, and a man dressed in blue surgical scrubs walked out of Aubrey's room.

Kate spun. "Dr. Vallano. How is she?"

"She's taken a turn for the worse." The specialist's face was grave. "I've never seen her so lethargic. Her despondent state is adversely affecting her health."

While Kate conferred with the doctor, Liam leaned against the door frame. He could observe the frail child inside, but Aubrey couldn't see him or Murphy, who napped across the hall.

He'd expected Aubrey to be blond. Instead, she was a tiny mirror image of Kate. Her pixie face was a delicate, pallid oval, too thin for her wide brown eyes, her hair a baby-fine fringe of brunette silk. Even her stoic expression reminded him of Kate. Judging by the kidlets he'd seen at K-9 public service demonstrations, she was not quite two. Just about the right age…

Queasy suspicion backhanded him and he staggered. He gripped the door frame and struggled to inhale air that stung his throat like accelerant fumes.

Had he and Kate conceived a child that fateful night? He'd been careful, and they hadn't even come close to a grand finale, but stranger things had happened.

Was that what Kate had meant by another impulsive decision that had cost her everything?

Chapter 6

5:00 p.m.

The doctor hurried away, and Kate turned to Liam, her pretty face furrowed into a baffled frown. Probably because he'd gone from leaning against the doorjamb to ramrod straight.

Her frown deepened. "Liam? Are you sick?"

He'd bet his beloved Mustang that his complexion was the same color as the trim—pea soup. "How…how old is she?" His hoarse question was as uneven as his pistoning pulse.

"She'll be three in March. She was born the night we met."

He wasn't entirely convinced. Then why had Kate been devastated that evening? Why had she been sitting in a bar, morose and alone, instead of celebrating the birth at the hospital with her family? "She looks a *lot* younger."

"She's small because of her condition." She reached for him, caught herself. "Liam, are you all right?"

"Ah. Makes sense." The ice thawed in his gut and his bunched muscles relaxed. If he'd had time to think it through, he'd have known she wouldn't blow off her own daughter. Especially to someone as harebrained as Janine.

Aubrey was not their child. The last complication they needed was a kid thrown into the volatile mix. Yet an odd, unexpected sense of longing ensnared him. "I'm okay."

"You still look kind of…seasick. Maybe you should go down to the cafeteria and grab a bite to eat and some coffee."

He arched a brow. "The pale pot calling the kettle peaked."

"I'll eat later." She absentmindedly rubbed her temples. A gesture she'd repeated many times over the past few hours.

Crap! He could kick his own butt for not honing in on the signal. "You have a headache, too, don't deny it. You've had one all day. Did you take anything for it?"

"I'm *fine.*" She made shooing motions. "Go do whatever you need to. I'll be finished shortly, and then we'll both eat."

He couldn't suppress a grin. "I don't remember you being this bossy, Just Kate."

Her reciprocal smile was genuine, if frayed around the edges. "And I don't remember you acting so maternal."

"Maternal? Just because a guy is concerned…" He narrowed his eyes. "Hell, you might as well slap a frilly apron on me."

Her smile twitched into a droll grin. "Whatever blows your hair back."

Chuckling, Liam loped down the corridor. He didn't need the red-lettered signs posted in the hallway warning that cell calls weren't allowed. He was familiar with RFI—radio frequency interference. RFI could detonate a bomb blast. Purposely or unintentionally—depending on the trigger mechanism. In a hospital, it affected vital functions like ventilators, monitors, pacemakers and anesthesia equipment.

At the nurses' station, his badge and a little banter snagged him two ibuprofen for Kate and access to a landline. As Riverside's Alpha SWAT team leader, Con had his hands full until the day shift was over, so Liam phoned Aidan and requested that he run Daniel through NCIC, the national crime information center computer. While he was at it, he contacted Alex and asked him to discreetly scrutinize Chuck Hanson's job performance. He didn't think the FBI agent was bent, just relentless. But you never knew. Relentless was one step away from fanatical.

His dislike of both men didn't figure into the equation—much. He planned to check out everyone connected to Kate. Stalkers were cunning, and adept at disguising twisted secrets behind "normal" personalities. Until an inciting incident flushed them out, they could work or socialize with the object of their obsession without the victims having a clue.

Causing lethal results.

However, her stalker could be a casual acquaintance, or a stranger. Someone obsessed with Renée Allete as a "celebrity." Any Beatles fan could tell you that scenario never ended well.

Liam narrowed his eyes. He'd have to constantly look over his shoulder. *Nobody* would hurt Kate on his watch.

His next call was to Zoe, superjournalist. He found her in the boutique at Paris, Vegas, with Con's wife Bailey.

Aidan could find out if Daniel had a record, but his sister-in-law would uncover any indiscretions Tyler had in his private life since preschool. Liam didn't even *want* to know how. With Zoe, a don't ask, don't tell policy was always wise.

He could also count on her generosity to provide free publicity for the auction. He related details, and Zoe promised to meet them at Kate's convenience for an interview.

He hung up, sweet-talked a can of soda from a nurse, then strode to Aubrey's room. He peeked inside. Kate sat on the edge of the bed, where the tiny girl lay limp and unresponsive.

Kate smoothed Aubrey's hair back from her wan face. "Where's my little sunbeam today?"

Aubrey's reply was barely audible. "I don't feel shiny."

"I have grape bubble gum in my pocket. Would that help?"

"No thank you, Auntie Kate."

Kate lifted a plastic cup from the bedside table and urged the child to take a sip from the straw. "What's wrong, sweetie?"

Aubrey hesitated. "Mommy was crying again."

Kate stiffened. "She'll be okay. She's…tired. You know how you feel cranky when you miss your nap?" Her voice was calm, but her awkward movements shouted distress. She set aside the cup o water. “Grandma took her home so she can rest.”

“Auntie Kate?” Aubrey’s lip trembled. “I don’t wanna die.”

“Oh, baby.” Kate bent and kissed the fragile little girl’s forehead “You aren’t going to die.”

“Mommy said Dr. Volcano said so.”

A muscle ticked in Kate’s jaw. “She misunderstood. Dr. Vallan said you’re going to get better.” She clasped Aubrey’s thin hand i hers. “We have special plans, remember?”

Aubrey nodded slowly, as if movement required extreme effort “We’re gonna swim. But I’m maybe not too strong.”

“You will be, soon. And then we’re going to snorkel in the Car ibbean. We’ll see all the pretty fish, like the little orange and whit striped guy in your favorite movie.”

“That fishie gots losted…and his daddy was sad. Will you cr like Mommy if I die?”

Kate choked, cleared her throat. “That…that is *not* going t happen. After the operation, you’ll be strong and healthy.”

“I’m scared, Auntie Kate. I don’t wanna go away.” Tears leake from Aubrey’s eyes and trickled down her gaunt cheeks.

Liam’s chest ached as if he’d stepped on a nail bomb and had hi heart driven full of rusty spikes. He strode inside the room “Someone told me there was a princess in here.”

Aubrey scrubbed her eyes with her fists. Her dainty brow quirked in surprise. “I’m not a princess!”

“What if you are, and don’t know it?”

Her too-wise-for-her-years gaze solemnly tracked him from hea to toe, then back. “My mommy isn’t a queen.”

Drama queen must not count. His gaze snagged Kate’s, and h smirked. She bit back a chuckle. “You are so bad.”

“Me?” He blinked, all innocence. “I didn’t say a word.”

Aubrey’s glance settled on his gun, and her face brightened. “A laser blaster! Are you a Power Ranger?”

He smiled. “No, I’m a police officer. My name is Liam.”

“Ohhhh! *Cops!*” The tiny girl clapped her hands and chanted theme song about bad boys.

He slanted a brow. “Isn’t *Cops*…advanced for a preschooler?”

Kate smiled ruefully. "Aubrey's not very active these days, and Janine keeps her occupied with lots of TV."

Queen Mum of the year. He handed Kate the ibuprofen. "Here ya go." He passed her the can. "And a miracle caffeine elixir to perform amazing feats of healing on your headache *and* your blood sugar."

Kate swallowed the tablets with soda. "I'll bet my Leica you've kissed the Blarney stone."

"Aye, that I have, Just Kate. As a wee lad o' twelve." He adopted Gran's Irish accent, which seemed to delight Kate. He'd been born a mimic, an advantage during speech and drama classes. As a kid, he used to perform a dead-on rendition of his father that never failed to crack up his family…including Pop. He hadn't had the heart to do it since Pop had been gone.

"What a surprise. Not!"

Aubrey sat up, more animated than he'd previously seen her. "I have weak kid's knees. They don't work, and make me sick."

Liam rounded the bed and perched on the edge opposite Kate. He plumped Aubrey's pillows to support her back, chagrined to see her collarbone sticking out above her pink Barbie nightie. "I know. But I hear you're getting a new kidney, soon."

"Yup." The little girl nodded. "In a oper-operation."

He nodded at the child, who was slurping on the straw. "She has an advanced vocabulary for such a young rug rat."

"She has a huge IQ. And she's been surrounded by adults all her life. She speaks French, too. I've read to her in both English and French since she was a newborn. She loves stories." Kate stroked Aubrey's baby-soft cheek. The night her niece had been born, she'd thought she'd lost everything. But she'd actually been given a different perspective…personally and professionally. Over the past two and a half years, she'd learned to settle for the hand she'd been dealt. Learned to squelch her yearning for things that had been snatched out of her reach forever.

"I thought you were living in Paris."

"I have been. Daniel is a senior exec for my father's environmentally friendly cleaning products company. He travels constantly, and Janine accompanies him. Mom can't keep up with a child, and my work is flexible. Aubrey has spent a lot of time in Paris with me." She mouthed the next sentence at him, so Aubrey couldn't hear. "She's only recently become so ill."

They shared silent worry across the bed. Kate looked down at Aubrey. Tortured anxiety shadowed the little girl's innocent brown eyes, and Kate's stomach rolled. No child should have to bear the wrenching fear of imminent death.

Nor should their loved ones. Dread coiled inside her. She couldn't lose Aubrey. The little girl was her one delight. Aubrey deserved a future, and Kate would make sure she got one.

Liam gently patted Aubrey's other hand. "You like stories, princess? You want to hear a *true* story?"

Aubrey's petite nose scrunched. "Are you any good?"

"I've been told I am." Liam chuckled. "I have plenty of experience. My baby brother Grady used to be afraid of monsters, and I would tell him stories to help him fall asleep."

"Okay, then." Nodding, Aubrey leaned back against her pillows. "Auntie Kate says it's 'portant to try new things."

Aubrey's tense little hand relaxed in Kate's. Enchanted, she listened to the misadventures of Murphy, the mischievous puppy. At Murphy's encounter with a hazelnut hurling squirrel, Aubrey's sparkling giggle floated out. Kate's delighted gaze met Liam's. Aubrey hadn't laughed for weeks.

Apparently, no females from three to ninety-three were immune to the O'Rourke appeal.

His tone went low and quiet. "Close your eyes, princess." Aubrey's lashes fluttered down on pale cheeks, and Liam's soothing voice spun the story's end. By the time Murphy the puppy fell asleep snuggled in a nest of baby kittens, Aubrey was also asleep, her breathing even, her tiny face serene.

Kate could barely speak around the lump in her throat. "Thank you," she whispered.

"My privilege," he whispered in return.

Hot tears pressured her eyelids. He had consoled the distraught child. He'd given Aubrey the precious gift of peace when nobody else could. Something strange had happened as he'd woven his comforting tapestry of words. As Kate had stared into his kind green eyes, listened to his smooth baritone, he'd cast a spell. With tender empathy, he'd consoled Aubrey.

And enchanted Kate all over again.

Just over two years ago, they'd shared the hot flare of desire. Today, they'd shared the enduring, steady warmth of compassion. Both connected them in a unique bond she'd never experienced with anyone. And she wanted more. She was so alone. So cold. Had never yearned so badly to take a chance. Longed to risk it all. Her pulse spiked on a sharp stab of fear.

She'd never been so scared.

Compelled to put distance between them, Kate moved silently to the window. She squinted at the sun-glazed landscape beyond the open blinds. If she risked everything, she would lose everything. She'd already learned that lesson…the hard way.

The relentless Vegas sun hovered in a blazing ball low on the horizon. Love was like sunlight. At first, it shone bright and beckoning, enticed you closer. Chased away the cold. Nurtured lovely green plants that shaded and nourished. When you got too comfortable, lingered too long unaware, it burned you. Blistered and blackened every living particle. Until your heart shriveled to arid wasteland…like the surrounding desert.

She couldn't count on anyone. Couldn't depend on anyone not to betray her. Couldn't trust anyone.

A brief interval of glittering warmth wasn't worth the inevitable scalding pain.

She straightened. Heck, scientists had proven that people who lived in cold climates were better preserved. She'd keep her emotions in the deep-freeze, where they would be protected.

Where she was safe.

Liam joined her at the window. "A penny for your thoughts."

"Don't waste your money." Aching from the effort to subdue her longing, she turned toward him. Golden light bronzed his exquisite face. Sunbeams played over the strong planes and kissed his shapely mouth, and warm highlights twinkled in his emerald eyes. An ancient god, formed from the gilded mist of Celtic legend. Ruler of all he surveyed. Charming, seductive and beautiful, conquering hearts wherever his arrows struck.

And it wasn't mere window dressing. Liam Michael O'Rourke was gorgeous inside and out. His beauty went soul deep. His intelligence, compassion and surefire humor were what made him so attractive. So hard to resist. So dangerous.

He was the one man who could pierce the glacier shielding her heart. Tempt her to tango *way* too close to the sun.

Soar like Icarus, melt her wings and plunge to her death.

She smothered dismay. If she played now, she'd pay later. Being sheltered in a layer of ice wasn't so bad. She'd grown used to the chill.

She had her life in Paris, her photography and visits with Aubrey. What more did she need? What she *wanted* didn't count.

Liam propped a hip on the windowsill, his fluid movements the opposite of his earlier unease. Some people couldn't handle intense medical situations, especially with kids. However, the devil-may-care bomb tech hardly struck her as the type to contract the queasies from a hospital. What had caused his earlier discomfort? He glanced at the sleeping child, his green eyes warm and tender. "She looks exactly like you."

"Much to Janine's distress. She wanted a blond baby doll."

He frowned. "As long as they're healthy, who cares?" He waited a beat. "Is your sister…ah…unstable?"

She shook her head. How to answer *that* question? "Janine was born with a heart murmur that corrected itself by age one. However, her infamous 'episodes' have incapacitated her since childhood with headaches, nausea and sobbing jags. In spite of CAT scans, MRIs and oodles of lab work, no doctor has ever offered a physical diagnosis." She sighed. "Mother had three miscarriages between our births, and my sister's well-being is her obsession."

"Your sis and brother-in-law are quite a pair."

"Yes, they deserve one another."

He studied her purposely bland expression. "Was that meant to be as snarky as you were careful not to make it sound?"

Kate started. Nobody read her like he did. She could fool everyone but him. With Liam, she couldn't hide inside her shell. He saw right through it, knew what she thought, what she felt. Could he also see the scared, uncertain woman she was, instead of the capable facade she presented to the world? A horrifying thought. "Um...probably." She pursed her lips. "Is that mean?"

"Hell, no. Compared to my opinion, it's charitable. I thought there was gonna be a nasty scene in the hallway."

"Like I'd make a scene."

He smirked. "Not you, *me.*" He took her hand. Though she hated to admit it, she appreciated the comfort. Seeing Aubrey in rapid decline had scared her beyond reason. His thumb stroked her palm in rhythmic circles. "Your mother is devoted to your sister. How does your dad fit in?"

"He's immersed in his company. We barely see him."

He didn't hide his dismay. "I'm sorry." His mellow voice was low and intimate. As his stroking thumb moved to her wrist, petals of warmth blossomed inside her. "That's rough on you."

Always self-reliant, she'd never questioned it. "Didn't your baby brother get all the attention?"

Liam smirked. "Grady is independence personified. His imagination never disengages, and constantly got him into scrapes."

"And you didn't get blamed?"

"Why would I take heat for his misdemeanors?"

"Whenever Janine got into trouble, she'd blink her big blue eyes and point the finger at me. Somehow I'd be found at fault."

He scowled blackly and tugged her nearer. "Hung by a kangaroo court, without a trial."

Liam's muscled body was so close, his heat, his invigorating scent sent desire soaring. Kate barely resisted the urge to lean into him. Lean on him. That path led to madness. "I just got grounded. I liked to paint and listen to music and read all by myself anyway. It was more retreat than penalty. That's when I got hooked on Phil Collins. Luckily, I enjoy my own company."

"You're a remarkable woman, Just Kate." Liam slid his arm around her waist.

It was an encouraging hug, one friend to another. Almost brotherly. *Yeah, right.* Like it mattered. Her hormones shot fireworks. Sizzling bursts of red and gold and brilliant green...the same color as his eyes. "I have a hard time buying that *you* never got into trouble, Saint Michael."

His scowl morphed into a grin. "Okay, I confess. I did, but only because Grady dragged me along for the ride. He was always taking stuff apart to see how it worked, or launching a daredevil experiment, and I was a more-than-willing accomplice."

"That sounds…fun."

"Mom and Pop might not agree." He chuckled. "When he was eight and I was ten, we accidentally blew up his bicycle, trying to attach 'rocket boosters.' Guess how I became fascinated by volatile chemicals?"

"My sister and I never had a relationship." Kate strove to banish dejection. "I give her the benefit of the doubt. Maybe she doesn't feel well." She drew a fortifying breath. "However, her outbursts seem to occur whenever she's been denied something, or lacks attention. I find it difficult to be patient when her daughter is gravely ill and all she thinks about is herself."

He stroked gentle fingertips down her cheek, making her insides quiver. "Don't beat yourself up, Kate. I'd have throttled the lot of 'em years ago."

"Don't think I haven't been tempted." Her uneven grin was half guilty, half conspiratorial. "I stick it out for Aubrey's sake. She needs a loving, stable influence in her life. If I give in to pettiness, the poor kid is on her own."

"Like you were." His warm hand cupped her face. "Like you *are.*" His gaze drew her in, enticed her into a shiny, intimate bubble where only they existed. He was so close, she could see each long, sooty eyelash, every golden speck dancing in his compelling green eyes. Could trace the sensual curve of his full lips. Soft lips that had cruised every inch of her bare skin. Commanding lips that had teased and tantalized until she'd lost herself in all-consuming need.

Kiss me! Kate locked her jaw to trap the demand inside. He had the ability to make her feel as if she were the only woman in the world. As if she were the center of his universe.

He apparently could make every woman feel that way. Which is why love 'em and leave 'em Liam had legions of adoring fans.

She yanked herself out of his embrace. "I don't need anybody."

Unhappiness darkened his gaze and his provocative mouth tipped downward. "Maybe that's the problem, sweetheart."

She didn't want pity. Or sympathy. "Don't you *dare* feel sorry for me. I do fine all by myself."

He shook his head. "Don't you want a little girl of your own someday?" He glanced at Aubrey, his face wistful. "With big brown eyes just like her mom?"

Her heart skipped a beat. Holy crow! He wasn't the first person to notice the resemblance between her and her niece. The reason he'd gone green when he'd first seen Aubrey and had asked about her age was because he'd thought she was Kate's…and his.

And the idea had made him sick.

She wrapped her arms around herself to ward off a foreboding chill. A man allergic to commitment would freak over having kids. Kids were definitely permanent. Yearning gripped her in a heavy fist, refused to shake free. Liam's babies would be stunningly beautiful. With their father's effusive, confident charm, and their mother's… She gulped. What did she have to offer? "I'll probably never marry, or have children."

"What?" Stunned, he straightened. "Why not?"

She was a realist. Realists faced life head-on, without knuckling under to pain. "I'm sure it hasn't escaped your notice that the women in my family aren't ideal models of motherhood."

"Wait a minute." He reached for her again, but she sidestepped. If he touched her now, when she was so vulnerable, she'd crumble. She couldn't afford to be weak. The weak got devoured alive. "You're great with Aubrey."

"Granting wishes as an auntie is vastly different from a mother's responsibilities. And I…my hands aren't reliable. Janine didn't let me hold her when she was a baby, because she was afraid I'd drop her. So was I, for that matter." She ignored the pain and raised her chin. "Heck, you probably possess more nurturing qualities than the Chabeau women combined."

"No freaking way." He gripped her shoulders and pulled her toward him. He was mad, but controlled. She might fear his passion, but she wasn't scared of his anger. "Drama Queen couldn't take care of a dog, much less a baby. You're buying into a lie. You *can* depend on your hands…*and* your instincts."

Fighting him was useless. She was as determined to keep her

distance as he was to bring her nearer, but he was far stronger. However, he couldn't make her come any closer emotionally. Unless she chose to. "My photographs are my children." She uttered a quavery chuckle. "Okay, maybe stepchildren. My paintings were the true creations of my heart, and I'd hoped they would be my legacy. But I've adapted. Over the years, I've grown fond of my photos." And if that affection didn't run quite as deeply or strongly as it had for her paintings, who would know? She was able to express her artistic urges, and they would pay for Aubrey's treatments. That was enough. Had to be enough. Life was short. You couldn't expect too much.

His grip gentled, and he released her. "I don't normally fly off the handle. You tangle me up…" He scrubbed a hand over his jaw. "How did you make the transition from painting to photographs?"

She knew exactly how he felt. He blasted apart her peace of mind with a mere look. "Actually, it was something you said to me the night we were together."

Staring out the window, he went rigid. "Hold that thought."

She looked at the baking cityscape, rush-hour traffic crammed bumper-to-bumper in the ruthless heat. "What's wrong?"

He spun her away from the window, his response rapid-fire, his voice low. "I saw a red flash. Maybe laser sights. We could be under surveillance, or we might be targeted."

"Are you sure?"

"No, but I'm checking it out." He swooped her up and sat her down on the bed. "You're safe here. I'm leaving the blinds open so he won't suspect I'm on to him. Stay away from the window." He sprinted toward the door. "I'll put Murphy on guard. He won't let anyone near this room until he receives my command."

"No! Wait…" But he'd already disappeared.

The man crouched in a stinking alley across the street, his rifle trained on the couple silhouetted in the hospital window. Black malevolence writhed inside his brain—a nest of poisonous snakes he couldn't exterminate.

She was supposed to die today.

He clenched his fingers around the gun stock so tightly it should have shattered. Katherine never did what she was supposed to. That was her entire problem.

Katherine's death would have proven that his explosive was no longer unstable in large quantities. Free advertising, repeated worldwide on CNN, in glorious Technicolor. Her demise would have made him rich beyond his wildest dreams. Set him free of the anger, indignation and resentment that boiled constantly inside him. Feelings he'd been forced to conceal far too long.

She was to have been his grand finale, his pièce de résistance before his rebirth from the ashes of mediocrity.

But he'd failed. And his disgrace was all *her* fault.

Everything was her fault.

Anger seethed, consuming him alive from the inside out.

Her policeman had made him look like a damned fool this afternoon. Had stolen his glory and riches.

He was out of patience. Finished with them both.

He fought the temptation to squeeze the trigger and be done with it. First, he would force them to play his game.

His rules.

His way.

His compatriots were becoming uneasy. He'd run out of options…and so had she. *Les Hommes de la Mort*—the Men of Death—would soon take matters into their own hands. They despised loose ends.

He glanced at his watch. He had mere hours, probably less before they intervened. Until then, Katherine's and her policeman's fates, their very lives, belonged to him. Power surged through him, making his palms slick with excitement. Making him hard.

If they survived his game, proved themselves worthy opponents, he *might* choose to spare them. For now. Or he might kill them anyway.

And revel in their dying.

His lips thinned into a grim smile as he holstered the rifle over his left shoulder.

Only time would tell.

Chapter 7

6:00 p.m.

Pulse galloping, Kate crouched protectively over her sleeping niece. Once Aubrey fell asleep it took an earthquake to wake her, especially after the ordeal of dialysis.

Kate fidgeted. She was used to solving her own problems. She couldn't twiddle her thumbs while Liam put his life on the line. She strained to look out the window, but saw only the glittering Vegas skyline. Liam had left Murphy to defend her and Aubrey. He'd rushed headlong after an armed assailant alone. Her heart skipped a beat. Without his partner. Without backup.

Though Liam hadn't mentioned it, maybe she should call 9-1-1. She glanced at the phone. What would she say? He saw a flash? *Maybe* someone is targeting us? Oh yeah, Chuck Hanson, gung ho FBI guy would *love* to document a false alarm on Liam's record.

She could do *something*. She attached the heavy telephoto lens to her Leica. With the strap draped around her neck, she crawled to the window. Crouched below the sill, she thrust up the camera and snapped. Long shots were her favorite technique. The distance gave the impression of an outsider looking in. Kept her emotions out of the picture and emphasized the scene.

That's what *she* envisioned. Liam had a different opinion. How odd that he'd mentioned "Man in the Shadows." She'd been wandering the streets of Paris at 2:00 a.m., unable to shake thoughts of Liam. The man's tall, limber frame; the wide set of his shoulders; the way his dark hair curled over his collar had jarred her with the similarities to her Irish charmer. She'd been missing him as much as she missed the use of her right arm when she'd captured the moody portrait.

Of all her photos, it was the first to sell. The only one she truly loved. The only one she'd kept a copy of. It wasn't stored in her studio safe with the negatives of her work. She took it wherever she went. It was currently displayed on her condo's bedroom wall, opposite Grandma's painting.

Grinding noises from inside the camera housing, followed by an abrupt pop, made her mutter a soft curse. The film had broken. Not an uncommon occurrence, but a pain in the derriere.

She risked a fast peek outside and saw nothing unusual. She crawled back to the bed, perched on the end, and then glanced at her watch. Liam had been gone over twenty minutes.

Kate stared at the telephone, racked by indecision. Because she hadn't seen or heard a commotion didn't mean he was all right. Guns had silencers. Knives didn't make noise. What if he needed help? What if he lay crumpled in an alley, bleeding to death? The agonizing image crushed her chest until she could barely breathe.

She checked her watch again. Twenty-six minutes. Way too long. She'd rather be labeled a fool than let something awful happen to Liam. Nerves jittering, she reached for the phone.

Suddenly the door opened and he strode inside. "Miss me?"

Heart in her throat, she whirled and frantically inventoried his body. No bullet holes, no knife wounds. No blood. Her trapped breath whooshed out. *"Finally!"* Her quiet tone didn't disguise the worried edge of anger. "Do you know how anxious…" Her jaw dropped as she saw what he carried.

"Mission accomplished." He held up a water-filled fishbowl,

where a small orange fish swooped in happy circles. The ensemble included rainbow colored gravel and a miniature Arc de Triomphe.

She blinked in stunned disbelief. "I'm being stalked by a goldfish? Gee, somehow I thought he'd be taller."

He laughed softly. "Officer O'Rourke always gets his ma—"

"Mackerel?" Shouting in a whisper wasn't easy, but she managed. "I was scared half to death…" Her voice quavered. "I was afraid you were wounded, or…" She choked, unable to say it. "And you were *shopping* for amphibians?"

"Well, technically, fish aren't amphibians—"

"Do you think I give a rip about a biology lesson right now?" Fear, relief and anger unspooled in rapid succession. "A dog isn't enough? You felt compelled to acquire another pet?"

He shrugged a broad shoulder. "By the time I hit the street, the spy was history. I reported it, but I doubt the local cops will find him. There's a pet store next door, and I was already there." He set the bowl on the bedside table. "The fish will give Aubrey something to care for. Something to do besides watch TV. I already cleared it with the charge nurse."

"Oh." She was so unaccustomed to thoughtfulness, it hadn't occurred to her he'd bought a gift for Aubrey. *"Oh!"* She groped for words. "She *adores* fish."

"So I gathered."

For the second time in less than an hour, unexpected tears threatened. "That is the sweetest thing I ever…"

His wolfish grin gleamed. "You were worried about me?"

"Of course not. You're a well-trained, armed SWAT officer. You can take care of yourself."

He wrapped his hand around her upper arm and drew her toward him. Even in the midst of a minimeltdown, she noticed he was always careful to grasp her uninjured arm. "You said you were scared half to death."

Kate pivoted to break his hold, and her back hit the wall near the door. *He's fine. Get a grip.* But the contrast between her earlier terror and his heartfelt gesture had hurtled her onto an emotional roller coaster. She raised her chin in defiance. "An expression people blurt without thinking—"

He planted both hands on the wall on either side of her shoulders, caging her in. "When they're upset?"

She swiped at her eyes, aghast to find them damp. Was horrified to discover she was shaking from forehead to French manicured toenails. What was *wrong* with her? "I am not upset!"

"Hey." His teasing grin vanished, and he brushed gentle fingertips over her lashes. "Those are real tears." He cupped her face in both hands. "And you're trembling. I thought you were kidding, but you *were* worried about me."

"You were gone so long. I didn't know…how to help you."

"I didn't expect you to help me." His glossy brows met in bewilderment. "I handle bombs and deal with bad guys every day. My family is packed with cops…all used to the lifestyle." Clearly amazed, he leaned down. "Nobody has concerned themselves with my safety for a long time. Nobody has ever *cried* over me."

"I'm *not* crying." She sniffled. "It's probably allergies."

"I'll buy that." His low, intimate whisper washed over her. "You're allergic to emotion." He eased closer, and she was caught between his hard-muscled body and the wall. Heartbeat thundered against heartbeat. He was warm, vital…alive.

And she was relieved, no…*overjoyed.*

Shock and surprise tumbled inside at the depth of her caring, at her strong attachment. She wasn't used to emotional upheaval. Struggling for balance, she studied the dark stubble that shadowed his jaw. Remembered the erotic tingle of his beard rasping her bare skin. She shivered. "I've dreamed about you."

The words had barely escaped before she cringed. *Ohmigosh!* Why had she spilled *that* horrifying secret?

Astonishment blanked his expression before he smiled gently. "It's okay to have feelings," he murmured. "To have dreams." His fingertips stroked her face, and she broke out in goose bumps. "People who don't have dreams, don't have anything."

"What…" She swallowed hard. The dizzying blend of his nearness and her blunder made coherency impossible. He'd be stunned by the hurricane whip of her feelings, by the bold demand of her dreams. "What do you do when your dreams get blasted apart? When they shatter at your feet?"

"Exactly what you've done." His gaze locked on hers as his clever fingers caressed her throat, grazed her collarbone. "Pick up the pieces and create something new. Channel the passion inside you to redefine something imperfect in a perfect way."

She wanted to believe him, but couldn't. "My pictures are far from perfect." They'd satisfied some of the yen to create, but didn't come close to baring her soul on canvas.

"I bought a gallery book of your work. I had no idea that you were Renée Allete." His eyes flared with a dangerous gleam. "The pictures tugged at me, drew me in. I couldn't resist. I like your photographs, Just Kate."

His praise sent happiness winging. "You do?"

"A lot." His husky whisper feathered over her lips. His green irises went smoky, and her stomach swooped on a flutter of anticipation. "God help me, I like *you.*" He breached the millimeters separating them and covered her mouth with his.

The first time, passion had rampaged between them, hot and fast. A flamethrower that had incinerated all reason. She hadn't had time to think, to breathe. She'd let herself be swept out to sea, riding the crushing riptide.

Now, his soft lips beguiled, coaxed her into the warm slide of desire. Her eyelashes floated down in willing surrender. Some things hadn't changed. Liam's tender touch, his intoxicating taste, his brisk scent all immersed her in him. Only him. Everything faded away. Nothing existed but her and Liam…and the seductive lure of shimmering pleasure.

"Mmm," she sighed into his mouth. Oh, she'd dreamed about his kisses. But dreams didn't even *touch* reality.

He cradled her head in his big hands and urged her nearer. His warm, silky tongue slid inside, flirted with hers…teased, withdrew, then thrust in again. Degree by exquisite degree, he notched up the heat. His fire licked at the wall of ice inside her, and melted her control.

She wrapped her arms around his neck and snuggled into him. He was hot and hard, and fiercely aroused. But it wasn't just chemistry. Their bond was more than physical. More than wanting. She cared about him in a deep, elemental way she'd never felt before. Didn't understand. Couldn't explain.

She told him the only way she knew how. She kissed him back, loosening her restraints on the deluge of emotions.

His heartbeat kicked against his chest. He groaned, and deepened the kiss. He drank in her essence, made love to her mouth as if he would go on kissing her until the world ended. Fine tremors vibrated in his steely muscles, restrained energy fighting to be freed. His need was as strong as hers.

She knew without a doubt that he *wanted* her—as she'd never been wanted before.

Her pulse scrambled and every neuron in her brain fired. She would give him anything.

She would give him *everything.*

There it was. The moment Liam had unknowingly waited for his entire life. The contented hum as the universe settled into place. Except it was more like a sonic boom exploding inside his skull.

He reeled, drunk on Kate's flower petal fragrance, on the feel of her skin, soft and sleek beneath his fingertips. On her taste, spun sugar melting on his tongue.

He was losing the battle for control. Losing his sanity.

Losing his soul. *Damn!*

It was a price he couldn't afford. Wouldn't pay. He yanked back, broke the kiss. Kate's small cry of protest, her fingers clutching his shoulders, bruised his already battered heart.

Fully engaged in survival mode, he panted for breath and propped his forehead against hers. "This isn't good."

"It isn't?" Her graceful features crumpled with hurt, and she tried to pull away. "I'm sorry, I'm terrible at this."

He held her tight. They were both trembling. "I didn't mean… You're *not* terrible at kissing." Good Lord, she'd short-circuited his brain. If she were any better, his boxers would have spontaneously combusted. He stared into her amazing eyes. They were dark and dilated with passion, her expression dazed.

His mouth slanted in wariness. "The kissing is good. No, make that *great.*" He released a sharp laugh. "Really great."

She worried her bottom lip between her teeth. He tracked the unconsciously sexy gesture, and his body twitched. He swore.

She frowned, visibly trying to mesh his words with his contradictory actions. She appeared as confused as he felt. "And that's bad?"

"No. *Yes!* Crap!" He propped his palms on the wall beside her and banged his forehead against it. He never had a problem with self-control before. Or self-expression. "Aw, hell, you have me stuttering like a rookie on his first bust."

"My kisses made Obi-O'Rourke, master golden tongue, stutter. Wow." Something that looked suspiciously like awe glimmered in her gaze. "So much for the gift of blarney."

A rush of adrenaline-laced fear zinged through his veins. He was in way over his head. And for the first time in his life, didn't know how to finesse himself out. His charm didn't influence her like it did every other woman. Kate demanded, and deserved, a higher standard he couldn't maintain.

She'd been worried about him for crying out loud.

Women never worried about him. Never shed tears over his welfare. He was careful not to get close enough to give them cause. He kept his relationships breezy and casual. And extremely short. However, around Kate, his best intentions took the express train to hell.

"You declared we should keep it just business between us." He flicked a glance at his watch. "Less than three hours ago. Even though I razzed you about it, I agreed."

"Yes." She rested her palm over his heart, which bucked in response. She was still trembling, her expression a tangle of shock and unsatisfied hunger. "Yet…"

"Yeah, here we are." He couldn't resist the urge to glide his fingers through the cool silk of her hair. He stifled a groan. He was in deep trouble. Up to his arse in alligators. "Why does this keep happening? Most important, how do we stop?"

She tried to mask the strain, but he saw it anyway. "Heck if I know. For one thing, don't buy Aubrey any more goldfish."

How was a guy supposed to think, with her so close, looking, smelling, tasting so damn sexy? "Who knew fish did it for you, honey? Damn good thing I didn't bring her an orca."

She fought a brief round with a wobbly grin and lost. "Technically, whales are mammals."

He eased back from the warm haven of her body. In spite of the cavalier attitude he'd donned for his own protection, he was painfully turned on. Distraction needed, fast. He made it to a three-count, then chagrined, shook his head. Not enough Gaelic in the freaking galaxy. "Do I look like I give a rip about a biology lesson right now?"

"It certainly feels like it." She gulped. "Guess it depends on whose biology you're studying, huh?" She shook her head. "You're right. We have to nip this in the bud."

Liam stroked a fingertip down her soft cheek, and she quivered beneath his touch. There was something strange at work here. A compelling force. He had power over Kate, and she over him. She wasn't like any other woman. Nobody had ever needed him the way she needed him. He'd never needed anyone the way he needed her. Around her, he found it impossible to be breezy and casual. The more they resisted, the more fate seemed determined to bring them together. Thunderstruck, his heart staggered in his chest.

Maybe Pop's wild claim *wasn't* bogus.

The revelation was exciting. Intriguing. His throat tightened. And scary as hell. What was he supposed to do now? He wanted to explore the possibilities. He wanted to turn tail and run. Circumstances, and Kate's safety, demanded he do neither.

He took a fortifying draught of oxygen. No matter how confused, how scared he felt, it was his job to jerk them out of the quagmire. And keep them there. At all costs, he had to protect her. "I'll keep my hands to myself, Just Kate."

"And your lips." She drew a quavery breath. Her gaze traveled down his body, and his skin tingled as if she'd run her hands over him. *All* over. "And your…goodies."

He chuckled unevenly. Yeah, especially the goodies. He strode to the door and swung it open. "Let's bug out." *Before I totally lose it, toss you on the floor and have my way with you.*

Kate tiptoed to the bed and tenderly kissed the sleeping child's forehead. "Sweet dreams, baby girl," she whispered.

Murphy pushed to all fours as they exited the room. The big canine stretched and yawned, showing a curling pink tongue and sharp white teeth. *No bad guys showed up. Let's eat.*

Kate squeaked and scurried to Liam's right.

They ambled down the hall, and Liam rested his palm on Murphy's soft, warm head. *She's terrified of your partner. Remember that next time you're tempted to taste her, boyo.* Priority number two, after Kate's safety, was clearing her with the FBI. As long as they suspected her of terrorist activities, neither of them were free. He had a buttload of obstacles to hurdle before he could even *think* about possibilities.

Kate stopped at the nurses' desk and requested they phone her immediately if the child's status changed.

They slogged five floors to street level, and walked out of the hospital into the blast of sunlight and grinding heat. Liam winced. He wasn't a fan of the desert climate, either. A true Oregonian, he slept best when a rainstorm drummed the roof.

He started to shove a Phil Collins CD into the player—another modern addition to his classic muscle car—thought better of it and switched to Queen. As they drove toward the Venetian, he watched his rearview mirrors, but no tail appeared. A grin sneaked out. Maybe biker dude had spread the word.

He caught Murphy's bright gaze in the mirror, and the dog grinned in response. *Yeah. Don't screw with Murphy and O'Rourke unless you want to lose some hide.*

Though regularly checking her side mirror, Kate was quiet and subdued in her seat. No doubt dealing with the backlash from their volcanic kiss.

"Do you keep a mailing list of gallery visitors and clients?" At her affirmative nod, he continued. "I'll need that, along with names of your doctors, physical therapists and anyone you regularly do business with."

"Okay. Mostly it's art supplies and photo developing…" She sat bolt upright. "I almost forgot! I was snapping shots of the outside of the hospital and my film broke. I need to drop my camera off at Custom Developers and have them extract it. Maybe I caught some evidence."

A cold fist gripped his gut, squeezed with icy fingers. "You stood at the window and took pictures…with a possible sniper gunning for you?" He stomped the brakes for a red light, jolting them forward. "I told you to stay clear."

"I'm not stupid. I stayed below the sill."

He fisted his hands on the wheel. If she'd gotten hurt…or

worse... He broke out into a cold sweat as the awful images scored his brain. Had she experienced this wrenching panic when he was outside and all she could do was wait? What did that say about the depth of her feelings? About the depth of his?

The car behind them honked, and he belatedly realized the light was green. He ground his teeth. The stalker could have sashayed right up to the car and blown her away while he was gobsmacked. *Get a handle on it, O'Rourke.* Blast it all, he was doing the work of three men—Larry, Moe and Curly.

She directed him to a small building tucked between a dry cleaner and a discount craft store in a nondescript strip mall. "It doesn't look like much, but they're the best in town."

"Don't argue with success." He made a covert visual sweep of the perimeter as he escorted her into the shop. Murphy trotted at his left, watchful but relaxed.

A stocky guy with short, curly blond hair challenged Liam the second they cleared the automatic glass doors. "Sorry, sir, you can't bring that dog inside." Of average height, skating toward overweight, he was wearing tan chinos and a white button-down oxford shirt. His red, yellow and blue striped tie matched the store's color scheme. Liam pegged his age around thirty. Way too old to be dressed for career day in junior high.

The guy did a double take and then paled. "Is that a *gun?*"

Liam plucked his badge from his back pocket and snapped it open. "Police K-9."

"Do you have police business here?" he shrilled.

Kate stepped forward. "He's with me, Brice."

"Ms. Chabeau! I didn't see you at first." Brice's amber eyes widened. "I hope there's no trouble."

"Officer O'Rourke is helping me with security for the Allete auction. We're on our way over there right now."

"Oh, wonderful!" The man slapped the counter, suddenly effusive. "It's been awhile. Work does get in the way of living your life." He nodded sagely at his own wisdom. "You look fabulous, as always."

Liam scowled. Nerd boy was a tad too enthusiastic.

"Nice to see you again, too." Kate offered her camera. "The film broke. And I need priority processing."

"Right away. I always give you my very best."

She smiled. "I appreciate it."

"Since the film is broken, you'll have to leave the camera. As long as you trust me with your treasure." Brice offered her a toothy grin, and the back of Liam's neck prickled.

This guy was too happy to be real. Too interested. Too *everything.* Liam would have Aidan and Zoe check him out, ASAP.

Brice wrote a receipt. "I'll phone you when it's ready."

When they were once again in the car and heading for the strip, Liam glanced at Kate. "How long have you known him?"

"I don't, really. I've used the shop for the past couple years when I'm in town visiting Aubrey."

"Happen to know his last name, or address?"

"Why?" She gasped. "You don't think Brice…"

"He blipped my weirdo radar. He likes you. And someone who specializes in custom developing is proficient with chemicals."

"He is a bit odd. But very sweet. He's never given me trouble, or any reason to think badly of him."

"Stalkers are clever. Devious. Evil. And they disguise it well. The whack job who's after you could be your best friend, and you wouldn't know until it was too late."

He grabbed his cell phone and called Aidan, then Zoe with Brice's info. Afterward, he checked in with the local precinct. Frustrated, he hung up and shared the bad news. "Biker dude escaped before EMS or the cops arrived."

"I feel so…violated." Kate shuddered. "Someone I might know wants to kill me, for whatever warped reason."

He clasped her hand and gave her fingers a reassuring squeeze. "Nobody will hurt you as long as I'm still breathing."

Fifteen minutes later, they arrived at the Venetian. Liam reluctantly accepted valet parking as the fastest way to get Kate to the relative safety of the hotel's interior.

The sun hadn't set, but the graceful white columned archways were lit, washing the facade in a welcoming glow. He monitored their surroundings as they entered the hotel.

Inside, Kate preceded him through the lobby and around the ornate gold fountain. The Renaissance art ceilings, imposing columns and intricate molding never failed to amaze. With Murphy following, they strolled down a side hallway.

The second they walked into the foyer outside a private reception room, a young man rushed them. Liam registered the guy's black leather pants, billowy red satin shirt and shoulder-length platinum hair in the same millisecond he whipped out his Glock. "Freeze!" he ordered. "Police."

Murphy stiffened and rumbled a menacing growl. The dog's ears flattened and his tail lowered. *Let me at him!*

The guy slid to a halt and flung his hands in front of his face as if to ward off bullets. *"Mon Dieu!"* he screeched. "Katherine!" He pronounced Kate's name *Cat-a-rin. "Aidez moi!"*

"Liam, *no!*" At the terrifying sight of Liam pointing a gun at her friend, Kate's heart jammed in her throat. She threw herself forward. Whirling to face Liam, she spread her arms, becoming a human shield. "This is my administrative assistant!"

"Dammit, Kate." Fury lit Liam's green eyes. He crossed the distance in three strides and yanked her toward him. The pulse in his neck throbbed a rapid tattoo. "I could have *shot* you."

She gulped down dismay and cast a distrustful glance at the bristling K-9. The hostile dog scared her way more than the gun. "You wouldn't have."

"Don't bet your life on it." He shook her. "Don't *ever* get between me and a target again. Do you hear me?"

His glare scalded her. She *knew* he wouldn't hurt her, yet she was spooked. And it was only a fraction of the intimidation he threw at the bad guys. Gad. It was a wonder they didn't wet themselves and surrender on sight. "Y-yes."

Panting, Etienne peered over her shoulder. *"Tres macho!"*

"Macho to the wazoo." Kate pressed a hand to her racing heart and waved with the other. "Officer Liam O'Rourke, this is my administrative assistant Etienne Duplais."

Metal scraped leather as Liam holstered his weapon. Murphy sat, his dark, observant gaze trained on Etienne. She warily eyed the dog. It was freaky how in a blink he could go from attack weapon to vigilant partner. Liam was obviously safer with Murphy on his side. She wasn't sure about everyone else.

Liam extended his hand. "Etienne."

"Mon plaisir de vous rencontrer!" Etienne sidled out and clasped Liam's hand. *"Le paradis sur terre existe!"*

Kate risked a cautious look at Liam. Not one flicker of a gorgeous eyelash. Whew! He obviously didn't speak the lingo.

Etienne still hadn't released Liam from his grasp. "It is my extreme pleasure to meet you, Monsieur O'Rourke."

Liam quirked an inquiring brow at her over Etienne's head. The intuitive cop didn't have any problem reading between the lines. Etienne's flamboyant awe was enough to make him wonder.

She shook her head in answer to his unspoken question. "Etienne has an eye for beauty…in all its varied incarnations." Etienne definitely loved women, and they returned his affection.

Liam finally extracted his hand from Etienne's fervent grasp. "Thanks, I think."

Etienne turned so he could look at both her and Liam. "*Mon coeur,* if you do not think this Irishman is *magnifique,* you need to have more than your vision checked."

Liam frowned. "How do you know I'm Irish?"

"Your name, it is not exactly *Italien.*" Etienne quirked a sardonic gilded brow. "Aside from that, it is obvious, no? The bone structure, the eyes, the hair…" Etienne's forehead furrowed. "Are you dating this policeman, Katherine? If so, we must have a talk, monsieur, how you say…man-to-man."

She tossed visual daggers at her friend. Could he get any more possessive and protective? "Knock it off, Etienne."

Etienne flapped his arms. "Where have you been, Katherine? I left message after message, and have worried myself silly."

If she mentioned the bomb, her young protégé would come unglued. She'd kept the stalker notes a secret from him for the same reason. "I was…at the hospital. Aubrey's worse, and Janine had a hard time dealing with it."

"The poor *bébé.* But your photographs will earn a great deal of money and she will be well soon." Etienne's lips pursed in a very Gallic moue. "Janine, now there is a woman with simple tastes. Why just look at some of her ex-beaus."

Liam's strangled cough sounded suspiciously like choked laughter.

"You're skating perilously close to the line, Duplais." There was nothing the outrageous Frenchman wouldn't do or say. A little over a year after she'd set up shop in Paris, he'd sauntered into her studio, literally off the street. In spite of his lack of experience and references, he'd dumbfounded her with his creative vision. She'd hired him on the spot.

Liam's intent stare tracked Etienne's athletic frame from leonine mane to pointed-toe boots. "Have an accident, boyo?"

Startled, she studied her assistant. In the chaos, she hadn't noticed the raw, scraped knuckles on his left hand.

Etienne's quicksilver eyes narrowed. "Your policeman is observant."

Deceptively casual, Liam rested his palm on his gun. "A fact you'd do well to remember."

"Subtle as a chainsaw, Ace." Surely he didn't believe *Etienne* was stalking her. Etienne wouldn't hurt a fly. Her admin was completely devoted. She sighed. As far as the conscientious cop was concerned, *everyone* was suspect until proven innocent.

"I wasn't going for subtle." Liam hadn't moved his laser gaze off Etienne.

Etienne shuffled his feet. "I was unpacking the shipment of photographs, and the wooden crate, she attacked. Fell on me."

Liam nodded. "Anything besides your hand damaged?"

"Thank you for caring, Monsieur Lucky-with-his-charms, *mais non.*"

"I hate to break up the testosterone patrol, but we have to get the photos arranged." Now that the crisis had passed, she needed to stay busy. Or she would dwell on *the kiss.* Would speculate on the implications of the searing connection. Yearn for the crazy sense of rightness, the warm welcome of belonging.

She was having an increasingly rough time wrestling her feelings into submission. It had taken the entire car trip to convince herself her lapse in common sense was simply temporary insanity caused by hormonal brain impairment.

Etienne gifted her with his impish smile. "When you did not appear, I hung all the photographs."

He extracted a key card from the pocket of his leather pants.

"Katherine possesses remarkable talent, monsieur. The instant I saw her brilliant photographs, I could not resist."

Watching Etienne closely, Liam crossed his arms over his chest, and his tanned biceps bunched. "I heartily agree."

"A man with much discernment." Etienne flung apart the doors. "*Mon coeur,* I think you will be happy with the displ—" Her admin broke off and his mouth dropped open. He blanched.

"Etienne?" Cold apprehension slammed her. "What's wrong?"

Aghast, he turned to Kate. Tried to speak, and failed. Tried again. *"Les photos ont disparu,"* he croaked."

Electric shock crackled over her. "What?"

"Volé!" Etienne whispered.

Kate rushed forward. Her horrified gaze flew inside. She gasped. The room was in chaos, furniture overturned, drapes torn. Except for dangling wires, the walls were bare.

Her photographs were gone!

They'd been stolen!

Chapter 8

7:00 p.m.

Liam said something from behind her, but Kate couldn't hear over the static buzz. A familiar-looking envelope was taped to the inside of the door. She tore it open with shaking hands.

Liam's hand cupped the back of her neck as he read the note over her shoulder.

She couldn't catch her breath. "Heed me, or they burn."

They watched as the paper blackened, then crumbled to ashes. Though the ibuprofen had dulled her headache, a tsunami of pain roared back, nearly bowling her over.

His fingers kneaded her bowstring-taut muscles, offering solace. "Are you all right?"

"I was merely absent for *un petite moment,*" Etienne raved. He paced in front of the open doors, babbling a stream of hysterical French she didn't dare translate.

Liam made a circular hand motion. "Murphy, search." The dog trotted into the room and began to sniff. Liam snatched his phone from his pocket. "Aidan," he said into the receiver. "Get the clan to the Venetian…yesterday! The Allete auction. And alert the locals to process a crime scene—grand theft."

Her vision blurred from the combination of suppressed tears and shock, and she staggered.

"Sit." Liam eased her onto a love seat, and then sat beside her, one arm around her shoulders. "We'll get your photos back."

"How? We don't even know who this lunatic is."

"Teamwork." He gave her a reassuring hug. "My brothers are on the way." He reached for his phone again and spoke to the head of security. Then he sent the still ranting Etienne for coffee. Coffee sounded good. A snifter of cognac even better. Liam gave her another squeeze. "Everything will be okay."

"Damn straight. The weirdo only *thinks* he's won." She dialed her cell phone. Puzzled, she listened to the busy signal. It was 4:00 a.m. in Paris. The assistant she'd hired should pick up from the apartment above the studio. Like Vegas, Paris was a twenty-four-hour city, but who would the woman be chatting with at the crack of dawn? Temporarily stymied, she hung up.

"It's all right to get upset, Kate. Perfectly natural under the circumstances." Liam rubbed her arms, and she realized she was shivering. "Let it out. I'm the only one here to see."

"Falling apart won't bring back my photos."

"You know, honey, constantly strangling your emotions is a formula for disaster. It's not good for your mental or physical health." He cupped her chin. "Everybody has to blow off steam."

"I'm fine." Not counting the brain-squeezing migraines.

"Now who's spouting blarney? You're a ticking time bomb. Nuclear fallout waiting to happen." He gently smoothed her hair. "Cry, scream, stomp, break stuff. You'll feel better."

"Not my style." She gave him a forlorn smile. "I leave the hissy fits to the professionals."

"Kate, if you continue to keep up the brave front, your ulcers will have ulcers."

A silver-haired man in a black suit hurried into the foyer and introduced himself as Mr. Baron, head of hotel security.

Liam surged to his feet. He displayed his badge and drew the man into a private confab. Speaking rapidly, he pointed at the open doors as Murphy ambled out and sat on his left.

His face grave with concern, Mr. Baron nodded in response. When their conversation was over, he hurried out.

Liam ordered the dog to guard the doors and returned to her side. "Baron is going to check the surveillance tapes."

She glanced up at the ceiling. After several months in Vegas, one tended to forget that the "eyes in the sky" watched and recorded everything that happened in the casinos.

Etienne bustled in, pushing a wheeled cart laden with a large coffeepot, mugs and a platter of hearty sandwiches. No surprise, Liam had pegged him at first glance. Her admin was calmer when he had purpose. "I fetched sustenance, as ordered."

Liam poured a mug of steaming coffee and added two sugars and a generous splash of cream. He placed a ham sandwich on a plate and then handed the mug and plate to her. "Eat something."

She sipped greedily at the brew, relishing the hot caffeine rush. "How on earth do you know exactly how I take my coffee?"

His roguish grin gleamed. "Anybody who drinks frappuccinos likes it smooth and sweet."

Exactly like his kisses. If you added *hot.* Against her will, her gaze lingered on his delectable mouth. He glanced down, caught her ogling and smiled.

Kate cringed. She was coming unhinged…in the middle of a crisis. She concentrated on her sandwich. Before long, three men and two women blasted into the foyer. She recognized the hunkalicious trio from the long ago night in Delany's Pub. Liam alone was breathtakingly beautiful. En masse, the sexy SWAT brothers delivered enough eye candy to throw a woman into diabetic shock.

Mother Nature's pheromone arsenal.

"Sainte Marie!" Etienne breathed. He slapped both hands over his heart. She hoped he didn't faint.

Liam drew Kate to her feet and tucked her against him. Solicitous, or staking a claim? Consideration, she appreciated. Possessive was a whole 'nother deal. "Kate Chabeau, meet Aidan, Con and Grady." Liam's brothers were luscious and lethal, and armed to their perfect, white smiles.

She murmured hellos, glad they were on her side. Liam introduced her to Bailey, Con's wife, the enviable owner of a shiny strawberry blond halo and creamy complexion, and Zoe, Aidan's wife, a pixie with short, dark curls and wise eyes.

"Nice to meet you, Kate." Zoe perused her with unabashed interest. "Your work is amazing."

"Thank you." Torn between pleasure and annoyance, she glanced sideways at Liam.

"Sorry." He murmured in her ear. "I had to burn your cover in order to brief them. They won't break your confidence."

"Please." Bailey waved at the love seat. "Sit down, finish your coffee. You've suffered a tremendous strain."

Liam urged her back down. "Where are the locals?"

"En route," Con said, passing his wife a coffee, and poured one for himself. Bailey set aside hers and dropped into a chair. Con moved behind her and rested proprietary hands on her shoulders. "The heat still bothering you, sweetheart?"

Overprotective DNA apparently ran in the family. Kate couldn't resist a tiny grin. When heaven was dispensing testosterone, the O'Rourke men had stood in line twice.

"I'm better now that we're inside." Bailey caught her eye and smiled. She patted her husband's arm. "Overwhelming at first, aren't they? You'll get used to it."

Yes, a woman could get used to being cherished. Kate rubbed her aching forehead. Not that she'd have the chance. Or wanted it. She didn't need a doting man.

Liam's phone trilled the chorus from Queen's "We Will Rock You," and he tugged it out. "O'Rourke." He frowned. "Say *what?*"

He disconnected. "The surveillance tape shows Elvira stroll past and appear to case the doorway. Then it turns to snow."

Zoe checked with a sandwich halfway to her mouth. "*Elvira?* As in, 'Mistress of the Dark'?"

"Yeah. 'She' appears to be a man, complete with Adam's apple. Apparently, 'she' also pitched a tantrum in the lobby, claiming 'she' was mugged." He shook his head. "Only in Vegas."

Zoe grimaced at Kate. "Are you okay? You're awfully pale."

"Just a headache. I'll be fine."

Zoe shrugged off the large battered canvas bag hanging over her shoulder. "I have ibuprofen."

"It's past that stage. I have prescription meds at home."

"Okay, gang, listen up." Liam addressed his family. "Bailey, help Etienne organize things here. Arrange the room to display the photos the instant we get them back."

Bailey nodded, and Liam continued. "Con, watch the crime scene processing—make sure they don't miss a speck. Follow up with hotel security. You're the best man to tightrope the fine line between assisting and overstepping the locals."

"Done," Con replied.

"Aidan, continue to run down the suspect list—off the record." Liam's implacable gaze briefly touched Kate's. "I have an addition for you. Call me with the reports, ASAP."

Kate watched Liam effortlessly take charge. She leaned into the cushions, resigned that he would investigate Etienne. Her Irish charmer was a very thorough man. Thorough with *everything*. Her stomach fluttered, and she gave herself a mental slap. *Stop!*

Neither brother balked at accepting orders from their younger sibling. A telling revelation of respect. She couldn't garner family cooperation for Aubrey's sake when she begged.

Liam turned to Zoe. "Geraldo, work the international angle using your journalism connections."

Zoe smirked. "Anything for you, Deputy Dog."

"Grady." Liam pointed. "Follow the Elvira lead. Be subtle. Blend. We don't want to spook the perp into destroying the photos. No pyrotechnics, no bullets and no taking prisoners."

Grady's dimples flashed. "Take no prisoners, ten-four."

"Subtle." Liam rolled his eyes. *"Blend!"*

"Sir, yes sir! No extreme measures…" Grady's grin widened, deepening his dimples. "Unless absolutely necessary."

As Grady sauntered away, Liam shook his head at Kate in mock exasperation. "That boy is a walking advertisement for judicious birth control."

She chuckled. The two younger O'Rourkes obviously shared a deep bond, but their relationship was refreshingly irreverent.

Everyone scattered, and Liam again dialed his phone. "Carson?

O'Rourke. Send the bomb squad to sweep Ms. Chabeau's apartment, code three. If you find a device, expect a double antitamper switch." He covered the receiver. "Address?" He repeated the location to Carson, and then hung up.

Kate gathered her hair off her nape, attempting to relieve the pressure on her head. "Is it wise to go to my apartment?"

"You need your headache meds." She started to speak and he held up a broad palm. "I swear, if I hear, 'I'm fine' pass your delectable lips one more time, I will turn you over my knee."

She bristled. "Watch it, Ace. I was under the impression that a bomb tech needed all ten fingers."

He laughed before quickly sobering. "We'll stay long enough to pack clothes and your valuables. Then I'll have Alex stash us at a safe house."

The thought of losing her only two treasures made her sick to her soul. Yet… "I have nothing worth risking our lives."

"I'm not risking squat. The bomb squad will clean house. That's what they do. And we have your neighbors to think about."

It was hard to accept that he would go to so much trouble and put himself in harm's way for her. Nobody had ever considered her comfort, her desires. It was unsettling. "I *would* like to get my grandma's painting…" She stopped short of mentioning "Man in the Shadows." He didn't know she associated the photo with him. No use calling attention to it. She set down her empty cup. "They're only things. I'm not sure we should—"

"Psycho is trying to steal your future. I'll be damned if I'll let him steal your past, too." He spoke through clenched teeth. "That painting means the world to you, like my car does to me. They might be 'just things,' but family ties keep you rooted. Give you hope."

Family ties! Appalled she hadn't considered it before, she jerked upright. "If the stalker wants to destroy everything I care about, he might go after Aubrey!"

"Already covered. I placed a call earlier when you made yours. Alex sent two teams of FBI agents to the hospital."

"Thank you." Having someone take care of her, someone she could count on, was a new experience. She wasn't sure how she felt. She couldn't depend on it. When push came to shove, most people moved their own needs to the top of the list, and damn everyone else.

She tried again to contact the temp in Paris. Maybe the woman had taken the phone off the hook when she went to bed.

Liam called Murphy over and fed him a sandwich. The dog's fangs demolished it in three bites, and she shivered.

The crimson sun blazed low on the horizon as the trio headed for the car. Liam navigated heavy traffic, vigilantly watching his mirrors. Odd. Even with a crazed stalker after her, she felt safer with him than she had in the past three years.

Police cars and a bomb disposal van crammed the parking lot of her condo. A chunky robot sat beside the front entrance, looking like an extra from a George Lucas movie. Carson met them on the second floor, at her doorstep. "We located two devices. One decoy and one live. All the neighbors were evacuated, and both devices were disarmed."

Liam shook his hand. "Thanks, we appreciate it."

Carson and the bomb squad departed. Kate moved to enter her apartment, but Liam blocked the doorway with his arm. "Hold on." He tucked her into the sheltered stairwell. "Stay here." He made the hand motion at Murphy. "Murphy, search." The K-9 trotted in.

"What are you doing?"

"Getting a second opinion." He followed the dog inside.

There he went again, putting himself in harm's way to protect her. She did deep breathing. He'd be fine. The bomb squad had just declared the place clean. She attempted another call to Paris. Got another busy signal.

After endless, anxious minutes, the dynamic duo returned. Liam swept a gallant bow. "*Now* you may come in."

She strode to the bathroom, gulped two migraine tablets and then leaned her throbbing forehead against the cool mirror.

"Are you all right?" Liam appeared in the doorway. At her nod, he looked skeptical. "Get packed."

"Since the bomb squad did their job, we're safe, right?"

"Not until Stalker Boy's crazy arse is in lockup."

Wonderful. She hurried into her bedroom and he followed.

His gaze traveled the Spartan room. She saw it through his eyes:

white walls, serviceable nightstand, chest and bed—draped with her one indulgence—a dove-gray silk comforter.

Compared to his homey Craftsman, it looked as bland and impersonal as Motel 6. "Daniel and Janine bring Aubrey to me in Paris when they're off on one of their junkets. I rented this place after she became so ill and I had to stay in Vegas. I didn't bother to decorate."

He smoothed his palm over the comforter, and her breath caught on the mental picture of his tanned, muscled body reclining in her bed. Gorgeous. Naked. Fully aroused. He pursed his lips. "You had to run clear to Europe to escape me?"

"No," she murmured. "To escape me."

He arched a thoughtful brow. "What's your Paris apartment like?"

"It's..." She hadn't bothered to decorate there, either. Stunned realization hit. No place felt like home. She hadn't been able to settle anywhere. She hadn't left her problems behind, they'd gone with her. She'd missed Riverside.

She'd missed *Liam.*

Shaking away the distressing thought, Kate lifted "Man in the Shadows" from the wall, and set it on the comforter. She pulled out her sturdy leather case she kept for transporting artwork.

"The book didn't do it justice." Admiration gleamed in his emerald eyes as he stroked a finger down the classic ebony frame that complemented the black-and-white photo, and her heart stuttered. She quivered as though his finger had stroked right down her center. "At the hospital, you were about to explain how you switched to photography before we got interrupted."

She looked down at the portrait. "Remember when we went back to your place the night we met?"

"I'll never forget it." Passion simmered in his deep, mellow voice as he turned his admiring gaze on her.

If he kept up, she'd have to grab a cold shower. "I left for Paris that morning. But you said something that stuck with me. You said, 'art is an unflinching expression of true self, no matter the medium. It's anything that arouses an emotional response in the creator and the observer. Anything that pulls both inside the experience and makes them participants.'" She slid the photo into the case. "I mulled that over for days."

"How did that lead you into photography?"

She snapped down the flap on the case. "Before my hand was damaged, I did renderings. Are you familiar with those?"

"Paintings with accurate perspective and details, where the artist makes the subject appear as realistic as possible."

"Rendering artists take photos to paint from. Art school profs loved my photo captures of light and shadow, and they raved over my compositions. After I came to grips with the fact that I'd never paint again, I pondered your words…and voilà!"

His intent gaze lingered on her face. "But it came hard."

Like ripping out my soul. She looked away from him, out the window. "Setting shutter speed and f-stops with my left hand isn't difficult. Manipulating the focus is a bit trickier, but manageable. Normally, I use a tripod to support the camera's weight and keep it steady, which leaves my hands free."

"Nice evade, but no escape. I was talking about emotionally."

She sighed. Deep down, she'd known he wouldn't let her get away with it. "The transition required significant emotional adjustment. But I made it. I didn't have a choice."

She walked to the opposite wall for Grandma Jane's painting, and then extracted a second case from under the bed.

His rapt attention focused on her, made her hyperaware. "Have you ever tried to paint with your left hand?"

"Yes." Under his close perusal, warmth shimmered over her skin. "But I…couldn't *feel* anything. I couldn't transfer emotion to the canvas." She shrugged. "I can't relate to abstracts."

He gestured at the painting she was easing into the case. "What do you feel when you see your grandmother's painting?"

"Inspired. Uplifted. Happy. But that's different." She paused, glanced down at the bold splashes of red, orange and gold scattered amidst slender strokes of green. "I'm connected to this painting. From my dad, I know how Grandma struggled. How no recognition didn't stop her from finding joy in painting. Her canvas isn't simply random brushstrokes. I see her steadfast hopes and bright dreams, like butterflies dancing over a field."

"You see it, but you can't paint it." His smooth voice went low, and he caressed her cheek. The zing glittered down her spine, clear to her toes. "Stifling your emotions is not only causing you headaches, it's smothering your creativity."

Stunned by his insight, she stared at him. She would *not* discuss this with the man who spun her emotions into wild loop-de-loops. "I'm perfectly happy as a photographer."

"Could have fooled me."

She stalked to the closet and yanked out a wheeled carry-on. "Are you going to stand there and drive me bonkers with amateur analysis, Dr. Phil, or do you plan to help?"

"I'm trying to help. You won't let me."

Her mouth slanted in exasperation. She was done with this conversation, and wanted him as far away as possible. "If I'm going to a safe house, I don't want to leave dirty dishes in the dishwasher. Could you start it up, please? Run the tap to prime the hot water first. Otherwise, they don't get clean."

"Sure. But I'd rather stay and pack your lingerie."

Glad to be back on firmer ground, she chuckled. "What would your mother say if she found out you were a pervert?"

Laughing, he left.

She kept her bureau—heck, her entire life—efficiently organized. In less than three minutes, she rolled her suitcase into the hallway. She tucked her art cases under her arm, pulled her phone from her purse and dialed her studio in Paris.

Liam met her in the living room. "There's no hot water."

"That's weird. I've never had problems with it before."

"Where's the water heater?"

"Inside the closet in the hallway, by the front door."

He walked to the closet, opened the door. "Hmm." Murphy padded out of the kitchen and peered over Liam's shoulder as he squatted to examine the fittings. "It has juice."

Finally, her studio number was ringing! The call connected, and a nasal recording announced in French, "The number you are calling has been disconnected or is no longer in service."

She hung up and squelched a spear of unease. European phone service was often sporadic. Kate tapped in the number for the family-owned bistro across the street. The owners would be up and busy in the kitchen, baking fresh bread and pastries.

"Bon matin," a breathless female voice answered.

"Margot? It's Kate. I'm calling from the States, and I can't get through to my studio."

"Kate? *Mon Dieu!* I was just about to call you." Margot erupted into a frantic tirade.

Kate listened with growing horror. She choked out pertinent questions, and then hung up. Numb with despair, she groped for the wall, found only air.

Liam was instantly by her side. His strong arms reached for her, supported her. "What's wrong?"

"My— My studio in Paris was bombed. The woman I hired barely escaped by climbing onto the roof. The blaze was so intense that everything…" She gulped. "Even my safe—and all the negatives inside—was destroyed. My apartment, my studio, all my work… The past two years of my life are gone."

She battled useless tears. *"Aubrey!"* Her knees buckled, as unsubstantial as cooked spaghetti. "Without the photos or negatives, there's no auction! No transplant!"

"Easy." He steered her to the sofa and sat beside her. "We'll get your photos back. Do they know what happened?"

"The investigator said the bomb was impossible to detect, because it was inside the water heater. It was activated by remote control, they think maybe the telephone. My temporary assistant got a 'hang up' call right before the explosion."

The implications hit home, and she gasped. She stared at Liam in terror-stricken disbelief. He stared back at her, the humming air electrified.

They both turned and stared at the water heater, situated between them and the front door. Between them and the way out.

A soft, ominous click sounded from inside the tank. They wouldn't have heard it with the door shut. Might not have given it a second thought.

Until Murphy sat on his haunches, his nose and ears pointed, his body quivering. *Heads up, partner!*

Liam swore. "He just alerted on a bomb."

Her apartment phone began to ring.

Chapter 9

8:00 p.m.

Kate didn't have a chance to blink. Liam snatched her art cases in one hand and grabbed her with the other.

"*Move!*" He hustled her to the patio door. Murphy jogged at their heels. Liam slammed open the glass door and shoved her out onto the balcony. He looked down at the pool. "Everybody in!"

He stripped her purse off her arm and tossed it and her picture cases over the iron railing. They banged onto the cement in a drift of dust two stories below. Her heartbeat thundering in her ears, Kate stared down at the tiny aqua rectangle. She gulped. If she didn't jump wide enough and missed…

Before she could worry, Liam scooped her up and flung her over. Flailing, she fell for forever. Shock crashed into her as her legs hit the cool water, and she inhaled before the waves closed over her head. Stunned, she sank to the bottom.

A splash to her right commanded her attention. Murphy floated down, and then thrashed upward. An ear-splitting kaboom rocked the world. The pool shook, and an orange glow flashed.

Kate bobbed to the surface and gulped in frantic breaths. Murphy paddled beside her. *Where was Liam?* Had he saved her and Murphy, and run out of time to jump? She'd only heard one splash. Distraught, her gaze tracked the roiling waves as fire rained from the sky.

"Kate!" She spun at the sound of his voice behind her. Weak with relief, she floundered. He grabbed her. "Take a breath!"

She obeyed and he pushed her under, followed her down. He wrapped his arms around her, sheltering her. She clung to him, and they flinched as chunks of flaming wood and blackened shrapnel plunked into the pool and sizzled out.

Just when she thought she'd suffocate, the bombardment stopped. They surfaced, gasped for air. Murphy paddled alongside unscathed. Hungry red flames spewed from the charred, gaping maw of her apartment, and oily smoke churned into the darkening sky.

Treading water, Liam surveyed the wreckage. "Damn! Inside the water heater, where the bomb squad couldn't find it without an X-ray. Surrounded by cool water, it wouldn't trigger a heat sensor, either. And impossible for the dogs to track." His brows winged up. "Man, this pyro is a genius!"

She stared at him, openmouthed with astonishment.

He gave her an abashed, waterlogged grin and towed her poolside. "Ah…in a scary, psycho killer sorta way."

"You bomb guys *really* get into your work." She spat chemically treated water, singed with the bitterness of smoke. "Mr. Wizard almost killed us!"

"Maybe." He lifted her onto the tiled edge and wrapped tense hands around her thighs. "He could have detonated the remote trigger anytime. If he'd wanted us to die in your apartment, we would have." He looked up at her, his face ragged with anguish. "It would have been my fault."

She stroked his cool, bristled cheek. "It would have been *his* fault. You took every precaution. You *saved* us." She brushed water from his dripping brow. "Why didn't he trip the bomb when we came in? And how did he know exactly when to make it go off?"

He planted both palms on the pool's edge. His thick biceps flexed below the navy T-shirt plastered to his sculpted pecs as he thrust his long, lean body out of the water like a spear. Standing on the concrete deck, he scooped aside his sodden hair.

Her concentration fractured into glittering shards. Liam O'Rourke wet. Yowza! His soaked, snug jeans left nothing to the imagination. Her imagination was *extremely* well-endowed. Her mouth went dry.

"Hel-lo. Earth to Just Kate."

She started. Shock had sent her round the bend. It was the only explanation. "I wasn't…um… What?"

"Busted, babe. Felonious ogling." His eyes twinkled, and his glorious mouth twitched into a brief grin. "As I was saying, I'd wager he had your apartment bugged. He's playing with us."

"This is his warped idea of *play?*" She stared at the burning wreckage. The destruction hadn't registered yet. Kate wiped stinging chlorine from her eyes. She couldn't afford to dwell on her loss now…she'd think about it later. *"Why?"*

"Unfortunately, lunatics are rarely stupid. Bombers seek out attention, and get a sexual charge from having power over life and death. They view people as objects to be manipulated, like pawns on a chessboard. It's a game." He leaned and hefted Murphy's front quarters out of the pool. "Winner take all."

Murphy scrambled out and shook himself. Droplets flew off his heavy fur, pelted her. Kate ducked behind Liam. "Yikes! I already had a shower today, thanks."

Something stung her upper arm. Puzzled, she glanced down, frowned at the splintered tiles, the thin line of blood trickling to her elbow. *What the heck?* Water didn't break ceramic. Water didn't sting. Didn't cut skin. A patch of tiles next to her hip blew apart, and fragments exploded into the air.

"Dammit!" Liam yelled. "The bastard's shooting at you!"

She stared at the small crater inches from her leg. A piece of broken tile must have flown up and scratched her arm. Her numb lips made it difficult to speak. "I don't hear anything."

"Silencer." Liam was already in motion. He yanked her up and towed her to a trio of steel Dumpsters in the alleyway behind the courtyard. Murphy followed at a fast lope.

"Down!" Liam pushed her into a squat. He yanked his gun out

of his holster. Knees flexed, he eased around the Dumpster and fired. Bullets pinged off metal as the stalker returned fire.

Liam pivoted, flattened his spine against the Dumpster. He fished in his pocket and tossed her his keys. "Make a break for the car and start her up. I'll cover you."

Icy fear snaked into her bloodstream. Not for herself. For him. "Who's going to cover *you?*"

"I'll meet you in front. Stay low." He slid around the corner again, fired another series of shots. Who knew a firefight was so *loud?* "Go!"

A deadly hail of bullets zinged overhead. Heart pounding in her throat, she crashed through prickly bushes and tore around to the parking lot.

Fumbling with the unfamiliar gearshift and clutch, she killed it twice before the powerful engine rumbled, vibrating the entire car. Finally! Kudos to the conscientious driver's ed instructor who'd insisted on teaching manual transmissions!

She twisted to look behind her, but saw only the deserted parking lot. The roar of distant gunshots told her Liam was still behind the Dumpsters. With no one to cover his escape, the shooter had him pinned!

He would run out of bullets soon. Did he expect her to save herself and leave him to die? She gritted her teeth. She'd dance onstage with the topless vampires at the Stratosphere first!

It took so long she nearly had heart failure, but she eventually wrestled the gearshift into Reverse with her left hand. Peering behind her, she wheeled the car in a three-sixty and backed down the alley as fast as she dared. She screeched to a halt beside the Dumpster. Half straddling the seat, she flung open the passenger door. "Taxi service. Anytime, anywhere."

Liam's astonished face appeared in the doorway. He grinned. "You talkin' to me?" He sounded more like De Niro than De Niro. Crouched low, he boosted Murphy onto the floorboards in the back, and then tossed in her art cases and purse.

"You went back for my stuff? While he was *shooting* at you?"

"I do love a challenge." Rounds whined over the roof as Liam leaped into the front seat. "Keep your head down."

Huddled over the wheel, her stomach pitched. She cursed her disability. Had she put him in worse danger by attempting a rescue? "We have to trade places. I can't shift *and* drive."

Bullets punched holes into the wooden wall of the building on her left. "No time." He grabbed the gearshift. "You work the gas and clutch, I'll shift. On the count of three."

Together, they finagled the car into first gear, then second. Liam grabbed two clips out of the glove compartment.

"Leave it to you, Ace, to travel armed to your eyeballs. Thank God," she added fervently.

He laughed. "Gunfighter's rules. Never go into a firefight without more ammo than the other guy." With his upper torso propped in the passenger window, he squeezed off departing shots as she sped out of the alley.

She charged through the parking lot and hastily assessed oncoming traffic. "Liam." She drove for several hair-raising beats while he shot behind them. "*Liam!* I need another gear!"

"Coming." He dropped back into his seat. "Stay cool."

"Sure thing. It's a hundred and ten degrees in Las Vegas and raining bullets!"

He helped her shift, and she merged into the stream of cars. Oncoming red lights strobed, and a convoy of shrieking fire engines rocketed toward her blazing apartment complex.

Anxiety niggled. "I hope none of my neighbors were hurt."

"The squad evacuated the surrounding buildings, remember?"

"Right. I'd forgotten in the melee." She released a sigh.

He fished his phone out of his pocket. "Crap. My cell drowned." He hung over the seat, giving her an exquisite glimpse of a tight, muscled tush hugged by damp denim. *Wow*. She yanked her gaze back to the road.

He emerged gripping her purse. "Damn good thing I rescued it." He extracted her phone and dialed 9-1-1 to report shots fired, and warned the firemen to wait for police backup.

He hung up and pointed to a sign for a park ahead. "Nobody followed us. Pull into that park and we'll switch."

Their motions perfected by practice, he shifted and she coordinated the pedals. They made a smooth left turn, and ended up safely slotted behind a screen of palms in the deserted park.

Kate rested her forehead on the steering wheel. “That was an experience I hope never to repeat in this lifetime.”

“We outsmarted Psycho.” Liam patted her shoulder. “We make a great team, Kate. Thanks for pulling my butt out of the fire.”

They *were* a great team. Unaccustomed pride winged through her. She’d mastered a physical challenge. She’d rescued Liam. “Thank *you* for saving me, my purse and my pictures.” If he hadn’t, she’d literally have nothing left.

He winked. “Murphy and O’Rourke, at your service. You can thank the mutt for alerting on the bomb so quickly. Otherwise, we might not have bugged out in time.”

An animal who terrified her had saved her life. And Liam’s. It disoriented her. As if she didn’t know up from down, right from wrong. She glanced behind her and stiffened. “Um…Liam?” Her heart sinking, she pointed to Murphy, who had clambered onto the seat. He held a familiar looking envelope in his mouth.

Liam swiveled. “Fan-freaking-tastic. Wonder what Norman Bates has to say now?”

“He’s probably gloating over his mass destruction of my life.” *Everything she owned was gone.* It was the last straw in a long, stressful day. She clutched the wheel so hard it creaked.

Liam turned to look at her, and his eyes narrowed. “Kate?”

Her breathing was ragged. “I. Can’t. Take. Anymore.”

Liam eased his arm around her as carefully as if she were a live explosive. “It’s okay. Let it out.”

The moment of reckoning crashed over her in a tsunami of pain. “He…he put a bomb in my car. Burned both apartments.”

“It’s okay, honey. Don’t fight it.”

At his encouragement, her words picked up speed and began to tumble over one another. “He stole my photos. Destroyed my studio and my negatives. *He’s annihilated everything I own except the wet clothes on my back and the pictures you saved.*” A knot of tears tangled in her throat. “He’s ruined the new life I worked so hard to build. Two years of struggle…gone!”

“I know.” He hugged her. “I’m sorry.”

Once released, her emotions poured out. “Worse, he’s put Aubrey in jeopardy." Though she fought it, anguish swelled into a choking burden. "He al-almost killed *you* b-because of *me.*"

"I'm not that easy to kill." His thumb caressed her nape. "Turn it loose. You'll feel better."

She swam against the overwhelming tide, but was wrenched under. "It's a nightmare! I have no control! I can't stop him!" Tears streamed down her cheeks. Ashamed, yet unable to pull out of the treacherous spin, she buried her face in her hands.

"Come here, sweetheart." He wrapped his arms around her and hauled her over the console and into his lap. She burrowed into his shoulder, and he stroked her hair. "Let go, Kate."

She didn't have a choice. Everything tore free. Wrenching sobs racked her body and eclipsed her ability to speak.

Strong and sure, Liam rode out the storm, kept her from sinking. He pressed a tender kiss to her temple. "That's it," he whispered. "Get rid of it."

Years of repressed grief spilled out. She sobbed, and he rocked her, crooning comforting nonsense as she cried.

She had no idea how long she cried before the torrent finally slowed. Breathing in choppy gasps, she clutched his damp shirt and fought to regain her composure. "Liam?"

His deep voice was calm, his capable hands steady as he rubbed her back. "Right here, Kate."

Despair devoured her alive. "What are we going to do?"

"Everything will be okay," his low, mellow voice rumbled into her ear.

"How can it be?" She sniffled, hiccuped. "How are we going to save Aubrey now?"

"I won't give up until we get your photographs back." He eased away and cradled her face in his hand. His green eyes burned with determination. "I refuse to accept the alternative."

His faith and confidence had never wavered. While she… Humiliated by her weakness, she ducked her chin. "I'm sorry."

"Don't." His warm breath feathered over her cheek. "The son of a bitch who torched your life has reason to be sorry. I'm gonna make him the sorriest bastard on the planet."

"I fell apart, acted like a big baby." She'd behaved as horribly as her hysterical sister.

"You expressed heartfelt emotion after a staggering loss. Perfectly normal." He made her look at him. There was no censure on his face, only kindness. "You feel better, don't you?"

It was the first time she'd unchained her feelings from their anchor. She was terrified by her loss of control, yet the constant, depressing weight had lifted from her shoulders. And her headache was gone. She'd released her burden to Liam, and now he carried part of it. "Surprisingly, yes."

"Way overdue." He snagged bottled water from a cup holder, broke the seal and held it to her lips. "Don't be embarrassed by your emotions. Your family expects an iron maiden, but you have a right to your feelings. No matter what they are."

She stared into his eyes, reassured by his warm compassion. What a remarkable man. Capable, self-assured, two hundred percent alpha male, yet unashamed to give tenderness and mercy. She gulped water. "Thank you." The words seemed so inadequate.

"Anytime." He gently wiped her damp cheeks with the hem of his T-shirt.

"I'm sorry I bawled all over you."

"No problem." His full lips curved into an irrepressible grin. "I was wet anyhow."

Murphy whined from the backseat, and she half turned. "Does he need to go outside?"

"He whined the entire time you were crying. He knows you're upset, and he's upset."

"No way. Animals don't understand people's emotions."

"Don't they?" He gestured. "Look at him."

The dog was curled on the seat with his muzzle between his paws. When she glanced at him, he whimpered. She stared into his liquid brown eyes and could have sworn she saw the same compassion expressed by his owner. How was that possible? Confusion backhanded her. Her gaze fell on the envelope, resting on the seat. "The note!" She gulped. "I don't want to read it."

Liam thrust out his hand. "Give it over, Murph."

Murphy picked up the envelope and delicately placed it on

Liam's outstretched palm. Surprise again winged through her at the depth of the dog's comprehension. Perhaps she'd underestimated both Liam and his partner.

Liam read the note out loud.

> "Katherine, my flower, I've hidden bombs in three populated locations. I can detonate them at will. Your policeman will never find or diffuse them all in time.
>
> Play by my rules, and win the photos. No police, no bomb squad, no public notice. Or the photos burn…and people die.
>
> Black and white, the key is in plain sight. One man's Silver is another's gold. You have until midnight."

"Sick bastard! I'll detonate *him* at will." Liam scowled. "Not exactly Ralph Waldo Emerson, is he?"

"I think better on my feet." She flung open the car door and got out. Her shaky legs barely held her up.

"Likewise. And Murphy needs to stretch." Liam followed and let Murphy out. "Good boy, Murphy. You found the bomb." He strode around to the trunk and retrieved a knotted cloth, which he held out to Murphy.

She stepped back as the dog growled fiercely and pulled on the cloth. "What's he doing?"

"He loves to play tug-of-war. All 'working dogs' are trained to do the job for their reward. This is his. Tug it, Murph." He pulled on the cloth and Murphy yanked back, nearly toppling him. Liam let go and the dog ran on the grass, viciously shaking the toy. Liam pursed his lips. "Black, white and gold could mean the blackjack table at the Golden Nugget."

She stared at the note, searching for clues before it disintegrated. "Would he put something in such a visible place?"

"I think Whack Job would post a neon ad in the middle of the strip. He craves your attention." He moved to her side, pointed. "Why is the word *Silver* capitalized?"

"I didn't notice that. Good catch." The paper shriveled, dusted into ashes. "Why would *silver* be capitalized?"

"A place?"

"There's a Silver Nugget, but it's in North Las Vegas. And a Silverstone Golf Club, but this says silver and *gold.*"

"A name, then."

"Silver…" Her pulse fluttered. "Long John Silver? *The middle of the strip.* Maybe black and white doesn't represent my photos, maybe it points to the Jolly Roger—the pirate flag!"

Liam nodded. "Gold could mean treasure. Treasure Island."

Her pulse tripled on a surge of fear-laced adrenaline. "He's put 'the key,' near the pirate flag on the ship, and we have to retrieve it to get my photographs back?"

"One fast way to find out." He found her phone in the car and dialed. "Con, still at the Venetian? Excellent. Confiscate a pair of binoculars and hightail it to the roof. Then call me back." He recited her cell number, and hung up.

Five minutes later, the phone rang. These SWAT guys didn't mess around. "Hey, bro. Look across to Buccaneer Bay, at the pirate ship's mast. See anything near the flag?" Listening, he tapped his booted foot. His brows rose. "Thanks. Stand by." He disconnected. "Con says a small plastic packet is dangling from a rope near the top of the mast."

She held Liam's calm gaze, struggling not to lose control. "What if the stalker tries to kill us again?"

"That's a given." He smirked. "But he's outnumbered, three to one."

She reached for his warm, sure hand and held on tight. "Why are you willing to risk your life to help me?"

"There's a little girl in a hospital who needs a kidney." He squeezed her fingers reassuringly. "And there's a woman here who loves her. A woman with heart and strength and courage."

"I'm not strong. Not brave. *You* are." She'd thought herself all cried out, but moisture welled behind her eyes. "And my heart froze solid a long time ago."

He wrapped his arms around her, enfolding her in warmth. "Bravery isn't always about bringing down bad guys and disarming bombs." He kissed her forehead. "Real courage is having the guts to climb out of bed in the morning and say, 'I'll start all over again today.' You resurrected your life after your dreams imploded. That takes heart *and* strength, Kate."

She'd thought his compassion and mercy remarkable. His intelligence and insight were *amazing.* She bit the inside of her cheek. "I can't take a chance with Aubrey's life, or on this stalker detonating those bombs. We don't have a choice. But he said no police, no bomb squad, no publicity. We'll be on our own."

"No worries. You have your own personal bomb tech."

For once, she didn't hesitate to share her feelings. Liam would understand. Her voice trembled. "I'm scared."

"Do you think I'm not afraid when I'm faced with a jumble of wires and C4 that could separate my head from my shoulders?" He smoothed her hair. "Damn straight I am. But I can't let *it* control *me.*" Resolve pulsed off him. "Fear is a survival instinct. *Accept* it. *Own* it. Use fear to give you the edge."

She dragged in a deep breath. Acknowledged her fear. Commanded mastery over it. And a miracle happened. Icy terror morphed into blazing fury. It felt *wonderful.* Empowering. The stalker might force her to play his deranged game, but *she* was in control of her responses, and he couldn't take that away.

"Who does he think he is? How dare he play God with Aubrey's life? With innocent people?" she spat. "He wants a scavenger hunt? Bring it on. We'll find my photos. Then we'll send him to prison, where he can play games for the rest of his sorry life. Like hide the soap with Bubba."

"That's my girl!" Liam's deep, wicked laugh made her supremely glad he was on her side. "Take back the power. Then, no matter what he does, we're playing by *our* rules."

She pulled away and glanced at her watch. "The Treasure Island show will be in full swing soon. We have zero time. How do we sneak aboard without being noticed?"

He rubbed his chin. "Know a fast place to rent costumes?"

"I only know of one costume shop and it's way downtown."

An ebony brow arched. "We might have to borrow some."

She groaned. "Why do I have the sinking suspicion that I'm going to hate this plan?"

Outside Madame Tussauds wax museum ten minutes later, Kate's anxiety spiked. Liam had aborted the campaign to convince the night manager to rent them costumes. The thin, balding supervisor was humor impaired…and definitely not of the female persuasion. A Riverside PD badge hadn't impressed him. In fact, he'd gotten huffy, and ordered them off the premises.

The Mighty O'Rourke had struck out.

Forced to go in undercover, they mingled with a busload of seniors. Murphy slipped in amongst the throng.

Once inside, no one gave them a second glance. The only perk of the stifling heat, their clothes were mostly dry. Not that it mattered. Tourists were encouraged to "interact" with the exhibits. Kate's nerves twitched. She and Liam would be interacting more than management anticipated.

Treasure Island was across the strip. With the clock ticking, they'd decided to change on the premises. Liam also hoped the costumes might confuse anyone tailing them.

He assessed the restrooms, located in a central area visible to both the entrance and gift shop. "Divert to Plan B."

Kate wrinkled her nose. "Exactly what *is* Plan B?"

"I'll brief you as soon as I figure it out."

They rushed ahead of the seniors, and she shot him a dubious glance. "Isn't 'borrowing' a murky area for a cop?"

"Emergency measures. Lives are at stake. We can't attract attention and risk Psycho burning the photos or detonating bombs. The museum will be reimbursed, no harm, no foul." Liam jogged past a familiar icon in a white sequin jumpsuit. "The King on a pirate ship? Don't they have anyone older?"

Dick Clark? Not. "We need to find the right section. She peeked inside a doorway. "Here, in this room!"

Liam glanced around and grinned. "Errol Flynn works for me." He pointed to a woman in an opulent red silk gown who was being held in the arms of a man standing beside a curtained four-poster bed. "Scarlett O'Hara looks about your size."

"Not quite the same era."

"It's *Vegas.* Nobody's going to scrutinize us that closely. "Pardon me, Rhett. Need to borrow your woman for a minute." Grunting, he flopped Scarlett onto the bed. "Take her dress."

She started unweaving the intricately laced bodice. "Dear Diary.

Tonight, I snuck into Madame Tussauds and stripped Scarlett O'Hara buck naked." In spite of the tense situation, or perhaps because of it, she giggled. She hadn't giggled since she was sixteen. "I'd rather do Errol."

"Now who's a pervert?" He grinned and dragged Errol over. He untied the blue satin curtains and pulled them shut, creating a makeshift dressing room inside the bed. "Behold, Plan B."

Murphy sat on guard at the foot while she and Liam climbed inside. They stood upright on the "mattress," which was a wooden platform draped with bedding.

Her hand circled. "Turn around."

"Spoilsport." Smiling, he complied. "I've seen you naked, Just Kate." His voice roughened to a sensual growl. "It's a beautiful picture I still carry in my head."

Her pulse leaped, and she lurched, dropped the gown.

Back to back, they undressed. The whisper of discarded clothing and Liam's soft breathing were unbearably erotic. Even after a dunking, he smelled clean and fresh, and all male. She'd never forgotten how awesome he looked naked, either. Had never forgotten the skill and strength coiled in his lean, powerful muscles. The supple warmth of his skin, dusted with dark hairs. The tenderness of his soft lips and clever tongue. Her abdomen clenched. She gripped the bedpost, overcome by the temptation to whirl around and press her nearly bare body to his.

"You ready?" he asked. "We need to hurry."

More than ready. He wouldn't resist. Caught in flagrante delicto by a busload of seniors from Yuma. Wouldn't that be special? She tossed petticoats over her head, followed by the dress, and fumbled with the bodice back. "Darn these laces."

"Let me." He scooped her hair across one shoulder, and his nimble fingers tied the dress closed. "All set."

She heard him pull the curtain and jump down. She turned and her breath hitched. A sexy pirate from her favorite romance novel awaited her. His tousled hair lent roguish appeal, and dark stubble dusted his cheekbones and framed his delicious mouth. The billowy white shirt open to his narrow waist revealed his spectacular chest and washboard abs. Knee-high black boots anchored strong calves and long legs. Tight brown breeches complete with a red sash tied above his gun belt hugged his muscular thighs. And oh, what those formfitting pants did for the rest of him. He brandished a gleaming sword in one hand. She groped for words with a mouth gone bone-dry. "Holy crow!"

His eyes sparkled. "You look damn fine yourself, Miz Scarlett. Red is a great color on you." He dropped his sword and lifted her, then spun her around before setting her down.

Dizzy from his nearness, she put a hand on his broad shoulder. She inclined her head at the mannequins on the bed. "We can't leave nekkid dummies for the seniors to find. Or to tip off management that the costumes are gone."

"If the seniors are anything like our neighbor, Letty, they might get a kick out of it."

They arranged the comforter over the dummies. Liam stuffed their street clothes into shopping bags they'd brought. Kate stepped back. Errol and Scarlett lounged nude between the sheets, while Rhett watched from beside the bed. She giggled again. "That is one disturbing little tableau."

Liam grinned. "Judging by Errol's satisfied smirk, he should be smoking a cigarette." He passed her the bags, then kicked his sword airborne and gracefully caught it. A thrilling swashbuckling move out of a Hollywood blockbuster. If she'd had time, she'd have surrendered to the urge to kiss him.

He took her left hand in his. "Let's make tracks."

They'd run halfway to the door, when he checked. "Crap!"

The distinct babble of female voices floated nearer. "Ooh, Shirley, I can't wait to see Errol Flynn. He's my favorite."

"Freeze," Liam whispered. "Murphy, *sit!*"

Caught red-handed, they froze in place as two women strolled into the room.

Chapter 10

9:00 p.m.

Liam remained motionless and unblinking while the elderly duo explored. In the enforced stillness, his thoughts wandered to Kate. He'd quashed his raging fury at the demented bastard who was toying with her, and put her and a gravely ill child at risk. Along with hundreds of innocent bystanders. Anger would only cloud his reason. Compromise his effectiveness. Psycho wanted to play? Liam tensed. He would play…hardball.

He would win this deadly competition.

Besides, Kate didn't need his anger. He'd finally breached her icy reserve. She'd let down her guard and admitted her fear. She'd sobbed out her anguish in his arms. She needed his tenderness and understanding. His heartbeat tripped. She'd begun to trust him…and he wouldn't betray her trust.

Should he push forward? Or hang back and let her make the tactical decisions? He gritted his teeth. He'd never teetered on an uncertain tightrope over a woman before. Just Kate.

"Shirley," the short, plump lady called. "Get a picture of the dog." She pointed to Murphy, immobile at Liam's feet.

"Rin Tin Tin!" The two women walked closer. "Isn't he realistic, though? I can almost see him breathing." Peering through thick lenses, Shirley inspected Liam. "Stars and garters! Forget the mutt, Jean. Check out the stud muffin."

"What a pretty pirate. I wonder who he's supposed to be?"

"The brochure said this was a 'hands-on' experience." Shirley uttered an impish chuckle as she snapped an instant camera. "I wouldn't mind a handful of that."

Liam bit his cheek to contain a snicker. Though the mission would be seriously screwed if they were discovered, the scenario was too ludicrous. *Watch those grabby mitts, grandma. Or you're in for a big surprise.*

Shirley's attention riveted on the four-poster bed. "My memory isn't what it used to be, but I sure don't remember Rhett catching Scarlett doing the mattress mambo with Errol Flynn."

"Mercy!" Jean huffed as the women hurried to the display. "What sort of museum *is* this?"

Clearly the more urbane of the two, Shirley snapped photos. "What happens in Vegas stays in Vegas, dear."

Liam slid a glance sideways at Kate. Her shoulders trembled with suppressed mirth, and bright laughter danced in her eyes. Moisture flooded his eyes with the effort to curb his chuckles. If his brothers heard about this, they'd bust his chops forever.

Shirley peeked into the next room. "Engelbert Humperdinck! Let's take pictures of us kissing him! We'll tell Willa and Bonnie back at Sunset Village that he was the real deal!"

"Ooh! They'll be so jealous!" Tittering, the ladies left.

A whoosh escaped Kate. Giggling, she doubled over. "Ohmigosh! If that woman had grabbed your buns..."

Letting his chuckles loose felt great. "Manager Snippy would be searching for a defibrillator." He snapped his fingers at Murphy and glanced around. "It's too crowded to bypass the door alarms. We'll have to try a covert exit out the front."

People had crammed the museum. Good. More bodies upped the odds of evade and escape. Tourists in Sin City expected spectacle, and nobody paid attention to their period clothing as they wended their way forward. Kate gazed at the canine. "I'm amazed by how still Murphy sat. He didn't twitch."

He gave his partner a fond glance. "Murph knows his stuff. He has to freeze on command, or we could both go kaboom."

Yeah, yeah, I'm not just another pretty muzzle. Murphy sniffed. *Rin Tin Tin, my tail feathers.*

They cautiously approached the main entrance, and Liam scowled. Probably suspicious after his unusual request, the manager lurked near the front doors. Had Lady Luck gone into a snit tonight? With a head case on the loose and three bombs threatening Vegas, he needed every ounce of good fortune.

He slid his arm around Kate's waist, halting her midstride. "Watch for an opportune moment," he whispered.

Vibrating with tension, she nodded. Trying to blend, they waited behind the shifting crowd. Eventually, the manager stalked to the far end of the foyer.

"Go for it." Arm in arm, they strolled out the doors.

Just as they reached the archway to the Rialto Bridge, the manager's nasal shout rang out. "Hey! You two! Come back here!"

Liam glanced over his shoulder and saw the guy running toward them. "Not in this lifetime, buddy." He grabbed Kate's hand. "Time to leave."

They zigzagged through the throng, with the manager screeching behind them. "Thieves! I'm calling the cops!"

"I *am* the cops," Liam muttered.

They hit the moving sidewalk that traveled over the Rialto Bridge. Kate stumbled, and Liam kept her on her feet.

"You haven't truly lived until you've jogged on a moving sidewalk wearing an antebellum ball gown," she panted.

"Pass. Petticoats are itchy." Worried about Murphy managing the Travellator, he looked to his left. Murph was fine. Hundreds of hours of obstacle course practice had paid off. Murphy loved "chase." Though usually, the dog was the one in hot pursuit.

Their eyes met, and the dog gave him a toothy grin. *Havin' some fun now, buddy!*

"Security!" the manager screamed. "Stop those two!"

"Just like a damn monkey on a cupcake." Liam towed Kate around knots of openmouthed onlookers. The safety-tipped sword he brandished in his right hand gave slow movers extra incentive to get out of his way. "Can't shake him loose."

He glanced back again and swore as three uniformed security guards joined the chase. "Great! The more, the merrier."

Kate looked behind them. "Should we stop and explain?"

He yanked her along faster. "And they'll believe us...why? The local precinct will get involved, and we'll be snafued in red tape for hours. Abby Normal said no publicity."

They charged into the second floor of the Venetian Hotel, connected to Madame Tussauds by the bridge. With seconds to spare, they piled into an elevator. Liam punched the button for the main floor. He pivoted Kate to the back wall and blockaded her view of Murphy. Gasping for air in the tight bodice, she didn't notice that she was in a confined space with the dog.

Liam's libido noticed the proximity to Kate. Her chest heaved, and the gown framed a mound of tempting cleavage. The scalding memory of her warm, soft breasts pillowed against his chest surged through his system, and he jerked his gaze to the ceiling. Damned inconvenient time for a lust attack. He whipped the sword against his thigh and focused on the sting. Hellfire, anytime she was in the same hemisphere, he got turned on.

Thankfully, the descent was fast. The elevator spewed them out into the lobby. Kate pulled his hand. "This way!" Since she seemed set on a destination, he let her take point.

Moments later, a second elevator pinged, and heavy boots thundered down the marble hallway behind them.

"In here." Kate blasted through an unmarked doorway around the corner from the check-in counter.

Baggage carts littered the room. "Where are we?"

She indicated a large conveyor belt. "At the entrance to an interior tunnel. It transports patrons' luggage so that the hallways are not cluttered." She stabbed a button on the wall, and the belt ground into motion. "All aboard."

"Jim!" A man bellowed outside. "Which way did they go?"

"Murphy, hup!" The dog jumped onto the belt. Gathering Kate

into his arms, Liam followed. He barely pulled her prone in time to avoid banging their heads as they chugged past a rubber flap and into the tunnel. The enclosure was about four feet square.

"Dammit!" A male voice shouted. "They're not in here. Check the corridor on the other side of the fountain." A door banged, and then the belt slid them too far into the tunnel to hear.

Side by side on the moving conveyor, Liam looked at Kate, snug in his embrace. "And a good time was had by all." She laughed, and he hugged her. "How did you know about this?"

"When my father won the contract to supply the hotel's cleaning products, the owner invited us for a tour and lunch." She grinned, and his heart flipped. He'd ensure she had reason to smile more often. "There's also a gigantic boiler under here. Aubrey was fascinated with everything. It was a fun day."

"And happily for us, informative." He glanced around the rapidly dimming tunnel. "Where does it lead?"

"To a centrally located area in the basement where the bags are collected and disbursed to individual floors."

He stared into her luminous brown eyes, mere inches from his. "This is the second time you've come to my rescue today."

"Merely returning the favor." Her shapely mouth curved in a grateful smile. "What would I have done without *you* today?"

As they descended into total darkness, the awful truth crashed into him. *She would have died.*

Compensating for lack of sight, his other senses sharpened. Painfully aware of the woman in his arms, he knew the instant the realization hit her. She jerked, stiffened. "Without you…" she choked. "The car bomb would have killed me."

"But it didn't." He urged her closer, delighted when she slid her arms around his neck and nestled into him. Her breath teased his lips, and her summer meadow scent curled around him. "Do you believe in fate?"

"I—I'm not sure. What exactly do you mean by fate?"

"I believe that we're born with a specific amount of time allotted by the Big Guy." He stroked the dainty contour of her ear, and she shivered. "I have respect, a healthy amount of fear, but I don't worry over each bomb. It's either gonna take me out, or it's not." He shrugged. "I could get flattened by a bus on the way to pick up Kung Pao chicken for Murphy."

"We were brought together today as part of a higher plan?"

"Not just today. Maybe it all started two years ago. Because your number's not up. We have places to go. A mission to complete." As the conveyor chugged along, Liam traced her collarbone with his fingertips. His palm grazed the enticing swell of her breasts bared by the gown. Her breath hitched, and his body tightened. *You're skating on dangerous ice, boyo.* Yet he couldn't stop touching her. "We have psycho butt to kick."

"I wish I had your unwavering faith, Liam."

"Faith is merely the ability to trust in what you can't see. I do it every day. So do you." He brushed her cheek with his knuckles. Her fragrant skin was as soft and delicate as a flower petal. "Most people don't have the fortitude to pick up the pieces after a disaster like you've suffered."

"I'm not anyone special." Her voice wobbled. "I did what I had to. I go one day at a time, and don't expect too much."

"Don't shortchange yourself." Inhaling her essence, he gave in to the temptation to cruise his lips down her slender throat. Was gratified when she trembled with need beneath his mouth. The same need that shook his very existence. "Life goes by fast, Just Kate," he whispered, nipping the sensitive cord where her neck joined her shoulder. "Live every moment to the hilt."

She arched beneath his questing lips. Her reply was a breathless gasp. "I don't know how."

"I do." Her fevered response to his touch hit him with a double whammy of dizzying power and fierce protectiveness. He longed to tuck her away in an ivory tower and keep her safe forever. He longed to strip off her clothes and bury himself in her heat, to thrust into her until she shuddered in completion beneath him. Until she cried out his name in surrender.

He submitted to his craving and captured her sweet lips. They parted on a low moan, and he sank into the hot silk of her mouth. Desire exploded, and the flash fire incinerated rational thought. He skimmed a hand down her spine, cupped her bottom. She rocked her hips against him, and he groaned.

She scrambled his circuits. Fired his blood. Made him ache with blazing need.

He pressed his lips to the swell of her breasts. She gasped as his tongue delved, feasted on her sweetness. His words ground out husky with passion. "You have on too many clothes." Engulfed in a white-hot haze, he struggled with the laces on the back of her dress. They tangled, and he groaned again. "No wonder those dudes in tights carried big-ass swords."

"Liam!" She murmured a shaky but insistent plea.

"I know, honey." He yanked at the knots. "I'll get it undone if I have to use my teeth."

All he could think about was having her. Possessing her. Gifting her with such staggering pleasure that she wouldn't be able to walk, talk or see.

He yearned to bind her to him body and soul…so she would never leave him.

She tried to speak again, but he stole her mouth, stroking his tongue against hers. He loved the way she felt, the way she tasted. The way she smelled. The way her lush curves cradled his hard angles. Loved how her body melded into his as if she were made for him. He loved her intelligence and courage and her loyalty to her undeserving family. He loved her artistic talent. Loved the quick, snarky wit she hid from the rest of the world.

Realization roared in his head, striking him deaf, blind and senseless. Shaking, he broke the kiss and buried his face in her neck. He couldn't breathe. His heart pounded so hard it threatened to burst from his chest.

He loved her.

Kate *was* his soul mate.

Pain tore his heart. And if she chose to walk away from him after this was over, he could not make her stay. Confronted by his worst fear, he swallowed a bitter lump of anguish.

All too soon, he might be forced to let go of everything he was so afraid to lose.

"Liam!" Kate said insistently into his ear. "We're at the end of the line."

Tell me something I don't know.

"Hey!" She tugged on his hair. "What's wrong with you?"

The sting jerked him back to reality. He looked up and saw a large room piled with luggage. The conveyor belt had spilled him and Kate halfway out onto a platform and then stopped. He had to try twice before he could speak. *"Hellfire."* He scrubbed a trembling hand over his jaw. "I've lost my freaking mind."

"It's okay. You had company." Her breathing was ragged, and she was quivering. She gave him a crooked smile. "We both got carried away. *Again.* Sheathe your sword, Ace."

Pull it together, boyo. Or your ass is grass, and Stalker Boy will be the lawnmower. He fell back on humor, his Kevlar shield against life's ambushes. "Don't invite a guy to sheathe his sword unless you're willing to accept the consequences."

Laughing, she sat up and attempted to smooth her tousled hair. Her gaze flew past him, and her chuckles died. "Um…is Murphy doing what I think he's doing?"

Murphy had exited the conveyor ahead of them. Sitting as rigid as a statue, the dog stared at the opening from which they'd just emerged. His nose was pointed, his ears stiff.

The hair on the back of Liam's neck prickled. Crap! The dog's shrewd gaze connected with his. *Lucky for you, partner, while you were nuzzling your female,* I *was on the job.*

"Kate, don't move." On his back, Liam slid past the rubber flap and into the tunnel. He glanced up at the roof and swore.

He eased out and stared at Kate's stricken face, and forced his tone to convey steadiness he didn't feel. If she panicked, they were dead. "You want the good news or the bad news?"

"G-good."

"We just found a bomb."

"That's *good?*"

"This one doesn't fit the pattern. Stalker Boy planted his earlier bombs in public arenas. This is his ace in the hole…he didn't expect us to find it. The cocky SOB thinks we're following his clues to Treasure Island. Now I have a chance to disarm the device before he's aware we've located it."

"Wonderful." She gulped. "What's the bad news?"

"We're next to the boiler." He inhaled deeply as the pressing weight of hundreds of lives settled on his shoulders. "If this puppy blows, it's gonna wipe out the entire block."

Horror assaulted Kate, and the room whirled. "Should we evacuate the hotel and casino?"

He shook his head. "If Psycho sees a mass exodus, he'll detonate. There won't be time to get everyone to safety."

"All right." Clinging to his steadfast green gaze, she drew a fortifying breath. "What do you want me to do?"

Liam slowly rose from the conveyor belt and patted Murphy. "Good boy. You did good, Murph. Stand down." The dog's vigilant posture relaxed, and he licked Liam's hand.

Liam tugged a Swiss Army knife from his pants pocket. "Search the bags, find a light." He strode to the door. "Duct tape, wire strippers and a blast suit would be handy, too."

"Right." She unzipped a suitcase. "What are you doing?"

"Jamming the door lock against unexpected company."

"What if we have to get out in a hurry?"

"If that scenario arises, we're already screwed."

For the second time that day, she looked into the spectral mirror of imminent death, and didn't like the reflection. She'd indulged in far too few pleasures. Had far too many regrets.

She'd spent so much precious time living in fear.

He returned to the tunnel, while she rifled through strangers' luggage. "Jackpot!" She set aside a stack of paperbacks on how to win at games of chance. "A book light."

"Great." His voice was muffled. Bring it."

"One more bag." She dug deep. "Hey. Duct tape!" She dumped out an eye-opening assortment. "You don't even want to *know* what else I found. But if you need batteries, we're loaded."

He laughed. "Sin City."

She carried the book light and roll of tape to the tunnel entrance. "Here's the stuff."

"Climb in with me. I need extra hands." His arm reached out to guide her. "Slide in on your back. Don't touch the walls."

Doubt taunted her. "I only have one hand to lend."

"I can't do it without you." His taut declaration hummed with significance, which she didn't have time to analyze.

Flat on her back, plastered close to his side in the confined area, she stared at the lethal tangle of wires and metal bristling from the tunnel's roof. Greasy dread churned in her stomach. "It will be fast, right? We won't feel anything?" And they would go side by side. Together.

"I won't let you down." Liam turned his head and stared into her eyes. "I won't let you die." He brushed a gentle kiss across her brow. "We're gonna neutralize Whacko."

He looked up and focused on the bomb. As he broke the connection between them, the jagged blade of loss staggered her.

Drawing strength from his calm tone, she resolutely shoved away disabling terror. She'd seen him in action. She had faith in his abilities. "Good thing you own a Swiss Army knife."

"Make the beam shine from the left." His movements slow but sure, he unscrewed plates and cut wires. "Pop gave each of us boys one for our thirteenth birthdays. We always carry them."

She went silent. He didn't need distractions. Liam at work was a picture of dangerous masculine beauty. Thickly-lashed eyes intense as lasers, chiseled features sharp with concentration. His wide chest rose and fell evenly, and his measured breaths echoed softly in the enclosed space. His hard biceps brushed her arm with warm, measured strokes.

Her injury had given her appreciation for hands that performed with unfaltering skill. She'd seen a breathtaking display of his eye-hand coordination when he'd flipped the sword. Up close and personal, his long fingers wove a tautly intricate ballet with precise grace. His hands exhibited the same skill and assurance as when they'd danced over her body.

Her pulse fluttered. Who would have guessed that watching him disarm a bomb would be so sensual? Drat, she wanted her camera. Liam in action would create a breath-stealing portrait.

As the minutes ticked past, pain thrummed down her arm, and she fought to hold the light steady. Sweat beaded on Liam's upper lip, and fear again gripped her. Perhaps things weren't going as smoothly as he made it look.

Holding his breath, he severed a black wire with his knife. "Take this wire. Keep it immobile and level with the device."

Anxiety made her go cold. "I-I'm not sure I can. Not and support the light at the same time."

"You have to." *Or else.* He didn't say it out loud. He didn't need to. His "no options" tone was enough. "Reach up and take it from me. Careful not to wiggle it."

"But…my fingers don't…" Either she helped him, or the bomb would explode. Her heart stopped. How could she possibly hold the wire still when her hand wouldn't cooperate? When her entire arm shook from the deadly combination of distress and weakness.

She would fail him. They would die. Hundreds of innocent people would die. And it would be her fault.

"You're here with me for a reason." Liam's low voice cut through panic, blanketed her with quiet assurance. "You *can* do this. I have complete faith in you."

Kate blinked back tears. Well, heck. She squashed the doubt demons. She couldn't give up and let the stalker win. Not without giving her all. In slow motion, she accepted the wire.

Liam briefly covered her ice-cold hand with his big, warm one, offering comfort and support. "That's it. Keep it steady." He quickly sliced wires. "Doing great, honey."

She struggled to take in air. Why was he suddenly moving so fast? What hadn't he told her?

"Interesting. Stalker Boy rigged this device differently." He cut a small strip of duct tape and efficiently taped off the silver end of a red wire. "That's unusual."

He was distracting her so she wouldn't be so scared. Her throat was too dry to swallow. "Oh?" was the most intelligent reply she could croak.

"A firebug normally sticks to a single design. They're organized, and above average in intelligence. In their warped minds, they're artists, who 'sign' their work by using specific materials and schematics. Once we figure it out, we can identify who built each individual bomb by the 'signature.'"

She forced her focus to the conversation. The information could be important. "Why didn't he put it directly in the boiler room? Wouldn't that make a hotter, more deadly explosion?"

"It would, yes. I wondered about that myself. Along with why he planted the first device under your convertible's seat. He'd have gotten a helluva lot more bang for his buck if he'd armed the engine.

Not to mention a guaranteed detonation when the ignition fired." His hands froze on the bomb. *"Hellfire!"*

"What happened?" She cringed. "Are we going to...?"

"No!" He swore. "I didn't mean to scare you." He took the black wire from her. Her aching arm flopped to her side, and she sighed. He twisted the black wire to a white one and taped them. "It just hit me why he put the bombs where he did. He must have to keep his explosive matter cool. It probably grows as unstable as its maker at higher temperatures."

"Lovely. In other words, if the bombs get too hot, they might go off by themselves, even without a detonator?"

"Right." He eased out what looked like a slice of pale green plastic. "Fascinating chemical composition." He slowly set it beside him. "Almost there." He cut and taped more wires, then put down his knife. He flexed his fingers and exhaled. "Clear."

"Wow." Relief made her giddy. "Impressive."

He shrugged. "All in a day's work."

"You just saved half of Las Vegas. What do you do on a second date?"

"This *is* our second date." He turned his head and his sinful grin flashed. "Don't tell me you've forgotten our first?"

She fumbled with the book light and avoided his gaze. "I wish *you* would. It was my most humiliating experience...ever."

"Yeah, we need to discuss that." He sat up, urged her up beside him. "It's been a long time coming, Kate."

Panic surged back full throttle. "I don't think—"

He shoved his knife into his right front pants pocket. "Unfortunately, there are more incendiary devices to disarm before we can deal with our personal fallout."

It was stupid to feel relief. To prefer facing a bomb instead of a heart-to-heart with him. Call her crazy, but she'd almost rather die than expose her ugly secrets and deepest hurts. At all costs, she tried never to let anyone down. And she refused to disappoint Liam. Once he knew the extent of her disability, he'd never again look at her the same way.

Personal demons aside, there was her fear of Murphy. She'd never trust the huge dog.

Involvement with the daring cop and his fierce partner was too dangerous—to her body and heart. She wasn't a risk taker. Not anymore. She'd sustained all the damage she could bear.

He stood and tugged her to her feet. "We have to get to Treasure Island." He flicked a glance at his watch. "Less than two hours left. One bomb neutralized, two to go."

Chapter 11

10:00 p.m.

They left their street clothes in the trunk of the car parked on the strip. Kate shook off melancholy. No time to navel gaze. She'd figure out how to avoid the talk with Liam later. *If there was a later.*

Followed by Murphy, they dashed across the pedestrian overpass between the Venetian and Treasure Island. Night shrouded the desert, and the Strip's rainbow-hued lights sliced a glowing corridor through the darkness.

The pirate show was already underway. Thanks to their borrowed costumes, a hotel employee readily rattled off directions to the cast entrance. They had no trouble slipping aboard the pirate ship floating atop the two and a half million gallons of water that comprised Buccaneer Bay. On the opposite side, the seventy-five-foot long Royal Navy British frigate rode the gentle swells.

Aboard the ship, a crewmember frowned at Kate. "When did production cast a girl?" He did a double take. "And a *dog?*"

Liam tossed off a shrug. "Equal opportunity employment."

The captain shouted, and the actor ran to the foredeck. Liam located a hatch, and she followed him down a ladder...not easy in the poofy dress. Murphy, equally hampered by his lack of opposable thumbs, also required Liam's assistance.

In the vast compartment, her commandeered book light was a godsend. Fascinated, she watched Liam and Murphy's seamless teamwork. The two communicated without effort, sharing one mind, one heart as they searched for a bomb. They didn't find one.

She peered out a porthole at the spotlights reflected off the bay. "Maybe he put it outside, under the waterline?"

"It's probably aboard the British frigate...the ship that sinks. If it blows, the audience will assume it's part of the show. Employees will think the pyrotechnics went wonky." Liam rubbed his stubbled chin, the epitome of a dark, sexy buccaneer. "Abby Normal is playing his evil head games. We'll nab the envelope first, then find a way over to the other ship."

Up top, amidst throaty male shouts and earsplitting explosions, the pirate ship commenced firing on the frigate. The boards beneath her feet trembled and the ship rocked. Kate grabbed Liam's arm. The staged battle felt disconcertingly real.

Liam slid one arm around her waist and his other hand shaded his eyes against the erupting flares as he looked upward. A small plastic bag dangled below the Jolly Roger, flapping at the top of the aft mast. "There's our target."

She stared at the trio of crow's nests towering thirty feet overhead, and her throat constricted. "That's awfully high."

"No taller than the oak in our backyard where my brothers and I built a tree fort when we were kids." He stepped back and saluted her with his sword. "A stroll in the park."

"I can't imagine raising four daredevil boys who grew up to be SWAT cops. Your poor mother." She shuddered. "Not enough antacid in the known universe."

"Our family motto is, 'Fortune Favors the Brave.'" He laughed. "Mom hauled timber and nails up the tree and helped us hammer Castle O'Rourke together."

Her mother would have hyperventilated at the thought. Kate

would love to meet Liam's mom. Maureen O'Rourke had attitude, strength and character. Kate strove to be that kind of woman. Would her fears thwart her? She studied Liam's twinkling eyes and confident grin. He'd followed his mom's example. While Kate had given up expecting too much, he lived life to the fullest.

He gestured upward. "If anyone approaches, run interference while I climb to the crow's nest and retrieve the note."

Kate glanced at the performers, rapidly loading cannons. Orange and red flashes scorched the black velvet sky, and white smoke boiled over the bay. She ignored the spear of uncertainty. She had the easy part. He had to climb the mast.

"Arr. Avast, me hearties!" a rough male baritone bellowed behind them. "Scurvy landlubbers!"

They whirled, and Kate gasped. Four pirates challenged them. Tall and beefy, built like Schwarzenegger before he got politics. The first man's pate was shaved bald. The second had long stringy hair, the third a bushy red beard, and number four sported a greasy blond mullet. Redbeard and Longhair wore crimson do-rags. All were outfitted in ratty leather pants and open vests that revealed tattoos and interesting piercings on sweaty bare chests. The motley crew was either a victim of bad pirate central casting, or a biker gang gone very wrong.

Baldie swung the thick chain dangling from his right hand. "You'd be here to hijack me matey's treasure."

Kate sidled closer to Liam. "Who's your *matey?*"

"Someone who pays cash up front and doesn't ask barmy questions." Staying scarily in character, Baldie ogled her cleavage and smiled lewdly. "Nice ballast, wench."

She swallowed hard. The stalker had hired them. Their stroll in the park had just turned into a midnight hike through Central Park.

Both Liam and Murphy rumbled out low, threatening growls. Suddenly grateful for the dog, she nudged Liam. "Now would be a very good time to draw your gun," she whispered.

His lips quirked. "Bloodthirsty wench," he muttered beneath the *kaboom* of the cannons. "We're surrounded by innocent bystanders. Bullets have a nasty habit of ricocheting."

She flicked a wary glance at the audience ringing the bay. She'd been so intent on the mission, she'd forgotten them. Luckily, Liam hadn't. Yikes! What now? "How about the sword?"

"I was theater trained to toss it around on stage," he muttered. "Which *looks* impressive as hell. But if you want a man who can actually fight with the damned thing, call Aidan."

He eyed the scruffy band and arched a mocking brow. "Ahoy, dudes. Axl Rose phoned. He wants his wardrobe back."

She shuffled on the swaying deck. "We need a man who can go toe-to-toe in a brawl, not someone who has fast hands and faster quips. Maybe I'm with the wrong O'Rourke brother?"

He chuckled, but didn't move his gaze off the pirates. "Watch and learn."

Without warning, Mullet swung a meaty fist. Liam dodged, but not quite quickly enough, and the punch grazed his jaw. Kate winced at the impact.

Liam staggered. Murphy's muscles bunched, and he snarled.

And then everything hurtled to hell in a handcart.

Mullet pulled a switchblade. Vibrating with fury, Murphy bared his fangs and growled. Liam shook his head. "Now you've royally pissed off my partner." He gestured. "Murphy, *bite.*"

The canine sprang and clamped powerful jaws on the man's bare right arm. Mullet screamed and stumbled backward. Murphy hung on and shook him like a rag doll. The weapon dropped from the man's torn hand, and blood spattered the boards underfoot.

Sick and paralyzed by the horrifying déjà vu nightmare, Kate stared at the bloody carnage.

"Kate!" Liam yelled from behind her. *"Down!"*

His shout snapped her to awareness. She jerked her gaze up to see Baldie advancing, whirling the chain. She dropped to the deck, and Liam leaped over her. He stepped into the assault and whipped up his sword. The chain wrapped around the blade, and Liam tossed the sword and tangled chain into the drink.

Baldie's face mottled red and he shouted an obscenity. Fists flying, he charged Liam. Liam blocked the punches, and threw a right cross that slammed into the big man's chin. The spectators, thinking it was part of the show, cheered loudly.

Brandishing a long, curved blade, Longhair rushed Liam. They were ganging up on him! As she scrambled to her feet, Redbeard grabbed her arm. Laughing, he crushed her to his chest and groped her butt. "I want in on the fun and games."

"Great. How about kickball?" She rammed her knee upward. Groaning, he crumpled. Kate's gaze spun over the deck. She needed a weapon! She snatched up a folded sail and a heavy metal hook attached to a rope.

She ran up behind Longhair, who slashed at Liam with the machete. Liam swerved as Baldie shoved him forward. The blade sliced Liam's side, and a line of scarlet blossomed on his shirt. She threw the sail over Longhair's head, blinding him. Left-handed, she swung the rope and smacked his spine with the hook. He dropped to his knees, and she used the hook to clobber him in the back of the head. He pitched forward and lay still.

Liam chuckled and thrust a thumbs-up. "Way to go, Miz Scarlett!" His eyes sparkled like he was having the time of his life as he danced away from another attack by Baldie.

She panted for breath in the restricting bodice and returned his thumbs-up. Gad, if she was going to hang out with a SWAT cop, she would have to work out more.

Baldie charged Liam, and he pivoted, putting his back to the rail. At the last moment, Liam crouched and grabbed the big man around the waist. Using Baldie's momentum against him, Liam surged to his feet and flipped him overboard. An Olympic-worthy triple gainer was followed by a geyser that splashed Kate. Raucous encouragement erupted from the audience.

With Longhair out for the count, Baldie in the bay, Redbeard cradling his family jewels and Murphy standing on a whimpering Mullet's chest, all four attackers were subdued.

The intense war between the two ships was reaching a crescendo. Kate barely noticed the thundering battle as she watched her sexy pirate shinny up the mast to retrieve the bagged note. Wow! Those pants were amazing. The *man* was amazing.

Was there *anything* he couldn't do?

She was so distracted by Liam's graceful athleticism, only a gasp from the audience warned her. Heart in her throat, she whirled. Redbeard was on his feet. Fury distorted his features as he grabbed

Longhair's fallen machete and advanced on her. His pronounced limp didn't make him appear any less menacing. "Knee me, will ya? I'll carve my initials into your face, bitch."

She retreated, but bumped into the rail. An anxious glance over her shoulder showed Baldie treading water. She stared at the madman lurching toward her. She wouldn't make it past him.

Kate glanced at Baldie again, and he leered. Nowhere to go. She had to jump. Burdened by the gown and petticoats, she didn't stand a chance of outswimming him. At least he was unarmed. She looked at Redbeard. His eyes smoldered, and the knife gleamed red from the reflected firefight.

She gulped, swung a leg over and straddled the rail. Mouthing a fast, silent prayer, she forced her clamped fingers to let go. Forced her stiff body to lean sideways and fall.

She never hit the water.

Instead, she was swooped up midtumble. Speechless, she stared at Liam, who'd swung from the mast by a long rope and scooped her out of midair. He held her securely in one iron-muscled arm as they sped high across the bay in a breathless arc. Flame-bright fireworks sizzled around them. Wind whipped through her hair, and the stars blurred.

Her stomach dropped from the dizzying ride. Liam whooped, and then they landed neatly on the British frigate's deck.

The bystanders roared approval drowned out the booming artillery. Liam grinned. "Talk about a head rush." He spun and executed a sweeping bow at the crowd.

Her mouth opened and closed three times before a croak emerged. "Holy crow!"

He cocked a glossy brow. "Wrong brother my ass."

She pressed a shaky hand to her galloping heart. "I thought you said you couldn't fight them?"

"I said I didn't *sword* fight. Hellfire, wench." His grin flashed white and wicked in his gorgeous, stubbled face, and her stomach flip-flopped for a different reason. "I grew up with three brothers. We were scrapping before we could walk."

One advantage to not avoiding conflict—apparently, you got very good at handling it. But then she'd established that, unlike her, he was good at *everything.* *"Wench?"* She scowled. "I might have to hurt you for that."

His grin widened, and his warm lips met hers in a hard, fast kiss that rocketed her heartbeat higher than during their swoop across the bay.

The crowd stomped and whistled, and she rolled her eyes. "I smell Irish cured ham."

He laughed. "C'mon, Just Kate. We have to get below decks."

The frigate rattled beneath the pirate ship's cannon barrage and sunk lower. The busy crew didn't notice as the pair stole below. Murphy, who'd been left on the pirate ship, barked.

She'd never blot out the picture of his violent attack. Of razor-sharp fangs tearing bloody flesh. She shuddered, suddenly queasy. She remembered all too well the horror and pain of a dog attack. She touched her twisted scars. As much assistance as Murphy had given them, as much as the attack had been necessary, she was thankful he wasn't nearby right now.

The dark, cavernous hold reeked of damp wood, and the air smoked with sulfur from the mock sea battle raging above. She rotated the book light as Liam conducted a quick visual search.

He strode toward the prow and pursed his lips. "Too easy." The bomb was in plain sight, anchored to a supporting timber.

"He's in a hurry, and getting sloppy?" She followed with the light as he circled the huge post, studying the bomb.

"Not freaking likely. What the *hell?*" He scowled. "A high school freshman with Internet access could have rigged this. It'll take all of ninety seconds to neutralize."

"Is it a trap of some kind? A decoy?"

He shook his head. "No, he wanted the explosive matter easily extracted. *Why?*"

Artillery fire boomed. The ship quaked again, and settled lower. Splashes echoed as the crew abandoned the sinking vessel. In this production, only the captain went down with the ship. Wetness sloshed her feet, and she glanced down. She was calf deep in water. Her heart lurched. *Warm* water. Water that had absorbed the super-heated Vegas atmosphere. Water that was maintained at a comfortable temperature for performers who got doused six times a night. "Liam? What temperature is the bay?"

He dipped his hand. "A few degrees over body temperature." He swore. "And when the chemical submerges..." He swore again. "Hot damn! This guy is the Einstein of explosives."

Pulse racing, she gestured at the plastic bag peeking out of his pants pocket. "Put it in the plastic bag."

"Not enough insulation." He grabbed her arm and spun her around, towed her forward. "Kate, bug out of here!"

She dug in her heels. "I got you into this mess. I am *not* leaving you!"

"No time for debate!" He gritted his teeth and yanked her toward the ladder. "Damn stubborn woman. Go!"

"Not on your life." She fought his pull. I'm sticking with you to the bitter end." She gasped. "*Sticking!* The duct tape! It's thick and waterproof!" She pointed to the roll at his belt. "Seal the explosive inside the tape!"

Admiration lit his eyes. "Yeah. Three or four layers might buy enough seconds to get topside." His glance ricocheted around the massive hold. "Dump the ammo from that metal tin and hand it over. Containing the explosive will reduce the impact."

The water crept above her knees as she emptied the tin and slogged to where Liam was disassembling the device. He slid the pale green sheet out of the metal casing and looked at her. Confidence gleamed in his gaze. "Hold out your hand."

Trembling, she did as he requested. He carefully set the explosive on her palm. She gulped. He trusted her to hold an explosive...standing thigh deep in warm water that would detonate instantly if she fumbled. She attempted to steady her breathing.

She'd better not fumble.

By the time he'd slashed the tape and sealed the explosive, water had hit her abdomen and was crawling upward.

He grabbed the tin from her, thrust the sealed explosive inside and rammed the lid shut. "Kate, *go*."

"What about you?"

"Almost done. Get the hell outta here!"

Floundering through waist deep waves in the sodden dress, she swam to the ladder. She spent precious seconds to strip off draggy petticoats and her sandals. Then she looked back at Liam.

He was furiously strapping the tin to a timber above his head. The ship moaned and heaved sharply to the side, and waves beat at his chest. "Climb, dammit!" he gritted.

Praying all the way, she scrambled up the rocking ladder.

When she reached the top, she struggled out onto the deck, and then turned and leaned into the hatch. "Liam?" she shouted.

"Behind you," he yelled from too far away. "Jump ship!"

Should she go back for him? *No.* She'd only slow him down. She staggered across the listing deck. The ship rode low on the waterline, the bay practically at her feet. *Liam, where are you?*

After a final agonized glance over her shoulder at the empty deck, she scaled the rail and jumped.

She hit the water at the same time an earsplitting boom shattered the night. Half the bay spewed up. The violent burst radiated shock waves, and tumbled her over and over underwater.

Unable to determine which way was up, she thrashed in blind panic. She couldn't see. Couldn't breathe. She was drowning.

Then something slammed into her and knocked her to the surface. *Liam?* Choking, gasping, she gazed wildly around. The ship's captain, the last actor in the water, was heaved ashore by crewmembers. She spun, searching the floating debris that bobbed beneath spotlights surrounding the bay. "Liam?"

Where was he?

Frenzied barking snagged her attention. Murphy had found them. Perched on a rock at the bay's edge, he leaned over and barked in frantic staccato. Was he pointing out the bomb? The dog's body shook, and his high-pitched barks rang over the water. When Murphy located a bomb, he went still. The dog was agitated.

She inhaled and dove. The spotlights offered limited vision in the murky depths. She searched the area below where Murphy barked, his voice muffled beneath the waves. The hull had split into three large pieces. With the dress dragging at her legs, she swam into the first section and found nothing but wreckage. She had to surface for air before searching the second.

Still nothing.

Her heart stuttered in fear. If Liam had survived the explosion, he would drown while she searched fruitlessly.

Ignoring her tortured lungs, she swam into the third section. She twisted through jagged, tangled timbers. Her hem caught on a splintered board and jerked her up short. She yanked, finally tore loose. Dizzy from oxygen deprivation, she didn't have time to navigate the slanted maze and laboriously make her way to the surface. Remembering lessons from long ago summers at camp, she went limp and let gravity float her upward.

She would die trying before she gave up on Liam.

Her head broke free of water, and bumped wood. She'd found an air pocket inside the upturned hull. Cracked boards allowed slender fingers of light to pierce the darkness. Her strained lungs inflated. Treading water, she clung to a broken plank.

A hand grabbed her shoulder from behind. She shrieked and spun.

Liam floated behind her in the claustrophobic space. "*Kate!* Are you all right?"

"Liam!" She flung herself at him. Wedged against the crisscrossed beams in front of him, she skimmed anxious hands over his face. A dark bruise shadowed his jaw, but she didn't see any blood. "Thank God!" I was so scared." She hugged him tightly. "Follow me. I'll show you the way out."

"I'd love to go with you." He smiled ruefully. "But I'm wedged behind two crossed beams. They're jammed against the bottom, and I can't get leverage in this cramped space."

She cupped his face. "Stay right here. I'll get help."

He chuckled. "Not going anywhere."

She let go of him and immediately sank. She flailed upward, spat water. "Shoot. This danged gown weighs a ton. I need to take it off." She turned around. "Unlace me?"

Amusement tinged his voice. "I thought you'd never ask."

"You're incorrigible."

"Yup. Incurable." His fingers tugged at her dress. He swore. "These wet laces won't budge. Grab my knife."

She rotated to face him and slipped her hand between the boards. His sash was in the way, and she tugged it loose. "Your gun belt is snagged on something. I can't get past it."

"Release the catch, but try not to let it fall."

She'd have to use her good hand to unhook the belt. Which meant catching it with her bad hand. Concentrating hard, she fumbled with the unfamiliar buckles in the narrow space. His gun belt came loose. For a second, she had a firm hold on it, then it slid through her weak fingers and sank like a rock. *Oh, no!* Except for his knife, he was unarmed. "I'm sorry."

"Don't sweat it. You did your best. Just get the knife."

Berating herself, she slid her fingers over his hipbone. It was hard to maneuver by feel alone.

He sucked in a breath. "That's not my knife, babe."

"Oh!" She snatched her hand back. "Sorry again."

His low laugh was wickedly sexy. "I'm not."

She found the knife on her second try. He cut the laces, and she managed to return his knife without groping him. His big, capable hands slid the dress down over her arms, and she wriggled out of the restricting garment. It fell away, leaving her in a black lace demi bra and matching bikinis.

He whistled in appreciation. "If that's the last sight I see on this earth, I'll die a happy man."

Raw fear sliced through her. "You're not going to die!"

"A figure of speech, honey." He smoothed his palm over her wet hair. "I have no intention of croaking anytime soon."

"You'd better not." She pressed her lips to his in a quick kiss. Free of the gown, she slithered through the wreckage. She surfaced, and her heart sank to the bottom of the bay. Everyone had left after the staged battle. As Liam had stated, they would have assumed the pyrotechnics had malfunctioned and wouldn't call the authorities. There would be no more shows tonight.

Terror twisted inside her. Except for Murphy, who stood trembling on shore, she was alone.

She could climb out and dash into the hotel. But by the time she explained, enlisted help and everyone returned to the pool, he'd have run out of oxygen in the tiny space. Or if the wreckage shifted and eliminated the air pocket, he'd drown.

No, saving Liam was up to her.

Nausea roiled in her stomach. She couldn't even remove his gun belt without fumbling. And she was supposed to save his *life?* But there wasn't anyone else. She inhaled and shored up her water-logged courage. All right, she'd save him. She dove again, and navigated the wooden jumble beneath the hull.

Liam's dazzling smile broke her heart. "That was fast."

She bit her lip. "Everyone's gone. It's just me."

"So what's the bad news, Just Kate?" His easy grin flashed. "We've worked together all day, with a hundred percent success ratio." He fished a rope out of the water. "I'll tie this to the front beam." He knotted the rope. "Loop it over the pole behind your head. Between both of us, it'll shake loose."

"I hope so." She eyed the heavy, crossed timbers imprisoning him in a wooden cage. "This seems risky."

"If you don't gamble, you never win."

She shot a scared look at her crippled hand. For his sake, this risk better pay off. "You never lose, either."

"Don't you?" He gave her a long, considering look. "No worries, Kate. Like you, my number's not up yet."

He passed her the rope. "You yank and I'll kick. Dive under the second it loosens."

Anxiety scalded her. If anything went wrong… Liam braced his palms on the roof. "Now!" His boot slammed the beam, and she strained on the rope. The barricade shivered, but didn't budge.

"Once more!" He kicked again, and she pulled with everything she had. The timber groaned, shuddered and a loud crack reverberated overhead. "Dive!" he shouted.

She jackknifed as the entire structure collapsed.

Kate surfaced and scanned the roiling water for Liam.

He didn't appear.

With horrific images searing her brain, she dropped under again and searched for him.

She found him on the bottom. He was conscious, but a huge beam had fallen on his right arm. No matter how hard they tugged and pushed in frenzied unison, they couldn't move it.

He was trapped.

Kate's aching lungs forced her to surface. She gasped in air and screamed for help. Murphy barked furiously.

Nobody came.

Desperate tears flooded her eyes, streamed down her face.

She hadn't saved Liam. She'd killed him.

Chapter 12

11:00 p.m.

Held captive at the bottom of the bay, Liam tried repeatedly to yank free. His brain quickly devised and discarded tactical plans. The scenario wasn't exactly loaded with options.

He couldn't gain leverage to budge the beam wedged across his right arm. Hell, he couldn't even turn over. He couldn't reach his Swiss Army knife to cut his own arm off, or he'd have done it. He pounded the timber. Trapped. Helpless. *Useless.*

He could only wait…and pray that Kate found help. Fast.

A bombshell of enlightenment detonated, and he reeled. This was how Kate felt. She constantly battled the fear and frustration of losing her right arm. She lived with ceaseless pain. She'd been forced to surrender her independence and dignity and depend on others.

His pulse stuttered in empathy. If a similar handicap had ended his career…if he'd been denied the release of driving his Mustang, or had to give up the creative pleasure of rebuilding his house, he would be angry and resentful. Yet Kate had overcome her obstacles vith determination and grace. She had reassembled the broken, loody pieces and started over. With no family encouragement. All lone on her gut-wrenching trudge to redemption, she'd learned not o count on backup.

No wonder she was scared to live life to the fullest. To take hances. No wonder she wanted to play it safe.

He didn't blame her.

His body screamed for air. He grappled with panic, strove to slow is heartbeat and conserve resources. He was rapidly running out f oxygen. Rapidly running out of time.

Harsh reality slammed him. Maybe his number *was* up. Maybe oday *was* his day to die.

He'd cursed, outsmarted and gambled with death. But he'd never ome face-to-face with the Grim Reaper. He'd never stared into his old, merciless eyes and seen his own end.

Regrets? Yeah, he had a couple. Like not being honest with his amily. They'd remember him as good-time Liam. Ready with a unny quip or a cheerful hand up. But would they know how much e loved them? He should have come right out and told them.

After Michelle had dumped him and Pop had been snatched away ar too soon, he'd taken refuge in humor. Starting at age nineteen, e'd hidden his pain behind a smoke screen of jokes and laughter. f he bounced from woman to woman, they couldn't leave him first. party-hearty guy had no time to notice soul-deep loneliness.

His pulse thundered in the taut silence. He hadn't been enjoying e present…he'd been running from his past.

He'd been so busy living in the moment, he'd never considered is future.

And he wanted a future…with Kate. She was the only woman e couldn't sway with charm. She called him out when he camou-aged his feelings with irreverence. She forced him to be real.

From their very first meeting, she'd seen past the blarney to the an beneath. *That's* why she'd fled from his bed. Somehow, she'd ensed his inability to commit. Intense, focused, loyal Kate wasn't woman who treated anything or anyone casually.

He ramped up his struggle to shift the massive timber. He ouldn't die now. Who would protect her from the head case stalker?

How would she rescue her photos? What would happen to the tiny, fragile girl waiting for a new kidney?

His diaphragm burned from holding his breath. "Experts" claimed drowning was peaceful. Painless. *Dead wrong.* There was too much time to ponder. To regret. To mourn. He'd never been scared of dying. He figured he'd go quick and clean, rocketed skyward in a bright, hot flash. He never expected to die alone in icy blue twilight, smothered by slow, agonizing degrees.

Near bursting, his lungs strained. Black spots blurred his vision. Though he fought to hold in every molecule of oxygen, he couldn't stop the insistent escape of air from his nostrils. He watched the bubbles stream upward. His final breath. He battled the irresistible urge to inhale, and his chest spasmed. His next breath would fill his lungs with water. Would kill him. Fear sank sharp talons into his spine, twisted in his gut.

Kate floated down in front of him, a beautiful angel of mercy. His laboring heart bucked. He wouldn't die alone after all. He reached for her. He yearned to tell her he was fiercely glad that her beloved face would be the last thing he saw.

She cradled his face in her hands. Her tender hands would be the last touch he felt. She pressed her mouth to his. Her soft lips would be the last to kiss him.

Black weight bore down, dimming his consciousness. Dragging him into the darkness. Racked by sorrow, shaking with desperate fury, he tangled his fingers in her hair, clung to her. *No, dammit!* He would not go! He would not leave her!

Pop, if you have any influence up there, help me!

The answer was swift. Unexpected. Kate breathed into his mouth, filled him with her breath. Her essence revived him. Her breath fed his starved lungs, chased darkness from his sight.

She grabbed the rope tied to the beam, gestured to tell him she'd return, and shot upward.

Dizzy from oxygen deprivation and relief, he closed his eyes. He'd received a reprieve from his date with death.

Treading water, Kate wound the rope over her shoulder and strove for calmness. Faced with failure, with losing Liam, she'd freaked. Splashed and shrieked for help that didn't come. While she'd been panicking, Liam had been drowning. She'd let her emotions run rampant, and they'd obliterated her common sense.

Because she'd let her emotions off the leash and stopped thinking clearly, Liam had almost died. He still might die.

Who did she think she was, trying to be his savior? She'd always played it safe. Taking chances caused catastrophes.

She gritted her teeth. The key to survival was to lock her feelings in a deep freeze…where they couldn't endanger anyone. The only way to save Liam was to entomb her emotions in a thick shield of ice. And never let them thaw out again.

Taking emotional chances ended in failure.

Kate stared at the dog standing guard on the rocks, and terror roiled inside her. She quashed it. No time to indulge in angst. She had to be hard and determined. Emotionless. Ruthless. To save Liam's life, she must confront her worst fear.

For him to live, she must kill her newly born feelings.

She stared at the jagged scars on her arm. A constant, ugly reminder of acting from her heart instead of her head. She forced herself to go cold and dead inside. Blotted out the awful mental picture of Murphy's recent attack. Made herself feel nothing as she swam to the outcropping, floated beneath the dog.

Her fingers shook as they fisted on the rope. She had one good hand. If it was destroyed… Her brain had to command her arm to move twice before it obeyed. Slowly, she lifted the quivering rope to the dog's lethal jaws. "M-Murphy," she croaked. "Tug!"

His head lowered, and she flinched away. Fighting the urge to flee, she tried again. Long, lethal fangs bit into the rope, and she snatched her hand back. "G-good dog! Tug!" He backed up, pulling hard, and she dove to where Liam waited below.

Moments ago, his luminous eyes had been haunted with pain. And the enraged knowledge of his own death. Her valiant pirate wasn't about to meekly shuffle through the pearly gates. Death would have torn him fighting from her arms.

His eyes shone with hope and gratitude as she gave him another breath. She went up for air, encouraged Murphy to tug, and then jackknifed. Bracing her feet on the floor, she strained against the beam's weight. The taut rope vibrated from Murphy's strong pull. Liam lent his left arm to the effort. As they pushed and heaved, the timber slowly rose the inches needed to conquer death. Liam slid his arm free. Together, they surged upward. Into the warm night's embrace. Into light. Into life.

Liam coughed violently, and she helped him flounder to the rocks. Murphy dropped the rope and snagged Liam's shirt collar. Kate heaved herself out of the water. With the dog's assistance, she dragged Liam onto dry land.

Panting, he flopped onto his back. She scrambled to his other side, opposite the dog, and sleeked thick strands of wet hair from his face. "I'll get an ambulance."

He grabbed her. "No." He coughed some more. "I'm good."

"Sure. Don't let a little thing like hacking up a lung dissuade you from seeking medical treatment."

He pushed to a sitting position, which brought on another bout of coughing. "How'd you get me out?"

"I had Murphy tug on the rope. Between the three of us, we had enough power to raise the beam."

Respect and approval glittered in his gaze. "Brilliant." He smiled. "You and Murph worked together?"

His hopeful smile battered the barrier around her heart. "It was necessary to save your life. Don't read anything more into it." What she'd known all along was confirmed beyond a doubt. She could never separate him from his partner. They were an incomparable team. Without Murphy, Liam would have drowned.

Yet after watching Murphy tear a man's arm to shreds, she could never trust him. Granted, he'd been protecting Liam. That didn't make her fear him any less. What if he mistakenly thought *she* was about to hurt Liam sometime? The risk was far too high.

Liam coughed again, and she rubbed his back. "Let me call your brothers. At least the one who is a paramedic."

"In this case, you're with the right O'Rourke, Miz Scarlett." His breathing eased, and she relaxed a fraction. "Those boys don't know nothin' about disarmin' no bombs."

She gestured at his sliced shirt. The water hadn't totally leeched away the bloodstain. "What about your knife wound?"

He peered at his side and snorted. "It's not even bleeding anymore. Takes more than an itty bitty scratch to slow me down."

She sighed. "Do you want me to go back in after your gun?"

He eyed the debris-littered pool. "I'd go after it, but it's buried, and the clock is ticking." He shoved to his feet. "We have one more bomb to disarm."

"Damn stubborn *pirate.*"

"Arr." He reached down a broad hand to help her up. His impudent gaze stroked leisurely over her, speeding her pulse, warming her skin. "Speaking of booty..."

Gad, talk about a quick rebound. "Don't start."

The horror of his close call suddenly shadowed his eyes. "Why the hell not? I could be dead tomorrow."

Memory's icy fingers scraped her spine, and she shivered. *She could be sobbing over his dead body right now.* His involvement with the stalker was her fault. His death would have been her fault. Her ultimate failure.

"I want you, Kate." His voice was tortured. Without warning, he yanked her against him, wrapped his arms around her and plundered her mouth with a desperate kiss.

His warm, wet body slicked along hers. His blazing kiss chased away cold, relentless fear. Threatened to melt her icy wall and bring her emotions roaring back full force. She longed to stand on tiptoe, wrap her arms around his neck and kiss him back.

Because she needed him desperately, she pushed him away. Nothing good could come of this. Trembling with despair, she touched her sensitized lips. How was she going to tell him the heartbreaking truth? He wouldn't want her once he understood the full extent of her handicap.

They also didn't have time to discuss it. Torn between angst and relief, she inclined her head. "The clock is ticking."

"Yeah." His voice was graveled. He tugged the plastic bag from his pocket. Miraculously, it had stayed put.

She opened the note. The message was short and to the point. *Is it Insanity to search for a needle in haystack?*

He pointed. "Another capitalized word."

"*Insanity.* The Stratosphere has a ride named Insanity. The point on the tower resembles a needle. Can it be that simple?"

"Simple." He snorted as the note disintegrated. "I just have to disarm a bomb on an amusement ride that's perched on top of a twelve-hundred-foot tower."

She gulped. "We'd better go." She strode toward the car. A strangled sound behind her brought her up short, and she turned.

Liam stood frozen, a poleaxed expression on his face.

"What's the matter? Are you hurt?"

He blinked. Then he chuckled and gestured at her body. "Talk about a moving violation."

Perplexed, she glanced down, and heat crawled up her neck. In all the angst, she'd forgotten she was only wearing a black lace bra and panties.

He unbuttoned his shirt, revealing a wide expanse of tanned chest dusted with dark hair. He shrugged out of the garment, making muscles ripple in interesting places. Her gaze snagged on the treasure trail of hair that started at his flat stomach and wandered beneath the waistband of his pants.

Holy crow! She bit her lip as he passed her the shirt. She fumbled it on and tamped down her rioting senses. *Think with your head, not your hormones, woman.* "We have to make a fast stop to buy shoes. My sandals are at the bottom of the pool."

"We'll bring our street clothes into the shop and change in their dressing rooms." He curled his big warm hand around the base of her neck, and delicious goose bumps prickled over her skin. "Let's rock and roll."

The man spying from his hidden hotel room twitched the heavy drapes back into place and threw down his rifle in disgust. He'd maneuvered them right where he wanted them. He'd been winning. Then Katherine had risked her life to save the cop. His lip curled. She'd even braved facing the dog.

She'd never belong to him…not now. He'd tried to make her love him. Instead, she ignored him. Just as his parents had.

And he despised her for it.

His parents had atoned for their sins…as would she.

He barked out a bitter laugh. Everyone thought they'd died of natural causes. He hadn't been able to take credit for his clever work. Nor would he this time. But no matter. Because Katherine would know him before she paid. Intimately.

He would make her scream out his name. Over and over.

He opened his laptop and hacked into her dictated electronic journal. Nothing new today. As he'd devoured her nightly entries, he'd felt as though she were confiding in him. Telling him her deepest fears, her secret desires. He scowled. He'd burned with fury when he'd paged back and read how she had wasted her innocence on the policeman. How could she, when she was supposed to be loyal only to *him?* He'd overlooked the offense only because she'd run away from O'Rourke. She'd lived alone in quiet torment, as celibate as a nun. Given time, he'd been sure she'd turn to him. After she'd groveled, he would have accepted her apology. Taken care of her forever. But now, the cop was back in her life...and his. Katherine had revealed her true nature. The whore was all over O'Rourke like a bitch in heat. He'd almost shot them both when the cop had kissed her on *Britannia*'s deck. That would have been too easy. Too merciful.

If they survived his next test, they would pay for his long, patient years of waiting. His scorching humiliation.

He would hurt the cop. Slowly. Torturously. No glorious explosion for O'Rourke. He'd seen one of his compatriots peel the skin off a man inch by inch. He'd never forgotten the white-hot power rush at the pain. The orgasmic satisfaction in the inhuman screams. He'd learned his craft from the best. He'd make O'Rourke plead for mercy. Beg for death.

The time for mercy was long past.

He'd force the cop to watch while he plucked his tarnished flower. He hardened, thinking about the exquisite pleasure her terror and pain would bring him. He would finally elicit a response from her. He would torment them with the knowledge that their lives were ticking away, second by second. He was their judge. Their executioner. Their god.

Blood beat in his temples with the thrilling swell of invincibility. His Katherine, as cool and untouchable as the calla lilies he left for her, would burn to ashes in the scalding fire of his rage. He would purify her. Purge her from his head, from his life. He would finally be free of her.

Then he would find a woman who truly deserved him. Move on with his life.

A much richer, and wiser man.

At the Stratosphere, a sign informed Liam that the upper deck was closed for a private wedding. He needed a way to clear the deck without arousing suspicion. He needed Zoe.

Using Kate's phone, he called Aidan. "I need to borrow your security pass and your wife, and she's not answering her cell."

"She's conspiring with Grady on a top-secret project." Aidan sighed. "She gets into enough jams without help, bro."

After a taut round of twenty questions—and a few choice words—Aidan agreed to send her to the Stratosphere.

Liam cased the lobby while he waited. Hot air balloons were featured in the decor. Even the lamps were miniature hot air balloons. In less than fifteen minutes, Zoe arrived with a portable TV camera. A scowling Aidan dogged her heels. Liam didn't blame big brother for guard dogging his woman. Because of Kate, he had a new perspective on the male protective gene.

Aidan pointed at his diminutive wife. "Ten minutes. Then I'm coming up and you're leaving, whether you're done or not."

Zoe grinned. "He never learns." She elbowed Aidan in the ribs. When he grunted and bent over, she kissed him. "Ease off the testosterone trigger, SWAT. I know what I'm doing."

Liam turned to Kate. "Distract security at the front desk so Zoe can get upstairs."

Kate headed for the desk, and Zoe patted Murphy on the head. "Hey Murphy. Keeping Deputy Dog outta trouble?"

The dog's tail swished. *I try my darnedest.*

She waggled her fingers. "See you in ten, boys. Don't do anything I wouldn't." She strode toward the elevator boarding area, which was constructed like a huge hot air balloon.

Aidan muttered and rubbed his ribs. "That woman is…"

Liam slanted him a wry smile. "Exasperating? Exciting? You can't stand to be away from her for a second, but at the same time, she scares the holy freaking crap out of you?"

Aidan's glance ricocheted to Kate, then back. He quirked a brow and his face creased in a grin. "Welcome to the jungle, little brother." He sobered. "Then you understand why I'm not thrilled by the idea of my wife in proximity with a bomb."

Liam wasn't thrilled with the entire scenario. But he and Kate had no choice. "I wouldn't endanger her or you. If Whacko's gonna detonate, he'll wait until I'm on scene." He scanned the perimeter. "What's the word on the background checks?"

"Hanson checks out. Some complaints about excessive force and aggressive behavior, but he's clean."

"And the others?"

"Daniel Tyler had trouble as a juvvie. Graffiti, drinking, one count of marijuana possession. He straightened out after his parents died in a car accident when he was twelve. He went to live with foster parents, now deceased. Graduated from MIT. Intel indicates he's anticipating assuming the reins when daddy-in-law retires. He appears devoted to his wife and child."

"Keep him on the list. Appearances can be deceiving. What about contestant number two?"

"Until six months ago, Brice Edwards lived with his mother. Father unknown, listed as deceased. Edwards Graduated summa cum laude from the most conservative college on the East Coast, then served a four-year hitch in the National Guard. He collects antique war weapons, including salvaged antipersonnel mines."

"Some of which can be triggered remotely. Freaky hobby."

"Freaky guy. His work associates describe him as brainy, but socially awkward. Talented at portrait photography. He's been saving to open his own studio, but his mom's medical bills and recent death wiped him out."

Aidan delivered the intel report without consulting notes. He'd always had a scary memory for detail. "Politically, he's so far to the right, he's in another continent. Quite the activist. Multiple counts of trespassing and disturbing the peace. He allegedly threatened the administrator of a women's clinic during a protest, but no charges were filed. The clinic was bombed two weeks later. Investigators didn't turn up anything."

"So Mr. Open-minded might resent women because his mother's

illness killed his dreams, and also a woman photographer's success. Especially if she's shunned his overtures."

Liam rubbed his chin. "And the third?" Kate's admin assistant sparked his intuition. He wasn't sure if it was because he suspected him of criminal conduct or because the model-perfect man's close relationship with Kate made him twitchy. Etienne's utter devotion to her reminded him of Murphy's dedication to him—and that mental picture was just wrong in so many ways.

Aidan's brows lowered. "According to Interpol, Etienne Duplais doesn't exist. Not until six years ago. No family. No birth certificate. No school records or work history. He materialized out of nowhere in Paris, with a passport, driver's license and spotty résumé as a sometime construction worker."

Liam glanced at Kate, engaged in animated conversation with the desk personnel. Did she know when she'd hired Duplais "off the street" that he had no credentials? "Did his construction work involve demolition?" Aidan nodded, and Liam frowned. "He'd be familiar with explosives, and have access." For Kate's sake, he hoped Etienne wasn't the perp. Having your closest friend turn Judas was shattering. He felt sick. Been there, done that. He'd hate to have to arrest him—and then break the bad news to Kate. And wouldn't *that* do a messy little tap dance all over his chances with her? "All three suspects have means and opportunity. That leaves motive. Which one do I focus on?"

Aidan shook his head. "What does your gut say?"

Grab your woman and get her the hell out of the kill zone. Kate had him twisted up in so many knots, his instincts were snarled by his feelings. Not good. He had to compartmentalize. Contain his feelings until Kate was safe. "Nothing clear, yet."

Murphy nosed his leg, obviously picking up on his tension. He stroked Murphy's back in reassurance. "Edwards has some photos for Kate at his shop. I need you to pick them up, bro."

The elevator pinged, and Zoe strode out, trailed by a Rio carnival wedding party. "The pen is mightier than the gun." She winked at Liam on the way out of the casino and spoke to the knockout bride. "We'll use the Strip for background shots. I'll bet you can't wait to see your wedding on the evening news."

Aidan started to follow his wife, but Liam stopped him. "Wait.

Your Homeland Security pass will help me convince the guards on the top deck to vacate for a 'drill.'"

Aidan turned. "What happened to your pass?"

"Long story."

His brother frowned. "I'll ride along."

"Nah. Other than eye color, we look alike. They'll never notice. Now if it were Grady, with those dimples…" His smile was strained. This was the tough part. "Take Murphy with you." Grady was the die-hard animal lover. Of his brothers, baby bro had the closest rapport with Murphy. But the canine would listen to Con or Aidan when ordered. "He can't navigate the roller coaster or the rides, and if the crap hits the fan up there, I'll have to rescue Kate. I won't be able to evac him fast enough."

"If crap flies, will *you* be able to evac fast enough?"

Liam shrugged, forcing nonchalance he didn't feel. "Hey, I'm the Gambler." His throat tightened. "If the worst happens and I go boom, tell Grady to take care of Murph for me."

Aidan scowled. "Wading ass deep in alligators, Liam?"

Liam raised his hand. "Don't go all caveman on *me.* If I need backup, I'll shout." Aidan had always fiercely protected his little brothers. Which made him the ideal rear guard for the SWAT team. Liam wouldn't want anyone else guarding his back. But to save a little girl, and scores of innocent bystanders, he and Kate had to play by Psycho's rules. They had to go it alone.

Kate must have seen Zoe leave with the wedding party, because she returned, warily staying far to his right. His spirits sank. He'd hoped that after working together, she'd learn to trust the dog. If anything, she was more leery than ever. Heart aching, he gestured. "Murph, go with Aidan."

Murphy stared at him, hurt in his sharp brown eyes. *What's this doody?* He whimpered. *You can't banish me. We're pack.*

Liam knelt and wrapped his arms around the dog. Murphy tucked his snout into his neck and snuffled with his cold, wet nose. A weird sense of loss assaulted him…as if he'd never see his partner again. *Don't be asinine*. Murphy would be safer with Aidan than on top of the Stratosphere. He rose. Gestured again. Made his voice stern around the lump in his throat. "Go!"

Murphy heaved a sigh, and slowly walked to Aidan's side. *If you say so. But I don't have to like it.*

With one last, yearning look, Murphy followed Aidan out. Kate's slow exhale and dropped shoulders gave her away. She might be relieved, but he was charging into a firefight naked. He had to go to work without his right-hand man.

The elevator zoomed them up one hundred and thirteen flights in thirty seconds. His ears popped twice on the way up.

Kate gasped. "Yowza! I've never been up here before." She grabbed his arm. "You have an affinity for fast rides."

The doors slid open, and he winked at her. Teasing helped ease the pain of leaving Murphy behind. "I'll have to take you on a long, slow ride sometime."

Her cheeks grew rosy, and she inclined her head at the two security guards. "Let's pretend we're actual professionals."

Aidan's Homeland Security ID, combined with a pitch loaded with cop jargon, convinced the guards he was there for an impromptu security drill. The FBI, in conjunction with SWAT, had been conducting them all week at tourist hot spots around town. Though the exercises were supposed to be a surprise, gossip had leaked among the casino personnel. Nobody wanted to flunk. The guards surrendered their keys and boarded the elevator.

Kate glanced around the deserted deck. "What now?"

"Stalker Boy has been putting the IEDs—improvised explosive devices—in plain sight. To cause maximum destruction, the bomb would be on the roller coaster track."

She grimaced. "Oh, goody."

He chuckled. "I've ridden everything up here a bunch of times. You've lived here a lot longer. How come you haven't?"

"I don't like thrill rides. My clothes and hair get all rumpled. I end up sweaty, hot and sticky. I'm dizzy for fifteen minutes afterward." She shook her head. "I hate being out of control, up, down, in, out while hanging on for dear life. Not to mention the involuntary screaming."

He arched a brow. "Are we still talking about roller coasters, babe?"

Her bright flush rivaled the neon lights shimmering a thousand feet below. Her expression suddenly vulnerable and uncertain, she turned away. What was that all about?

Compartmentalize. Get the job done. He paced the deck, conducting a visual inspection. Floodlights illuminated the area. Good deal, since they'd lost their light at Treasure Island, along with the duct tape and his Glock. Gaudy decorations continued the wedding's carnival theme. A thick rope anchored a real hot air balloon to one side of the structure, festooned with a banner that read: Congrats, Howie and Laverne! The bride and groom planned to depart in high style.

He studied each ride. He and Grady, the daredevil O'Rourke, had braved them multiple times. The Big Shot catapulted riders up the tower's mast with a 4 g-force. X-Scream was a giant, open car teeter-totter. Insanity's steel arm jutted individual swings over the edge and twirled hapless passengers facedown over the city. By comparison, the roller coaster had seemed tame.

He led Kate to a control box. "Move me slowly around the track until I tell you to stop. He climbed into the front car of the roller coaster, and watched the track as he traveled the loop. When he reached the bend where the track arched out over the city right next to Insanity, he saw it. "Stop!"

Hanging out of the car, he studied the device wired to the track. *Hellfire.* The IED at Treasure Island had been diagrammed from *Bomb Building for Dummies,* but this was a frigging masterpiece. The most sophisticated device he'd ever been pitted against. "Bring me back."

He had sixty seconds to think as the coaster snaked around the bird's-eye view of Vegas. But he'd made his decision the moment he'd assessed the bomb.

When the coaster lumbered to a halt, he jumped out. The confidence in Kate's eyes killed him. Blast it, he hated to let her down. The bomb tech wanted to go for it. But the protector who would die to save her prevailed. "The trigger has a fail-safe. No matter what I do, it's gonna blow." He shook his head. "A wise man knows when to cut his losses. We fold this hand."

Her jaw dropped. "Okay, where's the pod? I cannot believe that just came out of your mouth, Ace."

He couldn't believe it himself. He'd never backed down from a challenge. He clenched his jaw. Had he lost his nerve? Lost his edge? Before Kate, being cavalier was easy. He'd never had anything to really live for. Never had anything to lose. But he couldn't bear the thought of Kate dying.

Even if she lived only to walk away from him.

He took her hand. "I can jam it long enough for you to evac the upper floors. It's a big charge, but the tower is built to withstand a magnitude eight earthquake. The lower half of the structure would survive the blast. Everyone would get out."

"What about you?"

"I'll probably make it at least halfway down the stairs before it blows." He hoped. If he could run that fast. If the electrical circuits didn't shut down and leave him in the dark. If he didn't take direct backlash.

"Probably?" Her eyes narrowed. "I don't like the odds."

"They're the only odds we have."

Her mouth firmed in a stubborn line. He'd never seen her look that way before. Her fiercely determined expression did something funny to his insides—a lot like a spin on Insanity. "Will the people inside be harmed if we try to disarm it?"

"Not if I get the bomb off the structure, first. Then the concussion will affect only the very top, where we are."

"I vote we stay."

He dropped her hand and put distance between them. "This isn't the same as the other two bombs, Kate. The outcome is far less certain. I'm not wagering your life."

"You're wagering yours."

"That's different."

"Why?"

Aw, hell. Time to be a badass. "Because our only chance is to launch the bomb into midair before it explodes. We'd have to play a deadly game of hot potato. After I jammed the bomb, you'd have to catch it and toss it over the edge. If you missed, if you fumbled…" His voice was purposely hard. "I might still make it. You wouldn't. It's not worth the risk."

Searing hurt cannoned through Kate, stole her breath. The moment she'd dreaded had arrived. He'd finally admitted she was handicapped. Anger quickly followed. "This is *my* destiny. *My* decision. *I* am in charge of my life."

His green eyes were as cold as glaciers. "Or death."

"How *dare* you send me away and endanger yourself!" No way would he get downstairs in time. He'd die. Because they hadn't followed the rules, the stalker would destroy the photos. Aubrey wouldn't get her transplant. Liam's death would be wasted.

And she would lose everyone who meant anything to her.

She fought for control. *Stay calm. Don't think with your emotions.* What good was it to survive, if she was an empty shell? If she had *nothing.* "Those photos are the only things left of my new life. They represent years of grueling work and sacrifice. He's ruined *everything.* The photos are all I have left of *me.* They're my future. *Aubrey's* future."

"We'll find another way."

"Our family has tried for months. All their money is tied up in the company. They can't liquidate without going bankrupt. No way can we raise the money in forty-eight hours." She grabbed his forearms. "We can do it, if we stick together. After all we've been through, I can't believe you're giving up. You'll let him win?"

"Nobody wins this game. Playing I-have-bigger-cojones-than-you with Stalker Boy has lost its appeal." In contrast to his cold manner, he tenderly touched her cheek. "I don't want to lose you, just when I've found you again."

He had her mixed up with a woman capable of a relationship. But her physical scars had come between them…as she'd known they would. He didn't even know about her emotional scars. Her chest ached. Before long, he'd wise up and cut her loose.

First, she had to make sure he lived through the day.

"If we don't do this, I'll have lost *everything.* Including my self-respect." She squared her shoulders, steeled her resolve. "I've gone it alone, and alone is highly overrated. I'm not leaving you to face this by yourself." Her voice went soft and low. "Liam…I have more faith in you than fear of him."

He inhaled sharply. His eyes closed briefly, opened again. His face was stricken, his green eyes blazed. "What *is* it about you, Just Kate, that makes me crazy? What have you done to me?"

"Convinced you to allow me to help."

His slow sigh was resigned. "Don't rag me about the gift of blarney ever again."

Her most terrifying victory, ever. "What's the plan?"

"You get in a swing on the Insanity, and I'll put you over the edge. Then I'll jam the device, detach it and throw it to you. You pitch it out as far as you can. Exploding way up here in midair, it won't hurt anything, except—" He faltered.

"Except maybe us."

"Yeah." A muscle ticked in his taut jaw. "And you'll be closest to the blast."

He slid his arm around her waist as they walked toward Insanity, positioned at the edge of the deck next to the roller coaster. "Too bad the tape sank. I need something to cap the wires so they don't accidentally fire."

She felt her dress pocket. Aubrey's bubble gum was still there. She pulled it out. Water hadn't penetrated the foil package during either dunking. "What about a wad of gum?"

He grinned. "I'll be damned. You *are* brilliant, w—"

"I swear, If you 'wench' me one more time, I'm going to turn *you* over *my* knee."

He burst into laughter. "Nice to know you're into the kinky stuff."

Taking a leaf from Zoe's notebook, she elbowed him in the ribs. "Look who's talking."

Still laughing, he tore the wrapper and stuck the gum in his mouth. "Mmm. My favorite. Grape Ape."

The aptly named Insanity was a huge curved arm that supported a circle of swings. The ride was enough to freak her out, without the bomb. Her knees shook so badly he had to help her into the seat. "Good thing I'm not scared of heights." She glanced *waaay* down at the lighted strip.

"You'll do great." His hands were steady as he buckled the harness, but his breathing was accelerated. He held up his left hand. "Fortune Favors the Brave."

"I'll drink to that." Kate smacked him a left-handed high five. "After, you can buy me a bottle of Dom."

"I'll buy you a *case* of Dom." He yanked her to him, leaned in and kissed her. Hard, fast and very thoroughly. Her brains were scrambled when he turned her loose. "Stay safe."

He strode to the control panel. "Here we go!" he hollered.

Gears clashed, metal shrieked, and she swung over the rim. Her ɛet dangled into space, and she gripped the harness. Her seat jerked s he maneuvered her swing to the right of the coaster tracks. He vanted her strongest hand in the catching position. She gritted her eeth to keep from screaming. At least she didn't have to spin.

"Okay?" Liam yelled.

Suspended in the nylon harness, she stared down at the glitter-ıg city nearly a quarter of a mile below. The buildings and cars ɔoked like dollhouse toys. "Let's get this over with!"

She glanced at the roller coaster to her left. Horrified, she vatched Liam walk the tracks, arms outstretched. Her stomach ttered. Without anyone to man the controls, he couldn't use the oaster. And they called *her* ride the Insanity.

Strained minutes ticked past, and she wiped sweaty palms on her ress. She couldn't afford to slip.

"Kate!" Liam's shout made her jerk her gaze to him. "Heads up!"

She braced herself. Wiped her palms again.

"On three!" He crouched on the tracks, his body taut, his dark air blowing in the warm breeze. "One. Two..."

She sucked in a deep breath.

"Three! Here it comes!" In one fluid movement, he rose and ɔssed the device.

Praying like never before, Kate tracked the live bomb hurtling ɔward her.

Chapter 13

12:00 Midnight

Time slowed. The bomb took forever to reach her. Liam had tossed it high, in a perfect arc. It sailed up, up, before it reached its zenith, and then hurtled directly toward her. Holding her breath, she locked her gaze on the device.

The bomb finally zoomed into range. She whipped her arms over her head. Her fingertips brushed metal and missed. She frantically juggled the slippery missile. For terrified seconds, she fumbled, nearly dropping it into the seat with her. Then her sweaty fingers closed around the casing. She had it!

Liam yelled, "Pitch it!" and she heaved the bomb into space. "Duck!" he shouted.

She looked at him, and her blood froze. He was *running!* On a narrow track one hundred and thirteen stories above the ground! A puny metal railing was the only barrier between him and a thousand-foot plunge. *Damn him!* Instead of protecting himself, he was trying to reach the controls and yank her back.

"Crouch!" he yelled. "Cover your head!"

"You too!" She flung her arms over her head. An earsplitting kaboom rendered her temporarily deaf. A brilliant orange flash seared her vision through closed lids. Scalding heat boiled over her, and her seat rocked wildly. Shrapnel peppered the metal with loud clangs. She hunkered in her seat, forearms protecting her head. A piercing sting hit her left shoulder, another her right thigh, and she yelped.

Then everything went still and quiet.

Too quiet.

"Liam?" Her voice sounded muffled in her ringing ears. The track looked okay. But the concussion had collapsed the railing; the steel was folded and bent like crumpled playing cards. *"Liam!"*

Then she saw him. Her heart stopped, and she clapped her hand over her mouth to keep from screaming. He clung to a broken section of railing dangling over the tower's edge.

Oh, dear Lord! Hanging in the seat, suspended in space, she had to watch, powerless, as he struggled to hold on. The damaged metal shrieked, threatening to break free, and Kate's stomach flip-flopped as Liam froze.

He shifted gingerly, and the broken railing screeched out death throes and dropped six inches. He stilled again. When it settled, he began to climb. Stressed muscles bunched as he laboriously pulled hand over hand. She didn't dare speak and break his concentration. Each time the railing slid and screeched, he stopped. Agonizing minutes of slow progress later, he finally clambered onto the deck. Kate went limp.

He didn't even pause to catch his breath before he leaped to his feet and spun to check on her. "Are you all right?"

"Other than minor heart failure, just dandy. You?"

"Never better. You did *great,* Kate." He sprinted to the control panel. "I'll bring you back."

She couldn't *wait* to plant her feet on solid ground. The gears hummed, and the gigantic arm holding her seat swung backward. The machine emitted a loud bang and abruptly halted. Her seat bucked, and she clutched the harness.

Liam swore. "Shrapnel in the gear mechanism. I have to move it in the opposite direction." The ride reversed, swinging her farther over the city. The arm extended sixty-four feet before spinning the swings, but Liam hadn't sent her that far over the edge earlier. She wouldn't have been able to catch the bomb. Clatter erupted, and she lurched to a stop. Her swing tilted and rotated to face the tower. *Eek!* If she started spinning facedown, she was gonna hurl all over the Strip.

Inventive swearing roiled from the control box. Extra points for creativity. Liam appeared, his expression grim. "It's jammed. And the security doors automatically locked after the explosion. I can't get downstairs."

"My cell is in my purse on the deck. Phone for help."

His gaze traveled above her head, and he paled. "Don't move."

She rolled her eyes upward, following his gaze, and broke out in a cold sweat. A knife-blade shard of metal had lodged in the harness link, nearly shearing it off. "Time to call in the cavalry."

"I am the cavalry." He stretched out his hand as if he could reach her. "Stay calm. I'll get you down."

Yeah, a screaming hissy fit probably wouldn't help. She inhaled slow, deep breaths. "Unless you have a cape and pair of tights handy, I don't see how. Call 9-1-1."

"Don't panic. I'm coming." He disappeared from sight.

Why didn't he phone for help? A horrible suspicion assailed her. Unless he knew there was no time. He was coming? *How?* He was a resourceful guy, but he didn't have wings.

Suspended over the bustling city, she muffled her panic. She didn't dare move. Barely breathed. Aside from the breeze, the world from on high was eerily quiet. To keep her mind off plunging to her death, she studied the stars. As a girl, she used to stare out her window and wish. *Starlight, star bright, first star I see tonight. I wish I may, I wish I might...*

She closed her eyes to blot out the stars' mocking gleam. She no longer believed wishes came true.

It was windier away from the shelter of the building. The breeze picked up, rocking her swing. She bit her lip and clutched the harness. "Hurry, Liam," she whispered.

A clink sounded overhead, and the shard of metal fell, tumbling end over end until it disappeared in the darkened sky, far below. Uh-oh! *That can't be good.*

Suddenly, the connection popped, and she flipped backward. Her shriek abruptly cut off as the underside of the harness caught, and the breath was slammed out of her lungs. She dangled upside down a thousand feet in the air. *"Liam!"*

"I'm coming!" He sounded far, far away. "Hang on!"

Hysteria bubbled in her throat. She sure wasn't about to let go. Blood rushed to her head, making her woozy. The strained harness creaked. *"Hurry!"*

An aeon ground past before he shouted, "I'm below you!"

Hope collided with disbelief. *"How?"*

"I commandeered the hot air balloon."

"Thank heaven! Get me out of here!"

"I can't come directly to you. The swing will tangle in the balloon's ropes. You have to open the harness and fall to me."

Say what? "I can't see you." She couldn't see anything but vast, black sky. "I don't know which direction to go."

"It doesn't matter. I'm right beneath you. Unbuckle the harness and let yourself fall."

"Are you *insane?*" Her sweaty fingers dug into the straps. "Never mind, redundant question. *No way!"*

"*Do it.* I'll catch you."

Nausea churned in her stomach. She might hurl all over the Strip anyway. "What if you miss?"

"I won't." His tone was deadly calm. "Kate, listen to me. You feel safe because you have something to hang on to. But what you're clinging to isn't solid. It's broken. Faulty. It can't hold you up much longer. When it breaks, it will fling you into a free fall…in a random direction." His low voice caressed her, wrapped her in a warm cloak of reassurance. "Sweetheart, you have to let go in order to survive."

"I c-cant!"

"You *can.* I won't let you down. I'll catch you, I promise. Trust me enough to let go, Kate."

Oh, God, oh, God, oh, God. Deliberately releasing the harness and plummeting blindly into nothingness warred with every survival instinct she possessed. How did he boldly walk up to bombs every day and unflinchingly stare death in the face?

"C'mon, Kate," he urged. "I've wanted you to fall for me in a big way since we met."

Humor. He coped by using humor. Hey, if you can't beat 'em, join 'em. "O-okay. But if you let me go splat, I'm going to come back and haunt you forever."

"Deal." His laugh was strained. "Now unbuckle the straps and let yourself fall."

Amazing how finding a small shred of humor helped to make the situation less dire. She struggled to get free. Her handicap and suspended weight worked against her. The buckles wouldn't release. The stressed metal groaned, and she pried harder. At last, the catch snicked open, and she hurtled through space.

She didn't have time to say an entire prayer before Liam's arms closed around her. He grabbed her and swung her inside the basket. The balloon dipped sharply, and she gasped.

"I've got you." He adjusted his grip, slid her down the length of his body. Her knees buckled, and he held her tight.

Breathless and shaking, she flung her arms around him and choked back a flood of tears. No use blubbering now.

"Easy." He rubbed her back. "You're all right, Kate."

He was warm, solid, strong. She never wanted to let go. Her emotions were as fragile as the shredded harness. And just as apt to spin her into a deadly free fall.

He opened the burner jets. Flames hissed out, and the balloon drifted skyward. "Great night for a balloon ride."

She strove to regain composure. "W-when did you learn to pilot a hot air balloon?"

"I've never actually flown one, but I've ridden in a balloon race with Grady piloting. Couldn't be simpler. They operate with propane switches—just like a gas barbecue."

"I'm glad I didn't know your amateur status when I was dangling upside down nearly a quarter mile above terra firma."

He eased her into a sitting position and then sat beside her. Their shoulders touched in the small basket, and he had to bend his long legs at the knees. Trembling, she leaned against him. "Where are we headed?"

"As soon as we clear the populated areas, I'll bring her down.

Until then, we fly where the wind takes us." He held out his hand. "I brought your purse. Pass the phone, please."

"Who are you calling?"

"Air O'Rourke." He dialed. "Con? Why are you answering Grady's phone? Yeah, I've heard of call forwarding, Neanderthal. I have a message for him." He frowned. "You're *where?*" A huge, goofy grin broke over his face. "Way to go!" He chuckled. "When you come down, inform Grady that we're in a hot air balloon headed northeast. We'll need an extraction. Hang tough, bro."

Still grinning, he hung up. "Bailey passed out, and Con took her to the E.R. They thought it was the climate." He laughed. "Different kind of heat. I'm going to be an uncle." He slapped his knee. "Man, Mom and Letty, our adopted grandma, are gonna wig out."

She remembered how torn she'd felt when she'd discovered Aubrey was on the way. The news had been bittersweet, heavy on the bitter. His delight was contagious. "Congratulations."

"Yeah. I love rug rats. I want at least half a dozen."

Then he must anticipate eventually making a commitment. Maybe he was just waiting for the right woman. A lump formed in her throat. Obviously, he hadn't found her yet. "That's pretty ambitious. Maybe you should start with one and work your way up." He'd be a great dad. Loads of fun, but also caring, protective and responsible. Liam's children would never doubt they were loved. At the thought of another woman sharing that special intimacy with him, her heart ached. Was she destined to be always on the outside, looking in on the happiness of others? "What about Murphy? Won't he be jealous?"

"Nah, he adores kids. He'll be a big ole mama sheepdog and herd them into line." His green eyes sparkled, and she wished him that much joy always. She longed to be the one who brought the glow to his face, the light into his eyes. "What about you?"

What she wanted didn't matter. She had to settle for what fate had dished out. And be satisfied. No matter how much it hurt. "We've already had this discussion."

His brows lowered. "Nice step-ball-change, but you know exactly what I meant. You have a lot to give, Kate. You can't tell me that loving someone else's child is enough for you."

She stared down at her leg and saw blood snaking down her calf. "I'm bleeding." *And not just on the outside.*

He started. "How did you get cut?"

"I was hit by shrapnel. It's not bad."

His fingertips brushed her thigh. "It needs to be cleaned."

"I carry antibacterial wipes and bandages in my purse for Aubrey. She's klutzy like her auntie." She dug for supplies. He took the package of wipes, and she scowled. "I can do it."

He ignored her. One big hand closed gently over her thigh, and the other dabbed the blood on her leg.

"Have a hearing problem, Ace?"

His impish grin flashed. "Beg your pardon?"

She winced as the antiseptic burned. "Youch! Have mercy!"

"Sorry." He pursed his full lips, bent and blew softly on the wound. "Better?"

Pain was displaced by tingling warmth. Substituting one torture for another. *Better* was relative. "Sort of."

He carefully positioned two cartoon bandages over the cut. His concerned green gaze examined her from head to toe. He gently raised her arm. "Your shoulder is bleeding, too."

"It's fine."

"Now you sound like a SWAT cop." He chuckled. "Turn around." Not that she had a choice. His insistent hands on her shoulders positioned her back to him. He shifted behind her, and the zipper on her dress hummed. He skimmed the black linen down her arm, baring her shoulder. "Does it hurt?"

"Not yet." The adrenaline thrumming in her system dulled the pain. Cool wetness stroked her shoulder blade, followed quickly by the sting. She flinched, and Liam's breath immediately feathered over her skin. Though his caress was as warm as the desert breeze, she shivered.

His tender fingers smoothed adhesive strips on her shoulder. She tipped her head back, soaked up the reassuring heat from his body, breathed in his clean, woodsy scent.

His fingers combed through her tangled hair. The gentle massage felt like heaven. "Sure you're okay?"

He felt like a safe haven. If only she could curl up in his arms and ride out life's storms. He'd stayed steadfastly by her side through the entire, horrible ordeal today. Constantly put himself in harm's way to protect her. But was it the *illusion* of safety, like the damaged harness? She trusted him with her well-being. *Could* she trust him with her heart?

Or was he another person who would eventually let her fall?

She blurted out the truth. "I have no idea."

Vivid neon colors glowed below, city noises silenced by distance. Stars glittered overhead. The basket swayed in the desert breeze, ropes gently creaking. Peaceful moments were so rare, she could count them on one hand. She soaked in contentment, like the desert soaked in rare, precious raindrops. Snuggled close and steeped in quiet companionship, they floated through the air in a serene waltz.

If only the dance would never end.

Liam gathered her hair to one side and zipped up her dress. His fingers curled around her neck, and he leaned forward and brushed a soft kiss across her nape. "Kate?" His murmur tingled down her spine. "We started something two years ago. Don't you want to see how the story ends?"

She turned to face him. "I know how it ends. With you angry and disillusioned, and me with a broken heart." She released a slow, sad sigh. "Armageddon."

"That's bullcrap."

The waltz was over. Time to pay the piper. He'd finally recognized her handicap. She was obligated to complete the reality check. "I'm not capable of sustaining a relationship. I'm not just physically disabled. I'm emotionally disabled."

His forehead creased. "Translate that into guy-speak."

"My ability to trust has been damaged. I don't trust anyone. And I…I'm…" It was hard beyond belief to confess her failings to this warm, open, sexy man. But if she didn't, he might have expectations she'd only disappoint. "I'm…frigid."

Shock blanked his features. His mouth opened and closed several times before words emerged. "I've held you, kissed you. Made love to you." He snorted. "No way in *hell*."

"You don't understand." She shook her head. "I…I'm all right at the beginning. But I can't finish what I start."

Anger stamped out his bewilderment. "Some impatient jerk has been feeding you a line, sweetheart."

"It's true." She ducked her chin, wouldn't meet his gaze.

"Kate, you are warm, vibrant and responsive."

"No." Tears welled in her eyes. "I'm cold and dead inside."

He swore. "Honey, look at me." He cupped her face in his hands. "I don't know who's made you so confused. But there is no such thing as a frigid woman—just incompetent men."

"Well, the only man I've really been with is *you.*"

Horror rammed a spiked fist into his gut. He couldn't speak. Couldn't breathe. How could he have been so stupid, so insensitive? So freaking *clueless.* "That's why you ran," he whispered. "I rushed it. I hurt you. Scared you." He'd rather be gelded than have caused her that kind of damage. He went hot and then cold, fought the urge to be sick. "Words aren't adequate, but I'm sorry. I'll find a way to make it up to you. To fix it."

She gasped. "No, Liam!" She rose to her knees, gripped his shoulders. "It wasn't you. I had a bad experience before."

"Stop trying to salvage my feelings. I know damn well I was your first. And you said I was the only one." He clenched his jaw. "I should be shot."

"Now you listen to *me.*" She shook him. "I didn't go through with it before. With the other guy."

He battled for footing in the eye of the hurricane. Rage at himself. Fear for her. A blast of relief that her distress wasn't his fault. "Tell me what happened."

She stared at the horizon. "I've been geeky all my life. Unlike my pretty, popular sister, I never dated much."

"What was *wrong* with those guys?"

"Most of them were afraid of intelligent, 'artsy' women."

"I would have dated you in a hot second. I happen to love smart, creative women." Of course, he hadn't realized it until he'd met Kate. He'd been content with superficial party girls until she'd come along. He hadn't known what he was missing.

"People bandy that word around all the time, don't they? Like, 'I love chocolate.'"

Torn, he hesitated. Though he longed to tell her how he felt, she didn't want to hear it right now. As leery as she was about emotional involvement, she'd leap out of the balloon. He had to disarm her fears as carefully as a ticking time bomb. Or his hopes and dreams would get blown straight to hell.

She continued. "I was totally naive, a disaster waiting to happen. And boy, did it ever." She grimaced. "Shortly before the dog attack, I attended a presentation at the restoration firm I worked for on reducing ecological harm from artists' chemicals. The man who gave it invited me to lunch, and we started dating. Before long, I thought I was madly in love with him."

So, she'd once believed herself capable of love. A cautiously positive sign. "You *thought?*"

"In hindsight, I was more in love with his attention and compliments than him. But after a lifetime of coming in last to my sister, I was starving for it. Stupid, I know. *Now.*"

"When you're mired in a deeply emotional situation, it's tough to step back and analyze."

"Exactly my point." She frowned. "After a few months, he asked me to marry him, but I wanted to wait. He insisted my qualms resulted from poor self-image, and he could help. When I got hurt, he was there for me one hundred and ten percent."

"Good, he stepped up to the plate."

"At first, it was great. I was terribly wounded, physically *and* mentally. Family support was sporadic, and I clung to him. He urged me to marry him, and I agreed. I was so relieved he still wanted me—even with an ugly deformity. Who else would?"

He touched her cheek. "I do, Kate."

"A temporary bout of lust. It will fade in time."

The cynicism in her eyes lanced his heart. He swore. "Time will prove you wrong."

Her lips trembled, and she pressed them firmly together—as if she wanted to accept his challenge, but didn't dare take the risk. "Do you want to hear the rest?"

"You know I do."

"After I got out of the hospital, his concern became overbearing. He treated me like a helpless cripple. We had a huge fight." Lost in the past, she absentmindedly rested her hand on his thigh, and his muscles tightened. "I was devastated. The next day, he sent a lavish bouquet of flowers and an invitation to a 'romantic makeup dinner' at his apartment."

"Smooth."

"Very. One thing led to another, and we ended up in bed."

His stomach cramped. The thought of her with another man made him want to tear the guy's limbs off and feed them to him.

"Our misunderstandings kept compiling, like a car crash on the freeway that expands into a massive pileup. My scars bothered him more than he admitted. He didn't say anything, but I saw the disgust in his eyes when my arm brushed against him."

Liam covered her hand with his and gave her fingers a gentle squeeze. "He's an idiot."

"*I* felt like the idiot. It was like a switch flipped inside me and shut everything down. I couldn't go through with it. He was hurt and angry."

He battened down his rapidly rising temper. "Shallow, stupid *and* selfish. Not a winning combo."

"And yet he insisted he still wanted to get married. Believe me, I didn't need more pity. I got plenty from friends and coworkers." She sighed. "I questioned his motives. We had another fight, and I yelled that I didn't need a mercy…um…" She flushed. "Anyway, I threw his engagement ring in his face and slammed out in a righteous huff."

"Good for you."

"No, I reacted emotionally, instead of acting logically." She scowled again. "He may have tried his best to adjust to my injury, but wasn't capable of accepting it. The scars are ugly even after they've faded. They were *really* horrifying at first. Freddy Kruger had nothing on me."

His heart fisted. "Nothing about you is ugly, honey."

"Don't blow sunshine up my skirt. I have twenty-twenty vision." When he started to argue, she jumped in. "Anyway, I went back to apologize the next day. By then, I knew I couldn't marry him. I wasn't sure whether it was him or me, but I had too many doubts. However, he'd stuck by me through an incredibly difficult time. I owed him a civilized discussion."

"You were more forgiving than I would have been."

"You have the most generous heart I've ever known." She gave him a wobbly smile. "He wouldn't let me in. He told me at the front door he'd realized overnight that I was right. We'd stayed together for the wrong reasons. That it was over, and he was fine with it."

"He was still torqued at you and trying to get even."

"Oh, no, he couldn't get rid of me fast enough. 'Bye now, and have a nice life.'" She drew a quivering breath. "Remember when I said I'd also had that gut-deep 'something's very wrong' feeling? That's when it hit. Right before the woman in his bed came to the door. My sister."

His temper spiked hot and fast. As if she hadn't suffered enough. "Cheating bastards!"

"Sis treated men like Kleenex. Use and dispose." She struggled for control. "After I'd gone home upset, she'd run right over to 'console' him. Maybe my actions pushed him into her arms. Or maybe he *did* want revenge. Or perhaps they simply got carried away like they claimed. But Janine got what she always wanted—whatever I had at the time."

"I'm sorry." He pulled her into a hug. "You didn't deserve that, Kate. Any of it." He gritted his teeth. "Drawing and quartering is too good for them."

She gave a deliberate shrug, but her shoulders were stiff. "Back then, it ripped my heart out." She took a trembling breath, and then determinedly jutted her chin. "But it's water under the bridge. We've all moved on with our lives."

Maybe so, but she still suffered the consequences. Still lived with pain and doubt. "One incident doesn't make you frigid, sweetheart."

"But the same thing happened with you. I...switched off without warning. I froze."

"Yeah, and we'd just met. It was your first time, and whether you'll admit it or not, something else was going on with you that night. Give yourself a break. Even the major leaguers get three strikes."

"But I..." She flushed. "Look. I'll be perfectly honest with you. Sex is like figure skating. There's pairs and then there's individual freestyle."

"Ah." He nodded thoughtfully. "Maybe your triple lutz just needs work."

She averted her face. "I'm three for zero."

He scowled. She'd returned his kisses with inherent passion, had trembled with need beneath his touch. "Kate—"

She jerked her head up. "Is it my imagination, or are we sinking? *Fast.*"

He surveyed the landscape. *Crap!* He'd grown so absorbed in her, he'd forgotten to open the jets and heat the air. That wasn't like him. He normally multitasked with ease.

Kate's confession burned in his thoughts as he pulled open the parachute valve at the top of the balloon to slow their decent. Her struggle with trust was now painfully clear. Could he help her overcome her past, so they could have a future?

It was the most difficult, important challenge he'd faced.

The basket bumped to earth, bounced and then settled. His shoulders squared in resolve. He'd always loved a challenge. He was the guy to blow her faulty theory right out of the water.

As he helped Kate climb out, a chopper roared overhead. Grady, ever pushing the envelope. The chopper whirred down, kicking up a sandstorm. The aircraft's lights illuminated the desert. The passenger door opened, and Murphy bounded out and raced toward him. Liam knelt, and Murphy jumped into his arms.

Wriggling, the dog swiped his face with a wet tongue, and then sniffed him. *You've been cozying up to that female again.*

Liam laughed and hugged his partner. "I missed you, too, Murph." Kate made a small sound of distress, and he looked up in time to see her bite her lip and turn away. The day's shattering events must have caught up with her. She'd held together remarkably well during hours of intense pressure.

He rose, but before he could go to her, a woman hopped out of the pilot's seat and strode up to them. A big, brawny woman. Sporting long brown pigtails. And wearing a blue gingham dress, white pinafore…and combat boots?

"Yo, Dorothy." Liam stared at his baby brother. "I don't think you're in Kansas anymore."

Grady's gaze flicked to Kate and his dimples flashed. "It's not a flying monkey, but it'll get you where you need to go."

Kate collected herself, and her lovely mouth quirked in a half smile. The woman had grit. One of many admirable qualities. "Did you lose your ruby slippers and your munchkins?"

"Damn hard to pilot a chopper in high heels." Grady snickered. "But never fear, darlin', all munchkins are present and accounted for."

Liam arched a brow. Some secret project Grady and Zoe had been co-conspirating. "What in hellfire are you up to now?"

"Doing exactly what you ordered. *Blending.*"

"With *whom*?"

"The other 'girls' at La Cage. We're doing lunch tomorrow."

"You were dancing onstage at La Cage? No wonder you couldn't answer your phone."

Grady slid a manila envelope from beneath his arm. "Yeah, but I got your intel." Baby bro's eyes narrowed in an enigmatic look. "You'll need my phone." He handed it over, then turned and bestowed a disarming smile on Kate and offered his elbow. Liam's instincts shot to red alert as Grady escorted her to the chopper. Grady had passed him information that would upset her.

Liam tore open the envelope. Fear and fury whirled inside him as he examined the contents. Disheartened, he scrubbed a weary hand over his face. Why couldn't Lady Luck cut him a break? After tonight, Kate might hate him forever. A heavy sigh escaped as he lifted the phone and dialed.

Seated in the Mustang speeding through downtown Vegas, Kate glanced at Liam. "You've been uncharacteristically subdued since Grady picked us up. Is something wrong?"

Let me count the ways. "I have to go to work. I'm putting you in a safe house with Alex."

"Why? What's happened?"

You don't want to know. And I want to tell you even less. "Try to get some rest."

"Fine, keep me in the dark," she huffed. "But drop me at the hospital, so I can check on Aubrey. I won't be able to sleep, anyway." When he hesitated, she frowned. "The FBI agents are there, and Daniel usually hangs around at night."

"All right." He borrowed her phone once more to request that a

Fed meet her at the door. When the Mustang pulled up at the hospital, the agent strode out and waited on the sidewalk.

Liam turned to her, harsh lines of stress carved in his handsome face. "When I'm done, we have to talk."

Resignation coiled around her heart. They'd disarmed the bombs, and ended the stalker's game. An arrest must be imminent. Liam had done his duty. Was it time for the big brush-off? She firmed her chin. Not like she hadn't foreseen it. Or expected anything else. But she couldn't stop the tears that blurred her last view of him as he drove away.

Upstairs, Aubrey cried and fretted. A frazzled Daniel was pathetically glad to see her. They quieted the little girl, and then Daniel took his laptop to the lobby for an overseas teleconference. She felt sorry for him. Even exhausted, he still had to squeeze in work between a sick child and demanding wife.

Kate trudged to the cafeteria for a badly needed mocha. She chose a table in the corner and gulped the hot, sweet brew. Still no word from Liam. It was gonna be a long night.

Cell calls were allowed from the cafeteria, and she phoned Etienne. He was a night owl, and would be hitting his stride. "*Bonne nuit, mon ami.* How are the auction preparations going?"

"*Magnifique!* The mess has been banished! That Bailey, she is a wonder woman. I am at home now, verifying the *répondez s'il vous plaîts.* We will be a huge success!"

"Great! Thanks for effort above and beyond, Etienne."

"*Mon plaisir,* my lovely Katherine. When you are a rich and famous celebrity do not forget your lowly assistant's devotion."

She laughed. "I'll buy you that Jag you've been drooling over when you think nobody is looking."

"The scarlet one, *mon coeur.* Did you retrieve the photographs?"

Her spirits rose. If nothing else, she had a faithful friend in Etienne. He cheered her when she was down, encouraged her when she was hesitant and shared her artistic vision. She wouldn't have survived without him. Best of all, he was loyal to a fault. "Not yet, but I have a feeling Liam is hot on a lead."

"The, how you say, hunky Irishman, he is hot under any circumstances, *non?*" He chortled. "Ah, hold on, *ma petite.* Someone is at my door."

"At this hour?" She rolled her eyes. Probably a woman. Female admirers of all ages coveted the handsome young rascal like he was double chocolate fudge cake.

He set the phone down, and his bootsteps tapped across the floor. She smiled. Her assistant loved those crazy, pointy-toed boots.

A bang echoed, and she jumped. *What was that?* Amid shouts and thundering footsteps, Etienne screamed rapid-fire, unintelligible French. A sharp, short explosion rang out, and she gasped. *A gunshot?*

Etienne's screams abruptly cut off. Her heart stopped. "Etienne!" she shouted. "Are you all right?"

A door slammed. Ominous silence hummed over the line. "Etienne!" she yelled. "Answer me!"

Had the stalker gotten to him? *Why* had she tried to protect him by keeping it from him? Her heart galloped frantically as distant footsteps approached. A scraping noise sounded as someone picked up the phone. "Mr. Duplais can't talk right now."

She knew that voice. *"Liam?"* Icy horror stole her breath. *"What have you done to Etienne?"*

Chapter 14

2:00 a.m.

"*Kate?*" Liam's throat tightened. Damn! Had his last chance for a future with her just imploded? "I'm sorry you had to find out like this. I'd planned to tell you in person. Afterward."

"*What* is going on?"

"We…the SWAT team just arrested Etienne for stalking you." He winced. "And international terrorism."

"What?" she gasped. "Is he okay? I thought I heard a shot."

"We tossed in a smoke bomb and a flash bang. He's fine."

"Of course. It's only a bunch of Kevlar-suited, machine gun-packing warriors against one twenty-two-year-old French artist."

"Standard procedure. We aren't always sure what type of weapons or how many suspects are on the premises."

He heard her teeth grinding. "There is no way Etienne is a stalker *or* a terrorist. You've made a terrible mistake."

"You don't know all the facts. We have evidence—"

"I don't care, you're wrong! I'm coming down there!"

"*No.* Stay put. You can't see him. And until we find out if he has accomplices, you're safer with the FBI agents."

"It's *not him.* And he forgets English when he's flustered."

Hellfire, he was in for it now. "Ah...*je parle français.*"

A short, ominous silence ticked past. "You lied to me."

"I didn't say I couldn't speak French." He looked up as a team of Feds began to bag evidence. "Etienne was on the short list as a suspect from the beginning. I'd hoped he might slip up and say something he thought I didn't understand."

"What else have you been keeping from me?"

"Parlo italiano." He paused. *"Y español."*

"Very helpful, damn you!" Her fury vibrated over the line, scorched his ear. "Is Hanson involved?"

He hesitated again. "Yeah. He has to be."

"I will *not* allow that storm trooper to railroad my friend into prison! I am coming to the police station!"

"You can't see Etienne until after the interrogation. I'll make sure his rights are protected. You have to trust me, Kate."

"You didn't tell me you were going to arrest my friend." Hurt edged her rage. "You've been lying to me all along."

"I couldn't divulge classified intel." She was reasonable and intelligent. When she saw the evidence, she'd understand. *He hoped.* "And the language deal was actually a sin of omission."

"Don't juggle semantics with me." She inhaled unsteadily. "If you let them hurt Etienne, I will *never* forgive you."

He admired her loyalty, even when he was taking the fallout. "You know better. I'll see that he gets a fair shake."

"I don't know anything anymore." Desperation painted her quiet reply. "I feel so helpless."

"I understand. I've been where you are." Betrayal was always a cold shot to the heart. She thought *he'd* betrayed her. Later, she'd be forced to face the stinging truth about her friend. She'd experienced far too much treachery in her life.

After Etienne's final stab in the back, she might never be willing to trust anyone again.

Sorrow rode heavily on his shoulders. "I'm sorry, Kate." Damn, he wanted to be with her, needed to comfort her. But he had to do his job. "I have to be at the station when they bring him in. I'll call you when I can."

Ninety minutes later, Liam paced in front of the desk where Etienne was seated. He'd figured the volatile kid would break in the first quarter hour. Etienne was shaken, but firmly engaged in denial mode. The interrogation had been conducted in French, with the Feds observing outside. When Liam was done, he'd have to translate for *them.* "It'll go easier if you tell the truth."

Etienne groaned. "I have told you the truth."

Liam pinned him with his gaze. "'Elvira' told an undercover officer that a man with a French accent and long blond hair hired 'her' this afternoon to create a diversion at the hotel. The Frenchman met her in a dark hallway at the club and kept his face in the shadows. Nobody remembers seeing you at the hotel during that time period, and you have no alibi."

"I was in the storeroom unpacking the photographs." He waved his wounded hand. "That is when I scraped the knuckles."

Liam fanned out the pictures Kate had taken from the car. The blurry close-ups showed long blond hair protruding beneath a black visored motorcycle helmet. "Are you sure it wasn't when you wrecked your bike during this high-speed pursuit?"

"That is my Triumph, but it is not me driving."

"You didn't report it stolen. Yet investigators found the damaged bike under a tarp in your garage. Explain that."

Eitienne gave a very Gallic shrug. "It was not me."

"But you don't refute that this..." Liam threw down more photos—wired by Interpol. "*Is* you, chatting with a leader of *Les Hommes de la Mort,* the European terrorist group." Etienne appeared much younger in the photos and his crew cut hair was dark brown. "It *is* you stuffing a backpack into a locker at a subway terminal in London that was bombed an hour later. This *is* you snapping photos on a train platform in Barcelona the day before the commuter line was derailed and fourteen people died."

"*Oui,* many years ago. I was orphaned young and lived on the streets. I was starving and near to prostituting myself to survive.

This man..." He tapped a photo. "Henri Rouchard. He took me in. Fed me. Educated me. I had no idea he was recruiter for a terrorist organization. I did not know he used me. When I discovered it, I ran. Changed my appearance, my name. Stayed far away, for good."

"Why didn't you go to the police?"

"Do you suppose I would have lived to testify, *monsieur?*"

"So you worked under the radar, in construction. Specifically demolition. You're familiar with explosives." Etienne nodded, and Liam frowned and tried a new tack. "Quite a departure from your job for Katherine Chabeau. You just strolled in off the street and she hired you?"

"I approached her with plans for optimizing her market. She recognized my talent and potential, as I recognized hers. She rescued me from a life of mediocrity. She is my angel."

Liam clenched his jaw. Kate might have hired her own personal psycho. He extracted more photos and slapped them in front of Etienne. "These are close-ups of Kate's hands, along with a glowing accolade to her, written by you. Investigators found them in your bedroom."

"*Je ne comprends pas.*" Clearly bewildered, Etienne shook his head. "I have done nothing wrong in this."

"Why did you photograph her? Why did you write about her?"

"My Katherine, she uses a Leica. The company has a promotional campaign showing the hands of their photographers." He sighed. "One sees advertisements using models with faces of unattainable beauty. But it is the hands that make everything happen, *non?* They are the tools of the spirit." Tears glistened in Etienne's eyes. "Who has a more beautiful spirit than Katherine? She thinks her injury makes her some sort of monster. I wished to convince her otherwise."

Liam studied the black and whites. The lighting was exquisite. Showcasing only Kate's hands and the camera, Etienne had managed to capture her dedication and purpose, and the resourceful modifications that overcame her handicap. Her scars were visible, but the shot was angled so they weren't emphasized. The kid was almost as good as Kate. With maturity, he'd be in high demand. The pictures and testimonial revealed something more. Liam held Etienne's gaze. "You love her."

Unfazed, Etienne nodded. *"Oui."*

Liam's jaw tightened. *Objectivity, boyo, or you can kiss the interrogation goodbye.* "How does she feel about you?"

"She is my employer, my mentor, my friend. We are very much alike inside—misfits in this world. Though the bond between us runs deep, she does not wish to step across the line."

"Does that bother you? Does it make you angry?"

"Me, I do not need to force myself on women." What would have been obnoxious bragging from any other guy was blasé fact from Etienne. "There are plenty who are willing."

Liam studied Etienne's golden mane, quicksilver eyes and fit bod. *I'll bet there are, junior.* The kid had I-can-do-you-and-you'll-love-it confidence that drew the opposite sex like a tractor beam. Etienne's artistry with a camera wasn't the only thing that would be in high demand when he matured. He was used to having women fawn over him. Expected it. Was he truly as unconcerned about Kate's rejection as he appeared? "Have you sent her notes and flowers?"

"Non." He offered a roguish smile. "I gift her with Belgian chocolates upon occasion. She adores them."

Kate's fondness for chocolate was no secret. "Have you followed her, checked up on her?" He dealt out the photos Kate had taken from the hospital, showing the blurred silhouette of a man with long blond hair lurking in an alleyway. "Is this you?"

"Why do you ask this?" Blond brows knitted, and then he gasped. "Someone is stalking Katherine?" Bristling, he leaped up. "And you think it is *me?* Her devoted admirer and friend!"

"Sit." Liam leaned across the table. The kid was sharp. And his shock and anger genuine. Despite the evidence, Liam's gut believed him. Those instincts had kept him—and a lot of other people—alive through numerous bomb diffusals. "Has she had a disagreement with anyone lately?"

"Janine," he spat. "Always. She is pure bitch, that one."

A male voice intruded through the intercom. "O'Rourke, telephone. Female caller says it's urgent."

Kate had already called once, worried about Etienne and still wanting to come down. Liam hadn't been able to speak to her. "One sec." He made a split-second decision to toss the kid a grenade and see how adeptly he juggled it. "I doubt her sister has the skill to plant explosives in her car."

"Une bombe?" Etienne's eyes widened. *"Mon Dieu!* You should have said so!" He jumped up again. "Before he became CEO by marrying the bitch, Daniel developed chemical formulas for the company! He possesses both the knowledge and skill!"

Liam's pulse stuttered. "Whoa, that's a big leap in logic. Why would her brother-in-law want to kill her?"

He tsked. "Your investigators are lax, *monsieur.* Daniel was engaged to Katherine, and they had a falling out. They try to make nice for Aubrey's sake, but I do not believe he has ever forgiven her. When he looks at her, there is ice in his eyes."

Liam started. *Daniel* was Kate's ex? Damn, why hadn't she said so? Maybe she was embarrassed her fiancé had married her sister. When the intel hadn't sparked on Tyler, he'd assumed the vibes between them were family tension. He went cold. He'd blithely dropped her at the hospital. So much for gut instincts. They were screaming now. *Too late.* In all probability, he'd delivered her gift wrapped to the psycho intent on killing her. A madman likely angry and desperate after they'd beaten his "game." Time was up, and the stalker knew it. He would make his final move.

Checkmate.

"O'Rourke." The intercom crackled. "Your caller is insistent. She threatened to come down here and kick butt."

Kate! He had to warn her! He sprinted out and grabbed the phone. Murphy twitched his ears from his prone position beside the door. "Kate...listen. Have the FBI agents detain—"

"Liam, this is Zoe."

"*Zoe?* I'll call you back." He started to hang up.

"Wait! You need to hear this. It's about Daniel Tyler."

The hair on the back of his neck rose. "Spill it. *Fast.*"

"It was buried deep, but I followed a string of leads and hit the jackpot. Tyler has pulled off an identity switch, complete with dental records and fingerprints. His parents didn't die in a car crash, their car was firebombed. His foster parents died in a suspicious house fire." She snatched a quick breath. "And his maternal grandfather was *Phillipe Marché!*"

The mad bomber who'd run rampant in Europe before blowing himself sky high. The founding father of *Les Hommes de la Mort!* Adrenaline spiked. "Thanks! Gotta go!"

He punched in Kate's cell number. It rang eight times. *Crap!* He called dispatch and asked to be connected to the hospital. *C'mon!* His boot tapped a rapid tattoo as he was transferred to the fifth floor nurses' station. He said it was a police emergency and asked for Kate.

After an interminable wait, someone picked up. "I'm sorry," a female voice said. "Ms. Chabeau just headed to the elevator with her brother-in-law. They said they were meeting you."

The familiar sensation of drowning constricted his lungs. "Get the agents guarding Aubrey and have them detain Mr. Tyler."

"I'll try. But I'm not sure they can catch up with them."

He didn't waste a reply. Once Daniel lured Kate out of the hospital, Liam would never find her. He slammed down the receiver and spun on the officers clustered outside interrogation. His brothers weren't among them. Con and Aidan had returned to their wives after the bust. Knowing Grady, he was bungee jumping off Hoover Dam. "Send a black and white to the hospital—no lights or sirens! Detain Tyler, Daniel Ellis on suspicion of attempted murder, arson and terrorist activities. Dark blue Ford Five Hundred, get his plate number from dispatch. Consider him armed and dangerous." He thrust out his hand. "Phone and weapon." The group stared. "Toss me a friggin' phone and weapon! *Now!*"

A slender redheaded female detective threw him a flip phone, which he shoved in his pocket. Her 9 mm sailed through the air next. He thrust the gun into his waistband. "Murphy, come!" With the dog loping at his heels, he tore out of the station.

He broke every traffic law in existence and sped along the shoulder most of the way. He cruised the hospital's front parking lot. An empty police car was parked at the E.R. Apparently, lights and sirens trumped old-fashioned horsepower.

He pulled up behind it and downshifted. His peripheral vision caught movement, and he swiveled. A dark blue Ford nosed out of the parking garage and entered traffic. A man and a woman were inside. He verified the license number. Daniel and Kate.

Liam wheeled through the turnaround. Staying three cars behind, he drove with one hand and dialed with the other. He wasn't taking any chances where she was concerned.

Baby brother connected on the sixth ring. "Yo."

"Grady!" he barked. "Get your bird in the air and track me. I'm in the Mustang, tailing a dark blue Ford Five Hundred east on the twentieth block of Flamingo Road. Pull the uniforms out of the hospital and get their asses on the road. Mobilize SWAT and the bomb squad. I'm calling from..." He keyed up the screen and recited the cell number. "Stand by. I'll be in touch." He hung up and glanced at Murphy, on alert in the passenger seat. "Let's hope this is much ado about nothing, partner."

Unfortunately, his churning gut didn't believe it.

Liam kept his gaze fixed on the blue Ford. Tracking a dark car at night through an unfamiliar city wasn't his idea of kicks. He glanced in the mirror. Without backup. His fingers clenched on the wheel. If Daniel lost him, Kate was dead.

Kate glanced at Daniel's relaxed profile as he navigated an unfamiliar street. "This isn't the way to the police station."

"I'm thinking of buying and remodeling a casino as an investment. I was hoping you'd take a look. With your artistic eye, you're the best judge of potential."

"At this hour?" She frowned. "Besides, Liam asked you to bring me to see Etienne." She'd been in the elevator when Liam had phoned the nurses' station, and Daniel had taken the call. "I've been under Hanson's hammer and wouldn't wish it on my worst enemy. Who knows what they've done to him?"

He made another turn. "It'll only take a few minutes. I met an architect and designer on site this morning for proposals. When the hospital phoned about Aubrey, I left without the papers. They weren't cheap, and I need to pick them up." The car bumped down an alleyway, the interior eerily dark. They'd been the only car on the road for ten minutes. "Nobody in the family cares about creative projects. I'd appreciate your input."

His entreaty made her squirm. When Janine had announced her intent to marry him a month after the breakup, their father had promoted him to the top. And Kate had understood Daniel's true ambitions. He wanted to run the fast-growing company, and didn't care which sister he had to marry. He hadn't been able to push Kate to the altar, but Janine was all-too willing. When Kate had expressed reservations, the family had accused her of jealousy. A nasty scene she didn't care to repeat. She was the last person who wanted to collaborate with Daniel. He and Janine were manipulators, and she kept her distance. However, for Aubrey's sake, she always made the effort to be civil. "Make it quick."

He parked in front of a rambling, dilapidated building. She slid out of the car. The run-down area was sparsely populated and surrounded by warehouses and factories. What was he thinking? "You'll never convince customers to come down here."

"You'll understand when you see my plan."

Uneasiness crept over her. In spite of the warm night, she shivered. Suddenly, she did *not* want to go inside. Maybe the building was haunted. He tapped a keypad and opened the door. She backed away from the menacing shadows. "I've had a long day. I think I'll wait in the car. I'll see it another time."

"The deadline is tomorrow. This is your last chance."

Goose bumps prickled her arms. Okay, he'd officially creeped her out. Something in his mild tone was…off. What was up with that? She belatedly regretted not asking an FBI agent to accompany them. But she hadn't wanted to compromise Aubrey's protection. She shook her head. "Decide without me, then."

"You'll want to come inside, Katherine."

She took another step back. "Wrong."

A loud snuffle made her jerk her head up. A huge dog prowled around the corner. The brownish-black beast had a square head and massive jaws, and his shoulders reached her rib cage. A spiked metal collar protected a muscular neck as thick as her waist. He saw her and stopped, blocking her way to the car. His head lowered, and he rumbled a deep, menacing growl.

Heart racing, she stumbled through the doorway's yawning black maw. Any ghost lurking inside was preferable to that monstrosity.

Daniel waved. "Champion discourages the bad elements." His smile sent chills down her spine. "I paid a fortune for him. He was bred as a fighting dog, and has killed every opponent."

Bile stung her throat. "That's awful!"

"He gets the job done." He followed her inside and shut the door. Suffocating blackness closed around her like a giant fist. Daniel grasped her elbow. "This way."

She couldn't face the beast outside. She was forced to let Daniel lead her down the dark, twisting hallways, until she was completely lost. Casinos were built without windows and a purposefully confusing floor plan. If gamblers couldn't see outside, they had no sense of time passing. Making them wander through mazes of rooms enticed them to stay longer, spend more.

Daniel squeezed her elbow. "I have a present for you."

An unseen threat beat against the edges of reason, as formless as a crow battling a reflection in a window. Daniel was family, for Pete's sake. Yet she couldn't shake the foreboding.

To heck with reason, she wanted Liam. Kate slid her hand inside her purse. Her last call had been to the police station. She pushed the send button and forced a casual tone. "Where are we, Daniel?" She'd reveal her location through conversation. Liam would figure it out in a heartbeat, and come for her.

Daniel opened a door, and lights loomed ahead. Light should have helped, but fear had trapped her in icy claws. They turned a corner and entered a huge room. Slot machines hunkered on the floor, glowing eerily. A ladder canted against a wall, flanked by a toolbox and two large empty metal cages. More dogs? She shuddered. Black moiré silk-draped booths surrounded the perimeter. A single calla lily in a crystal vase speared from the center of each table. More black moiré smothered the walls.

She was locked in a giant coffin.

Panic bled through her. Her pulse pounded as she saw the spotlights angled from the high ceiling. Each cold, white eye was frozen on a picture. Her heart stopped. Her photos!

Daniel's lips thinned in a smug line. "I went to a lot of trouble to prepare this gift for you. Do you like it?"

Confusion tangled with horror. This had to be a freakish misunderstanding. Maybe he'd found her missing photos and this was his odd way of returning them. Ordinary men didn't suddenly turn into monsters. "I d-don't understand."

His face was as scarily impassive as his voice. "You're reasonably intelligent, Katherine. The game is over. You understand the matter at *hand*."

He'd deliberately emphasized the phrase to hurt her. Shock waves thundered, echoed and died, leaving vast, arctic silence. Shaking fear poured into the breach. *Daniel* was the man stalking her? The man she'd almost married. Janine's husband. Aubrey's father. The brother-in-law who'd sat across from her at holiday dinners, who sent flowers to her mother on her birthday. Her stunned mind couldn't comprehend it. Didn't want to accept it.

Daniel was the bomber who had tried to kill her and Liam.

Liam. Kate eased her hand inside her purse again and touched her phone. The unit's reassuring warmth met her chilled fingers. Their conversation was being transmitted to the police station. She only had to stall until the cavalry arrived. "I don't get it at all. Why don't you explain it to me?"

"Nice try." He smiled, but there was no feeling behind the vile gesture. "But it won't do you any good. I've blocked cell signals for a mile around the casino."

She started. "How did you know—?"

"I've watched your every move for over three years. You're nothing if not predictable."

She swallowed dismay. "Liam will find me." Her never-say-die bomb tech wouldn't let her down. She *had* to believe…or she'd wig out. Surviving Daniel's warped agenda required the same technique as surviving his bombs. If she panicked, or lost hope, she was dead. Meanwhile, she'd get out of here. "He'll come."

"Pathetic." His lip curled. "I don't know why I ever saw potential in you."

The retort escaped before she could stop it. "Likewise."

His glare made her go cold. "Don't count on rescue." He extracted a remote from his jacket. "The cops will be too busy picking up pieces of tourists all over the Strip." He stabbed a button…waited…stabbed it again. A scowl distorted his choirboy features. "What the—?"

Pride buffered her shock and fear. "If you're attempting to detonate the device at the Venetian, nice try. But it won't do you any good. We disarmed it."

He raised his head in ominous imitation of the menacing guard dog. "You think you've won." Ice frosted his gaze. "But I will take everything from you." He pointed the remote at the gruesome art gallery and pressed another button. A photo popped, sizzled and then blackened beyond recognition. "Your precious photographs are wired. The entire casino is one huge bomb."

Sick, creeping dread assaulted her, and hot tears pressed behind her eyelids. "Why do you hate me? Why are you suddenly determined to ruin everything that's important to me?"

"When we met, you were pitifully eager for my attention. So malleable. A lump of clay, awaiting a sculptor. Then your accident left you fragile and wounded. Lost. I wanted to save you. Instead, you pushed me away. Turned your back on me."

"*You* didn't want *me,* Daniel. Because of my scars." Scalding anger melted some of her terror. *Good.* Mad was better than scared. She raised her chin. "I saved myself."

"You would have been my greatest accomplishment. But you proved surprisingly stubborn. Annoyingly independent. You improvised a future without me. One you didn't deserve," he spat. "You got a glamorous career and international renown. I got saddled with a whiny, useless wife and a defective kid."

She grabbed the life preserver. "You dote on Aubrey. If the photos are destroyed, she won't get her transplant. No matter how upset you are with me, you'd never endanger her welfare."

"And the Oscar goes to..." He laughed bitterly. "I'm sick of the stench of hospitals. Of maudlin white coats dispensing hundred dollar pills and false sympathy. I don't give a rat's ass about the brat. She's not even mine."

Her jaw dropped. *"What?"*

"Ironic, isn't it? A doctor dropped that bombshell after tissue typing for the transplant. No wonder Janine jumped at my proposal." He grimaced. "I thought I was playing *her,* but your sister one-upped me. I've been forced to act the devoted family man until my plans were set. Between the sick kid and Janine's tantrums, my life has been a living hell. And it's *your* fault."

"Marrying my sister was *your* decision. I'm sorry it's been difficult." She held up a trembling hand. "But none of this is Aubrey's fault. You're the only father she knows. She looks up to you. Depends on you. She doesn't deserve to suffer."

"Collateral damage." His features hardened into a stranger's. "A favor, really. We put down dogs for less." The civilized mask disintegrated, and his vacant eyes revealed the horrifying truth. She faced a cold, amoral entity with no empathy. No conscience. He'd just pretended to be human. Driven only by ego, he felt no compassionate emotions. The embodiment of evil wouldn't be satisfied by destroying her possessions.

He planned to destroy *her.*

Dizziness threatened to swamp her, and she sucked in a deep, shaky breath. *Hold it together.* Keep him talking. Ego was his sole gratification and his greatest weakness. *Challenge it.* "The nurses know I left with you. Liam will never stop looking for me." *Dead or alive.* "He'll nail you. You *might* get your 'revenge' but you'll spend the next twenty years on death row."

He shook his head. "Thanks to electronic wizardry, 'Liam' called and requested I bring you to him. The nurse will verify it. Phone records will confirm it. I'll be back at the hospital with a rock-solid alibi while you and your lover are burning alive. After I'm done with you, you'll welcome death."

Fear tightened her chest. Daniel reeked confidence. "Like Liam will let you torture and kill us. Get real."

"He *will* come for you. After I invite him in—sans weapon—to save your life. Then I'll test him. How long do you think it will take him to break? To beg?" Triumph gleamed in his eyes. "He'll be revealed as your stalker—postmortem. Another tragic example of a man killing his obsession and himself."

Stay calm! Liam was too smart to fall for a blatant trap. Unless he lost all reason at Daniel's threats against her. He wouldn't… would he? She gulped. "That's totally implausible."

I've done my research. People know he's been obsessed with you since your one-night stand. He searched for you for months. A book opened to one of your photos sits on his coffee table. His jealousy caused him to arrest your admin assistant. The bulk of his evidence against Etienne will be revealed as manufactured and planted."

"*You* set Etienne up to be arrested! You jerk!"

Daniel smiled, hideous and empty. "Chemical residue will be found in O'Rourke's hotel room and car, as well as components for making the notes. One final note will declare he coerced you into disarming bombs in hopes he'd impress you by 'saving you.' But after you refused his advances, you had to die together."

"*Nobody* will believe that." At least Liam's brothers wouldn't. But she had the dire suspicion *her* family might. And the authorities, presented with tidy evidence wrapped in a black funeral bow, wouldn't waste time or manpower to search further.

"The fire will destroy all evidence of torture. They only have to believe until the kid expires. Then my unstable, grief-stricken wife will 'commit suicide.'" He sighed. "The mourning husband will leave for a new start in Europe." He deliberately set the remote on a table. "Powerful friends will give me a new identity and financing in exchange for my formula. Which I used your father's company and resources to develop."

The scope and cunning of his gruesome plan made her queasy. "You trust terrorists to help you? And you call me pathetic."

He stalked toward her. "Why didn't you just love me back, Katherine? Everything would have turned out differently."

She retreated and he advanced, hunting her. "You're obsessed with me. You want to control me. That's not love." It hurt to breathe. To speak. "But it's not too late. Nobody has to get hurt. We can just walk away and forget this ever happened."

"*Forget?*" He scowled. "You humiliated me. Wasted valuable time. Cost me years of needless effort. I'm not walking away." He lunged at her. "And neither are you."

Chapter 15

4:00 a.m.

Heart pounding, Kate spun and ran, zigzagging between slot machines. *Where was the door?* With the walls drenched in black silk and blacker shadows, she couldn't tell.

Daniel's harsh breaths rasped behind her. Ducking under the ladder, she shoved, and it clattered to the floor.

Please, slow him down.

"You have nowhere to run, Katherine." Daniel taunted from close behind her. Too close. "Nowhere to hide."

Her frantic gaze wheeled around the room, searching for a way out. For a weapon. Fear rose in a choking wave. Flight was impossible. Which left fight. Desperate, she turned and swung the only weapon she had, her purse.

The unexpected attack stopped him short. But before she could run again, he deflected the blow and caught her wrist. Laughing, he wrenched her arm. "You have more guts than I thought." Her hand went numb, and her purse thudded to the floor. He yanked her against him. "You reject *me,* run from *me,* but you're giving yourself to that cop, you bitch."

"No!" Terror screamed through her as she struggled to break his merciless hold. "Only once—the night Aubrey was born and my therapist told me I'd never regain the use of my arm! I'd lost you, I'd lost my career. I'd lost *everything.* I only slept with him because I was grieving and in shock."

"You both have to pay." He shoved her and she fell backward into a booth. He loomed over her, his eyes merciless. "Like my parents. My foster parents. And *Grand-père,* when he outlived his usefulness." He crushed full-length on top of her. "It's my obligation. My right. He taught me that when I was seven."

His fingers fisted in her hair and yanked her head forward. Pain stung her eyes, blurred her vision. He slammed his mouth down on hers. She sank her teeth into his lip and raked her nails across his cheek. He reared back, and she punched the heel of her hand into his nose. "You have no right!" she yelled.

Daniel swiped his palm across his face, and his fingers came away bloody. He spat a filthy name at her, captured both her hands in one of his and pinned them above her head. He slapped her. "Everybody has to pay." His hand slithered down her neck and crushed her breast in a punishing squeeze.

She screamed and tried to knee him. "Get off me!"

He forced her legs apart and held her down. She bucked and fought, but he was too strong. "The more you fight, the more I like it." He was breathing hard, his face tight with lust. "I'll teach you a lesson you'll never forget. And I'm going to make it hurt." He shoved her dress up, clawed at her panties. "When your cop arrives, he'll find you naked and used, and covered with my marks. He'll know you're my property."

A sob choked her. *Oh, God, she'd rather die.*

"No, you bastard," Liam snarled above them. "*You're* due a lesson." He yanked Daniel up. "And the teacher is in the house."

Daniel yelped. Stunned, Kate struggled to sit up. In a distant room, canine growling erupted into a brutal dogfight. Gunmetal flashed in Liam's hand. Something hissed. A shot rang out and a bullet slammed into the wall. Liam choked and flung an arm in front of his face. He stumbled, and Daniel chopped his wrist and wrenched the gun free. He threw it across the room, and then snatched the remote from the table.

Coughing and gagging, Liam lunged, and Daniel canted backward. He clutched the remote in one hand and a can of Mace in the other. "I wouldn't. My remote has a dead man's trigger, just like a grenade. I drop it and the entire place blows."

Liam froze, and Daniel cocked his head, listening to the vicious dogfight. "The guests are all here. Time to party."

Kate's throat closed up. The hellish dogfight revived her worst memories and fears. But this time, fear for Murphy's life overrode all else. He'd come to her rescue, and was in mortal danger. She couldn't help him. Nor could Liam.

Coughing violently, Liam scrubbed at his face. Moisture flooded his eyes as he squinted at Kate. "You all right?"

Shaking and cold and sick, she nodded, grasping for her shredded composure. "You got here in time."

"I can't shoot you without ruining my plans." Sounding perplexed, Daniel shoved the Mace inside his jacket. "I was prepared for your dog. And your violence. But you didn't wait for my invitation. I wasn't done with Katherine."

Liam gritted his teeth. "Be very glad. Now I'm just gonna haul your sorry butt to jail instead of castrating you first."

Daniel blinked. "You were supposed to come *after* I phoned."

"You whack jobs really get off on the planning and the hunt. And hurting defenseless women," Liam growled. "But you're not so hot at improv." His body language shouted aggressive male challenge. "Face me like a real man. If you can."

Daniel turned to face him, putting his back to her. "You were supposed to walk in unarmed, with your hands on your head, and surrender to save Katherine."

"Yeah. I'm gonna crawl in here with my tail tucked between my legs and offer myself up." Liam arched a brow. "Whatever you're on…dial down the dosage."

"Now you get to watch me teach Katherine her lesson." Daniel's shoulders twitched. "She's *mine,* to use and discard."

Kate took deep breaths and fought the urge to throw up.

"You are one sick puppy." Liam's watery glance briefly caught hers, and he casually gestured with the signal he gave Murphy to heel. "But you're out of business. Permanently."

From the gruesome sounds of the death match raging nearby, Murphy was unable to comply. She straightened. The signal was for her. Liam wanted her to follow his lead. Putting Daniel permanently out of business? She was so there.

Daniel jerked his head at the cages. "Get into the crate."

Liam snorted. "I know you're crazy, but do I look stupid?"

Kate eased unsteadily to her feet. Liam was goading Daniel. Distracting him. What did he want her to do?

"One button and this whole place goes," Daniel threatened.

Liam coughed, and then shrugged. "Fine by me."

Daniel's voice rose. "I'm in control here, not you!"

"You're losing control with each passing second. I'm pissing all over your precious plans, and you can't stand it." Liam swiped moisture from his eyes. His glance brushed a vase on the table beside her before staring fixedly at Daniel's forehead. "You've been out in the Vegas sun too long without a hat, Stalker Boy. You're touched in the head."

Got it. Loud and clear. He wanted her to bash Daniel in the head. Happy to oblige. Kate gulped. Did she have time before Daniel unraveled completely and killed them? She took another steadying breath. She had to trust that Liam knew what he was doing by baiting the monster. She stealthily reached for the crystal vase and slowly lifted it off the table.

Daniel waved the remote. "Ready to die, O'Rourke?"

Her movements furtive, Kate removed the lily. She set it on the table, and then smothered the vase in a wad of silk tablecloth and tipped, letting the fabric soak up the water.

"Try me. Hit the button, you cocky little bastard. Let's check in at the Pearly Gates together." Liam smirked. "Oh, wait. You're headed for a more southerly destination."

With the vase gripped in her left hand, she took a careful step. Then another. Liam had the sharpest eye-hand coordination and fastest reflexes she'd ever seen. But choking on the Mace would slow him down. Was he fast enough to grab the remote before Daniel blew them to kingdom come? She looked at Liam, all lean muscle and dangerous menace. Heck, even maced, she'd bet her life on his capable hands any day.

She was about to do exactly that.

She forced herself to tune out the ghastly screams and snarls of the dogs tearing each other apart on the other side of the wall. *Focus.* Palms sweating, she crept closer to Daniel's unsuspecting back. If he turned around…

Daniel stiffened. "*Obey me!* Or I'll—"

She moved behind him and held her breath, waiting for the right moment.

"You'll what? You should have finished using your brain before you donated it to science, whacko," Liam taunted as he subtly shifted closer to Daniel. If she hadn't been watching for it, she wouldn't have noticed. "If you think I'm gonna make it fun and easy for you, you've seen too many movies. I've spent the past fifteen minutes disarming most of your system."

Kate checked. He'd been here fifteen minutes? Had he heard her tell Daniel she'd slept with him in a fit of hopeless despair? She shook her head and crept forward. *Concentrate.*

"Impossible!" Daniel went rigid, his voice shaking with fury. "You don't have the intelligence to destroy my work!"

"What happened to the IEDs at Treasure Island, the Stratosphere and the 'hidden' device at the Venetian?" Liam grinned. "Big Bad Bomber loves manipulating authority. You'll have to get your jollies elsewhere." Outside, chopper blades thwacked overhead, and his grin widened. "Company." He thrust his fingers through his hair, positioning his arm to strike at the remote. "SWAT is about to crash your party. You're done."

"I have both luck and skill on my side." Daniel hissed, his body vibrating with tension.

"There's luck and skill, and then there's payback." Kate raised the vase, and Liam nodded. *"Do it!"*

She smashed the vase on Daniel's head. Crystal shards glittered to the floor, and he grunted and staggered.

Liam lunged for the remote. The men scuffled and jockeyed for control in a macabre, slow-motion tango.

Kate scrambled around the slot machines to the corner where

Daniel had thrown Liam's gun. She flung the ladder aside. The shadows were too murky. She dropped to her knees and groped along the floor. *C'mon!* The weapon had to be here.

On the other side of the wall, the dogfight reached a grisly crescendo. An anguished, mournful howl cut off, and then everything went dreadfully silent. Her stomach pitched. Had Champion scored another defeat? Had he killed Murphy?

"Champion's war cry!" Daniel crowed. "You forgot the Golden Rule of Vegas—the house always wins!"

Neither man would relinquish the trigger. Daniel had it clenched in his right fist, Liam in his left. Liam's grimace was tortured. "Here's your jackpot." He punched Daniel in the face. "And this is for hurting Kate." He punched him again.

A loud bang resounded from the wall, followed by a brilliant flash. Orange flames shot from half a dozen of her photos, which instantly blackened. Acrid smoke snaked to the ceiling. Her breath hitched in horror. One of them must have accidentally pressed a button. Liam hadn't disarmed everything.

Daniel's enraged scream sounded inhuman. "You're ruining all my plans!"

She gave up on the gun and dug in the toolbox. Clutching a thick crowbar, she surged to her feet. By the time she twisted through the slot machine maze, the wall had caught fire. Flames licked up the moiré to the ceiling, and smoke burned her eyes.

The smoke was attacking Liam's eyes and lungs, too. Already compromised by the Mace, his eyes streamed. He was coughing too hard to block Daniel's savage blow to his stomach. Neither man would let go of the remote. Liam doubled over, and the spotlights simultaneously exploded. Flames blasted the ceiling in a crackling sea of red heat. "Kate!" he croaked. "Get out!"

"Not without you!" Brandishing the crowbar, she ran toward him. Embers rained red-hot needles, and fire roared up the silk-draped booth next to her. She swerved and kept running.

"It's spreading too fast!" Liam slugged Daniel in the ribs, dodged and took a hit on the shoulder. "I can take care of myself. *You're a liability. Go!*" As he choked out the demand, the booths burst into flames, ringing the room in fire.

A flaming chunk of debris crashed at her feet, blocking her path to him. Liam jerked his gaze to her, horror in his eyes. Daniel seized the unprotected moment to slam a fist into his jaw. Liam recoiled as bone crunched flesh, and Kate flinched. Liam was right. He couldn't watch her when he needed to save himself. "Heads up," she hollered, and tossed him the crowbar.

She paused long enough to see him catch it on the fly. She'd done all she could. Agony choked her worse than the smothering smoke as she wove a crooked path to the doorway. She was going…but leaving behind her heart.

Wheezing, she battled the stinging smoke and searing heat and floundered into the next room. She stumbled over something and fell. She pushed up on her elbows and came face-to-face with Murphy, prone on the floor. His eyes were closed, his body torn and battered. He must have tried to get back to Liam and collapsed. *"Murphy!"* she called. *"Murphy, wake up!"*

He didn't move. Didn't respond. *Didn't breathe.* Her heart twisted. Liam would be devastated. Tears welled, and she placed a trembling hand on his blood-soaked fur. The valiant warrior had sacrificed his life for hers. "Thank you," she whispered.

Beneath her palm, the dog's side heaved in a slow, labored breath. He was alive! She glanced at the advancing flames. She'd be damned if she'd leave him to roast!

Arms up to protect her face, she dashed through the fiery doorway and charged back into the main room. Flames chased close on her heels. She couldn't see anyone in the hellish inferno. *Liam, where are you?* He hadn't passed her, and she hadn't seen any other way out. Her heartbeat thundered in her ears.

Please, don't let him be trapped.

The blazing barrier was too hot, too fierce to find him. She ripped moiré from a booth and stomped the smoldering edge. She sprinted back to Murphy, spread the fabric beside him and then rolled the limp dog onto the silk. "You weigh a ton, mutt."

Talking to him helped calm her terror, and she alternated between inane conversation and coughing as she dragged the unconscious dog down a black, smoky corridor toward what she hoped was an exit.

What seemed like an eternity later, she rounded a corner and gasped in dismay. She'd trudged in a circle, back to the center of the inferno. She retreated from the heat and dropped her face into her hands. She was lost. Trapped.

She was going to burn to death.

A tear slipped out, then another. *Smart, Kate. Blubber all over the place, maybe that will put out the fire.* Terrified, exhausted, she'd reached her limit. She dropped her hands and slumped against the wall.

Something cold and wet touched her palm. She squeaked and jerked her gaze down. Murphy stood beside her, wobbly, but aware. His warm, reassuring tongue licked the tears off her hand, and he nudged her thigh with his nose, as if pushing her up the corridor. What did she have to lose? "I hope you're a better navigator." She rested her hand on the limping dog's back and let him guide her through the black, smoky abyss.

After another eternity, Murphy led her into a room. She closed the door, shutting out the smoke. There were no windows, but a skylight provided enough illumination to take stock. They were in the kitchen. Another door faced the opposite wall. Kate ran to it and felt the panel, then the doorknob. They weren't hot. She cautiously opened the door and saw a large pantry stuffed with kitchenware and canned food. Her hopes sank.

There was no way out.

"Now what?" She turned back to the dog. Panting heavily, he lay beside the sink. *Think.* She rummaged through drawers and discovered a stack of towels and a few tablecloths. Thankfully, the water still worked. She soaked towels at the tap and then stuffed wet cloths around the door to block the smoke.

The dog's torn flesh was a vivid reminder of her own pain, and compassion welled inside her. She filled a bowl with water and offered him a drink. He couldn't raise his head, and she lifted it for him. His liquid brown eyes looked into hers with empathy and a depth of understanding that jarred her to the core. She'd never again doubt the dog's intelligence and reasoning skills. Or his devotion. He licked weakly at the water, and then dropped his head to his paws. He'd exhausted his energy saving them from the fire.

She located scissors in a utility drawer. Murmuring quiet nonsense, she used towels and strips of the moiré to bandage

Murphy's bloody wounds. He whimpered a few times, but knew that she was trying to help and didn't snap or bite.

While she worked, the fire's roar grew louder. Smoke crept around the wet towels. Hazy air heated to stifling, and sweat beaded on her forehead. Crouched beside the listless dog, she stared up at the skylight. There was no way to hoist herself up, much less Murphy. Coughing, Kate assessed the room again. She would not passively sit there and die.

Her glance snagged on the walk-in refrigerator. Lights had worked in the main room before the electricity shorted out. If the refrigerator was operational, the heavy steel appliance would be cool, well insulated, and smoke free inside. She jumped up, and flung open the doors. Cool air rushed out. *Yes!*

The gloomy interior appeared empty, except for metal canisters marked with the symbol for hazardous chemicals. Her stomach clenched. Daniel's explosive. She didn't dare remove it. If it didn't stay cool… She pushed aside uneasiness. Once the refrigerator's interior grew hot enough to combust the explosives, she and Murphy would suffocate to death, anyway. "C'mon, Murphy," she coaxed. "Come here, boy."

Murphy whined and struggled to get up, but couldn't. She eased him onto a tablecloth, grabbed the remaining towels and black silk and dragged him into the refrigerator.

She shut the doors, enveloping them in total darkness. The wounded dog needed to stay warm. By feel, she wrapped him in tablecloths and the silk. Shivering from the sudden drop in temperature, she spread a pallet of towels for him to lie on. She draped a towel around her shoulders and sat beside him. He lifted his head and rested it in her lap.

She stroked his soft fur. "Liam said the SWAT team is coming," she reassured him, and herself. "They'll call the fire department."

Misery seared her. Liam hadn't had Murphy to guide him. *Did he make it out?* Shaking, she huddled with the weak dog, sharing body heat. Or had he become disoriented and died in the blaze?

Alone in the cold blackness with a dying companion, she had nothing to do except torment herself with the cruel image. The barriers around her heart shattered into shards of ice. A sob burst free. Aubrey's chances for a future had burned up with the photos. Everything was gone. Had she lost Liam, too? Hugging Murphy, she sobbed out her sorrow.

Had Liam died without ever knowing that she loved him?

Kate had no idea how much time had passed. But the tears had long dried on her cold cheeks before she finally heard clanking and stomping. Numbly, she cocked her head, afraid to believe. Were those voices? "In here," she croaked. "Help!"

The doors swung open and a burly firefighter stared at her in disbelief. "I'll be damned! Are you all right, Miss?"

"Yes." She gestured at the dog, who was barely clinging to life. "But he needs help, fast. Can you carry him?"

"You bet." He lifted Murphy from her lap. Another firefighter helped her up. Her joints were stiff from both cold and trepidation. The firefighter offered to carry her, but she declined. She needed to walk, not be carried like a victim. He stripped off his coat and wrapped it around her, and she stepped out of the refrigerator and into warmth. Trembling, she leaned on his arm as she hobbled through the smoldering, stinking wreckage. The kitchen end of the building was still somewhat intact, but the outer perimeter was a charred shell. If Murphy hadn't led her to shelter, she would have died in the fire.

The man carrying Murphy followed. "The refrigerator was a clever shelter. But I'm glad we found you when we did. If you'd stayed in there, you'd have succumbed to hypothermia or suffocation."

Kate nodded. "I know." She'd considered both options before entering the refrigerator, and during the torturous vigil inside. Falling asleep in the pervasive cold and never waking up was preferable to burning to death. But dead was dead.

The firefighter supporting her patted her arm. "I didn't think we'd find any survivors after we discovered the bodies."

Bodies? Her breath stopped. Her heart stopped. The world stopped. "Wh-who were they?"

"One was a big dog." He grimaced. "The other we'll have to ID with dental records."

She swallowed hard. Willed herself to keep on slogging through the ashes of ruined dreams. *Who had died?* Daniel…or Liam? "D-did you find any others? Anyone who was injured?"

"Afraid not." Devastated, she bit the inside of her cheek to keep from bursting into tears, and he softened. "But we weren't the first responders. Were there others inside?"

"One man." *The man who meant everything to her.* Why had she clung to denial so long? Whey hadn't she told him how she felt? Now she might never have the chance.

"I'll notify the captain." He caught her as she stumbled through the blackened frame of the doorway. "Watch your step."

Bedlam assaulted her as she staggered outside. Choking gray smoke veiled the predawn air with spectral fog. Firemen and cops shouted and ran. Fire engines, police cars and ambulances flanked the burned ruins, harsh red-and-blue lights strobing. Dirty canvas hoses snaked along the asphalt. A steady, mournful drip echoed from the blackened skeleton.

So this was what hell looked like.

She turned to the firefighter behind her. "Take the dog to an ambulance. Maybe a paramedic can help him."

He frowned. "You need to be examined yourself."

"No." She had to find Liam. The ambulances were empty, so she checked each fire truck, each police car. He wasn't there. Starting at the beginning, she looked again. She circled the parking lot, searching every man's face. None was the familiar face she longed to see. She couldn't find his brothers, either. If Liam hadn't made it, they'd be with his body…in the morgue. Her heart labored in her chest, and it hurt to breathe. She did not want to accept the hideous possibility that Daniel had escaped and the ravaged body was Liam's. As wrenching minutes ticked past and she didn't see him, desolation crept over her.

Another grim circle later, she was forced to face the horrible truth. Broken and lost, she clutched the firefighter's coat around herself. Grief slammed into her. Tears she'd thought all cried out spilled down her cheeks.

Liam was dead.

She peered through tears at the ambulances nearly hidden behind the murky smoke. But Murphy was still alive. It was up to her to make sure he got medical treatment. Taking care of his partner was the final thing she could do for Liam.

She trudged toward the ambulances, dodging cops and firefighters. Just ahead, through the wavering haze, she saw a man coming toward her. A tall, broad-shouldered man, with thick dark hair. Her sobs jammed in her lungs, and she squinted, desperate to make out his features. A brief flicker of hope flared…then was snuffed out by dark despair. No, his stride was different. Instead of a confident, graceful lope, the man moved slowly. Painfully. Head down and shoulders slumped.

He walked closer. The smoky curtain parted. He lifted his head, and his face swam into clear view. Kate gasped. Reeled to a halt.

It was the man she never thought she'd see again. The only man she longed to see. *Liam!*

He saw her. He faltered, stumbled, and then his beautiful face creased in a smile. "Kate!" he cried hoarsely. He broke into a run, and scooped her into his arms. *"Kate!"*

Sobbing too hard to reply, she flung her arms around his neck. The coat fell away unheeded, and she hugged him tight. The sun grazed the horizon, flooded the sky with saffron light. His heartbeat thundered against hers, and she kissed his bristled cheek. He was warm. Vital. Alive!

He buried his face in her neck and hugged her tightly in return. "I thought I'd lost you."

"Mm-me t-too. I m-mean y-ou, too," she sobbed.

"Shh." He stroked her hair, rubbed her back. "It's okay. Everything is okay, now." He eased away, cupped her face in his hands. His gaze traveled over her. "You're not hurt?"

"N-no." She shook her head. "Y-you?"

"Minor smoke inhalation. Grady forced an oxygen mask on me for a while. No biggie."

She sniffled, for the first time unashamed of her tears. She had a right to cry. "Where *were* you?"

"Around back, showing my brothers and the investigators where I busted out." His thumbs gently wiped away her tears. "That crowbar saved my life. After I coldcocked Daniel with it, I lugged him away from the fire. I used the crowbar to smash through an outer wall. When I turned back to get him, he was gone. He must have crawled away, thinking he could escape."

She ran her fingers through his silky hair, traced his sculpted cheekbones, his soft lips. She couldn't stop touching him. "The firemen found his body. He didn't make it."

"I know." His voice was raw. "Neither did Murphy."

"Yes, he did! A firefighter brought him out right behind me!"

His green eyes lit up. "Where is he?"

"I think he's in an ambulance." She bit her lip. "He's hurt, Liam. I don't know if—" she couldn't finish. Instead she grabbed his hand. "Let's go find him. He needs you."

Hand in hand, they sprinted to the ambulances. The dog lay motionless on a stretcher inside the vehicle. Grady hovered over him, holding an oxygen mask to the canine's nose. An IV line trailed from a shaved spot on the dog's front leg.

Grady looked up at their approach, his face grave. Liam rushed to Murphy's side, and Grady patted Liam's back. "Easy." He hesitated. "It's bad, bro. His vitals are barely there."

Liam tenderly stroked Murphy's head. "What are you waiting for? Let's get him to the vet hospital."

"I had to stabilize him, or he wouldn't have made it to the hospital. Hop in the back with him." They complied, and Grady slammed the doors and sprinted around to the driver's seat.

Siren blaring and lights flashing, the ambulance tore out of the parking lot. Grady radioed ahead to the vet hospital. Kate clung to a support bar as they careened around a corner. "They let you use a people ambulance for a dog?" she called out.

"No," Grady hollered back, and she heard the wry smile in his voice. "But when did that ever stop me?"

A fast, wild ride later, the ambulance screeched to a halt at the hospital entrance. Grady wanted to stay, but dispatch said they needed the bus. Grady hugged his brother, and wished him and Murphy the best. He promised to have someone drop off Liam's Mustang, saluted Kate and sped away, tires squealing.

Liam and the vet tech wheeled in the stretcher bearing the unconscious dog. The vet tried to convince Liam to wait outside, but he insisted on accompanying his wounded partner. He'd warned her in the ambulance that Con and Aidan would be tied up at the crime scene, and couldn't be there to support them.

She dropped into a seat in the empty waiting area, wrapped her arms around herself and prayed.

After an endless, lonely vigil, the inner door finally opened. Liam slumped against the door frame. His face was bone-white and tears glittered in his eyes. Kate gasped. "Oh, *no!*" She rushed over and flung her arms around him.

He clung to her. "He—he made it through the surgery." He swallowed hard. "He needs to be kept quiet and rest for the next twenty-four hours. But the vet thinks he'll be okay."

She caressed his damp cheek. "Why are you crying?"

"Back at the fire site, when I thought I'd lost you, I—it ripped my heart out." He inhaled a trembling breath. "I never want to feel that way again." He dropped to his knees and wrapped his arms around her waist. "Nobody has ever put you first. Not your parents, not your sister, not your so-called fiancé. You deserve to always be first." He hugged her tight. "If you can't bear to be around Murphy, then I—" He choked, swallowed again. "I'll send him to live with Grady. He loves Grady, and I can visit him whenever I want. I need you, Kate."

The air rushed out of her lungs. Her knees went weak. Tears blurred her vision. Nobody had ever made allowances for her, much less the supreme sacrifice he offered. "That's the most incredible, generous wonderful offer I've ever received! But I can't allow you to do that." She smoothed his tousled hair. "If you guys don't live together, you can't work together."

His eyes swimming with anguish, he slowly rose to his feet. "I know what I'm giving up."

"No." She shook her head. "I'd never separate the team of Murphy and O'Rourke. *Ever.*"

The outer door crashed open, and two little girls rushed inside the clinic, followed by a man carrying a chubby beagle. "Our doggie is having puppies!" the smallest girl announced breathlessly.

Kate managed to smile at her. "How exciting!" She slid her arm around Liam's waist. He was shaking. "If you're ready to go, let's continue this conversation in private."

Chapter 16

7:00 a.m.

The local cops had delivered Liam's car. When Kate somberly passed him the keys, he opened the passenger door for her, and then slid into the driver's seat. He started the engine, and she looked at him, her fawn's eyes sad and vulnerable. She appeared ready to burst into tears. "I can't believe it's finally over."

He merged into traffic, and déjà vu whammed him back to the night they'd met. Then, it had been dark and rainy, but fiery anticipation had burned inside him. Today, it was sunny and mild, but apprehension chilled him to the bone. His worst nightmare would soon become reality.

Kate was about to walk away from him. Again.

His heart lurched. Watching helplessly as the casino had burned with her inside, he'd wanted to die. Losing Pop was the only thing that had come close to the agony. He stopped the car at a red light, idling in morning rush hour traffic. He couldn't bear to lose her. He'd offered to board Murphy so they could be together. Standing over his unconscious partner in recovery, the decision had torn his guts out. Yet he'd had no choice.

He gritted his teeth. She'd turned him down. She'd refused to separate them. His life was gridlocked, his hopes and dreams at a standstill like the dozens of cars backed up behind this never-ending stoplight. The signal finally flashed green, and he drove the Mustang forward. His future remained stalled.

He was about to lose her forever.

The sun blazed mercilessly, stinging his still sensitive eyes, and he flipped down the visor. He'd always loved sunrise. Each day brought a new beginning, a fresh start. Ironic. At the start of a new day, his life was set to crash and burn.

"Things didn't turn out the way I'd hoped." Her voice quavered. "And now I have to let someone down."

Here it comes. He braced for the blast. The shock waves of pain. The torment as his heart incinerated to ashes.

"Everything is ruined. Gone." She brushed a stray lock of hair from her face. "I can't pay for Aubrey's transplant."

His breath whooshed out. *Hellfire.* His fingers clenched on the wheel. He was a selfish bastard. Kate had run the obstacle course from hell, with more family fallout to come. Reaching over the console, he took her hand. "We still have another day. We'll think of a way, I promise. Try to put it aside so you can rest. You won't be any good to her if you're out on your feet."

Hope flickered in her gaze. "If we can't make it happen, nobody can." She rotated her hand so they were palm to palm, and linked her fingers with his. "Thank you. For everything."

Her hand felt so small. So fragile and trusting. Thoughts of what Daniel had nearly done to her clawed at his insides, and he swallowed a bitter wash of bile. He would die to protect her. He almost had. "I'd do it all again, Kate." *Everything. Anytime.*

"How did you know about Daniel? How did you find me?"

"Etienne told me Daniel was your former fiancé. The kid's statement plugged in the motive." Frowning, he changed lanes. "Sorry I had to arrest Etienne. The evidence was solid."

"I'm sure it was." Her voice was low, her body taut. "Daniel manufactured it."

"And did a damnable job." He headed toward the Strip. She'd need a hotel. "When Alex put you into my custody, he warned me the bomber might be involved with *Les Hommes de la Mort*. I couldn't take any chances. I had to lock up any viable suspect."

She gasped. "Why didn't you tell me?"

"I didn't want to scare you any more than you were."

"What does a terrorist group have to do with Etienne?"

How much should he divulge? Junior had had the guts to disown terrorists. His current record was as spotless as Granny O'Rourke's parlor. He released her hand to shift. "Ask him."

She nodded. "Etienne has traveled a rough road. When you look into his eyes, an old soul stares back. Whatever's in his past, there is no way he would knowingly hurt anyone."

"He's lucky to have you on his side." Her devotion was no surprise. "Etienne said you'd been engaged to Daniel. He also said Daniel had motive, means and opportunity to hurt you, and my instincts hit red alert. Then Zoe phoned with buried intel. Daniel is the grandson of Phillipe Marché, the infamous bomber. Everything jelled into a nasty picture."

She gulped. "Daniel claimed he killed his parents, foster parents and grandfather."

"I don't doubt it. Interpol thought Marché's last hit was a suicide bombing—more of Tyler's handiwork."

"He would have killed me." She fidgeted with her singed hem. "After."

"We beat him at his own game." Tyler hadn't raped her, either, luckily for the bastard. Liam snarled. He'd been serious as a heart attack about gelding him. "I phoned to warn you, but the nurse told me you'd left with him. I freaked. I was afraid I'd never make it in time." The excruciating interval counted among the worst of his life. "I arrived as you left the parking garage."

"The second time today a mocha has saved me." She gave him a wobbly smile. "I drank one earlier and had to stop in the ladies' room. I grabbed a few minutes to freshen up. I was determined to rescue Etienne, and didn't think I'd be very intimidating if I looked like something the cat dragged in."

He returned her smile. "Let's hear it for chocoholics."

"And for bomb techs. You disarmed Daniel's system."

"As much as I could. It was a piece of work." And he'd been in a bit of a rush.

"Talk about nerves of cold steel and bravery under fire." Her gaze glowed with admiration. "I was totally impressed. You were *amazing* when you called his bluff."

"Who was bluffing?" He hadn't *felt* cool or steely. He'd wanted to rip the SOB limb from limb. But Tyler had been prepared for him to attack. The only way to defeat sociopaths was to force them to deviate from their script. He glanced at her. Would she hate him for the truth? He gripped the wheel harder. He could never be less than honest with her. "He was determined to kill us. I was prepared for us to die rather than get in that cage and let him rape you. I forced him to accept my terms. No torture, no rape. I can't apologize for that."

"I don't want you to. You saved my life." She reached for him, but changed her mind. He cornered a tight left. So, they were back to acting like polite strangers. She was already leaving him. She stared down at her lap. "I'm sorry. Because of me, Daniel almost killed you and Murphy. I feel so stupid. I was engaged to him, spent years with him and never saw the evil. How could I have been so clueless?"

"There's no way you could have known. Sociopaths are ultimate actors. Women who are *married* to them for years don't realize they're cold-blooded killers until too late. We never see their true natures until they take off their masks." He was nearly to the Strip. Nearly at the end of the line. "Don't apologize for what he did. It's not your fault."

"You're a very forgiving man, St. Michael."

"Not so much." He turned onto Vegas Boulevard and tensed. Precious time was ticking away. "I don't regret that he's dead. He'll never hurt you again."

"No regrets here, either." She jutted her chin. "Not just because of us. Janine and Aubrey are safe from him, too."

"I got to you as fast as I could. He had the place booby-trapped. I heard him tormenting you." He braced himself. *Be straight with me, Kate. Even if it blows my heart to pieces.*

She paled. "Then you heard me say the only reason I slept with you was because I was reeling from a double shock."

His throat felt as raw as if he'd swallowed ground glass. "It explains a lot."

She placed her hand on his forearm. "During the fire, you yelled that I was a liability to you."

He hit the brakes a tad too hard. "I said it to make you leave. To save your life. I didn't mean it."

She squeezed his arm. "Yes, I got that."

He did a mental head slap. "You were buying time, to pacify Daniel." Liam slowly accelerated, thankful for perpetually snarled Vegas traffic. The all-night gamblers were just going to bed. He needed to finish this before she asked to be dropped off. The final showdown had been two years coming, and he had no idea if he'd ever see her again. "I understand why you felt so vulnerable that night with me. Why you couldn't go through with it. Why you ran. You were in emotional free fall."

"I was clearheaded enough to know that I wanted you. I knew what I was doing when I went home with you." She withdrew her hand. "But murmurs in the bar about 'Love 'em and leave 'em Liam' stirred up old doubts and new fears. Then the unexpected intimacy threw me into a spin. Instead of declaring my emotional independence, I faced an even more dangerous threat. I was too fragile. Another rejection would have destroyed me, and I went into survival mode."

She viewed him as an emotional threat? Was that good or bad? "You were overwhelmed. And left before I could leave you." Liam swore softly. "I'll be damned. Talk about karmic payback."

"Care to explain that cryptic statement?"

"I wasn't always commitment impaired." He sighed. "When I was a freshman at U of O, Pop was accused of skimming half a million dollars from an armored car robbery. He was framed, but couldn't prove it. I was engaged to my high school sweetheart, and we planned to marry after college. Michelle had big ambitions. She wanted to be the first woman president."

"You, hobnobbing with politicians?" She choked. "Somehow, I can't picture Officer Irreverence as the First Husband."

"Neither could she." His mouth twisted in a wry grimace. "When Pop was branded a dirty cop, she dumped me. She couldn't afford a scandal, blah, blah. Man, she was brutal. Cold. She flushed *three years* down the crapper without blinking."

"She'll make a perfect politician. No heart."

"No kidding." Why had it taken him so long to realize the flaw was in Michelle, not him? "When Pop was murdered, she didn't call. Hell, she didn't bother to send a card. One loss I could have dealt with. Two, sudden and brutal, knocked me off my feet." He pursed his lips. "The fall wasn't so bad, but the impact hurt like a bitch. I didn't want to get serious about anything after that. I fooled myself into believing I was enjoying the present. But I was just being a fool. During the last twenty-four hours, I've wised up."

"You have scars, too. Only yours aren't visible." Her voice was soft, her eyes luminous. "I'm so sorry I ran out on you and added to your pain. But I lost my way. Lost myself. I had to go…for my own survival. After rebuilding, I came back stronger, able to stand on my own. But I've also learned a lot since yesterday. And I'm finally sure of what I want."

Every muscle in his body went rigid. The moment he'd dreaded had arrived. "Tell me what you want, Kate."

"Take me home."

That was it, then. Pain graveled his voice. "Your apartment isn't livable, honey."

"Take me to *your* home, Liam. I want to discover the rest of the story."

Sounds faded, colors paled, and the world ground into slow motion. He blinked, and it returned to normal. Did she mean what he thought? Hope soared. He'd been given a second shot at winning her heart. Then wariness crept in.

If he blew it, there would be no more chances.

Liam supported Kate with a hand on the small of her back as they walked into the lobby of the Bellagio. Her taut muscles quivered beneath his palm. She'd claimed to be sure, but was as edgy as the point man in a minefield.

She stared up at the rainbow-hued ceiling. "No matter how many times I've seen these Chihuly glass flowers, I'm always awed at his talent. It's like being inside a kaleidoscope."

His feelings were a confused kaleidoscope. Green hope. Red desire. Black trepidation.

The elevator let them out on the tenth floor. He unlocked the door and followed her inside the room. She checked out the elegant decor in muted shades of mocha and cream with splashes of burgundy. The drapes were open, the famous fountains visible from both the living room and bedroom. "Lovely suite."

"Murphy needs space." Murphy's leash was draped over a chair near the door. Liam's guts cramped. He missed his friend with every fiber of his being. He picked it up and stroked the worn leather through his fingers.

Hellfire. His charm arsenal hadn't swayed Kate. All he had left to gamble was his heart. He sucked in a fortifying breath. "I love you, Kate."

Her eyes widened and she gasped. She tried to speak and failed, and he jumped into the breach. "But I don't want you to compromise your goals or independence for me. I don't want you to rush into anything. I want you to come to me on *your* terms. Complete. Whole."

"L-Liam" she stuttered. "I—"

"Hear me out." Determination blazed as bright as the sunrise, burning away fear and doubt. "If I have to wait for you, I'll wait. If I have to fight for you, I'll fight." His jaw tightened. "The only thing I will never do is give up on you."

"Oh!" She covered her face and burst into tears.

Well, crap. He wrapped an arm around her shoulders. "Not exactly the reaction I was going for."

"I'm just…thunderstruck." She gulped, pulled herself together. "You mentioned karmic payback." She rested her palm on his chest, and his heart stumbled. "When I came out of the fire, the only thing I wanted was to find you. To know you were okay. I hunted everywhere. Searched every face. I knew then how scared and confused you'd felt when I left and you'd looked for me all that time. I can never make that up to you. But I can try." She stepped back and gathered both his hands in hers. "Because you were right. Fish really do it for me."

He quirked a bewildered brow. "You lost me somewhere between 'you were right' and 'fish.'"

"When you brought Aubrey the goldfish, I tumbled headlong in love with you. I was terrified to acknowledge my feelings then…but not anymore." She smiled. "I love you, Liam."

Joy, yellow and warm, filled him, surrounded him. A grin burst free. "Come closer and say that." He tugged her to him.

She stopped him. "About Murphy…" The shine dimmed, and his grin faded. Happiness came with a steep price tag. He touched Kate's soft cheek. A cost he was willing to pay.

She kissed his fist, where he'd wrapped the leash around and around his hand and was clinging to it. "I didn't save the mutt's life just to send him to live with your brother."

Whoa! Say what? "You saved Murphy's life?"

"I found him knocked out in the next room. I rolled him onto a tablecloth and dragged him away from the fire."

He rubbed his chin and said, "As I disarmed the system, he alerted. I sent him to search out the threat." His brow knitted as he worked through the wrenching sequence. "It wrecked me when I heard him fighting the other dog. It *killed* me when I couldn't find him, had to leave without him." Astounded, he looked down at her. "You saved us both."

"He saved *me.* I got lost, and would have burned to death. But he woke up and led me to the kitchen. We sought shelter in the walk-in refrigerator, huddled together for warmth." She fingered Murphy's leash. "One dog took away my life…but another gave it back to me." She shook her head. "I don't want you to send him away. He belongs to both of us now."

Elation banished the last dark shadow inside him. "You must have had quite an epiphany, Kate."

"Only a fool wouldn't see the parallels. The refrigerator offered temporary respite. But we would have eventually died from hypothermia or suffocation. I locked my emotions in the deep freeze, thinking they were safe." She caught her bottom lip between her teeth. "Instead, they nearly suffocated to death. By not taking risks, I was clinging to a faulty, broken illusion of security. And headed for a disastrous fall."

He dropped the leash onto the chair. "You rebuilt your life from nothing, alone. You can be proud of what you accomplished."

"My 'accomplishment' is an illusion…just like the photos. I was so obsessed with not failing again, I held back, protected my heart. I settled for stark, flat, black-and-white existence. I achieved material success, but remained emotionally stunted." Her earnest gaze held his. "Sure, if I take chances, I might fail. But in not taking a chance, I *ensure* failure. Trusting you isn't a risk." She slid her arms around his waist and rested her cheek on his chest. "The riskiest choice I ever made was playing it safe. And the greatest risk is doing nothing."

"*Life* is a risk." He held her tight. "Bad stuff happens. But good stuff also happens. And sometimes..." He tilted her chin up and kissed her forehead. "Wonderful surprises happen."

"Yes, they do." She smiled. "And my new life, my *real* life starts here. Now...with you." Her smile wavered. "The problem is, I'm not sure how to let go. How to *really* live."

He stroked her tousled hair. "Stick with me, Kate." She swayed, and he caught her shoulders. "It's been a long day." He led her to the sofa. "Sit."

"Arf, Ace." She chuckled. "Are you aware that you frequently slip into dog commands?"

He laughed. "I'll watch that." He grabbed the room service menu. He wanted her more with every heartbeat, but she was wiped. He tamped down desire. He'd waited years to claim her...what was one more day? "You need food. What'll it be?"

"A giant hot-fudge sundae with extra whipped cream and sprinkles." When his brows rose, she shrugged. "Life goes by fast. Enjoy dessert first."

He shot her a wicked grin. "Best idea I've heard all year."

She self-consciously smoothed her singed, rumpled dress. "I'd like to grab a shower while you phone room service."

"You bet. There's an extra hotel robe in the closet. Do you want the bathroom with the luxury shower, or the whirlpool tub?"

"Shower. I'd fall asleep in the tub and drown."

He wiggled his eyebrows at her. "No worries. I'm proficient in mouth-to-mouth."

She rose and her lovely mouth curled in a slow grin that made his stomach swoop. "Tell me something I don't know."

Chapter 17

9:00 a.m.

Naked, Liam opened the glass door and stepped inside the large, steamy shower enclosure. Kate had turned on all of the showerheads in the ceiling and walls, even the massive rain shower overhead. Facing away from him, she slumped against the marble wall. In the soft golden light, her skin gleamed like wet alabaster. "Kate," he said quietly. "Are you all right?"

She gasped and lurched around. She didn't try to cover her body. Instead, she broke his heart by angling her right arm behind her. "Afraid I would run out on you again?"

Actually, he was afraid she'd pass out. "You didn't desert me once today. You didn't leave me to drown. You didn't leave me to fight alone in the fire, and you didn't leave Murphy to die. You've given me unquestioning loyalty, times ten. I'll never worry about you leaving me again."

Her eyes glowed. "Good, because I'm not going anywhere." She cocked her head. "Who's going to answer room service?"

"They're swamped with breakfast orders. It's gonna take thirty to forty minutes…so I came to wash your back."

Her luscious mouth quirked. "An offer I can't refuse."

"Service with a smile." He reached for the shampoo. "You can tip me later." Grinning, he motioned. "Turn around."

She obeyed, again keeping her arm out of sight. He dumped shampoo into his palm, and massaged it into her scalp. Lather foamed, and a soft but fresh scent mingled with the steam. He glanced at the bottle he'd returned to a built-in marble shelf to see what she'd chosen from the basket on the counter. Spearmint and chamomile. Smelled good enough to eat.

"That feels wonderful." Her taut muscles went lax beneath his fingertips. "It tingles."

Standing inches from her naked back with his fingers buried in her silky wet hair, he was getting a few tingles himself. He mentally conjugated French verbs. She'd had a traumatic day and was tired. He would not push. He shifted her beneath a stream of water. She tipped her head back, and he combed his fingers through the soapy strands until they were rinsed.

He soaked a washcloth and added shower gel. After scooping aside her hair, he gently massaged her shoulders, then her back.

She breathed a contented sigh. "You have beautifully talented hands, Liam."

You ain't seen nothin' yet. "So do you."

She hung her head. "Mine's ugly," she whispered. "Useless."

He dropped the washcloth on a shelf and turned her to face him. Reaching behind her, he drew out her right hand. "Your hands have helped me all day. They've comforted me. Saved my life." Holding her gaze, he raised her crippled hand into view. "What makes you special and beautiful and talented isn't in here." He kissed her scarred knuckles. "Or here." As he kissed the scarred path up her arm, her breath caught and she quivered.

"Your beauty and worth are *inside* you. Here." He touched her forehead. "And here." He settled his fingertips over her heart, where it galloped beneath his touch. "You have no limits except those you place on yourself, Just Kate."

Awed, Kate stared at her hand, clasped tenderly in Liam's. She'd been looking with narrowed perspective, had seen only distorted, weak muscles and jagged scars. His gentle words and tender kisses opened her vision to a wide-angle view. The complete picture finally snapped into full frame.

Her hand did not define who she was. Her potential wasn't restricted to her limited grasp.

Anything she could dream, she could achieve.

Her heart soared. He'd given her the most precious gift of all. He'd shattered the lock and freed her spirit from its frozen dungeon. And she wanted to give back.

Delight lit his green eyes. She deliberately poured shampoo into her bad hand, and then stroked it through his thick hair. His gaze warmed. He smiled tenderly, understanding the significance…as she'd known he would. "Ah, Kate." His voice was husky. "Do you know what it does to me when you touch me?"

Like she could fail to notice. A giddy rush of feminine power glittered through her veins, more intoxicating than the best champagne. She grinned and drizzled bath gel on his sculpted pecs. "I'm getting a great big hint."

A chuckle rumbled in his chest, and tanned, slick muscles bunched beneath her soapy fingers. With her index finger, she wrote her name in the layer of suds over his heart.

He glanced down and laughed. "You can't return me now."

"I'm keeping you, Ace." She sleeked her palms over his nipples, and he inhaled sharply. Avoiding the sword scratch, her fingers glided down his ribs and washboard abs to his flat stomach. "This is fun."

"Yeah. *Fun.*" He groaned. "Or torture."

"No." She pressed herself to him and rubbed their soap-slicked bodies together. "*This* is torture."

He sounded strangled. "I had to fall for a creative type."

Her giggle turned into a moan as he backed her into the wall. He slid his full length up and down her, all foam-sleeked skin and hard male muscle. The crisp hairs on his chest abraded her nipples and the huge ridge of his arousal teased her most sensitive parts. He kissed her, his tongue enticing hers to play. He touched and stroked her all over. The scented bubbles spread tingly friction everywhere naked, wet skin glided over naked, wet skin.

Suddenly, he went still. He broke the kiss and leaned into her. His sandpapered cheek brushed hers. "Kate." His husky whisper feathered into her ear. "If you're not up for this, tell me now. I can wait until you're ready."

"I'm way past ready, and nearly to begging," she murmured. Her nerves jittered, and she tensed. But what about her traitorous body? She'd never been able to complete the act. Not even in her dreams.

"You think too much." Liam planted both hands on the wall on either side of her head and pushed back. His smoldering green gaze burned into hers. "Sex is ten percent body and ninety percent brain. Relax, and let go."

It shouldn't surprise her anymore when he read her thoughts. "You mean it's okay to lose my mind?"

"Gamble it all." He grinned. "Go for broke."

She swallowed hard. How to cast aside a lifetime of rigid control? "Easier said than done."

He adjusted the showerhead, and water poured over them, sluicing the suds from their bodies. "Trust me." He bent and tugged her nipple into his mouth. Desire curled around her, through her. Her nipple puckered beneath his silken strokes, and pleasure pooled heavy and hot in her lower belly.

He suckled her nipples, alternating mouth and hands until she was squirming between his hard body and the wall.

His hands stroked her back, and his clever mouth cruised her ribs, kissing and tasting every inch. His fingertips danced over her, and every nerve ending sizzled alive. He courted and seduced and loved her until logic was drunk with desire.

He went to his knees. His fingers kneaded her bottom as he nibbled her belly. Warm water poured over her outside, and liquid heat streamed inside. His tongue dipped into her navel. "Do something for me." His black velvet murmur caressed her stomach.

Adrift in hazy passion, she panted for breath. "*Anything.*"

His broad shoulders eased her legs wide apart, and he licked the water droplets trailing down her thighs. Her heart somersaulted and butterfly wings fluttered inside her. She trembled with need, with longing. His big hands slid to her hips, held her in place, supported her. "Let go of the safety line." His heated breath brushed her curls, and her body tightened in shivery anticipation.

"Fall for me, Kate." Then his mouth covered her in the most intimate kiss of all. His velvet tongue swirled over her sensitized nub and delved inside.

Her inner muscles clenched at the sharp, erotic pleasure. Beneath the delicious onslaught of his mouth, she couldn't think. Couldn't breathe. Didn't care. She tangled her fingers in his hair, clung to him.

His tongue teased and stroked, weaving dark magic and building sweet promises. Tension built higher. Desire coiled tighter. Aching need grew unbearable.

Her eyes winched closed. Her head tossed back and forth. Completion shimmered at the edge of consciousness. But the harder she tried to grasp the bright, sparkling colors, the more they eluded her frantic reach.

She froze. For breathtaking moments, she was caught, pinned to the wall, helpless and shaking. "I can't!" Her hands fisted desperately in Liam's hair.

His voice answered inside her head. *Trust me enough to let go, my sweet Kate. I won't let you down. I'll catch you, I promise.*

Kate jerked in a shuddering breath and opened her hands. Opened her heart. Opened her soul.

Her body relaxed, and Liam's finger slid deep inside her. The slow glide hurtled heat into a burning flood, and passion burst free of her restraints. His swirling tongue pushed her over the edge of sanity…and the world exploded. Melted in a brilliant pool of colors. Wave after wave of achingly sweet release rocked through her, and she sobbed out her pleasure.

Losing her mind never felt so good.

A long time later, when she could hear and feel and think again, she opened her eyes. Liam was on his feet, holding her. His strong arms supported her boneless body, his cheek pressed to hers. He pulled away and grinned at her. "Welcome back."

She hadn't realized she was crying. Overjoyed, she dashed tears from her face. "I'm not frigid."

"Tell me something I don't know." Laughing, he kissed the tip of her nose. "I told you, honey. You're warm and vibrant and responsive."

"Only with you." She wrapped her arms around his neck. Though her body hummed with pleasure, her heart needed more. "Make love to me, Liam," she whispered shakily. "I want all of you. Now."

He hesitated. Ground his teeth. Sighed. "I can't."

Without warning, the past ambushed her. A knife blade of pain and disgrace stabbed into her chest, and she flinched.

He cupped her face. "Do *not* even go there." He brought her hand down to heated steel. "You know damned well how much I want you." His voice gentled. "We don't have protection."

"Oh." She thumped her head against the wall. "I'm a moron."

He grinned again. "I love you anyway."

She firmly shoved self-doubt outside and locked the door. The past was gone. Over. Liam was her future. And his naughty grin inspired all sorts of wicked ideas. "In that case…" Her fingers closed around his thick shaft. He was huge and hot and pulsing with need. "How about if I—"

A thundering knock rattled the front door. He swore. "Room service, with the worst timing in the universe."

"Ignore it." She stroked, felt him tremble.

The knock boomed again. He sucked in air through gritted teeth and gently disengaged. "You need food. Can't have you passing out on me…you'll require lots of energy later." His smile brimming with mischief, he kissed her. Slinging a burgundy towel around his lean hips, he stalked out.

Kate snatched a few minutes to blow-dry her hair before donning the plush hotel robe. Then she hurried into the bedroom.

Wearing the towel, Liam lounged on the jacquard bedspread. A cart was parked beside the bed, with a giant snifter containing a decadent chocolate fudge sundae. Snowy mounds of whipped cream, sprinkles and chocolate-covered cherries topped the confection. The rich scent of coffee wafted from a silver pot sitting beside a dewy bottle of Dom Perignon on ice. Her stomach rumbled, and her cheeks heated.

Liam chuckled. "I see I made the right call."

She rushed the cart. "We'll eat fast."

"Some things are better when they're savored." He smirked. "Nobody ever died from sexual frustration."

She poured coffee. Alternating sips, she lifted a filigreed gold paper bag from beside the coffeepot. "What's this?" She pulled out a large brown and gold box and opened it. She choked, spewed coffee. "You ordered *condoms* from room service?"

He shrugged. "They'll bring you all kinds of fun stuff that's not on the menu."

She snorted. "No wonder you didn't want to ignore the delivery." Gold script on the side of the box caught her eye. "*Chocolate* condoms?" Her jaw dropped. "Twenty-five assorted chocolate flavors from raspberry to hazelnut. Holy crow."

"They might last the day."

"Um…exactly how frustrated are you?"

He arched a glossy brow. "Two-plus-year's worth, honey."

She gasped. "You haven't been with anyone since…?"

"If I couldn't have you, I didn't want anybody."

Her lips wobbled. "I'll never again doubt you want me."

"You'll never have reason to." Smiling, he patted the bed. "Come here. I'm starving."

Leaning against the padded brown velvet headboard, they sat with the sundae propped between them. There was only one spoon, so Liam alternated between feeding her and himself.

They'd nearly finished when his hand jerked, dropping sundae into the vee of her robe. She jumped as the ice cream splashed the hollow of her throat. "That's cold!"

"My bad." His slow grin was wicked, and his eyes twinkled. "I'll clean it up."

Holding her gaze, he slowly, deliberately untied her belt and tossed it over the side of the bed. Desire shimmered inside her as, just as deliberately, he parted her robe and slid it down off one shoulder, then the other. He tossed it on the floor. His fingers roamed down her thigh, circled her knee, her calf, and then he snagged her ankle and tugged her prone. Fascinated, she propped herself on her elbows and watched him.

Still holding her gaze, he unfastened his towel and tossed it away. Naked, he prowled up her body like a big sleek jungle cat scenting prey. His gaze dropped to the ice cream and chocolate at her throat, and then wandered in a leisurely, arousing path down her body…and back. A sensual smile slid across his incredible mouth. "Mmm," he growled. "Looks delicious."

Need flared, hot and bright. She was still warm and ready from the shower. *"Now,"* she demanded, reaching for him.

He caught her hands. "I haven't finished dessert." He bent and licked the ice cream from her neck. After what had happened between them the first time, she expected fast and wild. Instead, he took his time, did a thorough job. She closed her eyes, flung her head back. The sensual tangle of cool, creamy ice cream and warm, silky tongue had her writhing in pleasure.

Something cold dribbled over her nipple. Her eyes flew open. Holding the spoon, Liam grinned at her. "Oops."

Her giggle ended in breathless moans as he proceeded to anoint and taste her, inch by inch. She discovered that each individual toe was a spine-tingling erogenous zone.

The mouthwatering fragrance of chocolate floated in the warm summer air, hazed with sunshine and happiness. Arousal built from a slow simmer to an overpowering cascade of molten need. Liam showed her what her body was capable of when held in the right hands…and the right heart.

He protected them, then moved over her and wooed her mouth in a long, drugging kiss. She gloried in the rich taste of chocolate and the dark, heady essence that was his alone.

He tasted like paradise.

"Look at me, Kate," he whispered against her lips.

Her eyelids drifted up, and their gazes locked. His knee grazed between her thighs, opened her. "Remember when I was trapped in the pool?" His low question was husked with passion.

"Yes," she whispered back. "I'll never forget."

His blunt heat pressed against her. Into her. "When you breathed into my mouth, it felt like my very first breath." He entered her in one long, smooth thrust. Filled her. Healed her. Made her whole. "Like I was reborn."

Their bodies and souls joined in complete harmony, he went still, holding her close. Their breaths mingled. Their heartbeats danced the same primitive rhythm. Searing intimacy permanently sealed the bond that had formed and then been torn apart nearly three years ago.

The best of both of them merged into one perfect creation.

She caressed his familiar, beloved face. He was her missing half. The one man with whom she could be real. She never had to hesitate before sharing her feelings with him, good or bad. She no longer had to protect her emotions.

She stared into his loving green gaze and entrusted her heart to him, forever. He was her haven.

"My sweet Kate." Liam began to move, and it was as natural and easy as breathing. Each long, exquisite stroke spiraled glittering pleasure through her.

Liam watched golden lights flare in Kate's soft brown eyes. He was drowning in her taste, her scent, in the liquid heat of her body. And he treasured every second.

He'd waited a lifetime for her.

With every moment, every beat of his heart, he showed her how precious she was to him. His eager mouth sought hers again and again. She rocked her hips in a rhythm that pounded in his blood, a siren's call that seduced his senses. He discovered the inner melody that belonged only to them, and spun out the pleasure, making it intense.

Her defenses were gone, her heart and mind fully open to him. He released his long-leashed desires, and possessed her. Claimed her. And received back far more than he took. Flickering flames exploded into an inferno, and their sensual ballet whirled into a fiery tango. As long as he lived, he'd never get enough of her.

She whimpered, close to the edge. He clenched his teeth. She arched beneath him, and his blood hammered in his ears. He wanted it to last forever, but the silky heat inside her ignited a consuming blaze in him. Every muscle in his body tightened and shook. Finally, he surrendered, and let the conflagration roar over him. He succumbed to the thundering crescendo and poured himself into her…and rejoiced in the moment when Kate cried out his name. When she trembled and clung to his shuddering body.

When she held his soul in her hands.

Shaking, he buried his face in her neck and wrapped his arms around her. She was his, and he would never let her go.

* * *

Liam unlocked the door to the suite. Kate had been asleep when he'd left. They'd laughed and talked and made love all afternoon and into the evening. The artist in her nourished the creative part of him that he'd never shared with anyone else. He grinned. His sensual artist had proven to be far more creative than he could have possibly dreamed.

He tucked the key card into his jeans pocket. He'd engaged in his fair share of sex. But he'd never felt the way he did with her. Each time was like the first. No other woman would ever trip his pulse. No other woman would ever weaken his knees. No other woman would ever hurtle adrenaline though his system with the same thrilling rush he got when he disarmed a bomb.

Just Kate…his very own personal incendiary device.

His grin softened into a tender smile. It wasn't just physical. They shared a perfect union of body and spirit that filled every empty corner of his heart. She knew who he was, knew what he was all about…and loved him unconditionally.

She completed him on every level.

Phil Collins's mellow voice beckoned him down the short hallway. Good thing he'd left a note saying he was going to visit Murphy and then had an errand to run.

He sauntered into the living room and stopped short. Kate was wearing one of his shirts and nothing else. The sleeves of the sapphire-blue dress shirt were rolled up, and her long shapely legs were bare. Her hair was piled haphazardly on top of her head, with wispy tendrils caressing her cheeks. His iPod blared music beside a bowl of gourmet chocolates on the coffee table. His body hardened. He was ruined for life. He'd never again get near chocolate without becoming violently aroused.

Kate hummed in a clear contralto as her left hand confidently stroked colorful swaths on a vivid canvas. The painting was a wild, exciting display of color and movement.

His heart stopped, and then bucked into a wild, joyous gallop. *She was painting!* "Who let Picasso into our room?"

She squeaked and whirled. "You're back. How's Murphy?"

"Better. The doc says he'll make a full recovery." He inclined his head. "Where'd you get the art supplies?"

She chuckled. "You're not the only one who can wheedle fun stuff from room service." Her eyes grew wide and uncertain. "I call it, *Love with an Improper Stranger.* What do you think?"

"Magnificent!" He grinned. "And the painting is great, too." He moved beside her and studied the mind-blowing canvas. "You said you couldn't paint with your left hand."

"I spent my entire life being scared. And what did it get me?" She put down her brush and turned to him. Yellow paint decorated her nose, and green streaked her temple. "You unlocked my frozen prison and showed me it was safe to let my feelings out. You brought warmth and color back into my world." She rested her hands on his chest. "I'm no longer afraid to try something new. Something risky and freeing and completely different from my renderings or black and whites."

A lump jammed his throat. He didn't think he could get any happier. He was wrong. He wrapped his arms around her. "*Je t'adore,* Just Kate."

She smiled up at him, eyes sparkling. "Your love gave me the courage to soar to new heights."

He could barely speak. "You humble me." He kissed her, long and deep. "Put that masterpiece on display, pronto."

"I'm offering it at the auction as an example of Renée Alette's brand new style, and I'll accept consignments for future works. I'll beg or borrow the rest of the money for Aubrey's transplant from the artist community."

"Zoe will be thrilled to drum up publicity." He handed her a cashier's check. "And this will help."

She goggled. "Where did you get this kind of money?"

He shrugged. "Investments."

"Liam Michael O'Rourke." She frowned. "What have you done?"

"Aubrey needed money, I got money. No biggie."

"*No way* you could reach a broker on such short notice. And on a cop's salary, you—" She blanched. "You sold the Mustang."

Hellfire. She was too smart not to catch on. He reluctantly confessed. "A high roller on the Strip gave me top dollar."

"Oh, no! *No!*" She tried to return the check to him. "That car means the world to you."

"I don't need it anymore." He set the check beside the chocolates. "Pop always had a spooky way of 'knowing' things. Maybe the car was his gift to us…for this exact purpose."

Tears dewed her eyelashes. Her uncaged emotions now surfaced easily. He loved that she finally felt secure enough with him to express her true feelings. "I promise, Liam, I'll make enough money with my paintings to buy it back."

"It's okay, honey. Pop's not in the car." He tapped his head. "He's in here." Tapped his chest. "And here." He held her gaze. "As long as you're beside me, I'll be happy. I'm done wallowing in the past…and firmly focused on the future."

Before she could protest any more, he swooped her up. He kissed away her tears and wiggled his eyebrows at her. "Those chocolates are making me ravenous!"

"Again?" She giggled. "We'd better call room service."

Epilogue

One week later
8:00 p.m.

Kate waited for Liam in front of the Bellagio fountains. They'd planned to meet for dinner after he'd visited Murphy at the vet's and she'd visited Aubrey in the hospital. The fountains played in a breathtaking ballet of water, music and pure white lights, and she hummed along.

So much had happened in a week. Using Zoe's information, Interpol had unearthed Daniel's real history. At his grandfather's urging, he'd firebombed his parents' car at age twelve. But instead of being sent to live with Marché, he was placed in a foster home. So he'd killed his foster parents in a house fire. Marché had raised such a committed, cold-blooded terrorist, Daniel had eventually killed him, too. Daniel had been using her father's company as a resource lab and reason to travel in furthering his development of a new explosive—hoping to make millions from his terrorist pals.

When Janine had discovered Daniel's duplicity, she'd dissolved into a self-pitying fit. Kate had realized they weren't doing Janine any favors by enabling her. She'd gently but firmly confronted her with the fact that her selfishness had nearly cost her everything—including her child. She'd pointed out that Janine was Aubrey's only parent, and her fragile daughter needed her more than ever.

Nobody was more surprised than Kate when a startled Janine had snapped out of her funk the next day and agreed. She'd started seeing a counselor, and the sisters had made tentative steps toward reconciliation. Rebuilding their relationship would take years of hard work, but it was progress. Kate smiled. Aubrey's surgery had gone perfectly, and her niece would live a long, healthy life. When she was stronger, counseling would help her deal with the death of the man she'd believed was her father. Janine intended to tell her the truth about her parentage when she was old enough to understand. Perhaps someday, she'd want to find her biological father. They'd take one step at a time.

Etienne was thrilled to be taking over her Paris studio, after he oversaw the rebuilding. He'd more than proven himself capable of handling the responsibility.

Awareness prickled over Kate's skin, and she pivoted. Liam strode down the sidewalk toward her with his easy, confident lope. He smiled, and her pulse kicked into double time. For as long as she lived, her heart would leap at the sight of her Irish charmer. Her best friend. Her lover. Her soul mate.

He reached her and tugged her close for a kiss. "I missed you."

"We've only been apart three hours."

"Feels like longer." He grinned. "Hungry?"

"Starving." She chuckled. "Can we have dessert first?"

"As long as it's chocolate." His green gaze sparkled with joy, and he laughed. "I have a surprise for you." He whistled, and Murphy trotted around the corner. His eyes were bright, his head high, his tail up and wagging.

She clapped. "You bailed him out of the hospital!"

Liam nodded, his face going oddly somber. "Because we have our most important mission to complete."

The dog ambled up to her, carrying something in his mouth. It was a small velvet box. Liam knelt at her feet. Her breath hitched, and tenderness swelled in her chest.

Still bearing the box, Murphy went down on all fours beside Liam. Liam gathered her hands in his…and anticipation swooped on fluttering wings.

"Kate." Two earnest gazes implored her, one brilliant green, one deep brown. "As bomb techs, Murph and I have always relied on Lady Luck. But now we want a sure thing." He gently squeezed her fingers. "Your hands saved Murphy's life. Saved my life. I want only your hands to make love to me. I want only your hands to dry my tears and comfort me through the years."

She was shaking from head to toe. His thumbs caressed her palms. "I want your hands to hold and rock our children…and our grandchildren." Poignant tears blurred her vision and spilled down her cheeks. Liam inhaled unsteadily. "And when I depart this world, an old, old man, I want your hands to be the last to touch me." His lips trembled. "Kate, will you marry me?"

Rapture. Jubilation. Exaltation. There were no words to describe the effervescent joy soaring through every cell of her being. Crying, she flung her arms around him. "Oh, yes!"

Grinning broadly, he took the box from Murphy and rose to his feet in front of her. He slid a glittering marquise cut diamond onto her ring finger. At that moment, the fountain lights burst into spectacular rainbow colors. They jetted toward the heavens and began to swoop and sway in time to Phil Collins's "Dance into the Light."

She stared at the waltzing water, then at Liam. "How—?"

He laughed, and Murphy barked and cavorted in happy circles around them. Liam opened his arms. "Dance with me, Just Kate."

Her spirit soaring with the music, she nestled into his embrace. Kate looked up at the man who held her future so tenderly in his hands, and smiled. "For the rest of our lives, Ace."

* * * * *

Set in darkness beyond the ordinary world.
Passionate tales of life and death.
With characters' lives ruled by laws the everyday world can't begin to imagine.

Introducing NOCTURNE, *a spine-tingling new line from Silhouette Books.*

The thrills and chills begin with UNFORGIVEN by Lindsay McKenna.

Plucked from the depths of hell, former military sharpshooter Reno Manchahi was hired by the government to kill a thief, but he had a mission of his own. Descended from a family of shape-shifters, Reno vowed to get the revenge he'd thirsted for all these years. But his mission went awry when his target turned out to be a powerful seductress, Magdalena Calen Hernandez, who risked everything to battle a potent evil. Suddenly, Reno had to transform himself into a true hero and fight the enemy that threatened them all. He had to become a Warrior for the Light….

Turn the page for a sneak preview of UNFORGIVEN by Lindsay McKenna. On sale September 26, wherever books are sold.

Chapter 1

One shot...one kill.

The sixteen-pound sledgehammer came down with such fierce power that the granite boulder shattered instantly. A spray of glittering mica exploded into the air and sparkled momentarily around the man who wielded the tool as if it were a weapon. Sweat ran in rivulets down Reno Manchahi's drawn, intense face. Naked from the waist up, the hot July sun beating down on his back, he hefted the sledgehammer skyward once more. Muscles in his thick forearms leaped and biceps bulged. Even his breath was focused on the boulder. In his mind's eye, he pictured Army General Robert Hampton's fleshy, arrogant fifty-year-old features on the rock's surface. Air exploded from between his lips as he brought the avenging hammer down. The boulder pulverized beneath his funneled hatred.

One shot...one kill...

Nostrils flaring, he inhaled the dank, humid heat and drew it deep into his massive lungs. Revenge allowed Reno to endure his imprisonment at a U.S. Navy brig near San Diego, California. Drops of sweat were flung in all directions as the crack of his sledgehammer claimed a third stone victim. Mouth taut, Reno moved to the next boulder.

The other prisoners in the stone yard gave him a wide berth. They always did. They instinctively felt his simmering hatred, the palpable revenge in his cinnamon-colored eyes, was more than skin-deep.

And they whispered he was different.

Reno enjoyed being a loner for good reason. He came from a medicine family of shape-shifters. But even this secret power had not protected him—or his family. His wife, Ilona, and his three-year-old daughter, Sarah, were dead. Murdered by Army General Hampton in their former home on USMC base in Camp Pendleton, California. Bitterness thrummed through Reno as he savagely pushed the toe of his scarred leather boot against several smaller pieces of gray granite that were in his way.

The sun beat down upon Manchahi's naked shoulders, grown dark red over time, shouting his half-Apache heritage. With his straight black hair grazing his thick shoulders, copper skin and broad face with high cheekbones, everyone knew he was Indian. When he'd first arrived at the brig, some of the prisoners taunted him and called him Geronimo. Something strange happened to Reno during his fight with the name-calling prisoners. Leaning down after he'd won the scuffle, he'd snarled into each of their bloodied faces that if they were going to call him anything, they would call him *gan,* which was the Apache word for *devil.*

His attackers had been shocked by the wounds on their faces, the deep claw marks. Reno recalled doubling his fist as they'd attacked him en masse. In that split second, he'd gone into an altered state of consciousness. In times of danger, he transformed into a jaguar. A deep, growling sound had emitted from his throat as he defended himself in the three-against-one fracas. It all happened so fast that he thought he had imagined it. He'd seen his hands morph into a forearm and paw, claws extended. The slashes left on the three men's faces after the fight told him he'd begun to shape-shift. A fist made bruises and swelling; not four perfect, deep claw marks. Stunned and anxious, he hid the knowledge of what else he was from these prisoners. Reno's only defense was to make all the prisoners so damned scared of him and remain a loner.

Alone. Yeah, he was alone, all right. The steel hammer swept downward with hellish ferocity. As the granite groaned in protest, Reno shut his eyes for just a moment. Sweat dripped off his nose and square chin.

Straightening, he wiped his furrowed, wet brow and looked into the pale blue sky. What got his attention was the startling cry of a red-tailed hawk as it flew over the brig yard. Squinting, he watched the bird. Reno could make out the rust-colored tail on the hawk. As a kid growing up on the Apache reservation in Arizona, Reno knew that all animals that appeared before him were messengers.

Brother, what message do you bring me? Reno knew one had to ask in order to receive. Allowing the sledgehammer to drop to his side, he concentrated on the hawk who wheeled in tightening circles above him.

Freedom! the hawk cried in return.

Reno shook his head, his black hair moving against his broad, thickset shoulders. *Freedom? No way, Brother. No way.* Figuring that he was making up the hawk's shrill message, Reno turned away. Back to his rocks. Back to picturing Hampton's smug face.

Freedom!

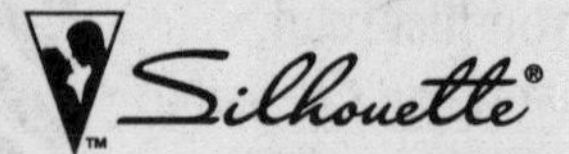

INTIMATE MOMENTS

COMING NEXT MONTH

#1435 JULIET'S LAW—Ruth Wind
Sisters of the Mountain
In a game of cat and mouse, can Juliet Rousseau and Officer Joshua Mad Calf solve a homicide that will prove her sister's innocence, while surviving their growing love for each other?

#1436 UNDERCOVER NIGHTINGALE—Wendy Rosnau
Spy Games
As the hunt for the elusive Chameleon continues, Agent Ash Kelly falls for a mysterious woman dubbed Nightingale, but quickly learns that in this game, appearances are more than deceiving—they can be deadly.

#1437 THE LAST WARRIOR—Kylie Brant
Tribal Police investigator Joseph Youngblood is sent to examine the attempted murder of a photojournalist and soon realizes that the attractive stranger could be the key to uncovering the mysterious deaths of three Navajo youths.

#1438 THE HEART OF A MERCENARY—Loreth Anne White
Shadow Soldiers
When nurse Sarah Burdett becomes a pawn in a deadly global game, she is thrust into the hardened arms of mercenary Hunter McBride. Now Hunter must battle his desires for Sarah while extracting her and a lethal pathogen out of the Congo in a desperate race against time....

SIMCNM0906